THE
DARLING DAHLIAS
AND THE
CUCUMBER TREE

THE
DARLING DAHLIAS
AND THE
CUCUMBER TREE

Susan Wittig Albert

BERKLEY PRIME CRIME, NEW YORK

THE BERKLEY PUBLISHING GROUP
Published by the Penguin Group
Penguin Group (USA) Inc.
375 Hudson Street, New York, New York 10014, USA
Penguin Group (Canada), 90 Eglinton Avenue East, Suite 700, Toronto, Ontario M4P 2Y3, Canada
(a division of Pearson Penguin Canada Inc.)
Penguin Books Ltd., 80 Strand, London WC2R 0RL, England
Penguin Group Ireland, 25 St. Stephen's Green, Dublin 2, Ireland (a division of Penguin Books Ltd.)
Penguin Group (Australia), 250 Camberwell Road, Camberwell, Victoria 3124, Australia
(a division of Pearson Australia Group Pty. Ltd.)
Penguin Books India Pvt. Ltd., 11 Community Centre, Panchsheel Park, New Delhi—110 017, India
Penguin Group (NZ), 67 Apollo Drive, Rosedale, North Shore 0632, New Zealand
(a division of Pearson New Zealand Ltd.)
Penguin Books (South Africa) (Pty.) Ltd., 24 Sturdee Avenue, Rosebank, Johannesburg 2196,
South Africa

Penguin Books Ltd., Registered Offices: 80 Strand, London WC2R 0RL, England

This book is an original publication of The Berkley Publishing Group.

This is a work of fiction. Names, characters, places, and incidents either are the product of the author's imagination or are used fictitiously, and any resemblance to actual persons, living or dead, business establishments, events, or locales is entirely coincidental. The publisher does not have any control over and does not assume any responsibility for author or third-party websites or their content.

PUBLISHER'S NOTE: The recipes contained in this book are to be followed exactly as written. The publisher is not responsible for your specific health or allergy needs that may require medical supervision. The publisher is not responsible for any adverse reaction to the recipes contained in this book.

ISBN 978-0-425-23445-7

PRINTED IN THE UNITED STATES OF AMERICA

*To my cherished herb and gardening friends,
who encourage me to keep my hands in the dirt
and my fingers on the keyboard.
The Darling Dahlias and I send you our love.*

Author's Note

Darling, Alabama, is a fictional town that is located in a real place: the beautiful wooded hills of southern Alabama, about seventy miles north of Mobile, west of Monroeville, and east of the Alabama River. If you'd like a map of the town, please visit the series website: www.darlingdahlias.com. You'll find other items of interest there, including: historical background of the 1930s, the period in which the series takes place; Depression-era recipes and household tips; and information about Southern gardens. I'll be adding new material frequently, so please bookmark the site and visit often.

A note about the language. When I was growing up in the 1940s, we lived on the outskirts of the African-American neighborhood in Danville, Illinois. At the time, my family called our neighbors and schoolmates "coloreds" or "colored folk" or "Negroes." Later, when I was in graduate school at University of California, Berkeley, and took an active part in the Civil Rights movement, we called our friends "Blacks" and "African Americans"; "Negro" had become an ethnic slur. (I notice, though, that the 2010 census uses "Negro" because many older African Americans self-identify with the term.) This historical series includes language and social practices appropriate to the early 1930s in the rural South. These may be offensive to some readers. Thank you for understanding that no offense is intended.

Susan Wittig Albert

Dear Reader,

The author of this book has kindly asked us—the officers of the Darling Dahlias Garden Club—to write this letter to you. She wants us to let you know that we've read this story and agree with her description of what went on during the month of May 1930, when some things happened that shouldn't have happened in any God-fearing town, much less in Darling, Alabama, which has 4 churches, 907 good Christian people (soon to be 908, because Mrs. Perkins is expecting any day now), and only a few Bad Apples.

Of course, in a story, it's usually the Bad Apples who get all the attention, so we want to warn you not to pay too much attention to them. You should look instead at the way everybody else is behaving and doing what they ought to do, which is to help one another and follow the Golden Rule, even though (as a certain few would like to have you believe) it sometimes turns out that he who has the gold, rules. In this case, silver and gold, both. But we won't say anything more about that, since we don't want to spoil the story for you.

Anyway, we just wanted to let you know that we recommend this book because it's true, most of it. And because the way the author has told it shows you how much the Dahlias care about our Darling and want to see things done right in our town, even when things are bad all over the country, with a lot of people out of work and the best help the Red Cross can offer is ten cents a day for food.

Well, that's enough of that. The Darling Dahlias always try to look on the bright side. As Aunt Hetty Little says, we keep our face to the sun so we can't see the shadows, which

*is why we plant sunflowers and marigolds and cosmos in
amongst the collards and sweet potatoes and okra in the garden. And speaking of gardens and such, we may not have just
a whole lot extra, but we're always willing to share what we
have. So we've given the author some of our favorite recipes
and tips for making whatever you've got go further, last longer, and taste better. She says she'll put them at the end of the
book. We hope they'll help you, if times are as hard at your
house as they are here in Darling.*

*We hope you'll keep looking on the bright side, too. And
remember what we said about Bad Apples.*

Elizabeth Lacy, president
Ophelia Snow, vice president & secretary
Verna Tidwell, treasurer

The Darling Dahlias Club Roster, May 1930

Miss Elizabeth Lacy, president. Secretary to Mr. Moseley, attorney at law, and garden columnist for the Darling *Dispatch.*

Mrs. Ophelia Snow, vice president and secretary. Wife of Darling's mayor, Jed Snow.

Verna Tidwell, treasurer. Secretary to the Cypress County probate clerk.

CLUB MEMBERS

Earlynne Biddle, married to Henry Biddle, the manager at the Coca-Cola bottling plant.

Mrs. Bessie Bloodworth, Darling's historian. Owns Magnolia Manor, a boardinghouse next door to the Dahlias' clubhouse and gardens.

Mrs. George E. Pickett Johnson, wife of the owner of the Darling Savings and Trust Bank. Specializes in pure white flowers.

Mildred Kilgore. A collector of camellias, Mildred is married to Roger Kilgore, the owner of Kilgore Motors, and lives near the Cypress Country Club.

Aunt Hetty Little, oldest member of the club, town matriarch, and lover of gladiolas.

Myra May Mosswell, owner of the Darling Diner and an operator in the Darling Telephone Exchange. Lives in the flat over the diner.

Miss Dorothy Rogers, Darling's librarian. Miss Rogers knows the Latin name of every plant and insists that everybody else does, too. Lives in Magnolia Manor.

Beulah Trivette, artistically talented owner/operator of Beulah's Beauty Bower, where small groups of Dahlias gather almost every day.

Alice Ann Walker, bank cashier. Her husband, Arnold, is disabled.

THE
DARLING DAHLIAS
AND THE
CUCUMBER TREE

ONE

The Dahlias in Full Bloom

Sunday, May 11, 1930

Elizabeth Lacy had been a member of the Darling Garden Club ever since Mrs. Blackstone started it in 1925, and president for the last two years. But she couldn't remember a more important meeting. Today was a special day. They were celebrating the opening of their clubhouse.

Their *new* clubhouse, Lizzy thought proudly, as she called the meeting to order after their tour of the garden—although of course the house wasn't new at all. It was the old Blackstone house at 302 Camellia Street, one block west of the courthouse square and one block south, next door to Bessie Bloodworth's boardinghouse, Magnolia Manor. Mrs. Blackstone, a lifelong resident of Darling, had died a few months before at the grand age of eighty-two, leaving her house to the club, along with almost an acre of garden in the back, a half-acre vegetable garden in the adjoining lot, and two beautiful cucumber trees, one in front and one in back.

As usual, Lizzy started the meeting with the roll call. All twelve of their members were present on this special occasion.

Since it was Sunday, the ladies were wearing their church out-
fits: summery flower-print cotton and crepe and rayon dresses
with pretty collars of organdy and piqué and dotted swiss and
hats with ribbons and flowers. Their skirts were safely below
their knees at last, now that the Roaring Twenties had stopped
roaring. They were all very tired of the flapper look (especially
since most of them had never been flappers) and ready for pleats
and ruffles and those cute, perky angel bell sleeves that were (as
Ophelia Snow put it) the very dickens to iron. Myra May was
the only exception to the summer-dress rule. As usual, she wore
trousers, light-colored, with a leather belt and tailored blouse.

After the roll call, Lizzy moved quickstep through Ophelia's minutes (adopted, with a correction by Earlynne Biddle,
who wanted it known that she had donated a book to the club
library) and Verna Tidwell's treasurer's report (five dollars and
fifty-two cents in the kitty). Bessie Bloodworth reported on
the upcoming plant sale, which would be held the next Saturday at the Curbside Market on the courthouse square, and
answered people's questions about where to go and what to
bring. She also invited people to volunteer for garden cleanup,
which (as they could see from their tour) was going to be a
big job. They would need all the help they could get.

Next, Lizzy took up the most important item of business,
which was renaming their club in honor of their founder and
benefactress, Mrs. Dahlia Blackstone. Henceforth and forever, they would be known as the Darling Dahlias, and their
clubhouse would be called the Dahlia House. Ophelia Snow
made the motion, Verna Tidwell seconded it, and there was a
loud chorus of ayes.

"Which is good," Lizzy said with satisfaction, "because
Beulah has already painted our new sign. It's leaning up
against the tree for now, but we thought we'd have a little
ceremony." She reached for her Kodak. "Why don't we go
outside and I'll take a picture for Friday's column."

For the last five years, Lizzy had written the "Garden Gate" column for the Darling *Dispatch*, which was edited and published by Charlie Dickens. The paper came out every Friday morning—unless there was a problem with the printing press, in which case it might be Saturday or even Monday, since Charlie would have to send down to Mobile for parts, and the parts would have to come back to Darling on the Greyhound bus. Lizzy loved writing the column, but she had a full-time job as secretary in Mr. Moseley's law office and had to do it after hours, on the Underwood typewriter at work. She never ran out of things to put in her column, though. There was always something pretty in bloom or something interesting going on in somebody's garden.

Outside, the club members gathered under the cucumber tree—so old and large and beautiful that it was one of the town's landmarks—to witness the unveiling of the freshly painted wooden signboard. Myra May Mosswell did the honors. "Ta-ta-ta-TA-ta-ta!" she cried, imitating a trumpet, and pulled off the bedsheet that Lizzy had brought to drape over the sign. Beaming, she flung her arm around Beulah Trivette. "Didn't Beulah do us proud, ladies? Just look at that beautiful basket of dahlias!"

Lizzy peered down into her Kodak, focused, and snapped. Beulah (whose talents as a hairdresser extended to all things artistic) had really outdone herself this time. She had painted THE DARLING DAHLIAS in big fancy letters, in vivid green on a white background, arching the words over a basket of dahlias in every imaginable color: red, yellow, orange, peppermint-striped, purple. It was really too bad that the newspaper photo would be just plain old black-and-white, Lizzy thought. If people wanted to see the sign in full color, they'd have to walk over to Camellia Street for a look.

"It was nothing, really," Beulah said in reply to Myra May. She tried not to look too pleased.

"Nothing?" Verna Tidwell chuckled. "Nothing short of gorgeous, Beulah. Beyond words." A wordless murmur of assent rippled through the group.

But Voleen Johnson had words, as usual. "Tad bit gaudy for my taste," she said, putting her head on one side. "Too many dahlias in that basket."

Lizzy sighed. When Voleen Johnson climbed onto her high horse, the best thing you could do was ignore her. "Okay, everybody," she called. "I've got a good shot of Beulah and Myra and the sign. So if you'll line up behind them, I'll get the rest of you."

Everybody dutifully lined up and put on their picture-taking faces. Lizzy looked through the camera, thinking that they were a fine group, in their spring dresses and perky straw hats—no more of those silly felt cloches that hugged your head and smashed your hair. They weren't spring chickens, though, none of them. At thirty, Alice Ann Walker was the youngest. Aunt Hetty, nearly eighty, was the eldest, now that dear Mrs. Blackstone was gone. Next oldest was Mrs. Johnson, at fifty-five. The rest were clumped in the middle, give or take a few years.

"I believe I'll just stand here," Mrs. Johnson said, planting herself comfortably next to Myra May in the front row. She always put herself out front, and why not? She was the wife of George E. Pickett Johnson, owner of the Darling Savings and Trust Bank. What's more, she was the spitting image of Mrs. Herbert Hoover, marcelled silver hair and all. Everybody thought so. Mrs. Johnson must've thought so, too, because she framed the cover of the May 13, 1929, issue of *Time* magazine, the one with Mrs. Hoover on it, with a string of real pearls wound around her throat and looped artistically down the front of her black dress. Lizzy knew this because Danzie, who did the Johnsons' laundry on Mondays, was sister to Sally-Lou, who worked for Lizzy's mother. Danzie had told

Sally-Lou (and Sally-Lou had told Lizzy) that the First Lady was hanging right beside Mrs. Johnson's dressing table.

"A tad too many dahlias," Mrs. Johnson repeated, putting up a hand to push her Mrs. Hoover white hair under her stylish purple hat, which she'd had made for her by a milliner in Atlanta, rather than Fannie Champaign, who had a shop right on Darling's courthouse square and made hats for every other lady in town. She said it a little softer this time, but Aunt Hetty Little was standing right behind her and heard it.

"That's only *your* opinion, Voleen," Aunt Hetty said tartly. "If you had your way, there'd be nothing but lilies growin' in this world." She raised her voice. "Beulah, those dahlias are just fine. You have done us right proud, dear. Now, smile, ever'body, so Lizzy can get our picture and we can get on with our meetin'."

This time, everyone agreed with Aunt Hetty, so enthusiastically that Beulah Trivette turned pink with pleasure and Mrs. Johnson pressed her lips together. Lizzy smiled as she snapped the photo. Aunt Hetty was the only person in town who could use that tone to Mrs. George E. Pickett Johnson. This was because Aunt Hetty really was Mrs. Johnson's aunt, although the Littles were a big family and Hetty was either aunt or cousin or other kin to just about everybody in town. And of course Aunt Hetty was right about the lilies, because Mrs. Johnson loved lilies with a passion, but only the pure white ones, never those common orange ditch lilies that everybody else had in abundance. The Johnson garden was full of white flowers, and Mrs. Johnson sent a big bouquet to the bank every morning all summer long, for the table by the front door.

Lizzy snapped another picture, and then a third, because Bessie Bloodworth was squinting. "All right, ladies," she said, "let's have our refreshments now. We can finish the meeting while we're eating."

The Dahlias were much too ladylike to shove, but nobody tarried. They trooped inside, the heels of their Sunday pumps clacking on the wooden floors, and straight to the back porch, where the table was spread with an embroidered cloth and decorated with a big blue glass vase full of flowers from the Dahlias' gardens: gladiolas from Aunt Hetty, iris and azaleas from Verna, cutleaf lilacs from Earlynne Biddle, Japanese cherry and dogwood from Lizzy, and lacy ferns from next to the back door for greenery. Times might be just a little difficult, but that didn't stop the spring flowers from blooming or the Dahlias from gathering big bouquets to share with their friends.

They'd brought plenty to eat, too. Bessie Bloodworth had piled a big plate high with those little deviled-ham finger sandwiches that are so light and tasty you could eat a half dozen before you knew it. Mrs. Johnson had brought a sandwich plate that was probably made up by her cook, Lucretia, with stuffed tomatoes and stuffed squash blossoms arranged around it so that it looked like something out of *Better Homes and Gardens*, where Mrs. Johnson had won a dollar the year before (and kept it, too) for Lucretia's butterscotch pie recipe. Most of the Dahlias didn't have time to stuff squash blossoms, even for a party, but they had brought their usual dishes of pickled okra and watermelon pickles and pickled eggs, along with spiced figs, pear compote, and fresh strawberries. Verna Tidwell brought molasses cookies, Mildred Kilgore brought her famous ribbon cake with peach filling, and Lizzy brought some of those little thumbprint cookies filled with raspberry jam made from the berries from the patch behind her house. Ophelia Snow had brought a couple of gallons of cold rosemary lemonade. She had extra ice from Friday's delivery, so she brought that, too, and the lemonade was frosty cold. When their plates were full, the Dahlias carried them into the parlor and settled down to enjoy their friends' cooking.

* * *

You're probably curious about the Dahlias' new clubhouse and gardens, so while they're eating and chatting, we'll have a quick look around. The house isn't very large, just two rooms in front, the parlor where everybody is sitting in wooden chairs, and the front bedroom, wallpapered in green and white roses. This room has been turned into a sitting room featuring photographs of old Mrs. Blackstone and her beautiful garden—the way it once was, years before—and shelves that now contain the club's gardening library. On the wall is a big gold-toned plaque from the Darling Town Council naming Mrs. Dahlia Blackstone Darling's Woman of the Year. She earned the plaque three years running, 1926, 1927, and 1928, which annoyed Mrs. Johnson, who has never gotten it even once.

Behind the front bedroom is the pink-check-papered bedroom, which the Dahlias are planning to use as a workroom. Behind the parlor is the kitchen, which has a gas range (installed just a couple of years before) and an icebox on one side, a sink under the window, and cabinets and a pine table with white-painted legs. The house, built sometime in the 1890s, is on city gas and water and there's an indoor bathroom at one end of the back porch. It also has electricity, for back in the mid-1920s, Ozzie Sherman installed a Delco generator to power his sawmill just outside of town. A smart businessman, he talked the Darling City Council into installing streetlights around the square and letting him run electricity through the town. Last year, the council took over the Sherman Electric Company and bought two new generators. If the money held out, they planned to run electricity all the way out to the Cypress County Fairgrounds.

Mrs. Blackstone's garden is much larger than the house itself. If you stand on the back porch and look down toward the creek, you can probably see why it has been written up in the Montgomery *Advertiser* and the Selma *Times-Journal* and who knows where else over the years. Back there beyond the trees are the ruins of what was once the splendid Cartwright mansion, Mrs. Blackstone's mother's family home. Built in the glory days of Old King Cotton, it burned to rubble after the Union troops occupied Darling during the War Between the States. Later—in the 1880s and 1890s—its manicured lawns and lovely gardens were carved into town lots along what is now Camellia Street. A row of houses stands there now, each one fronted by a white picket fence.

Mrs. Blackstone inherited the largest lots and a piece of the Cartwright gardens, which was only right, since her mother was the sole surviving Cartwright. Her share of the garden is full of blooming shrubs and trees—including another large cucumber tree—meandering down the hill and into the pines. Inside the fence that encloses the backyard are Mrs. Blackstone's wide, curving perennial borders, filled with iris, larkspur, phlox, and mounds of Shasta daisies and sweet alyssum. Mrs. Blackstone was sick the last few years of her life, so the borders are unkempt now and full of weeds, and the lilies she loved—Easter lilies, spider lilies, oxblood lilies, and those common orange ditch lilies—need to be dug and separated and replanted. There are tangles of sweet peas and cardinal climber and honeysuckle on the fences, and roses, roses, roses everywhere. Mrs. Blackstone was always very fond of roses, especially those big, floppy cabbage roses that smell like paradise, but all the plants are in need of pruning and general cleanup. Old Zeke, who lives in a tiny cottage the next street over, keeps the grass mowed but that's about all. The rest is a mess. If the Dahlias want to enjoy their garden, they've got their work cut out for them.

If you step off the porch and follow the path to the right around the back of the house, you can see the big vegetable garden plot at the corner of Camellia and Rosemont. Mrs. Blackstone always grew enough sweet potatoes and okra and green beans and squash for the whole neighborhood. The garden hasn't been planted for a couple of years now, and the Dahlias haven't yet figured out what to do with it. But the soil is rich, the space large and sunny, and if they want to, they can turn it into flowers or mow it, or whatever. They can even sell it, although times are hard and property isn't moving very fast in Darling. It might be difficult to find a buyer.

But we're not finished with our tour just yet. If you walk on around the house to the front yard, you'll see Mrs. Blackstone's prize hydrangeas, the old-fashioned weigelas that came from her mother, the wisteria climbing the front of the house, and the gorgeous azaleas, pink and lavender and white, massed under the front window, with a border of hostas at their feet.

And the cucumber tree, of course. It's such a big tree, and so pretty when it blooms, that it's earned quite a reputation. People driving or walking down Camellia Street always stop to admire it, especially at this time of year. It's in full bloom just now and covered with beautiful creamy blossoms as big as dessert plates, some of them. The flowers produce little red fruits that look like baby red cucumbers.

The cucumber tree. That's what everybody calls it, even though Dorothy Rogers, the town librarian and a Dahlia, insists that it ought to be called by its proper Latin name, *Magnolia acuminata*. But that particular tree and its twin in the back garden are both over eighty years old and have stood tall and proud since before the War Between the States. As far as people in Darling are concerned, they have always been cucumber trees, and cucumber trees they always will be. Aunt Hetty says that if you called it a *Magnolia acuminata*, nobody would know what in the Sam Hill you were talking about, and she's right.

For the club, inheriting the house (and the gardens and the two cucumber trees) came as a huge shock. When Mrs. Blackstone died, everybody in Darling quite reasonably figured that her property would go to her husband's nephew Beatty Blackstone, the owner of BB's Auto Repair Shop and the Sinclair Filling Station, and the only living Blackstone. That's the way property is handed down in Darling, from one family member to another. If you're next in line, it's pretty much a sure thing.

Beatty had it figured that way, too. He'd been thinking of this all the while his aunt was declining, figuring that he could sell the house or trade it to the bank in return for the mortgage on his repair shop. Either way, he'd be free and clear forever and wouldn't that just be swell? So on the day after Mrs. Blackstone's funeral, he locked up his repair shop, put on a clean white shirt and a tie, and sauntered jauntily over to Mr. Moseley's law office on Franklin Street to hear Mr. Moseley read the last will and testament of his aunt-by-marriage and pick up the keys to his new front door—only to learn instead that she had bequeathed the keys, the front door, the house, the garden, and the vacant lot at the corner of Camellia and Rosemont to the garden club. What's more, she had prepaid the taxes for three years, so the club would have a little time for fund-raising before they had to pay taxes again.

For Beatty, this was a stunning blow.

It was equally stunning for Lizzy, who was the first Dahlia to hear this news, partly because she was the club's president but mostly because she worked for Mr. Moseley. She was at her desk in the reception room, typing up the shorthand notes she had taken in a deposition about a cow that got loose and broke down a neighbor's fence, when Mr. Moseley opened the door to his office and asked her to come in and hear him read Mrs. Blackstone's will. He had a quirky smile on his face, which should have told her that something was up. Anyway, the next thing she knew, he was handing her the trust papers, the deed, and the key to Mrs. Blackstone's house, while Beatty Blackstone sat with his arms folded and his lower lip pooched out, glowering furiously.

Well, it knocked her for a loop, as she told Ophelia on the telephone the minute she got back to her desk. That was, the minute after Beatty had stomped out of the office and slammed the door behind him so hard that Mr. Moseley's framed Certificate of Recognition from the Darling Chapter of the American Legion fell off the wall and the glass broke. And since Myra May Mosswell (also a Dahlia) was on the board at the telephone exchange in the back room at the Darling Diner, the news of Mrs. Blackstone's astonishing gift to the garden club flew around town faster than you could say "Hello Central." Beatty's wife, Lenora, heard it from her cousin before her husband got home for lunch, and she gave him plenty of what-for-and-what-you-can-do-with-it. (It was Lenora's opinion that if Beatty would've been nicer to his aunt while she was alive, she would've been more generous to her nephew when she died.)

Beatty did get a consolation prize, however. His aunt left him her four-cylinder Dodge touring car with open sides and a canvas top, which hadn't been driven since Mr. Harvey Blackstone went to his grave in 1926, after sixty years of marriage. Oh, and forty-two dollars, which was what there was left in the checking account after Mrs. Blackstone's bills were paid, along with a big box of old Cartwright family papers and letters. These were of no interest to Beatty, since he was a Blackstone, not a Cartwright, and had no interest in Cartwright family history.

But the car, the money, and the family papers satisfied neither Beatty nor Lenora, who had been planning the new drapes she was going to hang at the front windows of

Aunt Dahlia's house ever since Aunt Dahlia got sick. Pretty soon, the story got around town that Beatty was going to challenge the will in court. That would cost him more than forty-two dollars, though, and Mr. Moseley advised him that his chances were about as good as a snowball's chance on the Fourth of July, so he let it drop.

Still, he slanted Lizzy a narrow-eyed, nasty look every time he saw her on the street and muttered something about fixing her wagon. Lizzy had the feeling that as far as the inheritance was concerned, they hadn't heard the last from Beatty. As events unfurled, it turned out that she was right.

Back in the Dahlia House parlor, Lizzy called the meeting to order again.

"Before we adjourn," she said, "we need have a look at the calendar for this coming summer and fall. Nineteen-thirty is going to be an exciting year, with more than enough to keep us busy."

"Any more exciting than 1929, and I don't believe we can stand it," Miss Rogers remarked darkly. As librarian and the organizer of the Darling Chautauqua series, she was the nearest thing the town had to an intellectual (and she knew it). She lived next door at Bessie Bloodworth's Magnolia Manor but was saving her money so she could have her own little house, the dearest dream of her heart. She had studied the stock market for several years, and in the spring of 1929, had taken all her savings out of the Darling Savings and Trust. She had wired it to a Wall Street brokerage firm to invest for her, with the idea of making enough money that she could say kiss-my-foot to Bessie Bloodworth and her Magnolia Manor. But her timing was terrible. After Black Tuesday, the only money Miss Rogers had to her name was a five-dollar bill in a mad-money envelope under her mattress. She had started saving again, but it would be a long while before she could recoup.

"We're all in the same leaky boat, Miss Rogers," Ophelia Snow said sympathetically. "But we'll bail it out. You know the old saying. 'Gardeners never give in; they—' "

"Just give out," the Dahlias chorused, in singsongy unison, and broke into giggles. Ophelia, round and bouncy, with flyaway brown hair and a sweet smile that never stopped, was an incurable optimist, and this was her favorite saying.

Miss Rogers bit her lip, and Lizzy was immediately sorry for joining in the laughter. Out loud, she said, "Miss Rogers is certainly right, ladies. None of us wants *that* kind of excitement, ever again. But gardening is a different kind of excitement. We've got a full calendar ahead of us, and I hope every Dahlia will roll up her sleeves and pitch in."

She began ticking things off on her fingers. "This coming Saturday is the annual plant sale. June is the Flower Show, July is the Tomato Fest, August is the Watermelon Roll, September we are having our Garden Tour, and October is the Harvest Festival. Oh, and don't forget: every Monday night, we get together for a game of hearts. Never let it be said that the Dahlias are lazy!"

Three or four people pretended to groan, but everyone else chuckled. There wasn't a lot of entertainment in Darling, but the Dahlias always managed to find something to do. Lizzy was about to ask for a motion to adjourn, but Verna Tidwell raised her hand.

"One more thing, Lizzy." The physical opposite of plump, pretty Ophelia, Verna was tall and thin, with an olive-toned complexion, a firm mouth, and intelligent, searching eyes. But while Verna was not everybody's idea of a Southern belle, she had a razor-sharp mind. She worked in the office of the probate court clerk, where she was in charge of keeping the records. This was a big job that involved shelves and boxes and cabinets of dusty plat books and details of property ownership, tax liens, wills, elections—papers and documents that went back generations. Verna always said that her job gave her a perspective on Cypress County that she couldn't get anywhere else.

"As club treasurer," she said, "I need to remind y'all to pay your dues. You can pay by the month—twenty-five cents. Or if you want to pay ahead, it's just two dollars and fifty cents for the full year. That's a savings of fifty cents."

Myra May cleared her throat. "I thought we discussed making it fifteen cents a month," she said. "I'm not speaking for myself, of course," she added hurriedly, although everybody knew that business at the Darling Diner had begun falling off even before the Crash. Myra May and her friend Violet Sims (they shared the apartment over the diner) were working two full-time jobs, supplementing the income from the diner with money they earned as telephone operators. Myra May always said the hours didn't matter—she and Violet were just glad to have the steady work. Everybody knew exactly what she meant.

"You know, Verna," Lizzy said, "Myra May is right about the dues. I think maybe you weren't at the meeting where we discussed this. But we did talk about dropping it down to fifteen cents." She looked around. People were nodding. "As far as the club goes, we'll be okay for money. Mrs. Blackstone paid the taxes on this house, so we won't have to worry about that for several years." She added, wanting to be fair, "Although there's the electrical bill, of course. And the roof."

They were lucky to have Dahlia House—there was no doubt about that. But the place was forty years old and hadn't been built all that well to start with. After the last hard rain, there had been puddles in the kitchen and the back room, and the leaks were only going to get worse. Sooner or later, and probably sooner, they would have to find the money to fix the roof.

Voleen Johnson frowned. "Personally, I think we should leave the dues right where they are. A quarter surely isn't too much to ask. If anything, we ought to raise them. We don't want to encourage—"

She stopped, because everybody knew what she had been going to say. She had been arguing for years that Darling's garden club should accept as members only people who were "serious" gardeners. Which meant people who had enough spare time to spend hours every day in the garden, or had the money to pay somebody else to spend the time, the way she did. The Johnson garden was a showplace, but Voleen Johnson never had dirt under her fingernails, like the rest of the Dahlias. And twenty-five cents a month, Lizzy was thinking, pretty much excluded the folks who lived over in Maysville, on the east side of the railroad tracks.

She saw that people were shifting on their chairs. "If somebody'll make a motion about the dues, we can discuss it," she said.

Aunt Hetty spoke up first. "I move that the 1930 dues be set at fifteen cents a month," she said firmly. "If somebody wants to pay it all at once, let's make it a dollar fifty."

"I'll second that!" Earlynne Biddle said, very fast. Her husband, Hank, was the manager at the Coca-Cola bottling plant. The plant was laying people off, and Earlynne knew that, for a lot of families in Darling, every nickel counted.

"I'll third it." That was Ophelia. Her husband, Jed—Darling's second-term mayor—owned Snow's Farm Supply, on the northwest corner of the courthouse square. He carried as many farmers as he could on credit, but the past several summers had been dry and most crops hadn't brought in enough for folks to pay their seed bills. Jed hadn't laid anybody off yet, but he'd had to cut the employees' hours. Like everybody else, the Snows were pinching pennies.

"Moved and seconded and thirded," Lizzy said. "The motion's on the floor." She looked around. "Is there any discussion?"

"Just one thing," Lizzy," Aunt Hetty said. "You're right about the roof on this house. We can probably get some volunteers to help, but we'll have to buy roofing material. We can't expect to pay for something that expensive out of what we collect from our members, though. I think we ought to lower the dues and find another way to raise money for the roof."

"Hear, hear," Bessie Bloodworth called from a corner of the room.

"I'm in favor," Mildred Kilgore added, and others were nodding. "If we lower the dues, maybe we'll get some new members. There's lots of work out there in the garden. They could help."

Silence. After a moment, Voleen Johnson said, in a sour tone, "Well, I've said my piece. Might as well vote, I suppose."

"Mrs. Johnson has called the question," Lizzy said crisply. "All in favor, say aye. Opposed, nay." There was a loud chorus of ayes. Mrs. Johnson didn't say anything.

"Motion carried," Lizzy said. "So everybody, pay your dues. At our next meeting, we'll discuss what we can do to raise money to fix the roof. But for now, could we have a motion to adjourn? And of course, there's still plenty of food."

"I move we adjourn," Beulah said. "I want a piece of Mildred's ribbon cake—if there's any left, that is."

Later, after the rest had taken their dishes and gone home, Lizzy, Opelia, and Verna put on aprons and tidied up the kitchen, washing the plates and silver, wiping the counter and table, and sweeping the floor.

"I sometimes wonder why she wants to belong to the Dahlias," Ophelia said. "Voleen Johnson, I mean." She put the clean forks into the silverware drawer. "The rest of us are way below her on the social ladder. Voleen was a Butler before she married into the Johnsons, you know."

Lizzy carried the enamel dishpan to the back screen door and tossed the water onto the trumpet climber that arched across the roof. "Maybe it's our friendly company she craves." She chuckled. "Must be kind of lonely at the top of that social ladder. Nobody can afford to climb high enough to join her."

Lizzy knew she was exaggerating, but what she said was mostly true. Darling had once had an aristocracy of sorts—the Blakes, for instance, and the Robbs and the Butlers and the Cartwrights, of course, Mrs. Blackstone's mother's family. They were the cotton kings and queens, with fine plantations on the richest bottoms and landings along the river, where the stern-wheel steamboats plied their weekly runs up from Mobile and down from Montgomery. The boats stopped at every landing to leave farm equipment and blocks of ice and barrels of flour and bags of sugar, and pick up bales of cotton and wool and bushels of corn and sweet potatoes and barrels of turpentine—a strong commerce built on agriculture.

But that was in the old days, before the War Between the States, before Emancipation, before the Depression of the 1890s, before the Great War. Everything was different now. The Louisville and Nashville railroad had taken over the river traffic. The boll weevils that munched through the cotton fields in the early 1900s had finished off what was left of the cotton fortunes. The aristocratic families had sent their young men off to fight, first Mr. Lincoln and then the Kaiser, and those who had managed to come back more or less unscathed had gone elsewhere to seek their fortunes: to Mobile, Atlanta,

Richmond, Chicago, even New York. There were no more Cartwrights now: Mrs. Blackstone was the last of that clan, just as Mrs. Johnson was the last of the Butlers. And now, the Darling Savings and Trust owned many of the old plantations and George E. Pickett Johnson (named for a Confederate general famous for his disastrous charge at Gettysburg) was the richest man in town. Voleen and George Johnson had friends among the professional people—the town's three lawyers, the circuit court judge, the probate court judge, the doctor, the president of the Darling Academy. But times had changed and there wasn't much in the way of a local aristocracy.

Verna put the broom back in the corner and replied to Lizzy's remark with an ironic chuckle. "Nobody can afford to do anything right now. Working in the probate office, I get to see how far behind on their taxes people are." She gave the others a sideways look. "Even some of the ones who act like they own the top of the ladder. And there are rules, you know." She picked the tablecloth up and took it to the back door to shake it. "Everybody has to play by them, like it or not. Eventually, they'll have to pay up." She folded the tablecloth and put it into the drawer.

Lizzy hung the dishpan on its hook under the sink, thinking that it sounded like Verna was talking about the Johnsons. But surely not. Mr. Johnson had the reputation of being a careful businessman and a person of solid strength in the community. He'd be the very last person to get behind on his taxes, if only because he didn't want his neighbors to think he was in trouble. And these days, people in the banking business couldn't afford to look like they were in trouble, or there would be a run on the bank.

Ophelia shut the silverware drawer and gave the others a quick smile. As the mayor's wife, she was right in the middle of all of Darling's current woes, but she tried as hard as she could to keep a steady outlook. And of course, she was an optimist.

"Folks do get behind, poor souls," she said sympathetically, "but I'm sure everybody will catch up. Times are hard now, but things'll get better soon. And in the meantime, we've got each other, and that's what counts. Friendship goes a long way."

"It does," Verna agreed in her usual blunt, practical way. "But friends don't pay your back taxes, Ophelia. At least, not that I've ever noticed. And they may line up to buy your house for pennies on the dollar at the tax sale, but I doubt they'll hand back the property deed just because they're your friends. Everybody's got a bottom line. Some are closer to it than others."

Ophelia shook her head, frowning, but Lizzy had to agree with Verna. She saw that kind of thing in the lawyer's office all the time: people trying to get as much as they could, even at the expense of someone else. Ophelia always liked to say that bad times brought out the good in folks. In Lizzy's experience, it was just as likely to go the other way.

When her friends had left, Lizzy took one last tour of the house, making sure that everything was in order. She locked the front door from the inside and let herself out the back, locking it behind her.

Until recently, most people in Darling hadn't bothered to lock their doors. But in the past few months, that had changed. Hobos, down on their luck and hungry, had begun jumping off the freight trains and going door to door, asking if there was any work they could do in exchange for food. Two or three had come to Lizzy's house, and she'd done what she could—asked them to chop kindling or clean up a tree that had come down in a storm, in return for a good meal and a couple of extra sandwiches. They were polite and nice enough and she hadn't been afraid. But if they found a house unoccupied and unlocked, it might be a different story. There wouldn't likely be any vandalism—they were just ordinary men and boys (and some of the boys no more than children), down on their luck and looking for a dry place to sleep. But she didn't want to take a chance. She wasn't as optimistic as Ophelia about people's good intentions.

Lizzy was going down the walk, thinking about this, when a low, cracked voice said, at her elbow. "Afternoon, Miz Lacy."

Lizzy jumped and put her hand to her throat. "Oh, Zeke!" she exclaimed. "You startled me!"

"Sorry," Zeke muttered. The old colored man was grizzled and thin, with a leathery face and a nose that was smashed to one side—he'd been a boxer in the old days, Lizzy had heard. He wore a shapeless felt hat mashed down on his head and bib overalls over a white shirt, clean, because this was Sunday. "Wonderin' if there was somethin' I could do to he'p out here." He gestured toward the garden. "Reckon the grass might oughta be mowed purty soon. An' there's plenty of snippin' an' clippin' and cleanin' in them flower beds." He shook his head. "Sho' looks a mess. Po' Miz Dahlia must be turnin' over in her grave."

Lizzy looked around. Zeke was right, she thought. The grass was ankle-high, and if it wasn't clipped soon, the job would be a lot harder—maybe too hard for Zeke, who must be in his seventies. But he was strong still, strong enough to make a living delivering groceries for Mr. Hancock and doing odd jobs around the neighborhood—when he wasn't drunk or recovering from an extended bout with the bottle.

"Thanks for pointing that out, Zeke," Lizzy replied. "Our club members will handle the cleanup on the flower beds, but maybe you could cut the grass for us." She looked again at the long stretch down toward the woods. "How much did Mrs. Blackstone pay you for the work?"

Zeke brightened. "A quarter's whut she paid, Miz Lizzy."

"Good." Lizzy opened her purse and took out a quarter. "Oh, and there's something else you might could do for us, Zeke. It doesn't have to be this week, but please dig a hole for the sign and plant it, out there in front of the house, under the cucumber tree. We want people to see it as they go past." Considering his habits, it would probably be better if she didn't give him all the money at once. "If you'll come by my house when you're finished, I'll pay you for it."

Zeke nodded, grinning a snaggletoothed grin. "Yes'm, I'll do that." He pocketed the money, giving her a questioning look. "What folks're sayin' is true, then? Mr. Beatty Blackstone ain't never gonna live here? This place don't belong to him or his'n?"

There was something in the tone that arrested her, but she only said, "No, Zeke. Mrs. Blackstone left the house and the lot next door to the garden club. The Dahlias will be keeping the garden up—as best we can, anyway—and using the house for our meetings. It's what Mrs. Blackstone wanted."

"Yes'm," Zeke said, and looked away. "Reckon you know about the Cartwright ghost."

Many Alabama houses have their resident ghosts, of course, especially if the house has had a history of tragedy. The Cartwright house was burned during the War (always spoken of in Darling with a capital W) and the Cartwright ghost, dispossessed, was said to wander through the old gardens looking for something she had lost, variously reported to be a baby, a family treasure, or even her shoes.

"I've heard about it, of course," Lizzy said. "I haven't seen her myself, though," she added.

"Lots of folks has seen it." Zeke was serious. "Never

bothered Miz Blackstone much, 'cuz it's her fam'ly ghost. She wuz familiar. But other folks might be afeerd, if they ain't never seen her."

"Have you seen her?"

Zeke looked wise. "Oh, reckon I have. More'n once, too, since I was a chile. Wears a long black cape, she does. Carries a spade and digs in dem bushes at the back end of the garden. You'll see her, too, if'n you come round here one night when the moon's full."

Lizzy nodded, although she had the feeling that Zeke's adult encounters with the ghost might be the product of his notorious adventures with the local moonshine whiskey—and his childhood sightings the product of an active imagination.

"Well, thanks," she said. "Let me know when you've put up the sign, and I'll pay you."

She walked away, wondering if there was a way the Dahlias could exploit the legend of the Cartwright ghost to help them raise money to fix the leaky roof. Maybe a moonlight garden tour, with one of their members dressed in a long black cape, playing the part of the ghost? She did a quick calculation. If the roof cost twenty dollars to fix and they charged a nickel apiece for the moonlight garden tour (half the price of a movie ticket), they would need four hundred people.

She laughed at herself. Obviously a silly idea.

They'd have to think of some other way to raise that money. But it wasn't going to be easy. Nobody in town had much of anything to spare.

TWO

Ophelia

Ophelia Snow didn't have far to walk home, for her house was around the corner on Rosemont Street, down Rosemont across Mimosa to Larkspur Lane, in a block that Ophelia had always thought was the prettiest in the entire town of Darling. (And since she believed that Darling must be the prettiest town in Alabama, that was saying something.) The well-kept houses, most painted white with blue or red or even yellow shutters, had wide front porches and green lawns under arching water oaks and magnolias and there were pretty flowers along the street all summer long. It was a place where kids could ride bikes and play wherever they wanted to, and where people cared about their houses and wanted them to look nice. It was the pride of Darling.

Ophelia had been glad when her husband, Jed, announced that he intended to run for mayor. The two of them had been born right here in Darling, had lived here all their lives, and felt a sense of responsibility for what happened here, good and bad. Ophelia's father, dead now, had been a lawyer and part-time pastor of the Methodist Church. Jed's family had been river-bottom farmers but his dad had sold out back in 1912 and opened Snow's Farm Supply, a few blocks north on Rosemont. Jed began working there when he came back from France in '18—all in one piece, thankfully. When his father retired a few years later, he took over.

Like Ophelia and Jed, most of the people who lived in Darling had been born there, or nearby. The town was located seventy crow-flying miles north of Mobile, in the modestly hilly region east of the Alabama River. It was named for Joseph P. Darling, who felt that a country rich in timber and fertile soils, with fast-flowing Pine Mill Creek close by and the Alabama River not far away, could benefit from a market town. He had planted his foot down right *there*, as Bessie Bloodworth (whose hobby was local history) liked to say. And where he had planted his foot the town had grown up, surrounded by farm fields and stands of loblolly and longleaf pines, with sweet gum and tulip trees in the creek and river bottoms, and magnolia and sassafras and sycamore and pecan.

Darling had grown apace without experiencing much in the way of noteworthy historical events, except for some brief but serious unpleasantness when Union soldiers occupied the town during the War Between the States and some considerable celebrating when the Louisville & Nashville Railroad came close enough to make building a rail-line spur and a rail yard a realistic scheme.

When the spur—the Manitee & Repton line—was completed, the town had blossomed. Now the seat of Cypress County, Darling was centered around a brick courthouse with a bell tower and a white-painted dome with a clock, the whole thing surrounded by a grassy lawn. The town's businesses were arranged around the courthouse square, and the oak-canopied residential streets were organized in a similar four-square grid, as logical and orderly as old Joseph P. himself. Around the town there were mostly corn and cotton fields and lots of timber. The past few years had been drier than normal—people were already talking about a drought—but Jed said the town's water supply was in no danger, and Ophelia believed him. She always believed Jed. Always.

"I'm home," Ophelia called, coming into the house through the kitchen door. She put her empty dish—the Dahlias had eaten every one of her stuffed tomatoes—on the kitchen table and went down the hall into the living room. Jed was just turning around from the telephone on the wall. He stepped to her quickly and gave her a hug. At six feet to her five-foot-four, he nearly dwarfed her.

"Have a good meeting?" He was one of those men who go on looking forty-five until they're seventy, brown-haired and brown-eyed, with square, capable hands and—usually—an open, pleasant look on his face. Just now, his brows were pulled together. He looked troubled.

"We did," Ophelia said, taking off her hat and fluffing her brown hair. "Except for Voleen Johnson, of course. She thinks Beulah's sign looks tacky. Well, I s'pose it is a bit colorful, but since Beulah painted it, we love it. Then we cut the dues, which annoyed Voleen even more. She thinks it'll encourage riffraff to join, although she couldn't quite bring herself to say it in so many words." She bent over and straightened the crocheted lace antimacassar on the arm of Jed's chair. "Really, I don't know why that woman bothers with the Dahlias. She—"

Ophelia straightened and caught the look on her husband's face. "Something's wrong?" She looked around uneasily. "The kids. Where are the kids?"

"Down the street at the folks'. Sis and her pair came over for the afternoon."

Jed's parents lived in a two-story white frame house

four doors down on the other side of Rosemont, where one or another of their grown children, along with their broods, usually showed up for Sunday dinner or homemade ice cream on Sunday afternoon. Sis was Jed's youngest sister. She lived out by Jericho. Her twins were only four, much younger than Ophelia and Jed's two, Sam and Sarah, now thirteen and eleven. There'd been another baby before Sam, their first boy, but he had died at birth. And then Sam came along, robust and squalling, and they had put their loss behind them and got on with what had to be done.

"That's good," Ophelia said with satisfaction. "They'll eat there, I reckon." She glanced at the clock—the walnut tambour clock Jed's parents had given them for a wedding present—on the shelf beside the radio. It was nearly six. "Are you hungry? We had refreshments—you know the Dahlias, plenty to eat. But I can fix you a sandwich. There's some ham."

Jed shook his head, and she saw that his frown was deeper. "Who was that on the phone?" she asked.

He hesitated imperceptibly. "Roy Burns."

Ophelia tilted her head. Roy was the sheriff. He and his deputy, Buddy Norris, kept close tabs on all the criminal elements in Darling. The job didn't amount to much, though, since the only people who came to Darling were friends and relatives of the folks who lived here or hoboes off the freight trains. Of course, there was the occasional crime of passion, some man getting liquored up and beating his wife, or a knife fight at the Watering Hole or the Dance Barn on Briarwood Road. There wasn't supposed to be any liquor out there, or anywhere else for that matter, but the moonshiners took care of that. The jail, on the second floor of Jed's Farm Supply building, had only two cells, which were mostly used to give drunks a place to sleep while they sobered up.

"What's wrong?" she asked. Today was Sunday. Why was

Sheriff Burns calling Jed on a Sunday afternoon, when families were settling in for supper and Sunday night church afterward and—

"Some sort of trouble at the prison farm. Dunno, exac'ly." Jed went to the row of pegs beside the door and took down his suit coat and his hat. "Reckon I better get on out there, Opie. See what's goin' on."

She went to help him on with his coat. "Out where?"

"Ralph's place." He jammed his hat on his head. Ralph Murphy was Jed's cousin on his mother's side. The two of them went hunting and fishing together as often as they could.

"But why? Why did the sheriff—?"

"Don't you worry your pretty little head about it, honeypie." He bent down and gave her a quick kiss. "Nothin' for you to be concerned about." He always said this and she always took it to heart, for Ophelia would rather look on the bright side whenever she could. The way she saw it, wasn't any sense to go digging up dirt when there was enough of it right under your nose. Same with trouble. And if Jed said there was nothing to worry about—well, there wasn't.

"You be careful, now," she said, and stood on tiptoes to kiss his cheek. "What time will you be back?"

"Look for me when you see me." He went out the door and clattered down the wooden steps. A few minutes later, she heard the Ford starting up, with its characteristic cough and chug, and Jed drove off.

Ophelia sat down in her husband's maroon plush overstuffed chair and turned on the table model Philco that had been the whole family's Christmas present. Jed liked to listen to Lowell Thomas read the news, and the kids loved to sprawl on the floor and listen to *Amos 'n' Andy*. Ophelia enjoyed music. The musical program that was on right now was the A&P Gypsies half hour on WODX, which broadcast from the Battle House Hotel in Mobile. Ophelia liked the Gypsies' music. Liked Milton Cross, too, who did the announcing, in tones that were considered "mellifluous." Frank Parker was singing "Just a Memory," one of her favorites, although it always made her feel sad.

She leaned her head against the back of the chair and listened for a moment, trying to imagine the Gypsies and Frank Parker and Milton Cross in a New York studio, playing this beautiful music just for her, sitting right here in Darling, a thousand miles away, with the sound rippling in waves like water, but through the air.

The music changed to a faster beat, something Latin, and she got up and began straightening things, picking up a stray sock, emptying Jed's ashtray, folding his *Mobile Register*. The article at the top of the page accompanied a photograph of Mr. Hoover, with a quotation from a recent speech: "We have now passed the worst and with continued unity of effort we shall rapidly recover."

Well, good! Ophelia loved it when the president sounded so encouraging. Encouragement was what everybody needed right now. If people believed that things would turn out right in the end and kept their spirits up, that's what would happen. And Mr. Hoover was doing all he could, reducing taxes and trying to get the states to spend whatever they could on public works. It wasn't his fault that Wall Street was in such terrible shape and people couldn't find jobs. She was sure that the president was doing the best he could.

She disposed of the sock and the cigarette butts, then collected her *Ladies' Home Journal* and put it back with the others in the rack on the end table by the sofa. The children's cat—an orange tabby named Rudy Vallée (because he was a vagabond lover)—came into the room and meowed plaintively. Ophelia followed him into the kitchen, where she opened the icebox and took out a pitcher of fresh milk and poured some into a saucer. Purring, Rudy lapped it hungrily.

She put the milk away, frowning. Ralph's place. Last year, Jed's cousin had married himself a new wife, Lucy—a little thing, pretty, with all that flaming red hair, but not very sensible. Ralph and Lucy and Ralph's two boys didn't live too far from the Jericho State Prison Farm. Occasionally there was trouble out that way, but why trouble at the prison farm should involve her husband, or why Roy Burns would call and ask Jed to drive out there, Ophelia couldn't fathom. It made her feel vaguely uneasy, as if a dark cloud were hanging over the horizon out in that direction, which of course it wasn't.

In fact, the sun was shining the same way it always did at this hour, the evening light slanting in through the window over the kitchen sink and turning Rudy Vallée's fur into bright gold. Ophelia looked around at the pleasant room, with its yellow wallpaper, starched white curtains, white-painted cabinets with red-painted knobs, and yellow linoleum on the countertop and the floor, which was as clean as Florabelle could make it. There was a pot of ivy on the windowsill and a red geranium in a yellow ceramic pot on the table. Red and yellow, her favorite colors, in a sunny, cheerful kitchen. Red and yellow made her smile.

Well. Jed was gone to Ralph's, the children were at Momma Ruth's, and the house felt empty. Ophelia went for her knitting bag, which held the socks she was working on. She'd just walk down the street and see if Sis knew anything about trouble out at the prison farm. They could sit on the porch and visit and watch the children playing hide-and-seek in the yard. She could knit and Sis could brag about how many quarts of green beans she'd already put up in that new National pressure cooker she bought last year—Ophelia wanted one, but couldn't justify buying it when her canning kettle worked just fine. After a little bit, Momma Ruth would put out the leftovers from Sunday dinner, fried chicken and new-potato salad and sliced tomatoes sprinkled with dill, and green beans and okra cooked up with onions and bacon. They would all help themselves, and then take their plates to the porch and eat, where it was cool.

Ophelia smiled happily to herself. She loved these late-spring Sunday evenings, before the brassy heat of summer settled in, the twilight falling softly across the familiar street, the shouts of happy kids, the contented squeaking of the porch swing, the sleepy melodies of evening birds and cicadas and frogs in the ditch behind the house. For her, this was the best time of the day and the week, the best time of the year, the best place to be.

Milton Cross and Frank Parker and the A&P Gypsies could keep New York.

She would rather be right here in Darling.

THREE

Verna

The Snows lived at Rosemont and Larkspur. Verna Tidwell's house was at the other end of Larkspur, just a block from Ophelia's, at the corner of Larkspur and Robert E. Lee. As she went up the steps to her front porch, she caught the scent of roses and took a deep, appreciative breath. The climber at the end of the porch, a Zepherine Drouhin, was covered with lovely pink blossoms, and the Louise Odier beside the steps filled the evening air with its rich, heady fragrance. Nothing like the scent of a rose, she thought to herself, to wash away your troubles, if you had any.

For the most part, Verna didn't, although she was always just as glad to borrow somebody else's. That was her nature, always had been, always would be, and it had driven her husband, Walter—now deceased—almost crazy. Walter had taught history and civics at the Darling Academy and always seemed to be living (or so Verna thought) in another time and place. He never paid enough attention to the real world or the minutiae of real life (except for his camellias, upon which he lavished hours every week). And he never was bothered by much of anything or anybody but Verna.

"Why are you so suspicious?" he would ask helplessly, when she raised a little question about this or that. "You're always poking around, looking for problems where they don't exist. Why can't you just accept things at face value? Trouble will go away, if you give it half a chance. Look at the Romans. And Hannibal. And the French and Indian War. All over now. All gone away."

Verna didn't quite get his point about the Romans and Hannibal, or about the French and Indians, either. But accepting things at face value wasn't her nature, which was good, given what she did for a living, working in the probate office. Her detail-oriented focus came in handy when she had to do a plat search or look up property records, and the people who worked with her had learned to rely on her ability to smell a rat when there was one in the neighborhood. Or not even a rat, necessarily, just something that wasn't right and needed fixing.

So Verna went on being naturally and happily suspicious and mistrustful and wary, and Walter went on being driven almost crazy by Verna until he died ten years ago, when he crossed Route 12 without looking up and the Greyhound bus ran over him. Verna always suspected that when it happened, he was crossing the Alps with Hannibal or building Hadrian's Wall with the Romans or was off someplace else where there weren't any buses but maybe a lot of camellias.

She opened the screen door and went into the cool, quiet dark. She still lived in the same small house that she and Walter had lived in. She liked it because it was paid for and Verna was always one to be careful about money, and didn't mind it being small because she didn't have any children.

Inside the door, she was met by her black Scottie, Clyde, who climbed into her arms and washed her face thoroughly while he was saying hello. Then he jumped down and ran into the kitchen to wait for her to open a can of Ken-L Ration—horsemeat, although Verna had never told him what it was. Clyde adored Racer, the bay gelding who belonged to old Mr. Norris, next door on the south. Mr. Norris' son Buddy owned a motorcycle, but old Mr. Norris refused to have anything to do with automobiles and hitched Racer to a two-wheeled cart when he had to go somewhere that was more than a good walk away. Racer spent his off-duty hours in the pasture behind the Norris house, where Clyde kept him company. Clyde would be horrified if he knew he was eating horsemeat.

Verna went into her bedroom, took off her hat, and put it on the dresser. Then she changed out of her brown-and-orange plaid dress and into her garden clothes—a pair of Walter's baggy green canvas pants and one of his old plaid shirts (Verna never threw anything away), and went out to the garden. Clyde immediately scampered off to see what Racer was up to and Verna went to her garden shed for the hoe, then headed out to give the weeds in the bean rows a quick haircut.

Walter had never cared much for vegetable gardening. It was flowers he had his heart set on. In fact, Verna always suspected that he loved his camellias a great deal more than he loved her. He had filled their backyard with them, big floppy bushes with big floppy flowers that she had never appreciated, never even liked very much. To her, they always seemed exotic (well, of course—they came from Asia, didn't they?) and overly demonstrative, flashy, flamboyant show-offs that took up too much room, took too much pampering, and seemed only too willing to surrender to root rot, dieback, bud drop, sunburn, scale, scab, and flower blight. And if Walter's anxious fussing enabled them to survive these afflictions, they were bound to keel over the next time the thermometer dropped down to twenty, which it did every three or four winters—just often enough to allow Walter to start his camellia collection all over again.

After Walter walked in front of the bus, Verna mourned for the requisite period of time, then invited all her camellia-loving friends to come and take starts from Walter's bushes. Then she had every last one cut down and the roots dug out, and Mr. Norris came over with Racer and plowed up about half of the backyard. Now she grew vegetables and a few flowering annuals and roses around front and felt like these were all the garden she wanted. More than she needed, actually. Which was why when she was done hoeing, she picked a tin lard pail full of green beans and carried it through the gate to the Norris house.

"Yoo-hoo, Mr. Norris!" she called, standing on the back wooden steps. She called loudly, because Mr. Norris was hard of hearing. "It's Verna, from next door. You here?"

Mr. Norris came to the screen. He had a water bucket in his hand and was on his way to the well pump on the cistern. Their street had been on the water main for ten years, but he refused to have city water. City lights, either, or city gas. Coal oil lamps had been plenty good for his momma and daddy, he said, and they were plenty good for him.

"Got somethin' for me?" he asked, and peered into the lard pail. "My, my, them's a nice mess o' beans, little lady." He eyed her mischievously. "Got some fatback to go with 'em?"

"Little lady" was a joke between them, because Verna was five-foot-eleven (taller, when she wore dress pumps with heels) and Mr. Norris, now in his seventies, was stooped, standing no higher than her chest. What's more, since she usually wore Walter's baggy old pants, she couldn't rightly be called a lady. And "fatback" was meant to be funny, too, because Verna didn't eat pork and Mr. Norris knew it. She had raised a pet pig when she was a girl and pork never seemed to taste right to her after that. Which was why she knew she shouldn't tell Clyde what was in his can of Ken-L Ration.

Verna walked to the well with Mr. Norris and watched him hang the bucket on the pump spout and raise and lower the handle. The water gushed out, clear and cool and every bit as good as the water that came out of the city mains. The full bucket was heavy and she took it from him.

"Buddy's not around to fetch water for you?" she asked. "He's out lookin' for a lady-friend?"

Mr. Norris' son's philandering was another joke, although sometimes not very funny. Buddy had got himself in serious trouble a couple of months before, when his wandering eye lit on another man's wife and the man took exception. Buddy had ended up with a broken arm and a black eye, which you might've thought would be embarrassing for a deputy sheriff.

But not for Buddy, who was never embarrassed by anything. He had gotten the deputy's job because he'd ordered a how-to book on scientific crime detection from the Institute of Applied Sciences in Chicago, Illinois, and had taught himself how to take fingerprints, identify firearms, and make "crime scene" photographs. When Deputy Duane Hadley retired earlier in the year and moved over to Monroeville, about fifteen miles to the east, to live with his married daughter, Buddy applied for the job. Sheriff Burns had been so impressed with his knowledge of fingerprinting and photography that he hired him on the spot.

Of course, the fact that Buddy rode a 1927 red Indian Ace motorcycle was probably the deciding factor, since Sheriff Burns had heard that the New York Police Department bought nothing but Indian Aces for their crack motorcycle police squad. Buddy's motorcycle gave Verna a headache every time he came roaring up to the house. But it gave Roy Burns the right to brag that Darling had the only mounted sheriff's deputy in all of southern Alabama.

"Buddy?" Mr. Norris shook his head. "Naw, he's out on a case." He liked this, so he said it again, louder. "He's went out on a case. Sheriff come by in his automobile and told him to ride out to the Ralph Murphy place. At the end of Briarwood Road, out by Jericho."

"What's going on out there?"

"Jailbreak." Mr. Norris was enjoying himself.

"From the prison farm, I reckon." Prison farm guards with rifles sat on their horses and watched the work parties, but occasionally somebody, or a pair or a trio of somebodies, would walk off and head for the trees. If they didn't get shot, they could be hard to find out there in the woods.

"Yup."

"Have they found them yet?" she asked. "The escapees, I mean." Verna wasn't all that anxious, but she knew that many people in town would be concerned. Once, years before, an escaped prisoner had made his way to Darling. Desperate, he'd broken into the diner for food and into Mann's Mercantile for clothing to replace his prison stripes. He'd jumped a train and gotten as far as Montgomery before the police caught up with him, and until then, everybody in town was on pins and needles, wondering where he was.

"Found 'em?" Mr. Norris said. "Haven't heard."

No, of course he hadn't. Mr. Norris refused to have a telephone, which made Buddy so mad he could spit. As a deputy, he said, he needed to be on the line, and kept threatening to get himself his own place, just so he could have a phone. As it was, if the sheriff needed Buddy, he had to call Verna or Mrs. Aylmer, on the other side of the Norris house, and one or the other would run over to get him.

They reached the back door, and Verna opened the screen and set the bucket on the wash bench just inside.

"Why don't you jes' come on into the kitchen and help me snap them beans?" Mr. Norris asked.

Verna tried not to laugh. If she went in with him, pretty soon she'd have all the beans snapped and he'd be asking her to cook them—and bake a batch of cornbread, to boot. "Sorry. I've got to get back and finish my hoeing."

He sighed. "Well, when Buddy gets home, you come on back over here an' he'll tell you all about the jailbreak." He slanted her a cagey look. "Or I c'n send him over there." Mr. Norris was always trying to persuade Buddy that he ought to court Verna, in spite of the fact that she was a dozen years older and a head taller.

"I'll come over if I'm not busy," Verna said briskly. She didn't want to encourage Mr. Norris' romantic efforts. She and Buddy definitely were not a match.

An hour later, garden chores done and Clyde whistled home from Racer's pasture, Verna settled down at the kitchen table with a peanut butter and grape jelly sandwich and two molasses cookies she'd saved back from the batch she took to the Dahlias' meeting that afternoon—which were all gone, of course. The Dahlias loved anything sweet, and these were just sweet enough, and spicy. She always put more ginger in them than most people did.

Finished with her meal, she settled down to drink her coffee and read her library book—*The Circular Staircase*, by Mary Roberts Rinehart. She had already read every single one of the detective novels the Darling Library had on its shelves (not a great many—it was a small library) and was reading the best ones for the second and third time. But that didn't spoil the pleasure, for it was her opinion that a good novel, especially a good mystery, deserved more than one reading. Verna was especially fond of sleuths like Miss Rachel Innes in *The Circular Staircase*, who was clear-sighted and practical and knew exactly what questions to ask, even when she was scared half out of her wits. And Maude Silver, in *The Grey Mask*, by Patricia Wentworth. Miss Silver was a former governess, fond of knitting and quoting Tennyson, who had set up shop as a private inquiry agent. Verna could almost imagine herself in the role of Miss Silver (except that she'd never had the patience for knitting) and fervently hoped that Miss Wentworth would write more books.

Her reading was interrupted by the telephone. Two longs and a short. It was Verna's ring, although the four other Larkspur Lane families who shared the line—the Wilsons next door, then the Newmans, the Ferrells, and the Snows at the other end of the block (their house fronted on Rosemont, but they were on the Larkspur line)—were probably picking up their receivers and putting their hands over the mouthpieces so nobody could hear them breathing and know they were listening in. This effort at secrecy was silly, of course, because everybody listened in and everybody else knew it. Some folks now were getting private lines, but most of Verna's friends and neighbors said they would rather be on a party line. How else would they get the news?

The call was from Myra May, on duty at the switchboard in the diner's back room. There were four operators on the exchange, Myra May, Violet Sims, Olive LeRoy (Maude LeRoy's youngest daughter), and Lenore Looper (Olive's friend). Each worked an eight-hour shift, so the board was covered twenty-four hours a day, seven days a week. There wasn't that much telephone traffic, though, so Myra May and Violet also waited tables and handled the counter at the diner, also not a very demanding job, now that the diner's business had fallen off.

"Verna, is that you?" Myra May asked when Verna said, "Hello." With so many people sharing a line, it always paid to know who was talking.

"Yes, it's me, Myra May," Verna replied. "What's going on?"

"Doc Roberts called for Buddy Norris. The doc asked me to ask you to go next door and tell Mr. Norris that Buddy'll be late gettin' home tonight, but not to worry. Doc Roberts is patchin' him up. He'll drive him home when he's done."

"Patching him up?" Verna asked, surprised. "Why? What happened?"

"I don't know the details, but there was some shootin' out at Ralph Murphy's place late this afternoon."

"Shooting!" Verna exclaimed. She knew perfectly well that Myra May wasn't going to tell her everything all at once. She always strung the story out as long as she could, so that everybody who wanted to get on the line had time to get there, and she didn't have to repeat. In Darling, this was a much appreciated courtesy.

"Right," Myra May said. "Shootin'. As in guns. Bang bang."

"Well, my heavens. Did Buddy get *shot*? I hope he isn't too badly hurt."

"Nope. It wasn't Buddy that got shot."

"Well, who?"

"The Negro who busted out of the prison farm. Didn't kill him, though. At least not so far as Doc Roberts said."

"What happened to Buddy, then?"

"Ran his motorcycle through Ralph's corncrib and broke his arm."

Verna had to stifle a laugh. "The same one that got broke before?"

"Nope. The other one. Jed Snow drove him back to town and dropped him off at Doc Roberts' office. Guess Buddy'll have to get somebody to fetch his motorcycle later. It's still stuck in the wall of Ralph's corncrib."

Verna, curious asked, "What was Jed Snow doing out there?"

"Lucy phoned and asked him to come out. I didn't take that call, it was when Violet was on the board this afternoon, but Violet said that Lucy was half hysterical. Jed is Ralph Murphy's cousin, you know. On his mother's side. He's out there a lot. Him and Ralph go hunting."

"Yes, I know, but—" Verna took a breath. "Ralph wasn't shot, was he?" She and Ralph had been high-school sweethearts back before she married Walter and Ralph had married Emma, who died of a cancer in her breast, leaving him with two very young boys. Verna had been glad when he married again, although it would have been better if he'd found somebody older and more firm-handed than Lucy. The boys—Junior and Scooter—needed somebody to whack their behinds and keep them in line.

"No. Ralph's working on the railroad and doesn't get home every weekend. Lucy was out there with the kids by herself and pretty scared. Guess she thought of Jed and felt like she needed a man around while the prisoners were on the loose."

"Oh," Verna said. "Did they catch both the prisoners?" She wasn't asking because she was anxious, but because she knew that everybody on the line would want to know.

"They caught the one they shot," Myra May replied, "but not the other one. Got clean away into Briar's Swamp, they said. He'll wish they'da shot him, I reckon. You go in there, you're gonna get eaten alive by mosquitoes." She paused. "You'll tell Buddy's dad?"

"I'm on my way over there right now," Verna said. Myra May hung up, but Verna didn't, not right away. She just stood there, listening, as Miss Silver might have done.

One. Two. Three. Four.

Everybody on the party line had heard the news.

FOUR

Lizzy

Monday, May 12, 1930

Mondays were always slow in Mr. Moseley's law office, which didn't bother Lizzy Lacy a bit. It gave her time to catch up on what she hadn't finished the preceding week. If she had a few minutes left over, she worked on her newspaper column, which was always due on Wednesday.

Today, there wasn't much work left over from last week, just some bills to pay (Lizzy did the office books and handled Mr. Moseley's personal accounts) and Lester Sawyer's will to type up, in triplicate, a job that Lizzy always hated, and especially in this case, because Lester Sawyer had a lot of property and was particular about who would get what when he was gone. She was a careful typist and didn't make many mistakes, but when she did, she had to get out the eraser shield and correct every carbon copy, which slowed her down considerably. There was also a list of telephone calls Mr. Moseley had asked her to make, as well as the court calendar to check, so she could have the necessary files on his desk before he needed them. He mostly did property and family law, with the occasional criminal case. There was nothing very exciting or even especially difficult about any of it, but it did require her to pay attention and notice things—which Lizzy considered to be a good thing, since she was a person who noticed.

Lizzy had come to work for Moseley & Moseley not long after she got her high school diploma. Benton Moseley had been a young lawyer then, handsome, bright, just out of Auburn Law School, in practice with his father, Matthew Moseley, a widely respected lawyer and, at one time, a state senator. The elder Mr. Moseley had died in the 1918 Spanish Flu, which carried off quite a few folks. But the younger Mr. Moseley—Bent, his friends called him—had carried on, following in his father's footsteps. He had even gone up to Montgomery in 1922 to serve in the Alabama Legislature, which meant more work for Lizzy, who had handled the office during the four years he was gone. In fact, she got to the point where she could do most of the things that Mr. Moseley could do, except go to court and argue in front of the judge. As it turned out, though, Mr. Moseley hadn't liked politics all that much. After one term, he came back to Darling and to the office full-time.

Lizzy was glad. She'd had a terrible adolescent crush on Bent Moseley in the early days of her employment and had mooned around, allowing herself to suffer greatly from unrequited love. But then he had married blond, beautiful Adabelle, a willowy debutante from a wealthy Birmingham family. They had two children, both girls who were blond and very pretty like their mother, and several years back had built a fancy house on the outskirts of town, near the Cypress Country Club. Adabelle's father had helped build the house. He had helped to further Mr. Moseley's political career, too, although it was rumored that he hadn't been too happy when his son-in-law returned to private practice. Now, Lizzy didn't allow herself to think of her earlier crush on Mr. Moseley— not very often, anyway. She just enjoyed working with him, did the best she could to make his work easier, and kept her romantic fire banked. These days, she wasn't even sure it was still burning.

This Monday was different from the usual because of the excitement of what had happened out at the Murphy place on Sunday afternoon, at the very hour that the Dahlias were holding their meeting. Mr. Moseley told her all the details when he came into the office. Two men had escaped from the prison farm. One had been shot in the shoulder—he was back at the farm, probably in solitary. The other had gotten away, Mr. Moseley said. He'd run back toward Briar's Swamp along the river bend, but the dogs had lost the scent, which was very odd, because Sheriff Burns was always bragging that the dogs were the best in the whole state. Anyway, they hadn't yet turned up his trail, as of this morning. Buddy Norris had tried to give chase on his Indian Ace motorcycle, but he hit a chicken, lost control, and rammed his motorcycle into the corncrib. The chicken only lost a few feathers, but Buddy ended up with a broken arm.

"The same one that got broken before?" Lizzy asked, trying not to smile. It wasn't funny, she supposed, at least, not to Buddy.

"The other one," Mr. Moseley replied. His tone was grave but his dark eyes were twinkling and the corner of his mouth twitched. "The one that didn't get broken . . . before." The husband of the woman Buddy had been too friendly with had consulted Mr. Moseley about filing for divorce, but he and his wife had apparently made up, or maybe they decided that a divorce would be too expensive. Anyway, the wronged husband hadn't kept his second appointment.

"I hope Buddy's going to be all right," Lizzy said primly.

"Doc Roberts says he'll be fine. Not too sure about that motorcycle, though. Jed Snow said the frame was pretty badly bent."

"That's too bad," Lizzy said. "Buddy's really crazy about that motorcycle." He rode it up and down Darling's streets on patrol—at least, that's what he called it. Lizzy supposed that patrolling was intended to be a good thing, except that Darling's residential streets weren't paved and Buddy usually rode so fast that if something was wrong or somebody was trying to flag him down or get his attention, he'd never notice. Mostly all he did was raise the dust, which hung like a cloud of smoke over the street long after he and his motorcycle were out of sight.

"I don't suppose he'd be happy patrolling on a bicycle, would he?" she added wistfully.

"I doubt it," Mr. Moseley replied. "But with that escapee on the loose, it would be a good idea to have somebody patrolling. I don't suppose he'll come in this direction—he's probably aiming to stay out in the woods. But some folks are going to fret until he's captured." He looked at his watch. "Well, now, Lizzy. Who've we got coming in first this morning?"

The morning's appointments marched briskly toward noon, when they closed the office for an hour. Mr. Moseley usually went home for a sit-down dinner with Adabelle, meat and potatoes and vegetables and dessert. But Lizzy always brought her lunch and ate on the grassy lawn behind the courthouse, under the chinaberry tree, where she was joined by two or three of the women who worked in the businesses around the courthouse square.

Today's group was small, just Bunny Scott (who sold cosmetics at Lima's Drugstore and gave makeup demonstrations for ladies' clubs in the area) and fellow Dahlia Verna Tidwell, who had some news about yesterday's prison farm escape and the efforts to capture the escapees. Verna, it turned out, had seen Dr. Roberts bringing Buddy home, his arm in a sling and a bandage across his forehead after he had wrecked his red Indian Ace at Ralph's place.

"Guess that'll teach him to ram that old motorcycle of his into other people's corncribs," Bunny said, and giggled in a way that told them she wasn't talking about motorcycles and corncribs.

"How you talk, Bunny," Lizzy said, pretending to be shocked.

Bunny (she hated her real name, which was Eva Louise) was in her early twenties and liked to shock. Today, she was wearing a lipstick-red silky rayon dress with a tantalizing V-neckline that exhibited her ample endowments and must have shocked some of Lester Lima's drugstore customers, including Mr. Lima himself, who was a deacon in the Baptist church. He had told Earlynne Biddle (Earlynne's son Benny was a soda jerk at the drugstore soda fountain) that he would never have hired Bunny, except that she was the Baptist preacher's wife's cousin's daughter. According to Earlynne (who had told this to Lizzy), the girl had grown up over in Monroeville, where she lived with her widowed mother until the previous winter, when she had moved to Darling.

However, since Bunny sold cosmetics, her peroxided hair, lacquered nails, and full figure weren't entirely bad things, at least as far as the drugstore's business was concerned. Benny Biddle had told his mother that Bunny was bringing in a whole passel of new customers. The men in town who would never be caught dead at a cosmetics counter were coming in to shop for perfume and lipstick and such for their wives and girlfriends. They didn't always have money to buy, Benny said, but they certainly liked to shop.

"Well," Verna said, "it must have been pretty scary for Lucy, out there with the two kids and those escapees on the loose. Guess that was why she called and asked Jed to come out."

"Oh, really?" Bunny took a shiny gold lipstick tube and a matching gold compact out of her purse. Looking into the mirror, she began to apply bright red lipstick. She pursed her lips, applied a second coat, then smoothed it with her little finger, the nail enameled bright red. "*Lucy* called Jed? Is that what you said?"

Verna nodded. "Myra May told me. She wasn't on the board when the call went through. That was Violet. But it was definitely Lucy calling."

"My, my!" Bunny's eyebrows, carefully plucked, were arched up under her bangs. "That's interesting, I must say." She closed her compact and put it away. "I was over at the Snows' last night—not Jed and Ophelia's place, but his folks'. I met Sis last winter when I first moved here, y'see, and I stopped to say hi when I saw her out front, keeping an eye on her kiddos. We all sat around and talked for a while. Jed's wife, Ophelia, was there. She said it was Sheriff Burns who called and asked Jed to go out to the Murphy place. She was kinda curious about that, which is why I remember it."

"Hmm," Verna said, in a skeptical tone that implied all manner of things.

Lizzy, who noticed Verna's skepticism, folded the wax paper in which she had wrapped her egg salad sandwich.

There was a silence. Bunny took out a tiny bottle of My Sin and began applying it to her wrists and behind her ears. She was wearing an expensive-looking bracelet with geometric silver-plated links and rhinestones that caught the sun and fired it back. "Far be it from me to gossip," she said carelessly, "but last week, Mrs. Adcock told me that Jed Snow and Lucy Murphy are quite the—"

"I'm sure there's nothing to it," Lizzy interrupted, before Bunny could tell them what Mrs. Adcock had said. Didn't matter whether there was any truth behind the talk—all by itself, talk could cause plenty of trouble. Working in a law office had taught her that, among other things. She folded the wax paper with her brown-paper lunch sack and put them both into her purse. "Anyway, it's none of our business."

But she couldn't help feeling sad for Ophelia, who was always so cheerful and never had a bad word to say about anybody. And for Ralph, who had met Lucy at a church social when she came over from Atlanta to visit her aunt Rachel. He'd been so smitten that he'd proposed to her inside a week, and they were married so fast it made everybody's head swim. Lizzy wondered whether Lucy had known what she was getting into. The Murphy place was a bit . . . well, primitive, especially for a girl who was raised in Atlanta, with all those modern things—electricity and flush toilets and trolley cars. And Ralph's boys were in their teens and sassy, since they hadn't had a mother for as long as they could remember. She wouldn't be surprised if Lucy gave it up and went back to Atlanta.

Verna took an apple out of her bag. "So," she said, changing the subject. "Anybody go to the picture show this weekend?"

She nodded across the street, where the marquee of the Palace Theater announced a double bill. *Applause* (a talkie starring Helen Morgan), paired with *Tarzan the Tiger. Tarzan* was a silent film, so Don Greer, who owned the theater, hired Mrs. LeVaughn to play the piano. The younger people like the talkies but the older folks said they liked it better when Mrs. LeVaughn played the piano and the actors and actresses didn't talk, leaving more to the imagination. In an effort to please both audiences, Mr. Greer usually tried to book one talkie and one silent.

"Haven't been yet," Lizzy replied. "Grady and I are going on Friday night." Grady Alexander, according to Lizzy's mother, was her "steady beau" and she couldn't understand what was keeping them from getting engaged. According to Lizzy, Grady was just a very good friend. According to

Grady—well, Lizzy knew he'd been hoping for more since they started seeing each other the year before. But she wasn't ready for that. Not yet.

"I went," Bunny said enthusiastically. "And let me tell you, Helen Morgan was just so swell—I cried buckets! My hankie was drippin', it was so wet." She wrung out an imaginary hankie. "And I always love Jane. She's kidnapped in this one, and Tarzan loses his memory when he's hit on the head. But he finally remembers who he is and rescues her, just in time." She rolled her eyes and heaved a Helen Morgan sigh. "What I need is a Tarzan to come and rescue me, y'know? Take me out of this dull little burg. Nothing excitin' *ever* happens here."

"What about the prison farm escape?" Lizzy asked. "That's pretty exciting."

"Pretty scary, too," Verna said. "Myra May says that the switchboard's been jammed all morning with people calling and wanting to know if the escapee has been caught."

Bunny shook her blond head disdainfully. "No, I'm talkin' *real* excitement. Whoopee, y'know? Music and lights and dancin' and people having fun." Another sigh, longing and wistful. "And men. *Real* men, I mean. Not like the country yokels around this place. They're just old flat tires."

"Maybe you ought to get on the bus and go down to Mobile," Verna suggested, in a practical tone.

"Or New York," Bunny replied. "I've been thinkin' 'bout that a lot, y'know. This isn't the first job I've had in cosmetics. I worked for a really classy drugstore in Monroeville until they had to cut back and I got laid off." She fluffed her hair with her fingers. "Why, with my training and experience, not to mention my looks, I bet I'd get a job on Fifth Avenue faster'n you c'n say scat. It would be a whole lot more fun than workin' for ol' Lester Lima." She made a face. "He ain't always the gentleman he seems to be, y'know."

Lizzy was about to ask what she meant by that, but Verna

spoke up, in a cautioning tone. "I wouldn't bank on getting a job in New York, Bunny. Times are pretty tough. Maybe tougher there than here. Lots of people are out of work. Don't you read the newspaper? Folks are lined up just to get a bowl of soup."

Bunny pushed her lipsticked mouth into a pout. "Oh, don't be such a wet blanket, Verna. A girl's gotta have a little fun in life, don't she? An' there sure as shootin' ain't no fun in this burg."

"Well, then, do it, Bunny," Verna said, with a shrug. "Go on. Try your luck in New York. See if you can beat the odds."

Bunny sniffed. "Y'know, I might jes' do that, Miss Smarty-Pants." Having delivered this telling blow, she scrambled to her feet and flounced off, hips swaying.

"Silly girl," Verna said, shaking her head ruefully. "Young and silly."

"But you like her anyway," Lizzy said, and chuckled.

"Yes, I do," Verna said candidly. "She has a lot of energy, and she wants more than most people want—or maybe she just wants it *harder*. Going to New York is probably a mistake, but I guess everybody's got a lesson to learn." She grinned. "With her looks, I doubt she'll starve."

Lizzy stood up and brushed the grass clippings off the skirt of her blue print dress. "Speaking of going, I'd better get back to work."

"I'll walk you," Verna offered, and the two Dahlias went across the street together.

"This business about Jed Snow and Lucy Murphy," Lizzy said, going back to the subject that most concerned her. "Do you think we should say anything to Ophelia?" She paused. "The thing is, if people are talking and Ophelia doesn't know anything, she'll feel even worse when she finally hears it." She hesitated, feeling torn. "But maybe she won't hear anything. Maybe Jed will come to his senses and start behaving himself."

Verna chuckled ironically. "You've seen Lucy Murphy. Do you really think that's going to happen?"

Lizzy thought about it. Lucy had the tiniest waist she had ever seen on a person, plus the most beautiful, naturally curly red hair and the creamiest skin. And she couldn't be a day over twenty-two. Whereas Ophelia was round and dumpy and . . .

She sighed. "So you think we should tell her?"

"I'm not sure we have to," Verna said mysteriously. "Myra May called last night, to ask me to go next door and tell Mr. Norris that Buddy'd broken his arm. She happened to mention it was Lucy who telephoned Jed, asking him to come out."

"So?" Lizzy asked, puzzled.

"So after Myra May hung up, I stayed on the line and counted. Four clicks. The Snows are on my party line. Somebody at Ophelia's house was listening."

"Ophelia?" Lizzy hazarded.

"Who knows?" Verna replied. "Jed might've been home by that time. But yes, it could have been Ophelia."

"So I guess we just wait, then," Lizzy said. She felt relieved.

"I guess," Verna said quietly. She took Lizzy's arm. "Listen, Lizzy, there's something else I need to tell you. Beatty Blackstone came into the probate office this morning. He wanted to see the plat record for the three hundred block of Camellia."

Lizzy felt immediately apprehensive. "Did he say why?"

"Nope. Just asked for the plat. When he was gone, I had a look for myself. It's interesting, the way they carved up the old Cartwright property when it was divided into lots and sold, back in 1890. Camellia Street was just a two-rut country road back then, running along the front of the Cartwright grounds. From the old plat, it looks to me like the lane that went to the mansion came right through where Dahlia Blackstone's house now stands."

"That makes sense," Lizzy said. She frowned. "I wonder what Beatty was after. I don't trust that man, Verna. He's . . . underhanded."

"Underhanded!" Verna hooted. "Lizzy, you're too kind. He is devious and dishonest, and I'm not at all surprised that Mrs. Blackstone didn't want him to have her house, especially since he's not her blood relative. Mrs. Newman—she's two doors down from me—says that when her husband got Beatty to work on that Nash of theirs, he charged them twice what they would've paid in Mobile. What's more, he only did half the job. They had to get somebody else to finish it."

"I just wish I knew why he wanted to see that plat book," Lizzy said thoughtfully. "I know that Mrs. Blackstone's house belongs to the Dahlias now, but somehow I keep feeling that there's another shoe out there somewhere, waiting to drop." And as if on cue, the clock in the courthouse struck one, a hollow, ringing *bong.*

Back at work, the long afternoon, warm and sleepy and always slower than the mornings, dragged on. Lizzy felt like she wasn't hitting on all four cylinders, as Grady liked to say. The law office was on the second floor of the Dispatch building, so when the windows were open, there was usually a bit of a breeze, which brought with it sounds and smells from all along the street. From downstairs came the staccato *clack-clickity-clack* of Charlie Dickens' typewriter. Next door on the west, tied to the rail in front of Hancock's Groceries, a horse whinnied—many of the farmers still drove horses and wagons when they came into town to trade butter and eggs and cream for sugar, flour, coffee, and tea. And from the direction of the Darling Diner, next door on the east, came the rich, sweet smell of stewing chicken. Euphoria, the diner's cook, always made chicken and dumplings on Mondays. Meat loaf, too, but meat loaf wasn't as aromatic as stewed chicken. The aroma of chicken was overlaid with the scent of warm dust stirred up in the street and the floral perfume of blooming magnolias from the trees around the courthouse.

Lizzy had a small electric fan beside her desk, but the air was heavy and the fan didn't do much to cool her off. There was still some coffee in the percolator on the gas hot plate in the corner, so she poured a cup to wake herself up, then finished the filing and a few other tasks for Mr. Moseley, who was out of the office for the afternoon. With nothing else to be done, she put a sheet of paper into the Underwood typewriter and began to work on Friday's piece for "The Garden Gate."

Lizzy had been writing the column since Mrs. Blackstone started the garden club five years ago, and it had attracted quite an audience. It wasn't just garden club news, of course, although there was always lots of that, because club members liked to see their names in print. It also included notes about the plants in local gardens, or wild plants from the woods and fields and streams roundabout. After a while, she decided that readers of the *Dispatch* must be sending clippings to their friends, because she started getting letters from all over— not just from Alabama, but from Florida and Georgia and Mississippi—asking gardening questions or telling her what they knew about the plants she had written about, or correcting her mistakes, of which there were plenty. The subject was complicated and she was no expert, so she always welcomed readers' additions and corrections. Sometimes they sent her seeds and bulbs, too, which was nice. She would grow them, or try to, and take photographs to send to the donors.

This week's column was what she called a "potpourri," since it was a collection of short items she had been saving. She was not quite half done with her draft when the tall grandfather clock at the top of the stairs cleared its throat and struck the half hour. Four thirty, and time to go home. She put her work away and straightened her desk, covered the typewriter, checked Mr. Moseley's office to be sure that everything was shipshape and ready for the next morning, and left, locking the door behind her, both at the top of the stairs and at the bottom, on the street.

Home was only a few blocks away. East on Franklin outside the Dispatch building, past the diner and Musgrove's Hardware, across Robert E. Lee to Jefferson Davis, and left on Davis. Halfway up the block, heading north, she reached her house. Her very own house.

She was turning up the path when she heard a shrill, quavering "Eliz'beth!" It was her mother, of course, calling from her front porch on the other side of the dusty, unpaved street. She was sitting in her rocking chair, her knees covered with a crocheted granny afghan. "Eliz'beth, Grady stopped by 'bout an hour ago. He left somethin' for you. A glass jar of somethin'. On the porch, right there beside the door."

"Thank you, Momma," Lizzy called, and waved, thinking once again that life would be much easier if she had a sister or two, or at least a brother.

No such luck. Her mother had been nearly forty when Lizzy was born. Her father had died when she was a baby, and Mrs. Lacy had lavished all her attention on her only child. For the first ten years, this was a privilege Lizzy had enjoyed. Mrs. Lacy loved to sew, so her daughter was always dressed in the prettiest dresses, organdies and sheer cottons, always white, with ribbons and embroidery. Lizzy's Mary Janes were always spotlessly white and polished. Her brown-gold hair was twisted up in rags every night so she could have bouncy banana curls.

But as Lizzy got older, her mother's fussing began to feel oppressive, to the point where it seemed that every action she took, every moment of her life, was watched, evaluated, criticized, and managed. When she was eighteen, fired by the desire to leave her mother's house, she had said an overeager "yes" to Reggie Morris and accepted the engagement ring he gave her. She began looking forward to having her own home and husband and children to take care of. In the meantime, when Reggie signed up to fight, she got a job at Moseley & Moseley and tried to learn how to wait.

But Reggie hadn't come back from France with the rest of the 167th Infantry. It had taken Lizzy a while to get over that, and then she had started carrying a torch for Mr. Moseley. That took a while to burn itself out, and by the time he married Adabelle, Lizzy was well on her way to spinsterhood. To her surprise, she found she didn't mind that much-maligned state very much at all. What she minded was living at home with her mother and being thoroughly *managed*. Why, she couldn't even have a cat, because her mother was allergic. As to a dog, that was out of the question, too. Dogs barked. It was becoming increasingly obvious (as her mother liked to say) that "a son is a son 'til he takes a wife, but a daughter's a daughter all her life."

Which was why, two summers ago, Lizzy did something highly unusual, at least by Darling's standards. Old Mr. Flagg had lived for many years across the street from her mother. When he died, Lizzy bought his white frame house, with sunflowers and raspberries in the backyard and a profusion of roses on the trellis and a little vegetable plot and a fence covered with butterbean vines. Mr. Moseley was in charge of handling Mr. Flagg's estate for the old man's out-of-town heirs. Lizzy was able to purchase the house privately, before Mr. Manning, the local real estate dealer, could get in on the act and add his percentage. She didn't tell her mother, or anybody else, for that matter.

Lizzy had been saving five or six dollars a week since she

had started working, so she was able to pay cash for the small house. She even had enough money left to get the old place repainted and wired for electricity (Mr. Flagg had liked his coal oil lamps). The work was done under the watchful eye of a local contractor whom Mr. Moseley had privately hired for her. When it was almost finished, Lizzy took the train to Mobile and treated herself to a new Tappan gas range and a GE Monitor-top refrigerator with coils on top, as well as a few items of necessary furniture, and arranged to have them delivered and installed. She didn't tell her mother about any of this, either.

All of this repair and refurbishment went on while Lizzy was at work. When she came home every evening, her mother couldn't wait to tell her in great detail what had been done during the day. The entire neighborhood was buzzing with curiosity, for no one except Verna (who had recorded the deed but was sworn to secrecy) had the slightest idea of who had bought the old Flagg house and was fixing it up. Not even Mr. Manning could provide a clue, which was nearly driving him crazy. It was a huge mystery.

All through that summer, the house was her mother's most significant topic of conversation. It had to've been bought by somebody from out of town, Mrs. Lacy decided—one of Mr. Flagg's large family of cousins, or somebody who had visited the house years before and liked it. But why hadn't the buyer come to see the work that was being done? And why wouldn't Mr. Moseley say a word—not a single, solitary word—about the purchaser? People had asked him, several times, and he had refused. Why? Why? Why?

All these questions were answered on the day the work was finally finished. Lizzy came home one evening bringing the key. She invited her mother to go with her across the street to see the house. This was natural enough, since Mr. Moseley had handled the Flagg estate, and Lizzy worked for him. Her mother was delighted to be let in on the process. They walked all through the house and yard, Mrs. Lacy ooh-ing and ahhing over everything and expressing her delight at the renovations and her continuing puzzlement at who in the world could have done all *this*.

They were standing in the new kitchen, admiring the Monitor refrigerator, when Lizzy told her mother that it was *her* house, and that she herself would be moving into it that very week. And yes, that sweet, affectionate orange tabby cat sitting comfortably on the windowsill, beside the pot of African violets, was *her* cat. Both were gifts from Aunt Hetty Little, who always had cats and African violets to spare. The tabby's name was Daffodil—Daffy, for short.

Her mother was so flabbergasted that it took a moment for the news to sink in. But when it did, she was mightily offended. There were tears and surprisingly loud recrimina-tions, given the fact that the kitchen window was open and a Southern lady (Mrs. Lacy was a Southern lady to the core) rarely raised her voice, at least not loud enough for the neigh-bors to hear.

But she had a right to raise her voice over this issue, didn't she? In Mrs. Lacy's generation, marriage was the only rea-son a woman ever left her mother's house, so she had happily embraced the notion that her spinster daughter—now past marriageable age—would never leave her, and would always be available to be *managed*. And now this! She (Mrs. Lacy) had devoted her whole life to Elizabeth, and how was she to be repaid? Why, by thanklessness and ingratitude, that's how!

Well, Elizabeth could just sell the house—that's what she could do. Now that it was fixed up so nice and furnished and all, and especially with that refrigerator, it would sell in a jiffy, and at a tidy profit. Or maybe it would be better to move the refrigerator across the street. Yes, that's what they should do. Sell the house, but keep the refrigerator. And the kitchen range, too. And if it didn't sell, Elizabeth could rent it. Why, just think of the income! They could afford to take a trip—go to Atlanta and see the sights, or add a room to Mrs. Lacy's house. They could do great things with the income the house would bring in every month!

But Lizzy's spine had become unexpectedly stiff. She took a deep breath, straightened her shoulders, and pointed out that she had been employed in Mr. Moseley's law office for fifteen years, during which time she had managed to save a tidy little nest egg, enough to move to—say—Montgomery or Mobile, where she could find a job in another law office without any difficulty at all.

So if her mother preferred that she sell the house, she would do so—and then begin looking for a new job elsewhere. Or she could stay right here in Darling and live in her own little house just across the street and look in on her mother every day to make sure that Sally-Lou was doing a good job. (Sally-Lou was the colored woman who lived in and did Mrs. Lacy's cooking and housekeeping, allowing her mistress to live like a Southern lady.)

There had been a few more tears, of course, but that was pretty much the end of it. Mrs. Lacy saw the wisdom of Lizzy's proposal—or pretended to, anyway. Lizzy and Sally had carried Lizzy's clothes and things across the street, and Lizzy had settled into her new home more happily than she could ever have imagined. Even today, two years later, she was filled with a very deep joy as she walked up the porch steps.

Her home. Her very own house and garden.

And there, by the door, was the present from Grady: a Mason jar filled with water and the cutting he had promised her from one of the farms that he visited in his job as county agriculture agent. It was already beginning to put out white roots and begging to be transplanted into her garden so it could settle in and start to grow tall and strong. It was a Confederate rose.

FIVE

THE GARDEN GATE

By Miss Elizabeth Lacy
Friday, May 16, 1930, Darling *Dispatch*

❧ Last Sunday, the Darling Dahlias held our first meeting in our new clubhouse at 302 Camellia Street, the former home of our club's founder, Mrs. Dahlia Blackstone. We had refreshments and transacted club business, including a reduction in the dues to just fifteen cents a month, so if you've been wanting to join, now's your chance. Also, we unveiled our new sign, painted by Beulah Trivette, noted local artist and owner of Beulah's Beauty Bower. The sign will be installed under the cucumber tree in front of the house sometime soon. The garden will be open during the Darling Garden Tour in September, the dates to be announced. If you'd like to add your garden to the tour, please contact Mrs. Hetty Little, who is keeping a list.

🐚 Earlynne Biddle reports that the best thing that's happened in her garden this spring is the unexpected comeback of her Butter and Eggs, which disappeared quite a few years ago and she thought was gone forever. It isn't where she saw it last, but that's a daffodil for you. She says that she was so glad to see it again that she didn't ask where it had been all those years.

🐚 Another nice thing that happened this spring, according to Miss Dorothy Rogers, Darling's intrepid librarian, was an automobile trip to the family cemetery, over near Monroeville. (Ask her how many flat tires they had going there and back.) Miss Rogers came home with slips from a beautiful rose, which she says was growing up into a tree beside the cemetery gate, almost twenty feet high. It was a single plant, but it was covered with blossoms in all different shades of pink, from carmine to mauve, different colors in a single cluster. She recognized it as Seven Sisters, an old rose that is thought to have been brought from Japan to Europe in 1816. Miss Rogers, who likes to use the proper names for things, says that we should call this *Rosa cathayensis platyphylla* or *R. multiflora grevillei*. Verna Tidwell says that we'll take Miss Rogers' word for it.

🐚 While I'm mentioning blossoms in different colors, I should like to say that I have just received a rooted cutting of a beautiful old Southern garden plant called the Confederate rose. You won't likely find this hibiscus (that would be *Hibiscus mutabilis,* Miss Rogers) for sale, but if you're really lucky, someone may give you a slip, which you can root in water. Here in south Alabama, the Confederate rose can grow into a small tree with several trunks, as much as ten feet tall. In late summer, you'll see clusters of round, fat flower buds on top of each stem, white as cotton, which is why it's sometimes called cotton rose. The flowers are single or double, about the size of a saucer. They're white when they open, then turn pink, then red, then a deep blood-red. Confederate ladies were said to have planted this hibiscus in honor of their brave soldiers. You can surely see why.

❧ Mildred Kilgore led several of the Dahlias on a wild-flower walk in Briar's Swamp a few weeks ago. They took their lunches and did not get lost. But they did see some beautiful spring woodland wildflowers, including shooting star; wild sweet William; giant chickweed (sometimes called dead man's bones); an unusual fire pink, or catch fly; white foam flower; and trout lilies—just to name a few. Spring is wildflower time in Alabama!

❧ The Dahlias are aiming to plant a bog garden in the wet area at the back of the Dahlia House garden. Some of the plants we are looking for include the wild blue flag, cardinal flower, great blue lobelia, false dragon-head, and golden-eyed grass. Miss Rogers will be glad to supply the Latin names (if you need them). If you've got any of these plants to share, stop by the library (Monday, Wednesday, Friday, noon to three p.m.) and let Miss Rogers know. She'll be glad to send somebody to dig them up. Dahlias: please contact Bessie Bloodworth and let her know when you're available for garden cleanup at the new clubhouse. That boggy area is going to be a challenge! (Wear old shoes. Or boots.)

❧ One last thing. These are tough times for everybody. The Dahlias are compiling a list of handy tips for what you can do to stretch what you have. We're calling it our "Making Do" list, and plan to publish it in a pamphlet. Your contributions are welcome. Just write them down and leave them for Elizabeth Lacy at the *Dispatch* office.

SIX

The Dahlias Gather at Beulah's Beauty Bower

Monday, May 19, 1930

Beulah Trivette discovered her talent for hair as a teenager, when she bobbed her own hair. Her friends loved it and begged her to bob theirs, which she did, to the horror of many of the mothers in Darling, who were convinced that bobbed hair was the first step on the road to perdition.

Beulah herself thought that her ability to do hair might be the first step on the road to a career. Right after high school, she took the Greyhound bus to Montgomery, where she got a job at a diner and worked her way through the Montgomery College of Cosmetology. She majored in hair and learned how to do a shampoo and head massage, cut a smooth Castle Bob (named for Mrs. Castle, the ballroom dancer who made it popular), manage a marcel iron, make pin curls and finger waves, and color hair. There was also skin care (facials), nails (manicure and pedicure), and makeup—all you needed to know, as the MCC advertised, "to make the ordinary woman pretty and the pretty woman beautiful." Beulah (who was already pretty and aspired to being beautiful) graduated at the top of her class in cutting and styling and then came back to Darling, fired with the ambition to introduce every woman in town to the fine art of beauty.

And so she did—in part because Beulah herself was a generous soul and genuinely wanted to help women make the most of whatever the good Lord had given them, whether it was a little or a lot. She was a perky, pretty blonde with a passion for all things artistic—not just hair, but drawing, painting, sewing, and flower arranging. She loved flowers with big, floppy blooms, especially cabbage roses and dahlias and sunflowers, and crowded as many as possible into her backyard.

After a couple of years of being eagerly courted by a great many Darling males (during which time she was thought pretty "fast"), Beulah married Hank Trivette. Most people were surprised, since they'd expected her to fall for one of the rowdy crowd that hung out at the Watering Hole, going out to the parking lot every now and then to pass their bootleg bottles around. Hank was a settled young fellow without much in the way of looks or gumption and he didn't spend much time at the Watering Hole. He couldn't dance, either, and pretty much steered clear of the Dance Barn.

But Hank (who had a few hitherto undemonstrated sterling qualities) endowed Beulah with something she wasn't likely to get from her other suitors: respectability and a marketing opportunity. Hank was the youngest son of the pastor at the Four Corners Methodist Church, where Beulah confessed her sins and joined on the Sunday before the wedding, wiping the slate clean and getting the marriage off to a good start. Before long, all the respectable Methodist women were coming to Beulah to get their hair shampooed and set, and then the Pentecostals joined the beauty parade, and finally even the Presbyterians. Beulah was on her way.

After the birth of Hank Jr., Hank (who knew a good thing when he saw it) bought a larger house on Dauphin Street, between Jeff Davis and Peachtree, and enclosed the screened porch across the back so Beulah could have herself a real shop. He installed a shampoo sink and haircutting chair and big wall mirror and wired the place for electricity for that new Kenmore handheld hair dryer that Beulah wanted.

That done, Beulah wallpapered the walls with big pink roses and painted the wainscoting pink. She painted the wooden floor pink, too, but pretty quickly discovered the problem with that and spattered it with gray, blue, and yellow. Then she painted a beautiful sign, decorated with a basket of pink roses, and hung it out front. Since Dauphin Street was the way most people came into town, lots of people saw the sign.

After a few months, the Beauty Bower was such a runaway success that Beulah had to put an advertisement in the *Dispatch* for somebody to help her out with shampoos and manicures. Bettina Higgens applied, demonstrated her skills on Beulah's very own hair and nails, and got the job. She was definitely not a pretty woman herself (she was tall and her brown hair was irredeemably thin and lanky) and she didn't have the advantage of cosmetology school. But she was a fast learner and Beulah was a good teacher, and within two weeks, they were working shoulder-to-shoulder at the now-twin shampoo sinks and haircutting stations.

The Beauty Bower opened promptly at nine in the morning, after Beulah saw Hank Jr. and daughter Spoonie off to school. Then she took out her hair curlers (she had traded her bob for curls), applied her makeup, and donned a freshly ironed pink-ruffled apron, with *Beulah's Beauty Bower* embroidered across the bib. Bettina, similarly aproned, was already at work, sweeping the floor, folding towels, and making sure that the customers' cover-up capes were clean and ready to be deployed.

Each day brought its regulars—the Mondays, Tuesdays,

and so forth. These ladies had gotten so used to meeting at Beulah's that it was more like a tea party than anything else, especially since somebody usually brought cookies while somebody else brought cupcakes, to go with the coffee percolating in Beulah's kitchen and the iced tea in the icebox. There were also the "irregulars," as Bettina called them, women who never could remember what day their appointment was or whether they had made one at all and just stopped by to see if Beulah or Bettina could fit them in. They usually could, after a short wait, which nobody minded because the Beauty Bower was such a good place to catch up on the news.

The Mondays included Myra May Mosswell and Miss Dorothy Rogers (nine o'clock), Mrs. Voleen Johnson and Leona Ruth Adcock (nine thirty). Beulah especially liked having Myra May first on Monday morning. That way, they got to hear a full report of all the weekend goings-on, straight from the telephone exchange and the Darling Diner. It got the week started off right.

"Well, dear?" Beulah asked, when Myra May was stretched out flat in the chair with her feet on a stool and her toes turned up in her peep-toed shoes (Myra May liked to paint her toenails red so they showed through her rayon stockings). Her eyes were closed, and her head lay in the shampoo tray. "Got any good news to tell us? Have they captured that escaped convict yet?" Beulah poured a pitcher of water over Myra May's dark hair.

Myra May opened her eyes and squinted up. "Water's too cold, Beulah. I like it hot, remember?" Beulah poured some more hot water out of the teakettle into the pitcher and tried again.

Myra May smiled blissfully and closed her eyes. "No, they haven't captured him. Sheriff Burns says they're still looking. But there's some other news. Somebody stole a car on Saturday night."

"Stole a car!" Beulah and Bettina exclaimed in astonished unison.

"Well, my goodness gracious," Miss Rogers said. She was in the same prone position as Myra May, toes up (sensibly shod) and head in the shampoo tray. "A car theft? In Darling?"

"Whose car?" asked Bettina, scrubbing Miss Rogers' gray hair energetically.

"Watch your fingernails, Bettina," Miss Rogers reprimanded. "And the water could be a little cooler. I don't like hot water."

"The car was a roadster," Myra May said. "Pontiac, near new. Stolen from in front of Fred Harper's house. Belonged to his brother. He phoned the sheriff around midnight Saturday night to say it'd been stolen."

"Who stole it?" Beulah asked, vigorously applying shampoo.

"Mr. Harper said he didn't know. A man and a young woman. They—"

"A woman?" Miss Rogers interrupted sharply. "Really. I don't know what girls these days are coming to. Dancing, smoking, drinking, taking the Lord's name in vain." She sniffed. "And now stealing cars. Society is going to utter wrack and ruin."

"Was Mr. Harper's brother visiting?" Beulah asked.

"No," Myra May replied. "He'd borrowed the car. Mr. Harper, that is. His brother is a dentist, lives over in Monroeville." She opened her eyes. "That feels lovely, Beulah, but you can rub a little harder."

"Lord sakes. A girl?" Bettina was shocked. "What'll Sheriff Burns do if he catches her? Will he put her in jail along with Clipper Rexnoth?" Clipper could be counted on to get roaring drunk a couple of weekends a month and be confined to jail to sober up safely.

"That will never do," Miss Rogers said definitively. She

fished for a hankie in her brown-checked bosom (Miss Rogers always wore brown—checks, stripes, plaids, or plain) and wiped a drop of water off her cheek. "The sheriff will have to find somewhere else to put her."

"There's an old lockup in the cellar of the courthouse," Bettina offered, pouring a pitcher of rinse water through Miss Rogers' hair. "I saw it once, years back. Used to be full of old records, but they got wet and mildewed, so they had to put 'em somewhere else."

"That won't do, either," Miss Rogers said. "It's like a dungeon down there. She'd catch her death of pneumonia."

"What did she look like?" Beulah asked Myra May. "The girl who stole the car, I mean."

"All I know is what Mr. Harper told the sheriff," Myra May replied. "She was—"

The telephone on the wall rang. Beulah was the one person on the street who had a private line, because the phone rang so often with calls from women wanting their hair done that the constant jangling would be a nuisance to anybody else on the line.

"If that's Olive LeRoy," Myra May said emphatically, "don't tell her I'm here. She wants me to work for her on the switchboard tonight, and I'm playing hearts at Ophelia's. Any of the rest of you coming?"

"Wish I could but I can't," Beulah said, as Bettina went to the phone, leaving Miss Rogers with her head in the shampoo sink. "I'm workin' on Spoonie's new Sunday dress. Promised it to her last week, but didn't get it done. It is the sweetest thing, blue and white checks with white ruffles and blue rickrack trim."

"I don't play cards," Miss Rogers said disapprovingly.

"Miss Rogers," Myra May said, "just what *do* you do for fun?"

"Fun?" Miss Rogers asked. "Well, I read. I'm reading *Wuthering Heights* right now."

"I thought that was 'withering,'" Beulah said, finishing with Myra May's rinse.

"Wuthering, my dear," Miss Rogers said, in a superior tone. "The word refers to the atmospheric tumult to which Thrushcross Grange is exposed."

It wasn't Olive LeRoy on the phone; it was Mrs. Johnson, canceling her nine thirty. "Says she's got a bad cold," Bettina reported to Beulah, returning to Miss Rogers.

"Must be really bad," Beulah said sympathetically. "Miz Johnson never misses an appointment. Likes to get her nails done on Monday so they look nice all week." Voleen Johnson didn't do any real work, except for cutting the flowers that went to the bank every day, so keeping her nails nice wasn't difficult.

"A cold?" Myra May was derisive. "Is that what she said? Well, I for one doubt it."

"Sit up, Myra May, and I'll wrap you," Beulah said, taking a towel. "Why do you doubt it?"

"Because she was perfectly fine yesterday morning in church. And because there's trouble at the bank, and she's probably afraid one of us will ask her about it." The minute Myra May said it, she pursed her lips, as if she knew she'd said something she shouldn't.

"Trouble?" Miss Rogers asked, pushing herself up from her prone position. She sounded alarmed. "What kind of trouble?"

"Wait," Bettina said hurriedly. "You're dripping. Let me get your towel." She wrapped Miss Rogers' head in pink terrycloth. "There. You look just like Cleopatra."

"You say there's trouble?" Miss Rogers frowned. "At the bank?"

Myra May tsk-tsked. "Now, Miss Rogers. You know I'm not supposed to talk about what goes through the exchange."

"But you told us about the pair that stole the automobile," Miss Rogers protested. "The man and the young woman."

"That's different," Myra May said defensively. "I could tell you that because you'll read all about it in the paper, and because once the report goes to the sheriff's office, it's public. Like the escaped convict business, stuff like that. I don't talk about the private things I hear. The things nobody's supposed to know about." She gave them a significant glance. "And there's a bushel of those, believe you me. I could tell you things that would curl your toes. But I don't. Because they are strictly private, and I am a professional telephone operator."

But her claim to complete confidentiality wasn't entirely true, and Myra May knew it. She sometimes passed on tasty little tidbits of this and that, even when she felt it was wrong—but only when it didn't matter too much and when it was just too good to keep to herself. Like the time old Mr. Beekins flushed his dentures down the toilet and Mrs. Beekins had to call Toomy LeGrand, the town's plumber, to come and fish them out. Everybody giggled when she told them that one. Or the time little Wilbur McWilliams swallowed a goldfish, and his mother called Doc Roberts to ask what to do about it, and the doctor said he should drink lots of water. That was always good for a laugh.

But Myra May also knew that she had slipped up in her remark about Voleen Johnson. She felt she was right—Voleen didn't want to have to face people just now, in case they asked too many questions about the situation at her husband's bank. Voleen didn't want to have to pretend that everything was hunky-dory when it wasn't.

Myra May had to admit that what she heard about the goings-on at the bank scared her silly, too. One of the Mobile banks had failed the previous November and Myra May's second cousin—her mother's sister's daughter's son—had lost every cent he had to his name. He'd left town on a freight train with his mother's last three dollars in his pocket and was somewhere out in Washington State, sleeping in a hobo jungle. Myra herself had money in the Savings and Trust, but she wasn't going to leave it there for much longer. The minute Beulah finished trimming her hair she was on her way to the bank to take that money out. She'd have to put it under her mattress, but if half of what she had overheard was true, it would be as safe there as in Mr. Johnson's Savings and Trust. Safer, probably.

"Of course you're a professional, Myra May," Beulah said in a comforting tone. "You're a professional through and through. Now, you just come on right over here to the chair, and I'll trim off those itty-splitty ends."

"But we are talking about the *bank!*" Miss Rogers exclaimed, dismayed. She sat down in the other chair and Bettina adjusted the cape around her neck. "That's where I have all my money! And not just me, either. The Savings and Trust is the only bank in town. We *all* have our money there—every single one of us! If something's wrong, we've got a right to know about it, haven't we?" Her voice rose to an unusual pitch—unusual for Miss Rogers, who was ordinarily very self-contained (except when it came to the possibility of losing her money—again).

"Sorry, Miss Rogers." And Myra May lifted her chin, took an imaginary key, and turned it in her lips.

Beulah picked up the scissors and began to trim Myra May's ends. "You said they haven't caught the escaped convict yet," she said, changing the subject. "But has anybody seen any sign of him?"

"Haven't heard," Miss Rogers said shortly.

"At church yesterday," Bettina said, "Mrs. Sidell—she lives on the road that goes out t'ward Springtown—said she lost two chickens and some eggs out of the coop and a sweet potato pie that was coolin' on the windowsill. Nobody saw who took it, but her husband said he figured it had to be the convict. Must be pretty hungry by now."

"Springtown," Beulah said thoughtfully. "Well, that's a ways south. Guess he's not headed in this direction. But somebody'll spot him, sure. They all have shaved heads, you know. The prison farm does that to keep 'em from gettin' lice, poor things." It was Beulah's opinion that having your head shaved was worse than going to jail.

"Wait, Beulah!" Bettina looked up, excited. "You know, I'll bet it was the convict who took that automobile! He prob'bly picked up a girlfriend and he was stealin' a car so the two of 'em could get out of town."

"You could be right, Bettina." Beulah put down the scissors and reached for the hand dryer. "I sure wish they'd catch him. Don't you, Miss Rogers?"

"I wish Myra May would tell us what is going on at the bank," Miss Rogers said crossly. "We've got a right—"

There might've been more words exchanged on this subject, but at that moment, the screen door opened and Sylvia Search lumbered in. Sylvia was just over five feet high and nearly that in girth. Next to Leona Adcock, she was the worst gossip in town.

"I cain't remember whether I'm down for nine thirty or ten," she said cheerfully, "so I thought I'd just come on over an' set 'til you're ready for me." She took a notebook out of her purse. "While I wait, I'll just take a minute to jot down some of those 'handy tips' Lizzy Lacy was askin' for in her garden column on Friday. We've been makin' do at our house for years and years."

"Actually, you're a Tuesday," Beulah replied, turning on the dryer. "But it don't matter at all, Sylvia. You want done on Monday, we can do you. Can't we, Bettina?"

"We sure can," Bettina chirped. "Just so happens that Miz Johnson canceled not five minutes ago. You just sit there, Miz Search. We'll get to you in two shakes. And maybe the rest of us can help with those tips. We've been makin' do, too."

And that, Myra May thought with relief, was the end of that conversation. Nobody would say a single thing of any consequence as long as Sylvia Search was in the room—not unless they wanted it broadcast to the rest of Darling.

But it wasn't the end of the troublesome subject of the bank.

An hour later, freshly combed and dried and turning away from Alice Ann Walker's window at the Savings and Trust with fifty-three dollars tucked carefully into the lining of her pocketbook, Myra May bumped into Miss Rogers. She hung around long enough to see the librarian push her savings book across the counter and hear her say, with her accustomed firmness, "I wish to withdraw the money in my savings account, please, Alice Ann. All of it."

And at noon, Beulah and Bettina hung the Closed sign on the Beauty Bower's door and went together to the bank, where they stood in line with three or four other citizens of Darling, all looking warily uncomfortable.

And in his bank president's office, watching through the glass window as one after another of the bank's customers made a withdrawal, Mr. George E. Pickett Johnson was becoming nervous.

SEVEN

Ophelia Lends a Helping Hand

It wasn't Verna or Lizzy who told Ophelia about her husband carrying on with Lucy Murphy, after all. That responsibility was assumed by Mrs. Leona Ruth Adcock, who lived kitty-corner across Rosemont from the Snows. Mrs. Adcock always took it on herself to make sure that everyone in the neighborhood stayed firmly on the straight and narrow. Or if they strayed, that the appropriate people knew about it. She and Sylvia Search had a reputation for gossip that was excelled by none.

It was early Monday morning, just about the time that Beulah and Bettina were opening up for business. Ophelia, who liked to get into the garden while it was still cool, was spading a hole beside the corner of her front porch for her new angel's trumpet, properly called *Datura arborea*, according to Miss Rogers. Ophelia had swapped Bessie Bloodworth an early-blooming double white peony for it at Saturday's plant sale. (She didn't know the peony's real name because it had come from her mother, who always called it Aunt

Polly's peony because that's where *she* had gotten it.) Bessie, who "specialized" in angel's trumpets, had taken half a dozen cuttings in the fall and carried them over the winter on her south-facing back porch, just for the sale. This one was supposed to be creamy yellow and would probably get about six feet tall. Ophelia wanted it by the porch where she could enjoy its sweet scent when the trumpets unfurled in the evening, but she'd have to remember to tell the kids to leave the seeds alone. They were poisonous, although Bessie said that her grandmother had smoked the leaves to relieve her asthma. Ophelia didn't think she'd try smoking it, even though Bessie said her grandmother (who had died on her hundredth birthday) thought the smoke helped to take the edge off her troubles.

Mrs. Adcock—an older lady with a sharp, ferrety nose and a pointed chin with two or three stiff hairs growing out of it—was returning the cup of brown sugar she had borrowed the week before. But that was only the ostensible reason for her visit. Her real reason became clear when Ophelia (who tried to be neighborly even when she didn't particularly like the neighbor) invited her into the kitchen for coffee. Mrs. Adcock wanted to let Ophelia know that certain folks in town—she didn't like to name names—were saying that Jed was fooling around with his cousin Ralph's young wife while Ralph was away, working on the railroad.

Of course, Mrs. Adcock went on piously, she never liked to interfere in people's private business. But she did think it was her bounden duty to let Ophelia know what was being said. Not that there was necessarily anything in it, she hastened to add, since even Christians were always going to gossip. No matter what the truth of something was, they'd have it told six ways from Sunday, and there never was any real knowing just what the facts were.

Still, she was sure that Ophelia would like to hear about

this, 'cause goodness only knew, it was terrible when people you thought were your friends were talking about your husband and his cousin's wife behind your back and you didn't know a thing about it.

Having delivered this nasty bit of news, Mrs. Adcock smiled in a neighborly fashion, changed tacks, and opened a new subject. "Have you heard about the ghost?"

"What ghost?" Ophelia asked blankly, trying to get her mind around what Mrs. Adcock had just said about Jed and Ralph's wife. Of course it was all a pack of lies. Jed would never—

"Over on Camellia Street. The Cartwright ghost. She was wanderin' around in Mrs. Blackstone's garden Satiddy night, pretty as you please."

"Oh, really?" Ophelia murmured distractedly. She didn't believe for a minute that Jed might be hiding any sort of—

"Really." Mrs. Adcock picked up her coffee cup. "Mrs. Sedalius saw her and told me all about it after church yestiddy mornin'." Mrs. Adcock was one of the faithful at the Four Corners Methodist Church. "Mrs. Sedalius lives at the Magnolia Manor, you know, right next door to the old Blackstone house. She has a very nice second-floor room, facin' south, where she can see out of her window into the garden. That's where she saw her. The Cartwright ghost, I mean. The one that haunts the old mansion that was burned during the War."

"Hmm," Ophelia said. Jed wouldn't. Not with Lucy, not with anybody. But there was that telephone call—

"Exactly, my dear. That one." Mrs. Adcock sipped her coffee. "It was 'bout ten o'clock, an' Mrs. Sedalius was gettin' herself ready for bed. She looked out the window toward Mrs. Blackstone's garden, and what did she see but the ghost, wearin' a long, dark cape an' carryin' a spade, way she always does." Mrs. Adcock leaned forward and lowered her voice.

"Mrs. Sedalius said it was a full moon out there an' she saw that ghost just as plain as if it was bright daylight."

"What did she do?" Ophelia asked, wrenching her attention away from Jed and that phone call. Jed had said it was from Sheriff Burns, although that had struck her as odd at the time. Why would the sheriff—

"Do? Why, she ran out in the hall an' banged on Bessie Bloodworth's door an' called her to come have a look. But by the time they got to the window, the moon had went behind a cloud and they couldn't see a blessed thing. Mrs. Sedalius said it was black as the inside of a wolf."

Ophelia didn't ask how Mrs. Sedalius knew what the inside of a wolf looked like. "Well," she said doubtfully, "I suppose she might have been—"

Mrs. Adcock sat back in her chair. "That's exactly what Bessie said, too. She was sure that Mrs. Sedalius was imaginin' it. That ghost ain't been seen for quite a while, you know, and folks're figurin' she found what she was lookin' for and wouldn't be around anymore. But later that night, after everybody had went to sleep, Bessie herself heard it."

Ophelia frowned. "Heard what, exactly? How do you hear a ghost?"

"Why, the sound of the spade, that's what! The ghost was diggin' out yonder, at the back of the garden where it's all marshy an' wet, by that cucumber tree. Bessie said at first she thought she was dreamin'—you know, after hearin' all about the ghost from Mrs. Sedalius. But she got up out of her bed an' raised her window an' heard it loud an' clear. Clink-clink-clink." Mrs. Adcock picked up a spoon and rapped it against her cup. "Jes' like that. Clink-clink-clink."

"And then what?"

"Well, I don't rightly know, dear." Mrs. Adcock put the spoon down. "Somebody come up to us jes' then to ask Mrs. Sedalius 'bout the Sunday School party, an' she didn't finish her story. But if it was me, I'd've run right straight back to bed an' pulled the sheet right up over my head. Wouldn't you, if you heard a ghost diggin' in the backyard?"

"Probably," Ophelia said. She was going to see Bessie in the next day or so, to help clean up the garden. She made a mental note to ask whether Bessie had looked around to see if there had really been any digging.

Mrs. Adcock said she reckoned that the ghost was looking for the buried coffin of that dead baby, or a lost pair of shoes, or maybe a box of family silver—she'd heard the story three different ways. She added that she was keeping all her doors and windows locked, so that if that escaped convict came around looking for food or money, he couldn't get in. Then she thanked Ophelia for the coffee and borrowed an egg (so she'd have an excuse to come again, when she had another piece of gossip) and went back across the street, saying that she had to get ready to get her hair done over at Beulah's Beauty Bower.

After she had gone, Ophelia sat at the table for a moment, thinking that it was a good thing that Mrs. Adcock had come over while Florabelle was out in the backyard hanging out the wash. Florabelle absolutely believed in ghosts. If she thought the Cartwright ghost was walking again, she'd throw her apron over her head and go sit with her face to the wall.

Ophelia was also glad that Florabelle hadn't heard the other thing, too—although if people around town were talking about Jed and Lucy, the colored folks already knew it. Florabelle lived in Maysville, on the east side of the railroad tracks. When she went home at night, she caught up on the news from all her cousins and friends who worked for the white families in Darling. Ophelia considered asking Florabelle what people were saying about Jed and Ralph's young wife. But Florabelle was like most of the colored women

Ophelia had known in her life, kind and thoughtful, with a sturdy, innate dignity. She might've heard something, but she wouldn't tell Ophelia what it was. It would be too embarrassing to both of them.

Ophelia got up and wiped the red-and-yellow-checked oilcloth with a dishrag, then got the broom and began to sweep. She was remembering the phone call a week ago yesterday, the one Jed had said was from Sheriff Burns. She was also remembering what she had heard on the party line that same evening, when Verna and Myra May were talking about Buddy breaking his arm when he drove his motorcycle into Ralph's corncrib. Myra May had said it was Lucy who called Jed, not the sheriff, the way Jed claimed.

Ophelia hadn't thought much about it at the time. There must have been a lot of excitement at the switchboard that afternoon, with telephone calls flying back and forth about the prison farm escape. It would've been easy for whoever was on the board at any given time to misremember who called who and what they said. Ophelia had meant to ask Jed when he got home, but Sam had fallen and scraped his knee when he was roller-skating, and by the time she'd patched that up, she'd forgotten all about it.

Ophelia wasn't inclined to pay a lot of attention to Mrs. Adcock's story. But there were a few other things, now that she thought about it. Little things, like Jed's increasingly frequent visits to the Murphy place. And people who stopped talking when she came into the room, as if they didn't want her to hear what they were saying. Were they talking about Jed and Lucy?

But Ophelia didn't believe in stirring a big pot of troubles until her mind and heart got stewed into mush. So she stopped thinking and went out to the washhouse to give Florabelle a hand with the wringer. Jed's pants were heavy when they were wet and the wringing went faster when there was one to feed and one to turn the wringer crank.

By the time Jed's pants were on the line, Ophelia had decided what to do. She put on a fresh cotton dress, combed her hair, put on her second-best hat (the straw with the blue silk flowers) and reminded Florabelle that Jed wouldn't be home to noon dinner because it was the third Monday, the day the Elks held their monthly meeting at the Darling Diner. Florabelle could go ahead and give the children their dinner—she would eat when she got home, which might be later in the day. Then she went to the garage and carefully backed out the Ford sedan. She was going out to see Lucy. She didn't have a plan—Ophelia wasn't the kind of person who thought ahead about what she wanted to say. She just wanted to see Lucy and try to figure out what was what, that was all.

Really, she told herself. That was all.

The Murphy place was at the end of the Briarwood Road, about four miles west of town, just at the edge of Briar's Swamp and not far from the river. It was Ralph's daddy's home place, but Ralph had built an addition on the house when he and Emma—Ophelia's best friend—got married years ago. Emma had been a solid, sensible girl, and she'd started having babies right away. But she'd died of a cancer too young, leaving Ralph to cope with Junior and Scooter, who were as free-spirited and independent as might be expected of youngsters who didn't have a mother. Ophelia didn't like to criticize, but Lucy wasn't old or heavy-handed enough to take Emma's place. The boys needed a switching every now and then, which wasn't likely to happen, with Lucy being as soft as she was and Ralph working on the railroad and gone all week, even some weekends.

Ophelia pulled up at the gate. When Emma was alive, she had kept up the yard, but now there wasn't much to it but dirt and weeds and a few straggly flowers along the porch, where a pair of dominecker hens were scratching under the watchful eye of their red-wattled rooster. A white goat was tethered beside the fence, thoughtfully nibbling what was left of Emma's favorite Ducher rosebush—a white China rose, the only white one Ophelia had ever seen.

Ophelia tootled the horn, and in a few moments Lucy hurried out onto the porch, waving when she saw the car and starting eagerly down the rock-bordered dirt path. But when Ophelia got out and Lucy saw who it was, she dropped her arm and stood still.

With some wistfulness, Ophelia had to admit that Ralph's wife was a beauty. She wasn't more than twenty-two or twenty-three, and her thin cotton dress was buttoned tight across a full bosom and snugged in to a small waist. She was barefoot and her red hair was twisted up carelessly to keep it off her neck, but the untidiness only added to her loveliness, making her look like a child. There was something of the child in her face, too, a welcoming eagerness, even when her visitor turned out to be somebody other than the person she might have been expecting. She was wary, yes, in the way a child is wary of a stranger. But who wouldn't be on her guard, living out here, with the nearest neighbor—the Spencers—three-quarters of a mile away, back toward town?

Seeing the eagerness, Ophelia took heart. This girl is just plain lonely, she thought. Ralph's boys might be company, but she's happy to see anyone who might pay her some attention, break up the monotony of an isolated life. Maybe she would have preferred it to be Jed, but his wife would do almost as well. Of course, she was an optimist, Ophelia reminded herself, but it wouldn't hurt to start off thinking like this, until she was proved wrong.

"Why, hello, Opie," Lucy said warmly. "I wasn't expecting anybody this morning. So nice of you to come by."

"I was just out this way," Ophelia said, "and I thought I'd stop and see how you were doing." Of course, if Lucy gave it a moment's thought, she'd know this wasn't true. Ralph's place was at the end of the road, which dead-ended in the swamp just behind that clump of trees to the west. You wouldn't come this far unless you were coming *here*. But maybe she wouldn't think about it. "You okay?" she added.

Lucy crossed her arms, hugging herself. "Well, to tell the truth, it's not been any too good the past week. Ralph is away, workin', and it's hard, bein' here alone with the boys." Her voice was light and soft, like lemon meringue fluff. "They're at school today, and on weekends, they're off in the woods, huntin' and fishin.' Mostly, it's just me, by myself."

"And now there's that convict on the loose," Ophelia said. "It's been a whole week. I'm surprised they haven't caught him yet. Somebody said they all have shaved heads at that farm. Shouldn't be too hard to spot him." At the plant sale on Saturday, she'd heard that the dogs had somehow got confused on the scent, some going one way, the others going a different way. In the muddle, they'd lost the trail. They were good dogs, trained bloodhounds, and it wasn't often that they lost their quarry. But Sheriff Burns was still saying it was only a matter of time before they had the convict under lock and key again.

Lucy looked away. "I reckon he's a smart one, knows how to live off the land back there in the swamp. Either that, or he's gone clean out of the county by now."

"You'd think somebody'd see him and turn him in," Ophelia said. "A colored man with a shaved head wearing a striped prison suit—a dead giveaway, seems to me."

"He's probably wearing Tad Spencer's overalls by this time," Lucy said with a little laugh. "Miz Spencer missed 'em off her clothesline, along with Mr. Spencer's blue work shirt. And he's not colored."

"Oh, really? I just assumed—"

Lucy let out her breath uneasily. "'Course, I haven't seen him, but that's what they say. Young, too, no more'n a boy. But old or young, I couldn't take a chance. I was sure glad when Jed came out here and took a hand with Junior and Scooter the Sunday the posse was here."

"Oh, did he?" Ophelia felt a vast sense of relief. Of course, that didn't explain why Jed had told her that it was the sheriff who asked him to come out.

"Yes. They were wild to go with the sheriff and the dogs to hunt down the escapees, and I knew I couldn't keep them at the house for long. So I ran to the Spencers' and called Jed. I don't think he raised a finger in anger, but he cert'nly put the fear of God into those boys. They've been a little more mannerly to me since."

"I'm glad to hear it," Ophelia said, and smiled happily, thinking that she *was* glad. "Jed has always been good with Ralph's kids. You have any more trouble making them mind, you let him know and he'll give 'em a good talkin'-to."

"Oh, I will." Lucy tilted her head. "I'm sorry, Opie. I'd offer you some tea, but I don't have any. I need to do some grocery shoppin' when I can get a ride to town. I've got some garden coming on out back, so there's plenty of peas and greens and the like, and I'll be putting up beans and tomatoes before long and we'll have okra and corn come summer. But right now, I'm about out of anything other than garden truck and bacon and sausage from that pig Ralph butchered last winter."

Ophelia was surprised, then realized she shouldn't be. "The Studebaker isn't running?"

Lucy shook her head. "Ralph is bringing the parts with him when he comes home next time. I could hitch up Junior's horse, but he's limping pretty bad on his right foreleg, and I don't want to risk making it worse with an eight-mile round trip." She shrugged. "It hasn't been too bad, I guess. Tea and coffee are what I miss most."

"Well, for pity's sake," Ophelia said warmly. "You can't go without coffee and groceries, Lucy. Get dressed and comb your hair. I'll take you into town and bring you back."

"Really?" Lucy's luminous gray eyes opened wide. "Oh, Opie, that would be swell! I can't tell you how much I appreciate—"

"You don't have to," Ophelia said, shushing her. Doing good was its own reward, she'd always thought. "Did Ralph leave you some money?"

"Enough," Lucy replied. "And the hens are laying. I've got a couple dozen eggs to trade." She hesitated uncertainly. "Listen, I'd ask you in, but the place is kind of—"

"That's all right," Ophelia said. "I'll just wait in the car."

"Oh, good. I'll go and put on a different dress, then. I'll be just a jiffy."

Lucy was true to her word, and startlingly lovely in a yellow print dress with a white collar and piping down the front, her red hair loose and flowing under a ribbon-trimmed felt hat, her gray eyes sparkling with excitement. "It is so kind of you to lend a helping hand," she said, when she got into the car beside Ophelia. "I sure hope Ralph gets that car fixed soon."

When they drove into town, Ophelia made a detour past the Dahlias' new clubhouse so Lucy could see it. She had invited Lucy to become a member, and Lucy (who confessed that she really was awfully lonely) had agreed. She noticed that Beulah's beautiful sign was still leaning up against the cucumber tree and made a note to let Liz know it hadn't been put in the ground yet. Just then, she saw her neighbor walking down the block toward home, her hair freshly curled.

"That's Mrs. Adcock, just back from Beulah's," Ophelia said, and added, with just a touch of spite, "Let's wave, Lucy."

So they both waved merrily and Ophelia honked the horn. She was gratified to see Mrs. Adcock's prissy mouth drop open when she saw who was with her. She drove down another block and then up to the courthouse square, which she circled twice, very slowly, waving at Beulah and Bettina, who were walking out of the Savings and Trust, and at Verna, who was just going into Lima's Drugs. She nosed the Ford into the curb in front of Hancock's Groceries, next to a dusty old roadster with patched tires and a ripped cloth top.

Ophelia and Lucy went into the store. Mrs. Hancock was behind the counter, and from the way her eyebrows went up when she saw the two of them together, Ophelia guessed that she had heard about Jed and Lucy. Ophelia gave her an extra-large smile.

"Lucy needs to stock up on staples, Mrs. Hancock. Lucy, where's your list?"

Lucy handed over her list. Mrs. Hancock swallowed her surprise and got to work. Flour, sugar, salt, cornmeal, coffee, tea, macaroni, navy beans, two pounds of prunes, a bag of potatoes, three pounds of corned beef, and a couple of cans of mackerel, along with two bars of Fels-Naptha laundry soap, a bottle of Mrs. Stewart's bluing, a bar of Lifebuoy soap, a bottle of arnica, and some iodine and rubbing alcohol.

"The boys are always scraping themselves," Lucy said, at Ophelia's questioning look, and added a bag of chocolate candy for the kids.

Mrs. Hancock put everything into cardboard boxes and the grocery boy carried them out to the Ford, while Lucy handed over her fresh-laid brown eggs and paid the rest of the bill in cash. Mrs. Hancock, who was used to the people of Darling putting their groceries on credit, acted almost as if she didn't know what to do with real money. She stared down for a moment at the bills in her hand, and Ophelia felt sure that Lucy had just made an indelible impression. But then, Ralph had a job and sent money home. These days, not every husband could do that—and some wouldn't, if they could.

The groceries safely loaded, Ophelia and Lucy were getting into the car when Jed came out of the diner on the other side of the Dispatch building, with three or four Elks. They stood and talked for a moment, their heads close together, as if they were discussing something troublesome. Then Jed turned. When he saw the two women, his eyes narrowed and his glance slid from his wife to Lucy and back to his wife again in a way that told Ophelia that while there probably wasn't any truth behind the rumors that were flying all over town, Jed had been wishing.

Good enough for you, fella, she thought to herself with a grim satisfaction. And then she thought, half-wistfully, *Well, I can't blame you, I reckon. Lucy is a beautiful girl, and young. So very young.*

A moment later, Jed had joined them. "Well, hello," he said, smiling uncomfortably.

"Hello, honey," Ophelia said, and stood on her tiptoes to kiss him on the cheek. "Lucy and I have just been doing some shopping." She smiled at Lucy. "Nice to have the whole morning for some girl talk."

"Oh, yes!" Lucy smiled back, radiantly. "Jed, I can't tell you how glad I was that Opie drove out to the place and asked if she could take me to get groceries. I don't think we would've starved out there, because the boys can always shoot squirrels and the garden's coming on. But we were out of flour and coffee and sugar and just about everything else."

Jed gave his wife a small, weak grin. "I'm glad, too." He turned to Lucy. "Next time you write to that man of yours, you tell him it's high time he came home and took his wife to get her groceries. Tell him I said so."

"Oh, I will, Jed," Lucy promised, in her lemon-meringue voice. "I surely will." The clock in the courthouse bell tower struck. "Listen, I hate to rush us, Opie, but I need to get on back. The boys will be coming in from school before long."

"Don't forget, Opie," Jed said. "I've got City Council tonight." They held the meetings at the courthouse, where there was room if any of the townspeople wanted to come. Mostly, they didn't. "We had a big dinner just now—meat loaf and potatoes. A sandwich is all I'll want for supper."

An hour later, Ophelia was putting the Ford back into the garage. As she came around the house, she saw her neighbor sitting on the front porch in her rocking chair, her lap full of the peas she was shelling. Ophelia waved.

"Hello, Mrs. Adcock," she called cheerily. "Isn't it a beautiful day?" She looked up. "Not a cloud in the sky—blue as blue can be."

"A tad warm," Mrs. Adcock replied, with a frown. She tossed a handful of peas into the pan at her feet. "Sun's been hot all day, seems to me."

"Well, I guess a little sun won't melt us," Ophelia answered. "Beulah got a good do on your hair," she said. "Looks pretty." She was rewarded with a tart smile.

In the kitchen, Ophelia saw that Florabelle had finished and gone home. She glanced at the clock. It was only three. She needed to telephone Bessie Bloodworth and tell her that she'd be glad to help out with the garden work the next day, morning or afternoon, whatever was best for Bessie. She wouldn't ask her about that ghost, though. If she did, everybody listening in on the party line would hear it. She'd ask her tomorrow.

And after she finished talking to Bessie, she'd make some tapioca pudding and open a jar of those spiced peaches she had put up last summer. Peaches and tapioca pudding—Jed's favorite dessert, to go with his sandwich. It wouldn't hurt to be a little nice to him, after his disappointment.

And while she was at it, she'd make some peach cobbler. It was her turn to host the Monday night game of hearts, and the Dahlias loved her cobbler.

EIGHT

Verna Tidwell, Amateur Sleuth

Verna and Lizzy ate their Monday lunch on the courthouse lawn, as usual, under the chinaberry tree. Today, they were joined by Alice Ann Walker, an enthusiastic Dahlia and one of the two cashiers at the Darling Savings and Trust Bank. Alice Ann's husband, Arnold, had lost a leg in a railroad accident and was now permanently disabled, so Alice Ann was the family's chief breadwinner. She'd been at the bank since she graduated from high school and was a more-or-less permanent fixture there. A few moments later, Myrtle Suggs sat down with them. Myrtle worked in dress goods at Mann's Mercantile and did Mr. Mann's bookkeeping. She brought a cheese-and-bacon sandwich and a hard-boiled egg. Alice Ann had brought her usual peanut-butter-and-grape-jelly sandwich. She had a grape arbor in her garden and made enough jelly to give every Dahlia a jar at Christmastime.

Since the four of them worked around the square and could see what was going on with Darling's businesses, their conversation was a little gloomy. Verna (from her vantage point in the probate office) said that property tax collection in Cypress County was down and the county commissioners were wondering where in the world they were going to find the money to fix the bridge over Pine Mill Creek that got washed out in the April rains.

Alice Ann said that it had been an unusual morning at the bank. "Seems like half the town is taking their money out of their accounts. When I left, there were three people waiting in line." She leaned forward and added that foreclosures were up and about to go higher, and that if she named names, they would all be surprised at who was about to get foreclosed. But they wouldn't have to wait too much longer to find out, because the list of properties the bank intended to sell would be in the *Dispatch* at the end of the month. Everybody would get to read it.

Myrtle, not to be outdone, said that if she told them who in town was so far behind in what they owed at the Mercantile that Mr. Mann wasn't letting them have any more credit, they would probably have a big laugh, because it was good comeuppance for some who lorded it over others. But of course that list would never be in the newspaper, so maybe she should just whisper a few names—

Lizzy said no, she shouldn't, because things were hard enough for people without having their dirty laundry hung out all over town for everybody to see and point fingers, and anyway, judging from the number of bankruptcies that Mr. Moseley was filing, lots of folks were in the same sad situation. At which Myrtle had the grace to look ashamed and say that she was just having a little fun but maybe it wasn't funny after all. She changed the subject.

"Anybody goin' to the Elks' picnic on Saturday?" she asked brightly, and the conversation moved on to other things while they all finished eating, then folded up their lunch bags and got ready to go back to work.

"I wonder where Bunny is," Lizzy said to Verna as the others left. "You know, I think I actually miss her. I get impatient with her because she's such a silly kid, but when she's around, she keeps us from getting so down in the dumps. She always finds something to tease us about and make us laugh."

"I'm curious, too," Verna said. "First time she's skipped lunch in quite a while." Verna agreed with Lizzy about Bunny. Her perfume and makeup and flouncy ways were sort of silly, but it was a youthful silliness that livened you up when you were feeling dark and gloomy. "Maybe she just got busy at the drugstore. I'll drop in and say hi."

Lizzy nodded. "See you at Ophelia's tonight for hearts?"

"I'll be there," Verna said. "What are you bringing?"

"Haven't decided," Lizzy said. "Cookies, I guess. That's easiest. I'll have time to bake after work. See you tonight."

Bunny wasn't at the drugstore, as Verna discovered. Her glass display case gleamed and the cosmetics on the shelves behind it were attractively arranged, but Bunny herself was conspicuously absent.

"Dunno where she is." Lester Lima was behind the pharmacy counter in the back of the shop, dressed in his usual long white coat, recording a prescription in a ledger. He glowered at Verna over the tops of his gold-rimmed glasses.

"Really?" Verna asked, surprised.

"Didn't come in to work this mornin'. Didn't let on she wasn't comin' in, either. You see her, Miz Tidwell, you tell her that she's not gonna have a job here if she doesn't come to work tomorrow, or at least tell me when she *is* comin' to work. She's too flirty, anyhow." At Verna's raised eyebrow, he cleared his throat and added sourly, "Likes to make up to the menfolks more'n she should."

Verna suppressed the observation that Bunny's flirtiness was probably good for business, although since Mr. Lima was a Baptist deacon, he likely took a dim view of that kind of advertising.

"Maybe she's sick," she said, now genuinely concerned. "Maybe I should ask Reverend Bledsoe's wife. She's cousin to Bunny's mother, isn't she? Maybe she knows—"

"Miz Bledsoe's up in Nashville," Lester Lima said. "Daughter had a baby last week." His smile was a taut stretch of thin lips across stained teeth. "Anything I can help you with today, Miz Tidwell?"

Verna, feeling as if she'd just been told to go back to her pew and shut up, looked over his shoulder to the shelf behind him. "A bar of Camay soap, please," she said, and handed over a nickel.

Verna was already thinking what to do. After work, she would walk over to Mrs. Brewster's boardinghouse on Plum Street, where Bunny lived. The girl had probably come down with a cold and hadn't thought to let Mr. Lima know that she wasn't coming in.

The afternoon moved along briskly, as it usually did. Until last month, Coretta Cole had worked full-time with Verna. But tax revenues were down and Mr. Earle Scroggins, the probate clerk and Verna's boss, had cut staff hours. Now Coretta only worked mornings, so Verna had the office to herself in the afternoons. She had a strongly managerial bent and enjoyed keeping things organized and straight, so she spent her time checking records, filing documents, and recording a few property tax payments (but not nearly enough to replenish the county coffers). She issued a license to Junior Prinney and Mary Louise Towerton, who were getting married at the First Baptist Church on Sunday afternoon, registered a birth certificate for the newest addition to the Ollie Cox family, and logged in a surveyor's report on a property just outside of town.

She also dealt with Beatty Blackstone, who came in for

his third visit in a couple of weeks. This time, he asked to examine the plat that included Mimosa, the street behind Camellia, where Mrs. Blackstone's house—now the Dahlias' clubhouse—was located. He didn't just study the pages with a furrowed brow, either, as he had done earlier. He made notes. Detailed notes, to judge from the busy sound of his pencil scratching.

Verna wondered what Beatty Blackstone thought he was doing, searching through those old property records, but she didn't ask. Mr. Scroggins was very strict about not asking questions, which she supposed was right, most of the time— although sometimes people got up to monkey business, especially where property titles and deeds and liens were concerned. Mr. Scroggins had been the probate clerk of Cypress County—that is, his friends and relations had reelected him to that important office every six years for the past eighteen. But he usually came in only once or twice a week, to ask if there was anything he was supposed to do, which there usually wasn't. Mr. Scroggins had instructed Verna to take care of just about everything (even signing his name on official documents), and if people didn't bother to read the name painted on the glass in the office door, they'd think she was probate clerk. Unless there was a good reason, she usually didn't bother to enlighten them.

When the courthouse clock struck five, Verna put everything away, tidied the office, and watered the mother-in-law's tongue in the green jardinière in the corner. Then she closed the venetian blinds on the tall windows and left.

There were several places to board in Darling, depending on who you were and how long you planned to stay. Traveling salesmen or people in town for just a day or two stayed at the Old Alabama Hotel and took their meals in the dining room or across the square at the Darling Diner. Single fellows and men who worked on the railroad boarded by the week with Mr. and Mrs. Meeks, in an unpainted frame house two blocks west of the rail yard, and ate breakfast and supper at the Meeks' table.

Widows and spinsters of a certain age who couldn't or didn't want to live by themselves boarded by the month with Bessie Bloodworth at the Magnolia Manor, next door to the Dahlias' new clubhouse. The Manor had a vine-covered veranda across the front, where Bessie's boarders sat out every night after supper with glasses of cold lemonade and their knitting until it got too dark to see. Bessie said she didn't want people calling it the old-ladies' home, so she named it Magnolia Manor and got Beulah to paint a pretty sign, which she hung beside the door.

The young working women in town—the two school teachers, Miss Patricia O'Conner, the new home demonstration agent, and Bunny—boarded with Mrs. Brewster, over on Plum Street. Mrs. Brewster was the soul of respectability and had a reputation for being strict, even by Darling's standards. Curfew was at nine on weekdays and ten thirty on weekends. At the magic hour, Mrs. Brewster herself went around the house, locking all the doors and checking to make sure that "her girls" were in their rooms, where they ought to be. Breakfast was at six thirty in the morning and supper at six thirty in the evening (Mrs. Brewster didn't serve noon dinner because all her girls went out to work). Those who missed breakfast or supper went hungry, since they weren't allowed in the kitchen and weren't permitted to have food in their rooms. There was a washhouse out back where they could do their laundry and a corner in the basement where they could iron. Or they could pay Cleo (the colored girl who came in on Mondays and Wednesdays) to do their washing and ironing for them. It wasn't included in their board bill.

But Mrs. Brewster wasn't entirely heartless. They could entertain their men friends on the front porch or in the parlor and were free to use the wind-up Victrola, so long as they played their own recordings (softly) and refrained from dancing. They could sit out with their men friends on the front porch until it got dark. Then they could sit in the parlor (on separate chairs, but not side by side on the sofa), so long as the door to Mrs. Brewster's sitting room was left open. Mrs. Brewster herself always said she stood *in loco parentis*, which was supposed to mean that she was only doing what the mommas and daddies of "her girls" would want her to do. But her boarders thought she was just plain loco, and most moved out as soon as they could.

Verna had met Mrs. Brewster at numerous Darling events, but if she had expected to be greeted cordially, she would have been disappointed. Mrs. Brewster herself answered the front door and returned a grim frown when Verna asked to see Bunny.

"Miss Scott is not here." Mrs. Brewster, a bosomy lady who always wore long-sleeved black with a little white lace around her throat and wrists, was from Chicago. She had married Mr. Brewster (now deceased) at the end of the Great War and had lived in Alabama ever since. But she had never "assimilated," to use her word. She liked to say that she might've come to live in Dixie, but that didn't mean she had to think Dixie or talk Dixie. She clipped her words and spoke in short sentences like a proper Yankee. "She has not been here since before breakfast on Sunday."

Verna (who had convinced herself that Bunny was sick—or pretending to be) was surprised. "She's been gone since . . . Sunday morning?"

"That's what I said," Mrs. Brewster snapped inhospitably. "Miss Scott has broken a cardinal rule: being absent without explanation or permission. She did not attend Sunday breakfast, nor has she come home since. I run a respectable boardinghouse and I expect my girls to behave themselves. Miss Scott has exhibited previous difficulties observing the rules, and this is the last straw. She is no longer welcome under my roof." She began to shut the door.

But Verna put her foot in it. "Excuse me," she said firmly, "but I am asking about my *friend*." Before this minute, Verna hadn't thought much about whether Bunny was really a friend or just somebody she ate lunch with on the courthouse lawn. But in the face of Mrs. Brewster's vehement wish to shut the door, she thought that Bunny ought to have at least one friend, and the sooner the better.

"Bunny didn't come to work today, and she didn't let Mr. Lima know she wouldn't be there," she said crisply. "Now you say that she hasn't been home for nearly two days. So where is she?"

"I have no idea," Mrs. Brewster replied, "and I do not want to know." She made another move to close the door.

"Well, then." Verna removed her foot. "I suppose I'll just have to go and get the sheriff."

The door was four inches open. "The sheriff?" Mrs. Brewster sounded surprised.

So was Verna. The statement had come, she supposed, of reading detective novels and the occasional true crime magazine. But the door stayed open, so she went on.

"An attractive young woman is missing. I am her friend, and I want to know where she is. If you can't help, I'll ask Sheriff Burns. He'll probably bring a search warrant and—"

"A search warrant?" The door opened a little wider. "Why would he do that?"

"Because we might be talking about a case of foul play." Of course, Verna didn't think this for a minute, but characters in true crime stories were always wondering about foul play, and it sounded good. Or bad, depending on how you looked at it.

She thought of something else, and added, "Especially with that escaped convict still on the loose. We can't be too careful, can we?"

These last remarks gave Mrs. Brewster pause. Finally, much put-upon, she heaved a sigh of patient exasperation. "Just what is it you want to do, Mrs. Tidwell?"

"I'd like to see Bunny's room." This was another thing Verna hadn't thought of before she heard herself saying the words, but now that she had, it seemed like the right thing to do. It was what Lord Peter Wimsey had done in *The Unpleasantness at the Bellona Club.* He had gone to have a look at the dead man's rooms. What's more, he had taken a camera. Briefly, Verna regretted not having thought of that.

"But Miss Scott is not *in* her room," Mrs. Brewster protested heatedly. "And if she did not go to work today, it's because she has left town. She's been talking about that for weeks, you know. She's very dissatisfied here."

Mrs. Brewster was right about that. Bunny had it in her mind that she would be happier somewhere else—Mobile or Atlanta or even New York. Verna was about to give up and go away, when she thought of one more thing.

"Did she take her clothes? And her jewelry?"

"Well . . ." Mrs. Brewster hesitated. "No," she said at last. "That is, I don't think so."

That decided it. Bunny wouldn't leave town without taking every scrap of clothing and jewelry she owned.

"I can either see her room or I can bring the sheriff," Verna said.

Another sigh, then: "Oh, very well." Mrs. Brewster stepped back and pointed up the stairs. "Second floor. End of the hall, on the right. The door isn't locked. I don't allow any of my girls to lock their doors. They have nothing to hide from one another or from me."

The stairs were steep and the second-floor hall was long,

narrow, and dark, with a window at the very end that let in a dim light. Verna shivered, thanking her lucky stars that she had her own home with a yard and a garden and didn't have to live in a boardinghouse. At the end of the hall, she pushed open the last door on the right and stepped into a small dark room that smelled strongly of talcum powder and My Sin. She went to the single window and rolled up the water-stained window blind, which was ripped on one side. There were no curtains. Perhaps the girls were meant to supply their own, Verna thought sadly, like the Victrola recordings.

The unforgiving light flooded the room. Verna saw a narrow bed made up to look as if someone were sleeping in it, with the coverlet pulled over a pillow. If Mrs. Brewster had opened the door and looked in on Saturday night, she probably thought that Bunny was there, asleep. Verna had to smile at that, because she had played the same trick when she was a young girl living with her parents, although her truancy had never extended to staying out all night, let alone for the weekend.

Bunny had indeed not taken her clothing with her—or at least, she hadn't taken much of it. The chair in the near corner was almost hidden under an untidy heap of skirts, blouses, and dresses. Items of gauzy underwear, including a slinky, silky black teddy, littered the floor like dying moths. In the far corner was a pink-painted dressing table with a small round mirror and a pink bench. The top of the dressing table was covered with bottles and jars and tubes of lotions, potions, and makeup. Long ropes of beads and other costume jewelry dangled from the mirror. In lieu of a closet, a curtain was fastened diagonally across another corner, to hide hanging clothing. A basket on a battered four-drawer mahogany chest was filled with a tumble of colorful silk scarves. A cheap cardboard suitcase sat on the floor next to the chest. Verna hefted it. Empty.

She went to the dressing table, aimlessly turning things over. All of it was very much Bunny, she thought. A hairbrush with strands of bright blond hair, a cheap rattail comb, a pair of fancy tortoiseshell combs, bobby pins, spilled face powder, a bottle of fire-engine red nail enamel, an open inkwell, a pen. Several scraps of paper, as well, filled with a loopy, childish script. *Eva Louise Woodburn. Bunny Woodburn. Mrs. Maxwell Woodburn.*

Verna frowned down at the paper. Woodburn? She didn't recognize the name. There were no Woodburns in Darling, so far as she knew.

There was a drawer in the dressing table, and she opened it, seeing that it was filled with emery boards, eyelash curlers, and the like. But in one corner, half hidden under a stack of cheap five-and-dime hankies, Verna saw a small wooden box, the polished top inlaid with colored mosaics and mother-of-pearl. Curiously, she picked it up, and then saw, beneath it, a small paper-bound savings account record book from the Darling Savings and Trust, with the name *Eva Louise Scott* written on the front. A small photograph was stuck inside the book: Bunny, squinting into the sun, wearing a lacy black teddy (probably the same one on the floor) and a pair of high heels. She was posed like a glamorous femme fatale on the front hood of a racy-looking roadster with an Alabama license plate. Her ample endowments were amply visible under the less-than-ample silk that barely covered them. The man taking the photo had cast a shadow in front of him. And yes, it was a man—or a woman wearing trousers and a fedora.

Verna (who didn't shock easily) was shocked, and her estimation of Bunny shifted a point or two to the negative. She knew that women out in Hollywood posed for similar photographs—she had seen them in magazines. But this was Darling, and something like this was unusual.

Still thinking about the photo, she opened the deposit

book and was surprised to see the amounts listed in the deposit column: regular deposits of ten dollars a week over the past six months. Two hundred and seventy dollars—not a huge amount of money, maybe, but pretty impressive for a girl who worked at the cosmetics counter at Lester Lima's drugstore, where she probably earned no more than seven or eight dollars a week.

Verna put the deposit book back, her estimation of Bunny shifting a notch or two back toward the positive. She had pictured the girl as a spender, not a saver. But if she was saving ten dollars a week, how did she pay her board and room? Where was the extra money coming from?

The wooden box was still in her hand. Verna lifted the lid and was startled to see a pair of pearl earrings—real pearls, from the look of them—nestled against folds of blue velvet. In tasteful gold letters, inside the lid, was the name *Ettlinger's Fine Jewelry, Mobile.*

Her eyes widened at the sight. If the pearls came from Ettlinger's, they had to be real. Where had Bunny gotten the money? Or if they'd been a gift, who in Darling could have afforded to give them to her? And then she thought of the bracelet Bunny had worn the other day. It had looked expensive, too. Where—

Verna's questions were interrupted by a light rap at the door. A young voice asked softly, surreptitiously, "Bunny? You in there, Bunny?"

Verna opened her mouth to answer, and then changed her mind. After one more knock, the door was pushed open. Verna swiftly pocketed the little jewelry box. Mrs. Brewster might be confident in the integrity of her girls, but it wasn't a good idea to leave obviously expensive jewelry lying in an unlocked drawer in an unlocked room in a house where nobody had anything to hide.

Verna spoke crisply. "Hello."

The girl jumped, and her hand went to her pretty mouth. "Oh!" she cried. "Oh, my goodness! Oh, Mrs. Tidwell!" It was little Miss Amanda Blake, the elementary school teacher, who had come from Montgomery at the beginning of the school year. Verna had met her at a Presbyterian ice cream social the month before. She was wearing a green wrapper and her hair was wet under a towel turban. "You startled me. I thought there was nobody here." She gulped. "I mean, I thought Bunny was—"

"You were looking for Bunny?"

Miss Blake looked flustered, and her glance flew from one side of the room to the other. "Not exactly. I mean— Well, Bunny borrowed my red blouse last week. I thought, since she wasn't here, I'd just come in and see if I could—" She pounced on a bit of filmy red fabric hanging over the seat of the chair. "There it is! Oh, goody, goody gumdrops!"

Verna suppressed a chuckle. Miss Blake had tried to appear so grown-up when they met at the social. At the moment, she looked as if she were fourteen. "When did you see Bunny last?" she asked.

"Bunny?" Miss Blake frowned and puckered up her mouth. "Well, I'm not sure. I suppose it was Saturday evening." She thought for a minute more. "Yes. Saturday. She wasn't here for breakfast or supper yesterday, or breakfast this morning." She lowered her voice. "Mrs. B is fit to be tied. She says she's throwing Bunny out."

"You saw Bunny at supper on Saturday?"

"Not then." Miss Blake shook her head. "It was at the picture show. Johnny Potter and I went to see Helen Morgan in *Applause.*" She clasped her hands and rolled her eyes in a fair imitation of the melodramatic Miss Morgan. "She was so swell. Helen Morgan, I mean. Really, truly she was. I cried and cried. Have you seen it yet, Mrs. Tidwell? If you haven't, you must. You'll just love it. Oh, and there's a Tarzan feature, too. But it's silent. *Applause* is a talkie."

"You said you saw Bunny," Verna prompted.

"Oh, sure. I saw her coming out of the ladies' when I went to get popcorn for Johnny and me. But we just waved; we didn't speak."

"Who was she with?"

"Why, nobody." Miss Blake held up her blouse, frowning at something she saw on the front. "Just look at that," she muttered. "Grease. Or maybe coffee. Bunny is so careless."

"She went to the picture show by *herself*?"

Miss Blake looked up. "Oh, I meant that nobody was with her coming out of the ladies'. I don't know who she went to the picture show with."

Verna gestured to the bed. "Mrs. Brewster said Bunny was here on Saturday night. What do you think?"

"I think . . ." Miss Blake hesitated. "Well, personally, I don't think she slept here. I doubt she came home after the picture show."

"Where do you suppose she is?"

"Don't have a clue." Miss Blake gave Verna a half-defiant look. "But it isn't the first time she's been out all night. Oh, she's always here when Mrs. B checks the beds, or she makes it look like she is. And she's always back in time for breakfast. Until now, anyway."

"Oh, really?" Verna asked, surprised. "But I thought Mrs. Brewster locked the doors. How does she—"

"I'll show you." Miss Blake stepped out into the hall. Verna followed her.

"This window," Miss Blake said in a low voice. "Don't tell Mrs. B, but the girls use it sometimes. To come and go after hours. You can climb down the porch pillar, and there's a trellis—a little shaky, but almost as good as a ladder for getting back in. Nobody can see you from the street, because of that big tree and the bushes. Not that I've done it myself," she added righteously. "But Bunny has. And the others, too. But mostly Bunny."

"Ah," Verna said. "Of course."

Experimentally, she raised the sash and put her head out. The porch roof wasn't at all steep. If you were young and agile, it wouldn't be much of a trick to climb out. And if the trellis bore your weight, you could use it to climb back in again. She put the sash back down, noticing that it moved easily and quietly. The girls probably promoted that with a bit of Vaseline on the cords.

"Well, I guess this tells us something," Verna said.

"Shhh!" Alarmed, Miss Blake put a finger to her lips, glancing over her shoulder. "You don't want to go giving away our secrets, do you? If Mrs. B found out—"

"I won't tell her," Verna said reassuringly. She paused. "Tell me—do you know the names of the young men Bunny has been seeing?"

"Well, there are several." Miss Blake stuffed her red blouse into the pocket of her wrapper, then pulled the towel off her damp hair and shook it loose. "There's Pete Crawford and Willy Warren and somebody else . . . Can't remember who; somebody she knew when she worked over in Monroeville. Bunny isn't just real crazy about him, but he's got more money than most, so she sees him sometimes."

"What about Maxwell Woodburn? Is he the one she met in Monroeville?"

"Woodburn?" Miss Blake frowned, shaking her head. "No, he's her pen pal up in Montgomery. He writes to her a lot. But as far as the boys here go, she always says they're hardly worth thinking about." She sighed plaintively. "It's hard these days, you know? A boy maybe likes you, but he doesn't have the money to take you out, so he doesn't let on. That he likes you, I mean. And those that have money, you don't like. I don't mean *you*, exactly," she amended hastily.

"I'm sure," Verna said, very glad that she was past all that liking business. She paused for a moment, thinking. "What about the other girls who live here? Are they friends with Bunny? Would they be likely to know where she is?"

"No, not really," Miss Blake said. "The home demonstration agent is a lot older, almost an old maid, and the other teacher says Bunny is wild." She stopped, frowning, sounding worried. "You don't suppose something's happened to her, do you? I mean, they . . . they haven't caught that convict yet."

"I don't have any idea," Verna said honestly. "What do you think?"

"What do I think?" Miss Blake sighed and rubbed the towel through her hair. "Well, I guess maybe she just got tired of Darling and ran off. She talked about that a lot. She was always threatening to get on the Greyhound and go down to Mobile, or even up to New York. She said she knew a lot about selling cosmetics, and that she could get a job pretty easily, with her looks and all." She rewrapped her turban. "But it's kinda funny that she didn't take her clothes and her jewelry. I mean, if I was leaving town, I'd sure as shootin' clean out my room and take a suitcase. Wouldn't you?"

"Yes, I would," Verna said, thinking regretfully of the clothes on the floor and the empty suitcase. "I would definitely do that."

NINE

Lizzy Makes an Identification

Lizzy finished up her Monday afternoon work at the usual hour, but Mr. Moseley was still at his desk. In fact, he had been there since right after lunch, working on a stack of documents he had brought into the office with him. He had made several telephone calls direct from his phone without asking Lizzy to get the other party for him, the way he usually did. He kept the door shut while he was talking.

Usually, Lizzy knew everything that happened in the office, so she was intensely curious. Whatever was going on, it involved Mr. Riley, the certified public accountant who sometimes worked on cases that required an auditor. It also involved Mr. George E. Pickett Johnson, who had already called twice and had sent a packet of papers over from the Savings and Trust in the middle of the afternoon. There had been two or three other calls, as well—the same man each time, but he refused to identify himself and asked to be put straight through to Mr. Moseley, after which Lizzy was instructed to hang up. After the first call, Mr. Moseley told her to cancel the two appointments left on the day's calendar. She knew that something very mysterious was going on, especially when he was still at his desk at the end of the afternoon.

Lizzy rapped on his door, and when she heard a grunt, she opened it. "It's five o'clock and I was thinking of going home. Are you going to want me again today, Mr. Moseley?"

Mr. Moseley glanced up from his work. His brown hair fell in a boyish shock across his forehead and he pushed it out of his eyes. He had taken off his suit coat, undone his blue tie, and was working with the sleeves of his white shirt rolled up on his forearms. His forehead was creased, but his eyes lightened when he saw her.

"I'll always want you, Liz," he said, in a joking tone. "You know that."

Lizzy felt herself blushing. She understood that it was just his way of saying that she was a good secretary and he liked her work, but his tone made the compliment sound more . . . well, more personal than he probably meant. It was disconcerting. It renewed the romantic dreams she had folded and put carefully away, like old linens closed in a drawer with lavender.

She pressed her lips together. "Yes, Mr. Moseley," she said evenly. "Would you like me to stay a little longer? In case you need me for something?"

He looked back down at the papers on his desk. "No, you go on, Liz. I'll be here for a while. And I'm expecting somebody, so please leave the downstairs door unlocked." He leaned back in his chair and stretched, arms over his head. "There is one thing, though," he said casually—too casually. "Do you have much money in the bank here in town?"

She frowned at the unexpectedness of the question. "In the bank?" She thought. "Well, not a lot. Maybe fifty dollars or so. I'm saving for some more work on the house. Why?"

"It might be a good idea if you took that money out." He glanced at the clock on his desk. "They're closed over there now, but you could do it first thing in the morning. You can keep it here in the office safe if you don't want that much money in the house."

"Take it out of the bank?" she asked uncertainly. "But why would I—"

His eyes narrowed and his tone became stern. "Don't ask," he commanded. "Just do what I say. And don't tell anybody else about this. Got it?"

"Yes, sir," she said.

"Don't tell *anybody*," he added emphatically. "That's an order."

She nodded, perplexed, and felt the prickles of apprehension on the back of her neck. Something serious was going on. She didn't know what it was, or why it ought to involve her, but—

"And don't worry," he said, and gave her a lopsided grin. "Just do what I say and you won't have anything to regret."

Which perplexed her even more. But she had never questioned Mr. Moseley and she wasn't about to start now. She got her purse out of her bottom desk drawer and went down the stairs to the street, thinking that she'd better go next door to Hancock's and buy some sugar. She'd stop at Mrs. Freeman's house and pick up some eggs, too. Mrs. Freeman had a dozen laying hens that produced more eggs than she could use, so she traded the extras to the neighbors. Lizzy was already in debt to her for three quarts of raspberries, to be paid off when the berries were ripe.

But just as she stepped onto the street, a blue Ford coupe pulled up in front of the building and Grady Alexander jumped out. He was wearing his working clothes—blue shirt with the sleeves rolled above the elbows on tanned, strong arms, dark twill wash pants, sweat-stained felt fedora. He had what Lizzy thought of as that "Grady look" on his face, the intent look he wore when he had his mind on something serious.

Seeing him, she felt herself flushing, remembering Saturday night, when things between them had almost gotten out of hand. After the picture show, they had driven out to the bluff just beyond the Cypress County fairgrounds, where they parked under the shadowy trees. The flickering stars seemed brighter in the absence of the moon, and the languid music of the frogs and night birds drifted through the open windows of Grady's Ford. Maybe it was the romantic scenes in the picture show that pushed him into that restless, urgent mood. Or maybe it was just what he said, that they had been seeing each other long enough and it was high time they made up their minds to get married—meaning that it was high time that Lizzy made up her mind, because Grady had already made up his.

Whatever it was, things had definitely gotten a little steamy between them in the humid, breathless dark, certainly a lot steamier than she had intended. She had pushed his hands away and made him stop at the point when she knew that if she didn't make him stop right that very second, she would stop wanting him to stop and—

It wasn't that she was a prude, or that she was saving herself for marriage, as her mother insisted she should. No. And it wasn't that she didn't want it, too, because she did, probably more than she was willing to admit. And she might've, if the question of doing it weren't so tangled up with the puzzle of love and marriage. Grady seemed to have the idea that you only did it with someone you loved and meant to marry, either soon or someday. If they did it, he was bound to think she loved him and meant to marry him, and she didn't want him to think that. Not yet, anyway. The days when she knew she didn't mean to marry Grady still outnumbered the days she thought she might want to, someday.

"Hello, Grady," she said, as casually as she could.

"Hullo, Lizzy," Grady replied brusquely, and strode past her. Then he stopped and turned and snatched off his hat, and the sternness in his high-cheekboned face softened. Somewhere in his family, far enough back so that nobody quite remembered where or when or who, there had been an Indian—Creek maybe, or Choctaw. The lineage might be forgotten, but the lines on his face were clear enough. "Sorry. It's not you, doll. I'm in a hurry. I gotta talk to Charlie."

Doll. She wished he wouldn't call her that, but there was no point in saying so—again. "What is it?" she asked, caught by the intensity of his expression.

"Come inside," he said, and pushed open the door, standing back so she could go first. Grady had graduated from ag school at Auburn and was educated in the latest farming methods, but he was still a Southern gentleman. Or at least he had been, until Saturday night.

The *Dispatch* office was the size of Moseley & Moseley upstairs, but was just one large, tin-ceilinged room, with a wooden counter built across the space about ten feet from the front door. Behind it, Charlie Dickens was typing at his battered old desk, wearing his usual green eyeshade, a white shirt and tie, and a sleeveless gray vest. A cigarette dangled from one corner of his mouth. Behind him, at the back of the room, the newspaper press sat silent—he wouldn't crank it up and start printing until Thursday evening, after Lizzy and Mr. Moseley had quit for the day. It made a lot of noise.

"Charlie," Grady said urgently. "Hey, Charlie."

Charlie glanced over his shoulder. He was a large man, past middle age, fleshy and half-bald, with hard, penetrating eyes that didn't seem to go with the plump softness of the rest of him.

"Hey, Grady." Charlie stopped typing, rolled his chair back, and stood, stretching. "Afternoon, Lizzy. Say, Miz

Search dropped off a page of tips on makin' do for that pamphlet your garden club is compiling." He began sorting through the litter of papers on his desk. "Now, whut the heck did I do with it?"

Charlie's skills as an editor and his command of standard English were impeccable, but he preferred to 'talk 'Bama,' as he put it. He said that folks felt a little easier talking to him if he didn't put on the dog.

Grady put his hat back on, all business. "Charlie, there's been a bad accident. I was out having a look at Harvey Jackson's hogs when his boys came in and said there was a car wrecked and somebody dead in it, down in Pine Mill Creek. Harvey and I drove over to look; then I hightailed it back here to town to tell the sheriff. Figured you might want to get out there and take some pictures. Looks like a newspaper story to me."

Charlie stopped messing with the papers on his desk and jerked off his eyeshade. "Get out where? Where's the wreck?"

"Where the bridge on the county road has been out for the past three weeks. A girl drove through the barrier and into the ravine. She's dead."

Lizzy bit her lip. "Oh, dear! Oh, Grady, that's awful! A girl? Who?" Darling was small and its families, neighbors, and kinfolk were all knitted together in a dense fabric of relationships. When somebody died, it left a hole. Everybody felt the loss, one way or another.

"You can say that again," Grady replied tersely. "Purely awful. The car rolled a time or two before it got to the bottom, and it landed on top of her. She's smashed up so bad I couldn't tell you who. She's a blonde is all I can say."

A blonde? Lizzy stared at him, her heart beginning to pound.

Charlie was reaching for his suit jacket. "Don't have any film in my camera," he said, shrugging into it. "Used it up on Saturday, shootin' the Vo Ag boys out at the fairgrounds. Lester ordered it for me this mawnin'—be here on tomorrow's bus. Lizzy, you got film in that Kodak of yours?"

"Sure," Lizzy said. "You can take my camera." She was trying to sound normal. "What kind of car is it, Grady?"

"Pontiac roadster, green, pretty new. It's upside down in the rocks by the creek."

"Roadster?" Charlie frowned. "Whose 'ud that be? Didn't know we had any Pontiac roadsters in town." Darling was small enough so that everybody knew what everybody else was driving, how long they'd had it, and what they'd paid for it.

"Dunno," Grady said. "Didn't recognize it m'self. I can give you a lift out there if you want, Charlie. I left Harvey Jackson's oldest boy with the wreck. I told his dad I'd bring him home, so I'm going back out there. We can stop at Lizzy's house on the way and get her camera."

"Fine with me," Charlie said, shoving a small notebook into his coat pocket and grabbing his hat. "Let's go."

"I'm going too," Lizzy said.

"Sure thing," Charlie said, opening the front door. "We'll leave you at your house after you give me your camera, and then we can—"

"No," Lizzy said firmly. "I mean I'm going out to Pine Mill Creek with you. I want to see the wreck."

"Absolutely not," Grady said flatly. He went to the Ford and opened the passenger door with a Southern gentleman's flourish. "Trust me, Lizzy. This is for your own good. You do not want to see this wreck. Now, get in the car. Charlie can ride in the rumble seat as far as your house."

"Maybe Liz oughtta ride in the rumble," Charlie said. "She's skinnier than I am. How 'bout it, Liz? You're gettin' out first."

"But I might know who she is," Lizzy objected. "I know

all of the women in this town. I might be able to identify her." She lifted her chin and hardened her voice. "And if I don't go, neither does my camera."

"Forget it," Grady said. "You are not going. It is not a thing for a woman to see."

"All right, then." Lizzy folded her arms. This was so like Grady, always trying to tell her what she should and shouldn't do, which was one of the reasons she was not going to marry him. "I'm not going, and neither is my camera."

Charlie scowled. "Hey, you two. Stop bickerin' and let's get goin'." To Grady, he added, "Woman is too damn stubborn for her own good. If she wants to see a dead body, let her. What the hell—won't hurt her none."

"Exactly," Lizzy agreed. "It won't hurt me. And I might be able to help."

"Help? I don't see how you can help." Grady glared at her.

"I might be able to identify her."

Grady made a skeptical noise.

"Maybe she can," Charlie said. He was trying to cram himself into the rumble. "Come on. Let's get that camera."

"You'll faint," Grady said.

"I've never fainted in my life," Lizzy said. "But if I do, you can pick me up."

Grady's voice was hard. "Lizzy Lacy, I swear. You are the stubbornest woman God ever put on this green earth. Get in the damn car."

They stopped at Lizzy's, where she picked up her Kodak and turned it over to Charlie. Back in the car, she sat as far over against the door as she could, but it was a tight fit and she could almost feel the heat of Grady's thigh and the angry thrust of his muscled arm when he shifted gears. What's more, she could still feel the heat they had generated in this very same car on Saturday night. Neither of them spoke for the five- or six-mile drive.

Pine Mill Creek lay at the bottom of a wooded, steep-sided ravine, some thirty feet deep. The muddy waters had run high during the April rains, and the worst of the floods, laden with downed trees and other debris, had taken out the wooden pilings that supported the rickety wooden bridge. There wasn't enough money to replace it with a modern structure, and the county commissioners hadn't yet figured out what to do. In the meantime, the local residents were driving ten miles out of their way to cross the creek farther from town, and the county had put a couple of yellow-painted sawhorses across the road, with a sign that said BRIDGE OUT.

Now one sawhorse had been shoved aside and the other was splintered, where the Pontiac had smashed through the barricade. Sheriff Burns met them, a big wad of tobacco tucked in one cheek. His Model A was parked across the road, and Buddy Norris, his arm in a sling, was at the bottom of the ravine, with a young man dressed in overalls. The two of them were conducting a search around the wrecked car, which lay, wheels up, twenty feet down, at the edge of the running water. It had somersaulted at least once before it landed, and pieces of automobile wreckage—a bumper, a fender, a wheel, a headlamp—were scattered across the hillside. Carrying Liz's Kodak, Charlie started down the bank.

The sheriff looked at Lizzy and his eyebrows went up.

"Miss Lacy thinks she might know the dead woman, Roy," Grady said in an even tone. "Okay if she goes down and takes a look?"

The sheriff grunted and spit a string of tobacco juice. It splatted into the dirt. "Not a pleasant sight, Miz Lacy. That gal down there is tore up purty bad. Squashed flat when the car landed on her."

"I want to do it," Liz insisted.

The sheriff rolled his eyes. "Think you can handle it?"

Now that she was here, Lizzy wasn't so sure. But she nodded, not trusting her voice.

"All right, then." He looked at her shoes. "Not goin' to be
an easy climb down an' back, neither."

Lizzy pulled herself up. "I can do it."

The sheriff twisted his mouth skeptically, but his desire
to get the victim identified won out. "Well, then, let's get on
with it."

It wasn't an easy climb. It had rained the previous afternoon, and the clay hillside was wet and slick. Lizzy's feet and
legs were muddy by the time she reached the car, and she was
out of breath and a little dizzy. Even dizzier when she saw
what was lying under the car.

The dead woman wore a lipstick-red silky rayon dress.
Her peroxided head was turned away from them, dried blood
crusting her pretty blond hair. One braceleted arm was flung
out, red-enameled nails clawing at the ground as if to seize
the last glimmering instant of life as it slipped away from
her. The bracelet was made of geometric silver-plated links,
with rhinestones.

"Well?" the sheriff demanded. "Know who it is?"

"Bunny Scott," Lizzy said numbly. Her lips were cold and
she began to shiver. "Eva Louise Scott. She works at Lester
Lima's drugstore, in cosmetics. We eat lunch together most
days." Grady's arm went around her, and she leaned gratefully against him.

Charlie went around the Pontiac to snap a photograph.
The sheriff took out a notebook and a pencil and wrote down
Bunny's full name, spelling it aloud. "E-v-a L-o-u-i-s-e Scott.
Not married?"

"No. Not married."

"Any near kin around here?"

"Her mother's dead. Mrs. Bledsoe is her cousin, I believe.

Bunny lives—lived—at Mrs. Brewster's boardinghouse." The sheriff licked the tip of his pencil and wrote this down.

"Is that her car, Lizzy?" Grady asked softly.

"She doesn't have a car," Lizzy said. "I didn't even know she could drive."

"Oh, she c'd drive, all right," the sheriff said, with what sounded like satisfaction. He spit tobacco juice. "That there car is stolen. Reported stolen late Satiddy night."

"Stolen!" Lizzy exclaimed, and pulled away from the shelter of Grady's encircling arm. "But Bunny wouldn't—I know she wouldn't, Sheriff. She's young and a little flighty but she's a good girl. She wouldn't steal a car!"

"Well, she did," the sheriff said. "The fella she took it from telephoned it in. Said he saw her take it." He shifted his chew from one side to the other. "Well, not her by name nor nothin'. Somebody fittin' her description." He flipped a couple of pages in his notebook and read, squinting. "Short blond hair, red dress. In her twenties, staggerin' a little, like maybe she was drunk. She was with some man. No description on him."

"But Bunny didn't drink," Lizzy objected. "She might've been a little wild, but—"

The sheriff cleared his throat loudly. "Like I say, she was drunk. You just bend down and take a look under that car, and you'll see a bottle of moonshine whiskey, broke, lyin' right up next to her. Buddy found another, just up the hill." He raised his voice. "Buddy, show Miz Lacy that empty bottle you found."

Buddy Norris held up the bottle.

The sheriff went on. "Figger her'n the man took the car, maybe just meanin' to go on a little joy ride, out to the Waterin' Hole, maybe, then put it back. But they was liquored up enough so that they just kep' on drivin'. Drove right through that there barrier."

"Where's the man?" Grady asked.

"Figger he jumped outta the car a-fore it went over," the sheriff said. "Still on the loose."

"I still don't believe it," Lizzy insisted. "Not Bunny."

The sheriff closed his notebook and pocketed it. "'Scuse me, Miz Lacy, but we're lookin' at the ev-i-dence right here in front of us. 'Course, I reckon you could say the fella who had the car was careless, leavin' the key in the ignition the way he did. But this is Darlin', after all. Folks don't steal cars in Darlin'. Much less a girl."

"Well, I guess this'un did," Buddy Norris said, coming around the car.

"She didn't!" Lizzy protested. "Sheriff—"

The sheriff turned his back on her. "Buddy, is that the doc's car I'm hearin' up there on the road? You climb up the hill and see if he needs any he'p gettin' down here. Meantime, Grady and Charlie, whyn't you boys give me a hand in gettin' this car off the body so Doc Roberts can have a look-see. With that broke arm of his, Buddy is worthless as tits on a boar hog."

It was no good protesting. Lizzy turned away from the men and scrambled up the hill, unaided, trying not to think of the mangled body under the car. She didn't look back. A little later, Grady joined her in the Ford, accompanied by the young man in overalls, who climbed into the rumble seat. They dropped him off at the Jackson place, then drove back into town together, still not speaking. Lizzy sat, hunched and miserable, against the passenger door.

They were just coming to town when she said, "I need to go to Verna Tidwell's house, Grady. The corner of Larkspur and Robert E. Lee."

He gave her a concerned look. "That's pretty far from your place, isn't it? Four blocks, almost five. You'll have to walk home. I'll wait for you."

"No, thanks. But maybe you could wait until I see whether Verna's at home."

"This has been hard on you, Liz. I don't think you ought to—"

"Just do what I say," she said wearily.

Still objecting, Grady pulled up in front of Verna's and waited while Lizzy ran up the porch steps and knocked at the door. When Verna opened it, she turned and waved at him. He sat there for a moment, then waved back, reluctantly, put the car in gear, and drove on.

"Well, come on in, Lizzy," Verna said. Her black Scottie was eagerly sniffing Lizzy's shoes. "Clyde, you stop that," she reprimanded. She looked down at Lizzy's feet and up again, with a sly grin. "My goodness gracious, Liz. You look like you've been scrambling around in the mud. You and Grady out sparkin' in the woods?"

"Nothing like that," Lizzy said. "Pour me some tea, Verna, and I'll tell you about it."

TEN

The Dahlias Play Hearts

Monday evening was the City Council meeting and Ophelia's card night. The Dahlias' weekly card game traveled from house to house, but tonight, it was here. Ophelia sent the kids to Momma Ruth's for supper and the evening, to get them out from underfoot. Jed came home from the feed store late and wolfed down a ham-and-pimento-cheese sandwich, two deviled eggs, and a bowl of tapioca and peaches. Then he changed into a fresh white Sunday shirt to go and "act like I'm Darling's mayor," as he put it. He always downplayed the importance of the job, but Ophelia knew that he loved it, just as he loved Darling. He might not love everybody in it, but he loved the town.

Ophelia was helping him with his tie when Jed put his hands on her shoulders and looked her straight in the eye.

"I want you to know that there wasn't ever anything at all between me and Lucy Murphy," he said firmly. "Whatever you've been hearin'."

So he had heard it, too, she thought. Aloud, she said,

"Actually, I had a little visit from Mrs. Adcock this morning. She just had to tell me . . . Well, you know. Such a blabbermouth. Of course, I know better," she added, in a comforting tone and adjusted his tie. "You wouldn't do a thing like that."

Jed looked down, away from her. "No, I wouldn't," he muttered. "I just felt like—Well, hell, Opie. Ralph ain't doin' right by that little girl, leavin' her out there with those two half-grown boys and a busted-up old car and a bunged-up horse. He oughta know better."

"He ought," she agreed. "And he probably does. But he's got to make a living, like everybody else. He probably figures he's lucky to have a job, so he doesn't say 'can't' to his boss as often as he maybe ought to." She paused. "And maybe—"

"I know, I know. I shouldn't've taken it on myself to look after her. Wa'n't a bit smart, given the way people in this damn town like to talk." He bent over and kissed her on the nose. "You did right, sugah-pie, goin' out there and gettin' Lucy and bringin' her into town. That fixed their wagons."

Ophelia nestled against him. "Thank you," she whispered, putting her arms around his neck.

He kissed her quickly. "Anyway," he said, disengaging and stepping back, "folks'll have something else to talk about tomorrow."

"Not us, I hope. What is it now?"

"You wait and see," Jed said. His face darkened. "It's not goin' to be good, Opie, but I've taken care of us. You and me and the kids—whatever happens at the bank," he added, "we got nothin' to worry about."

"Taken care of *what?*" Ophelia asked, now alarmed. "*What* don't we have to worry about?"

"Can't rightly say just yet." Indulgently, he patted her on the cheek. "But I don't want you frettin' your pretty head about it," he said, and was gone.

* * *

Ophelia was still pondering Jed's mysterious words as she set up the card table and got out the cards and paper and pencils for scoring. The Dahlias' Monday evening card party was open to all the club members, but not everyone came. Miss Rogers and Aunt Hetty Little didn't play cards, and Bessie Bloodworth had Bible study at the Manor on Mondays. Alice Ann Walker often played with them, but she had left a message with Florabelle, saying that she wouldn't be able to make it tonight. So it would just be Verna, Myra May, and Lizzy—four, counting herself. Which was fine for hearts. They could play with as many as seven, but it was a little awkward.

She made tea, cut the still-warm peach cobbler, and laid out her prettiest lace-trimmed napkins (the ones her mother had embroidered with pansies). She was moving the chairs when she heard the knocker. As she opened the door to Myra May, Verna and Lizzy were coming up the walk.

"Good timing," Ophelia said cheerfully, trying not to look at the dirty hem of Lizzy's skirt. It looked like she'd been rolling in the mud. "Only have to answer the door once."

A few minutes later, they were settled around the card table, glasses of iced tea at their elbows. But they weren't playing cards. They were staring openmouthed at Lizzy, who had just told them that Bunny Scott had died in an automobile wreck. She had stolen a nearly new green Pontiac and crashed it through a barrier and into the Pine Mill Creek ravine.

"Dead!" Myra May exclaimed. "So *she* was one of that pair of thieves?"

Ophelia gasped. "That pretty little blond thing that works in the drugstore stole a *car*? Why, she's no more than a child!"

"The sheriff says she stole it," Lizzy said grimly. "But to tell the truth, girls, I can't believe it, either. Verna and I have lunch with her every day . . . *had* lunch with her. Bunny was always kind of silly and flighty, but she didn't have any meanness in her. She'd never steal a car."

"A green roadster?" Ophelia asked, frowning. "I don't think I've ever seen a green roadster in this town. Who did it belong to?"

"The dentist in Monroeville," Myra May said. "Fred Harper phoned the sheriff around midnight Saturday night to report it stolen—his brother's car, he said. I was on the switchboard," she added, in answer to the raised eyebrows. "I heard him. Said he couldn't see the man very well, but he gave a pretty good description of the woman. She had short blond hair and was wearing a red dress. In her twenties. Staggering, maybe, like she was drunk."

"Bunny was wearing a red dress," Lizzy said quietly.

"Who's Fred Harper?" Verna wanted to know.

"The chief cashier at the Savings and Trust," Myra May said.

Verna rolled her eyes. "Oh, that one."

"You've met him?" Ophelia asked Verna.

"Only through the teller's window. He's thin, kind of bony, actually. Pale hair, steel-rimmed glasses, no eyebrows. Sort of . . . finicky." Verna looked at Myra May. "It wasn't his car?" She answered her own question. "I don't suppose it was. Somehow, he doesn't strike me as the roadster type. More like a bicycle sort of person." She raised her eyebrows. "I could see him on one of those old-fashioned high-wheelers, like my old granddaddy used to ride."

Myra May nodded. "He told the sheriff that he'd borrowed it from his brother, which I guess made it worse, far as he was concerned. He was half hysterical. Kept saying he didn't know how he was going to explain it. To his brother, I guess he meant."

"If he saw somebody stealing his brother's car," Ophelia

said reasonably, "why didn't he just go out there and stop them? Why was he wasting time on the telephone, for pity's sake?" She shook her head. "If Jed saw somebody stealing our Ford, he'd pick up his gun and stomp out there and haul them out of the car before you could say Jack Robinson. Then he'd tie them up with the clothesline and *then* he'd call the sheriff." She smiled a little, as if she was proud of Jed's ability to act in this strong, manly way.

"Well, I don't know," Myra May replied, frowning. "I seriously doubt that Mr. Harper has a gun. He's renting the old Lewis house, next door to my cousin Mabel, so I see him sometimes, puttering around in the backyard. Doesn't strike me as the gun-totin' type. And if he had one, he probably wouldn't know how to shoot it. Or the robbers would've grabbed it and shot *him* and then stolen the car. Things like that happen, you know."

She was right. Darling itself was law-abiding and so safe that people had never felt it necessary to lock their doors—until the hobos had made them nervous. But just down the road at the Watering Hole, people got shot up all the time. Moonshine whiskey and guns didn't mix.

"Maybe it was the escaped convict," Ophelia suggested. "From the prison farm. They say he's not much more than a boy, but I guess he's old enough to steal a car."

Verna shook her head. "I still can't believe that Bunny would do that. And she certainly wouldn't be hanging around with an escaped convict." She chuckled sadly. "She had other fish to fry."

Myra May pursed her lips. "Lizzy said she was driving the car when it went into the creek. Sounds like pretty clear evidence, if you ask me."

Nobody said anything for a minute; then Lizzy spoke. "Fred Harper," she said thoughtfully. "I've met him—at the bank. He hasn't been here in Darling more than a few months. He came from a bank somewhere else. Can't remember where. But there's more, ladies." She turned to Verna. "Verna and I missed Bunny at lunch today, so Verna went to the drugstore and found out from Mr. Lima that she hadn't come in to work. Tell them the rest of it, Verna."

Verna filled them in on the general outline of her visit to Mrs. Brewster's boardinghouse and her informative talk with Amanda Blake.

"You actually went to Bunny Scott's room?" Ophelia asked admiringly. "You went through her things?" She sounded as if she thought Verna had done something brave.

"I didn't intend to, but I'm glad I did. Seeing her room— well, it's sad, that's all. Just a little hole in the wall. And Mrs. Brewster is a witch. You can't blame Bunny for wanting to escape." She glanced inquiringly around the table. "Anybody know Maxwell Woodburn?"

The others shook their heads. "Why?" Ophelia asked. "Who's he?"

"Somebody Bunny was apparently thinking of marrying. She'd been practicing 'Mrs. Maxwell Woodburn' on a scrap of paper. Amanda Blake thinks he might be her pen pal, in Montgomery. And what's more—" She told them about the deposit book.

"Two hundred and seventy dollars!" Myra May exclaimed, her eyes widening. "Where in the world did that girl get that kinda money? Why, she couldn't be making as much as I do, and I sure as shootin' can't salt away ten dollars a week! Hardly a dollar, truth be told."

"It's nice that she was saving it, though," Ophelia remarked. "If everybody would save, we'd be better off. And if she was thinking of marrying this Woodburn fellow, why, of course she'd save, bless her heart."

Myra May rolled her eyes. "Well, sure, sweetie. But where

did she *get* all that moola? Was she lifting it out of the drug-store till?"

"I guess it would be easy enough to do," Ophelia said slowly. "But she wouldn't take the same amount every week, would she? That would be a dead giveaway."

"There's more," Lizzy said. "Tell them, Verna."

"There was a jewelry box in the drawer of her dressing table," Verna said. "Really pretty, with little bits of colored mosaics and mother-of-pearl." The box was in her purse at this very moment, but she didn't want to show it to them. She had told Lizzy about the earrings, but she hadn't confessed to taking them. That was too much like theft. And now that she had them, she couldn't think how to put them back.

"Tell them what was in the box," Lizzy urged.

"Pearl earrings," Verna said. "Large pearls. From Ettlinger's."

"Oh, my!" Ophelia breathed, wide-eyed. "I love pearls. Do you suppose they're *real?*"

Myra May laughed. "Honey chile, if she bought them at Ettlinger's, they're real. That's the fanciest jewelry store in Mobile."

"Who says *she* bought them?" Lizzy asked wryly.

"Lizzy's right," Verna said. "Girls as pretty as Bunny don't buy jewelry for themselves."

"Well, then, who?" Myra May was puzzled. "None of the single guys in this town have *that* kind of money." She shook her head. "I mean, think about it, girls. Do you know any men in Darling who could give Bunny something like that?"

"Hardly," Verna said.

"Maybe they're from her pen pal," Ophelia said. "The one she was thinking of marrying."

Verna laughed. "Maybe that's why she was thinking of marrying him. Because he could afford to buy her pearls."

"Or maybe the man who gave them to her isn't single," Lizzy said uncomfortably. She was remembering something Bunny had said about Lester Lima not being quite the gentleman he looked to be. Which made her remember something she'd heard about a girl who had worked there the year before. Nadine, wasn't that her name? Yes, Nadine.

"Not single!" Ophelia exclaimed, and colored. "What makes you say a thing like that, Lizzy?"

"Well, I just think we ought to keep all the options open," Lizzy said. "I mean, if we're going to solve this mystery—"

"What mystery?" Ophelia asked. "The poor little thing got so desperate to get out of town and meet up with the man she wanted to marry that she stole a car. Not much mystery there."

"Anyway, that's what we pay the sheriff for," Myra May retorted. "It's his mystery. Let him solve it."

"He already has," Lizzy replied. "He says she stole the car. Bunny and an unidentified man. But I don't think so." She looked around the table. "Well, I'm sorry. I just don't."

"But she was *in the car*," Myra May repeated emphatically. "For heaven's sake, Lizzy, you said that yourself. And there was booze. You told us that, too."

Lizzy couldn't think of anything else to say.

"For what it's worth, I don't believe it either," Verna put in. "It just doesn't seem right to me."

"Well, then, what are you going to do about it?" Ophelia asked.

Lizzy and Verna exchanged looks. Then Lizzy nodded, and Verna spoke.

"Lizzy and I are going to investigate. The sheriff obviously thinks he knows everything there is to know about this case, and we don't agree. So we've decided to conduct our own investigation."

"An investigation," Ophelia said admiringly. "You girls are *brave*."

Verna nodded, accepting the compliment. "We thought we'd talk to Don Greer at the picture show first. Bunny was there on Saturday night. He might be able to tell us who she was with."

"We thought we'd talk to Mr. Lima, too," Lizzy said. "Maybe he can tell us who she was seeing." She looked around the group. "If you hear of anything that might help, please let us know."

The clock on the wall cleared its throat importantly. Ophelia glanced up at it, startled. "My gracious, look how late it is! We'd better get our game started. Oh, and Lizzy, before I forget, I drove past the Dahlias' house this morning, and saw that our sign is still leaning against the cucumber tree out front. I thought Zeke was going to plant it."

Lizzy sighed. "He will, when he gets around to it. Or maybe I'll do it myself, if I get tired of waiting. It's not a huge job."

"Let me know and I'll come help," Ophelia offered. She picked up a small glass bowl and dropped a handful of jelly beans into it. "Who wants to be the bank?"

"I will," Myra May said.

The hostess always dealt first, so Ophelia picked up the deck and began dealing, cards facedown.

Lizzy picked up her cards and frowned at them. "Speaking of banks, I wonder—have any of you heard anything about the Savings and Trust?" Mr. Moseley had ordered her not to tell anybody that he had told her to take her money out. He hadn't said she shouldn't *ask* about the bank.

Ophelia looked up from her hand. "Is there something wrong? If anybody knows anything, tell me. Jed was dropping mysterious hints tonight, but I couldn't make out what he was saying, except that I'm not supposed to worry." She made a face. "Which is what he always says when he's worrying."

Verna shrugged. "Haven't heard a word. But the bank is right across the street from my office window, and I noticed a fair amount of traffic in and out of there today." She glanced at Myra May. "Did I see you go in there this morning? Looked like you from a distance, anyway."

Myra May kept her eyes fixed on her cards. After a moment, she said, "Voleen Johnson canceled her hair appointment at Beulah's this morning."

"She *did?*" they all chorused, wide-eyed, immediately seeing the significance of this surprising event.

"Oh, golly," Verna said, in an awed tone. "Whatever is going on, it must be serious. Really." She took three cards out of her hand and passed them to Myra May, who was sitting on her left.

Ophelia looked around the group. "All right. I want to know what's happening. Does anybody know? Please tell me!"

"It's a mystery to me," Verna replied.

"Me too," Lizzy said.

Myra May put her cards down. The time had come to tell her friends what she knew. Which wasn't much, but just enough.

"Have you ever heard of a bank examiner?" she asked.

ELEVEN

Ophelia Learns Some Surprising Facts

Tuesday, May 20, 1930

Bright and early on Tuesday morning, as soon as she had got Jed off to the Farm Supply and the kids off to school, Ophelia put on her gardening clothes (green twill pants, a long-sleeved blouse, and old shoes), took her floppy straw hat and a basket of garden implements, and walked to the Dahlias' clubhouse, up Rosemont and around the corner on Camellia Street. She and Mildred Kilgore had volunteered to help Bessie Bloodworth in the overgrown back garden, pulling weeds and clearing underbrush. It was a beautiful morning, with the bluest of blue skies and a mild breeze, a perfect morning for working outside, as long as you were out there early, before eight o'clock, before the sun climbed high into the sky.

Mrs. Blackstone's gardens had been a paradise of flowers, fruits, and vegetables for many years. Even in her mother's day, back in the 1840s and '50s, the gardens around the Cartwright mansion had been a sight to behold, according to all reports. Bessie, who was Darling's unofficial town historian, had once shown the Dahlias several old photographs of the mansion's gardens—every flower bed managed and maintained by slaves, of course.

Those days were gone, thank goodness, and everybody was free and equal. (At least, that's how Ophelia liked to think of it.) But there was no money, and even if the Dahlias could find a few dollars, it would have to go to repair the roof. If they wanted to resurrect their part of what had once been that lovely garden, they were going to have to roll up their sleeves and do the work themselves.

When Ophelia came around the corner of the vacant lot, Bessie Bloodworth was standing out in front of the clubhouse, her hands on her hips. In her early fifties, Bessie was a tall, energetic-looking woman with thick, dark eyebrows, silvery-gray hair, cut short, and square, capable hands. She was wearing bib overalls and a hat and she had a rake in one hand.

"Looks to me like we don't have a lot of work to do out here in front at the moment," Bessie said, surveying the wisteria and the weigelas. "That snowball bush seriously needs cutting back, but most of the pruning here in front can wait until late fall or early spring. I think we ought to concentrate on the back garden. You agree?"

"Beulah's sign still isn't up," Ophelia said, pointing to the painted sign that was leaning against the cucumber tree.

"That's Zeke for you." Bessie chuckled. "Lizzy asked him to dig a hole for it, but he does things on his own calendar. I suppose he'll get around to it sooner or later."

"Maybe we should do it ourselves," Ophelia suggested. "Wouldn't take long."

A horn tootled and they turned to see a blue 1929 Dodge four-door sedan slow to a stop. It was Mildred Kilgore, an avid camellia collector. If there was a camellia anywhere that she didn't have, she'd move heaven and earth to get it, even if she had to pay good money for it. She could do that, though. Her husband, Roger, owned Kilgore Motors, just off the courthouse square. It was a Dodge dealership, and Mildred always drove the latest model.

"Sorry to be late," Mildred said, getting her gardening implements out of the car. She was dressed in a neat khaki skirt and plaid blouse, and looked so natty that Ophelia immediately felt grubby—but then, Mildred always had that effect on her. "Today's ironing day, and I had to get Jubilee started on Mr. Kilgore's shirts. Have I missed anything important?"

"We were just discussing what to do about the sign," Ophelia told her.

Mildred frowned at it. "We should install it. Leave it leaning against the tree like that, somebody might come along and steal it."

"Let's take it around to the back," Bessie said. "That way, if we don't get around to it today, it won't be out in plain sight."

With Bessie carrying the sign, they went around to the back garden and stood for a moment, surveying the scene. The iris and lilies and roses were blooming in sweet profusion, and so were the weeds, which almost smothered the flowers. The honeysuckle was about to completely overwhelm the cardinal climber, and the foot of the garden, a boggy area, was a sea of green ferns.

"Whew. Just look at this mess." Ophelia shook her head. "There's certainly plenty to do back here."

And there was. The grass had been recently mowed, but the borders needed to be cleaned out, the dead vines pulled off the fences, the low-hanging tree branches cut back, and the shrubs pruned. Some of the work—pruning the roses and dividing the lilies and other bulbs—would have to wait for the proper season. But the clearing-out could be done now, or at least started.

"Where do you want us to begin, Bessie?" Ophelia asked.

"Anywhere," Bessie said, waving her arm. "Just choose a spot, any spot. Let's pile all the weeds and debris in the middle of the yard for now. There's a compost pile behind the vegetable garden—when we're finished for the morning, we can carry everything over there. Mrs. Horner, over on Mimosa, promised Lizzy that we could clean out her henhouse in return for the chicken manure. It makes a really nice hot compost."

"Sounds good to me," Mildred said. "That's what we like. Plenty of hot compost." She pulled on her garden gloves and headed for the fence to take control of the rampaging honeysuckle, while Bessie started for the perennial border. Ophelia went to work beside her, and they began yanking weeds— Johnson grass, dog fennel, henbit, and ground ivy—throwing them onto a large pile on the grass.

After they had been working for a few minutes, Ophelia said, "What's this I hear about the Cartwright ghost, Bessie?"

"Ghost?" Mildred turned, her clippers poised for attack. "Somebody's seen the Cartwright ghost?"

"My goodness," Bessie said, sitting back on her heels. "Where'd you hear that, Ophelia?"

"Mrs. Adcock," Ophelia said. "She got the news from Mrs. Sedalius at church on Sunday. She told me about it yesterday."

"Word gets around, doesn't it?" Bessie chuckled. "Well, I'll tell you, Ophelia. I've lived in this neighborhood since I was a girl, and I keep hearing tales about folks seeing the Cartwright ghost. Over the years, dozens have told me they've seen her. But I've never seen her myself, and I didn't believe

Mrs. Sedalius when she said she'd seen her—black cloak, spade, and all. I figured she'd had too many nips of that bootleg rum she hides under her bed."

Ophelia laughed. Since Mrs. Adcock only knew Mrs. Sedalius as a fellow churchgoer, she probably didn't know about the bootleg rum. "But you changed your mind?"

"Well, not exactly," Bessie said. "I still don't believe in ghosts. That's not my style. However, I will admit to a shiver or two when I heard that spade clinking."

"Spade?" Mildred asked.

Which meant that Bessie had to tell the whole story, from beginning to end. When she had finished, Mildred asked slyly, "So when you heard the ghost digging, did you jump right out of bed and come down here to see what was going on?"

"Not in the dark, you silly goose," Bessie replied, and they all laughed. "I waited until it was bright daylight, before church. Then I came back here and looked all around. I didn't see a thing."

"No holes?" Ophelia asked. "But if you heard the sound of digging—"

"Nary a hole," Bessie said firmly. She glanced toward the back of the garden. "Although I didn't go poking around down there, where Miss Rogers thinks we ought to put the bog garden. It's damp and overgrown, and I was wearing my Sunday shoes."

"I've never been back there," Ophelia said. "There's a creek, Lizzy said."

"Well, sort of." Bessie got to her feet. "Actually, it's more like a seep spring, which is why Miss Rogers thinks it will be a good place for a bog garden. But it's going to take a lot of work. Most of those ferns will have to come out, and there's sedge grass and burdock. Come on back and let's have a look."

"I'm ready for a break," Mildred replied, stripping off her gloves. They walked toward the rear of the garden, past a fragrant gardenia bush and a pretty clump of flowering agapanthus. "I enjoyed seeing the pictures you showed us of what the garden looked like in the days when the Cartwrights were living in the mansion," she added.

"It was beautiful," Ophelia agreed. "Acres of lawn, and all those azaleas and weeping willows and oaks hung with Spanish moss."

"They had plenty of slaves to keep it that way," Bessie said, matter-of-factly. "You can't have a garden like that now—not unless you have more money than you know what to do with, or a dozen friends who will work for nothing."

"Or a dozen garden club members," Mildred put in dryly, "who work for the love of gardening—and the chance to take home a few passalong plants for their own garden. Like those spider lilies over there. They really need to be dug and divided." She paused. "Didn't you tell us that it was Dahlia Blackstone's mother who designed the original garden?"

"I didn't know that," Ophelia said. "Must've been a long time ago. Mrs. Blackstone was in her eighties when she died, wasn't she?"

"Eighty-two," Bessie replied. "Dahlia's mother—Cornelia, her name was—came here as a young bride in the 1840s, back when the place was new-built. She put in the gardens before the War, Dahlia told me, before Mr. Lincoln freed the slaves. Which was long before the mansion burned."

"I don't think I've ever heard the real truth of that story," Ophelia said. "Just a lot of rumors. Did the Union troops torch the house?" After the fighting was over, soldiers had looted and nearly destroyed the town of Claiborne, not far away on the Alabama River, then had made their way to Darling, wreaking havoc as they went.

"Nobody seems to know just what happened," Bessie said.

"Dahlia's father, Colonel Cartwright, was away in Virginia, where he had been fighting alongside General Lee. He didn't get home until several months after the War ended, and by that time, his wife was dead and the house was gone."

"Such a sad thing," Mildred said mournfully. "To fight all that time, and come home and find nothing left."

"I'm afraid there were plenty of other situations just like this one," Bessie said. "The Cartwright place was the largest house in the area, and Dahlia—who was only thirteen or fourteen when the War broke out—said that her mother was terrified that the place would be ransacked and they would all be murdered. Mrs. Cartwright had her jewelry and the family's valuables hidden, in an effort to keep them from being stolen."

"The same thing happened in my family," Ophelia put in reminiscently. "My grandmother was living in Atlanta. When she heard that Sherman and his Yankee rabble were coming, she pulled a brick out of the fireplace and put her jewelry behind it. The soldiers searched the house, but they didn't find a thing."

Bessie was rueful. "I'm afraid it didn't turn out that well in this case. Dahlia never liked to talk about it, or about the ghost, either. In fact, she thought the ghost was a lot of nonsense. But she did tell me once that the man who was responsible for hiding the family treasure had been killed. Her mother—she had consumption—was dead as well. They searched and searched, but the family's valuables never turned up. Whether they were lost or stolen—nobody knows. Whatever the truth, it's hidden in the mists of time."

"And the mansion?" Ophelia asked. "How did it burn?"

"When Cornelia got sick, Dahlia was sent to Mobile to stay with her grandmother. She didn't come back until her father returned from Virginia. By that time, the place had burned to the ground. Could've been Union looters, although they didn't burn anything else in Darling. Maybe it was an accident. Or—" Bessie shrugged. "Dahlia said she never knew for sure and never really wanted to find out. She didn't like to think back on those days. She had lost too much. It was too painful to remember."

"We think we have it hard now," Mildred said seriously, "and we do, with people losing their money and their jobs. But it was a lot worse back then. The War changed everything. You wonder how people managed to survive."

"A lot of them didn't," Ophelia said. "Unless you had a garden, you and your kids could starve." Walking slowly, they had reached the edge of the grassy lawn. "Is that the spring down there?" The area was green and thick with clumps of green ferns and shrubby bushes and shaded by low-hanging branches.

"This is it," Bessie said ruefully. "As I said, if we're going to plant a bog garden here, we've got a lot of work to do. It's a jungle." There were a number of square-cut stones scattered randomly among the underbrush. "I wonder if there was a garden area here before. Those stones—looks like they might have come from a wall. Maybe a seating area, too?"

"It would have been beautiful," Mildred said, looking up. "These are gorgeous old trees. Just look at that huge sycamore, with the lovely peeling trunk. And that cucumber tree, in bloom. Must be the same age as the one out front, on Camellia Street."

"Dahlia said that her mother planted a half dozen or more cucumber trees along Camellia Street," Bessie replied. "Back then, you know, it was just a country lane, running along the front of the mansion's grounds." She sighed. "The trees are all gone now, except for the one in front of the Dahlia House. There was a splendid tree in front of Magnolia Manor— growing there since before the house was built. It was a sad day when it got struck by lightning. The cucumber tree has to be the prettiest tree God ever invented."

"*Magnolia acuminata,*" Ophelia amended, in Miss Rogers' prim voice, and all three of them laughed.

Mildred had wandered a few steps away, looking curiously at an area of broken ferns. She bent over and parted the greenery to have a closer look, then called over her shoulder, "Girls, come look at this."

"What is it?" Bessie asked, looking over her shoulder.

"Looks like somebody's been digging up plants," Mildred said. "In the last few days, too. The dirt is fresh." She stepped back, frowning. "I thought people were supposed to donate plants for the bog garden—not come and dig them up."

For that's what they were looking at: a half-dozen mounds of freshly turned soil, among the stones scattered under the cucumber tree. A few of the holes were quite large and deep.

Ophelia and Bessie exchanged wide-eyed glances.

"The ghost?" Ophelia asked breathlessly.

"Ghostly spirits don't dig real holes," Mildred pointed out.

"Ghostly spades don't clink, either." Bessie frowned. "You don't suppose somebody was looking for a plant, do you? But if that's what it was, why didn't they just ask, for pity's sake?"

"Might've been a rare plant," Mildred remarked. "Maybe we'd better put up a no-trespassing sign." She looked at her wristwatch. "Listen, girls—I've only got another half hour to work on that honeysuckle. Then I have to get back home and see how Jubilee is coming with the ironing. Last time, she had to do two of Mr. Kilgore's shirts over again."

"What about putting up that sign out in front?" Ophelia asked Bessie.

"We can do that another day," Bessie said. "Let's just finish that bed, tote the rubbish to the compost pile, and call it quits. It's getting hot, anyway."

They went back to work, and when it was time to stop, Mildred offered to give Ophelia a lift home.

"Thanks, but it's just a couple of blocks," Ophelia replied. "I can walk."

"Nonsense," Mildred said, opening the car door. "We haven't had a chance to talk in weeks. Get in."

Ophelia climbed into the front seat. The two of them had been best friends once, but Mildred and Roger had built a big house not far from the Cypress Country Club and they didn't see as much of each other now as they used to. But the old friendship was still there, and when they got together, it wasn't long before they were chattering like a couple of teenagers.

Mildred turned the key in the ignition and started the car. "Did you hear about the girl who stole the car and drove it into Pine Mill Creek and killed herself?"

"Bunny Scott," Ophelia replied. "Lizzy and Verna said they sometimes ate lunch with her, but I only knew her from the drugstore. Actually, I bought some lipstick from her a few weeks ago. Tangee. She said it would look natural, and it does. Did you know her?" she added curiously. There must have been some point to Mildred's question.

"No, not really," Mildred said. She shifted gears, glancing at Ophelia. She had the look of somebody who is carrying a huge secret and is just bursting to tell it. "But I know something interesting about her. I didn't want to talk about it in front of Bessie. You know how she hates anything that sounds remotely like gossip—even though most of that history stuff she's so crazy about is nothing but old folks' gossip."

Ophelia frowned. She didn't like gossip, either, but there might be something here that Verna and Lizzy ought to know about, for their investigation. "What do you mean, Mildred? What do you know?"

Mildred looked straight ahead, both hands on the wheel. "Well, on Friday afternoon, I happened to go into the drugstore to buy a bottle of Bayer. When I went in, I couldn't see anybody. Bunny Scott wasn't there, nor Mr. Lima, either. Which I thought was sorta odd, you know, because Mr. Lima never leaves that store untended, not after he had all that trouble with boys coming in and stealing candy bars. That's why he put the candy behind the soda fountain counter, where they can't reach it." She sighed. "Really, I just don't understand modern children. They are so undisciplined. Where are their parents? Don't they learn anything at Sunday school? Why, when we were girls—"

"You're right," Ophelia broke in. Once Mildred got started talking about undisciplined children, she'd never stop. "So what happened when you went into the store?" she prompted.

Mildred turned the corner onto Ophelia's street. "Well, like I said, I didn't see anybody right away, so I went toward the back, where the medicines are. You know the curtain that hangs over the door between the pharmacy area and the storage at the back?"

Ophelia nodded.

"Mr. Lima and Miss Scott were behind the curtain," Mildred said avidly. "I could see their shadows." She turned to look at Ophelia, her eyes very wide. "He was kissing her, Ophelia! Not in a friendly way, either. Passionate, just like in the movies."

"Oh, my gracious!" Ophelia was utterly shocked. "Mr. Lima? Why, he's a deacon in the Baptist church! What was *she* doing?"

Mildred gave what sounded like a snicker. "Well, of course

I couldn't exactly see, since they were behind the curtain. But she definitely wasn't fighting him off. In fact, I'd say she was giving every bit as good as she got, if you want to put it that way." They had reached Ophelia's house. Mildred pulled up in front and turned off the engine.

"But Mr. Lima is married!" Ophelia protested. "Plus, he must be thirty years older than Bunny is. Was," she corrected herself quickly. And really, there was no point in passing judgment. Whatever Bunny Scott had done, it was all in the past. Nobody but the good Lord could judge the poor girl now, and maybe He'd be lenient, seeing that she was so young and hadn't had proper bringing-up.

Mildred leaned both arms against the steering wheel. "Plus," she added in a knowing tone, "Mrs. Lima is the jealous type. Remember Nadine Tillman?"

"Nadine Tillman." Ophelia pursed her lips, frowning. "I know who she is, but I don't exactly remember . . . Didn't she work at the drugstore a while back?"

"Last year, after she got out of high school. But Mrs. Lima found out that Mr. Lima was getting fresh with her."

"Mildred!"

"Exactly. And this is no gossip, Ophelia. I know it for a fact, 'cause Mrs. Lima's maid is my Jubilee's cousin. Jubilee said they were talkin' about it all over Maysville. You know you can't keep a thing from the help—especially something like this."

Knowing what she knew about the way news got around, Ophelia could not discount this source. And by now, she was deeply interested, in spite of herself—not to mention that this shocking information seemed like something she ought to share with Verna and Lizzy.

"What happened when Mrs. Lima found out about Nadine Tillman?" she asked.

"Well, I don't know what Mrs. Lima said to Mr. Lima, of

course. But I can tell you that he fired Nadine. Just flat-out fired her, no notice or anything. The girl left town. Nadine's mother said she was headed to Chicago to look for work, but she's never heard from her. Not a peep. Never even got a postcard. Just plain gone. And that's been over a year ago. For a while, Mrs. Tillman talked about hiring a private detective, but Mr. Tillman got laid off out at the Coca-Cola plant, so that's out."

"My goodness," Ophelia said weakly. Of course, young people these days didn't always keep in touch, but this definitely sounded suspicious.

"Which, to tell the truth," Mildred added in a significant tone, "is why I was curious about Bunny Scott. I was wondering just how she managed to drive into Pine Mill Creek." She paused. "I mean, I have never been one to cast aspersions. If I didn't already know what I know about Nadine Tillman dropping off the face of the earth, maybe I wouldn't think anything of it. But it does seem to me that it is just too coincidental. Don't you think? Nadine disappearing the way she did. And then Bunny Scott driving into that creek."

Ophelia shivered, not liking what she was hearing. "They didn't see you, did they?" she asked apprehensively. "Mr. Lima and Bunny Scott, I mean."

Mildred shook her head. "I decided the aspirin could wait. I went to Hancock's and bought some groceries and went back to the drugstore after that. When I walked in, both of them—Mr. Lima and that girl—were as cool as cucumbers. You'd never know anything had happened between them." She turned the key in the ignition and the Dodge started smoothly. "Well, I have to go. Thanks for letting me dump all this. As I said, I'm not one to cast aspersions. But I just had to tell *somebody*. And you're such a good listener. Really, Ophelia, we ought to see more of each other."

"Sure," Ophelia replied, and said good-bye. By nature, she

was not a suspicious sort of person. But as she went up the steps to her front porch, she couldn't help wondering whether Mrs. Lima knew about Mr. Lima and Bunny Scott. And if she did, what she might have said. Or done.

She frowned. This wasn't the kind of information she wanted to pass along on the party line. She looked at her wristwatch. It was just past ten, and the courthouse was only a couple of blocks away. She would drop in on Verna in the probate office and deliver this surprising fact in person.

Verna and Lizzy were conducting an investigation into Bunny's death. This was something they needed to know.

TWELVE

Myra May Learns Some Startling Facts

Myra May Mosswell's daddy had been a doctor. When he died, he left his only child a small house and a nice little bundle of money, not very big, but big enough to get her started in a business. Myra May, who was a practical sort of person with a good head on her strong shoulders, spent several months considering in a logical, rational way what she wanted to do with her inheritance. Did she want to move to a big city that would offer exciting opportunities for a woman of ambition and common sense? Memphis, maybe, or Mobile or Atlanta? Or did she want to invest her money in Darling and live in a small, comfortable, but essentially boring town for the rest of her life?

While Myra May was turning these important questions over in her mind and trying to decide what she wanted to do with her life, she was managing the dining room and kitchen at the Old Alabama Hotel. As things turned out, however, staying in Darling was not a calculated decision based on a commonsense approach to planning for the future. It was sheer, random happenstance—a bit of luck. Or, as Myra herself said afterward, a piece of stunning good fortune. Just before Labor Day brought a close to the long, hot, boring summer (during which Myra had just about decided she'd be better off in Atlanta) a young woman got off the Montgomery-Mobile Greyhound bus and came into the hotel looking for work. Her name was Violet Sims. She had curly brown hair and a sweet voice and she was very pretty.

Now, Myra May was not what anybody would ever call pretty. She had a strong jaw, a broad forehead, a firm mouth, and a way of looking at people—especially men—as if she might bore a hole right through them with her eyes. When men were around her, they had a tendency to stumble and mumble and make themselves scarce as soon as they could. She had never yet met a man she wanted to marry and by this time (she could see thirty in the rearview mirror) she was pretty sure that she never would. Women liked her because she was strong and a straight shooter, but they were afraid of her, too, although not as much as the men.

Violet, as it turned out, was not at all afraid of Myra May. She had been born and raised in Memphis and had seen enough of the city, as she put it, to last her for a couple of lifetimes. She and Myra May hit it off at once—"It was just like we'd known one another forever," Myra May said in astonished delight—and for the next six months, they worked shoulder-to-shoulder in the Old Alabama dining room and kitchen. By Halloween that year, Violet had moved into Myra May's house, and by Christmas, Myra May had decided that she definitely wanted to stay in Darling, at least as long as Violet was there.

And then there was another piece of luck. Mrs. Hooper, who had owned the Darling Diner for over thirty years, began to have trouble with swelling in her legs and decided it was time to put the business up for sale. It had a fine location on

Franklin Street, across from the courthouse, between the Dispatch building and Musgrove's Hardware. The serving area featured a long linoleum-covered lunch counter with a dozen red leather–covered stools and a half-dozen wooden tables and chairs. Behind the counter was a pass-through to the kitchen, and at the back of the building was the small room that housed the town's telephone exchange. Upstairs was an attractive, sun-filled apartment with its own porch and private entry, where Mrs. Hooper herself had lived. The building needed some painting and fix-up, but the kitchen equipment was in good shape, and the diner had a reputation for serving good food at fair prices—unlike the Alabama Hotel, where the food was good but the prices were out of sight.

Myra May and Violet inspected the property and discussed the matter for several days. Then Myra May went to Mr. Manning, Darling's real estate dealer, and made an offer to trade her house and some cash for the diner, as long as Euphoria Hoyt (who was known as the best chicken fryer in southern Alabama) was part of the bargain. Mrs. Hooper was in the market for a small house where she didn't have to walk up stairs, and Myra May's house suited her just fine.

Euphoria was happy to agree as well. "Whoo-ee," she said. "I's real relieved to jes' keep on fryin' chicken. That's whut I does best in this world. That, and make meat loaf. Oh, an' bake. I do love bakin' pies, 'specially ones with meringue on top." It was a fact that Euphoria's fried chicken and mouthwatering meringue-topped pies—lemon, coconut, chocolate, and especially peanut butter—were spoken of with great fondness as far away as Monroeville. When Myra May chalked up "Peanut Butter Meringue Pie" on the menu board, it was gone lickety-split.

The papers signed, Myra May and Violet quit their jobs at the Old Alabama and moved into the apartment over the diner. Olive LeRoy, who had worked at the telephone exchange since the system was first installed, taught Violet and Myra how to manage the switchboard, and the three of them, with Olive's friend Lenore Looper, set up a regular rotation for trading shifts, so that the board was covered all day and all night. Of course, there weren't many telephone calls at night, but somebody had to stay near the board in case of an emergency, so there was a cot in the room for whoever was working the night shift.

Myra May herself usually opened the diner at eight and cooked and served breakfast. She always tried to be downstairs by seven, so she had time to stir up a batch of biscuits, cook up the grits and red-eye gravy, and make coffee. Once that was done, all that was left was frying bacon or ham and cooking up eggs, which she did to order, as people came in.

Business had fallen off a bit lately, but the breakfast trade was still pretty good. She could usually count on filling at least half of the counter stools at any given moment, and one or two of the tables. Of course, not everybody came in at the same time, which was good, because if they did, she'd have to get Violet to come down and help.

This morning—Tuesday morning—the crowd was the usual. There was Charlie Dickens from the *Dispatch*, Jed Snow from the Feed Supply, Marvin Musgrove from the hardware store next door, and J.D., Marvin's helper. All of them sat, as usual, at the counter. Charlie Dickens and Jed Snow seemed glum, but the other two were talking up a storm about the Elk's Club picnic, coming up on Saturday, and wondering whether Sparky's arm was going to be in shape for the baseball game. Then the sheriff came in, smoking his usual smelly cigar, and Myra May had to tell him, as she usually did, to leave it outdoors. As usual, he glared at her, but complied, putting it on the outside windowsill where he could pick it up on his way out. Buddy Norris was with him, and the two of them, plus Tom Hinks from the Circuit Court office, took their usual table in the corner.

When Myra May carried the coffeepot to the table to pour their first cups, the sheriff and Buddy and Mr. Hinks were talking about Bunny Scott, and how she had died, and why they were sure she'd been driving the stolen car when it went into the creek, and drinking, to boot. They still hadn't figured out who her accomplice was. Buddy thought it was most likely the convict, but the sheriff had a different opinion. He thought the convict was out of the state by this time.

The men didn't try to keep their voices down, and Myra May listened carefully and made mental notes. However, they said nothing that she hadn't already heard from Verna and Lizzy the night before, except that Bunny Scott's body was over at Doc Roberts' office this morning, where he was giving her a good looking-over before she was moved to Noonan's Funeral Home. Mrs. Bledsoe—the girl's mother's cousin— was up in Nashville, helping her daughter with a new baby. The sheriff was trying to get in touch with her for the names of other relatives.

Then the door opened and Hiram Riley came in. Myra May knew him because he'd done an audit of the hotel accounts the year before. With him was a well-dressed stranger. Everybody in the diner turned their heads, watching as they went to the table in the farthest corner.

Charlie Dickens leaned toward Jed Snow. "Bank examiner," he said in a low voice.

"Bad news," Jed Snow returned, under his breath.

Hiram Riley and the bank examiner had their heads together, talking in low, serious voices, so that nobody at the counter could hear what was being said, even though they strained their ears. But when Myra May took them their hot plates of ham and eggs and grits and gravy, she heard enough to startle her so that she almost dropped a plate. She hurried back with an extra bowl of grits, and after that, another plate of biscuits, just so she could hear the rest. It was dynamite.

Impatiently, Myra May bided her time for another hour, until Euphoria came in to start cooking for the dinner bunch and Violet came downstairs to handle the counter. Then she took off her apron and hurried straight over to the courthouse. Luckily, the probate office was empty, except for Verna. She was sorting a stack of documents into alphabetical order, a pencil stuck behind her ear.

"What's going on?" Verna asked, riffling through the papers.

"Have you heard about Alice Ann?" Myra May asked urgently.

"Alice Ann?" Verna looked up. "Heard what? She was supposed to play hearts with us last night, but she didn't show up. Is she sick?"

"No. She's being questioned."

"Questioned?" Verna put her papers down and stared. "Alice Ann? Who's questioning her? About what? Why?"

"Mr. Johnson at the bank," Myra said tersely. "And the bank examiner. About embezzling money. They haven't brought the sheriff into it, but that's the next step."

"Embezzling? Alice Ann?" Verna was shaking her head. "That's ridiculous! What in the Sam Hill are those men thinking?" She narrowed her eyes. "How'd you hear about this, Myra May? On the switchboard?"

"In the diner. Hiram Riley, the accountant, was discussing it with the bank examiner while they were having breakfast this morning." She laughed bitterly. "It's a good thing that it never occurs to men that the women putting their food on the table might be interested in what they're saying. They just go on talking as if we're invisible."

Verna pushed out a long breath. "But I don't understand how anybody could think that Alice Ann Walker was involved in anything like that. She's just a cashier, and not even the head cashier at that!"

"I don't know the full story, of course," Myra May said, "but from what I picked up this morning, Mr. Johnson thinks that Alice Ann has been stealing money from people's accounts. 'Jiggling the books,' he calls it. A little bit here and a little bit there, but it's added up. Almost ten thousand dollars. Maybe more. All in the past five or six months."

Verna gasped. "Ten thousand— Why, I don't believe it, Myra May! If she did it, what's she done with the money? The Walkers certainly aren't spending it."

"Seems very strange to me, too," Myra May said. "Apparently she hasn't been charged yet, maybe because they don't have enough evidence."

Verna narrowed her eyes. "Evidence?"

"Well, Hiram Riley was saying that the bank's records show that the money is gone—it's been jiggled out of various accounts, but they haven't figured out what she's done with it. They've looked at the Walkers' bank account, which is no more than you'd expect, apparently, and at the accounts of her relatives—her cousins, her sisters, her parents. They went to her house, which didn't strike them as being anything fancy, and questioned her husband. Alice Ann says she can't tell them what she did with it because she didn't do *anything* with it, and Arnold denies knowing anything about it, as well. But Mr. Johnson says she probably hid the cash someplace and has just been waiting for a chance to run off with it."

"Run? Alice Ann?" Verna hooted incredulously. "Where would she go? She's lived in Darling her entire life. What's more, her whole family is here, and Arnold's family, too. Of course, she would never leave Arnold, never in the world. And maybe it's cruel to say so, but Arnold couldn't run off with her—he's crippled. It's kind of hard to run if one of you is in a wheelchair."

"You're right. But the money is definitely gone, according to the examiner. What's worse, the bank was already in trouble because it doesn't have enough capital. This theft—and the withdrawals in the last day or so—might push it over the edge. At least, that's what they were talking about this morning." Myra May's voice, always so strong, trembled. "That would be terrible, Verna. Every business in town needs that bank. We can't survive without it!"

"You're certainly right about that." Verna shook her head. "But this business with Alice Ann—why, it's just crazy. As nutty as Bunny Scott stealing a car and driving it into the creek."

"Speaking of Bunny," Myra May said, "I heard this morning that Doc Roberts has her in his office, doing an autopsy, I guess."

"Why an autopsy? She was killed in the car wreck."

Myra May shrugged. "I guess it's standard operating procedure. Anyway, after that, they'll take her to the funeral home. There's some question about the funeral and where she ought to be buried. They're trying to find out who's next of kin."

"Mrs. Bledsoe," Verna said. "I think the rest of Bunny's family is either dead or gone."

Myra May nodded. "Well, I need to get back to work, Verna. I just thought you ought to know about Alice Ann. And you're right. It really does seem crazy." She turned to go.

"Thanks, Myra May," Verna said. She was still shaking her head over the news when Ophelia opened the door and came in.

"I've got something to tell you, Verna," Ophelia said breathlessly. "You're not going to believe this, but—"

"If you've come about Alice Ann," Verna broke in, "I already know. Myra May just told me. It's the craziest thing I've ever heard."

"This isn't about Alice Ann," Ophelia said with barely suppressed excitement. "It's about Bunny Scott and Lester Lima. Something Mildred Kilgore just told me. You'll never guess, Verna, not in a million years!"

Verna sighed impatiently. She hated it when people said that. "No, I'll never guess, Ophelia. You'll just have to tell me."

Which was what Ophelia did.

THIRTEEN

Lizzy Learns Some Dismaying Facts

While Myra May was finishing up with the diner's breakfast crowd and Ophelia was working with Bessie and Mildred in the Dahlias' garden, Lizzy was standing outside the bank with three or four other people, waiting for it to open—waiting nervously, for the usual opening time of ten a.m. came and went, and the doors remained shut.

While she waited, Lizzy was going back over all the recent excitement in Darling. The escaped convict, Bunny's death in that stolen auto, and now some sort of trouble at the bank. She swallowed hard, remembering what Myra May had told the Dahlias the night before, when they were playing hearts.

Bank examiner. After reading about so many bank failures all around the country in the past few years, Lizzy shivered at the words. What if the bank examiner had come to Darling yesterday, studied the bank's account books, counted the bank's money, and ordered it to be closed? Overnight, her fifty dollars (which she hadn't thought was very much money, compared to what she had already spent on the house), had ballooned into what seemed like a huge amount. It was all she had, besides her paycheck. If she lost it, she'd be sunk.

But far, far worse, everybody in town would lose their money. The businesses, the people, everybody. They'd *all* be sunk!

The group grew larger, and people began to whisper anxiously. But when the doors of the Savings and Trust opened at last (and only eight minutes late), it seemed that the worry was for nothing. There was the usual bouquet of Mrs. Johnson's flowers on the table just inside the door. Mr. Johnson himself greeted Lizzy pleasantly, asking after her mother's health as if everything was perfectly normal, as perhaps it was.

But Lizzy knew what she needed to do. She returned Mr. Johnson's smile, straightened her shoulders, and headed for Alice Ann Walker's window. When she saw it was closed, she turned to the chief cashier's window, presenting her deposit book and saying, in a clear voice, "I'd like to withdraw my savings, please."

"How much?" asked the chief cashier, Mr. Fred Harper. Verna's description had been accurate. He was thin and pale, with pale hair and pale, thin eyebrows behind steel-rimmed glasses. His fingers were long and thin, with well-manicured nails. If he was worried about the bank, he didn't let on.

"All of it, please." Lizzy wanted to ask him to tell her exactly what it was that he had seen on Saturday night when he reported a woman and a man stealing his brother's car. But now wasn't the time. Now was the time to get her money, in case the bank— She made herself stop.

Mr. Harper looked into a drawer, then stepped away from the window and came back with a packet of bills. While she watched, he counted out the money—fifty dollars in fives—put it into an envelope, and passed it to her through the window.

"Thank you," she said.

"You're welcome," he replied crisply. He looked over her

shoulder at the line of silent, nervous people behind her. "Next," he called.

Her withdrawal secure in the office safe, Lizzy worked through the usual Tuesday morning tasks, typing, sorting, filing, and paying the bills that had arrived in the mail the day before. Mr. Moseley phoned at ten thirty to tell her that he would be late. Mrs. Moseley phoned (from Birmingham), demanding to talk with her husband and all but accusing Lizzy of lying when she said he wasn't in the office. There were several other calls—one from Mr. George E. Pickett Johnson, another from Mr. Riley, the accountant, and a third from a Mr. Matthew Bogard, who didn't identify himself. Then another call from Mrs. Moseley. And then, just after eleven, a call from Grady.

"I need to talk to you." He sounded urgent. "Are you busy? Is it okay if I come to the office?"

"Well . . ." Lizzy said hesitantly, looking at the half-finished page in her typewriter. "I guess I can take a little break. But I'm supposed to meet Verna at noon." The two of them were going to the Palace Theater to ask Don Greer if he remembered seeing Bunny with anyone on Saturday night. "When do you think—"

"In about three minutes," he said. "I'm next door, at the diner."

It took him less than three minutes.

Lizzy nodded toward the percolator on the hot plate. "There's coffee. Shall I pour you a cup?"

He shook his head. "Just had some." He took off his fedora and dropped into the chair beside her typewriter table, stretching out his long legs. "I was at the diner when Doc Roberts came in a few minutes ago. He had just turned in his autopsy report on the girl's death." He looked straight at her, his eyes dark. "It wasn't the car wreck that killed her, Lizzy."

"Bunny?" For a moment, she couldn't make sense of what he was saying. "It wasn't the wreck? Then what?" She looked at his face, tense and strained. "What, Grady?"

"She was shot." Grady was his usual blunt self. "Back of the head, behind the left ear."

"Oh, no!" Lizzy exclaimed.

"It's a fact, Liz," Grady replied. "Doc Roberts said it was hard to spot. Her skull got pretty well mashed when the car rolled over on her."

Lizzy shut her eyes, but she could see the image anyway. Bunny under the car, her blond hair crusted dark with blood. "Then . . . Then how does the doctor know?" She opened her eyes. "That she was shot, I mean."

"Because he retrieved the bullet. It was still inside her skull. A twenty-two caliber. Not a very big gun, but big enough to do the job."

Lizzy stared at him in wide-eyed dismay, still trying to put it all together. "But I don't . . . The left side? You mean, somebody shot at her through the car window? While she was driving? Is that why she crashed through that barricade and into the ravine?"

"Uh-uh." Grady shook his head. "Not through the window. The driver-side door flew off in the tumble and the window stayed intact. It was rolled up, and there was no sign of a bullet hole in the glass. Anyway, Doc Roberts says it was point-blank range. Whoever did it was close enough to put the gun right up to her head."

"But I don't see—" She tried to puzzle it out. "Point-blank range. But that means . . . That means she was sitting in the car, Grady. On the passenger side. And somebody else was driving. The same man—"

"The same man that Fred Harper reported seeing when the car was stolen," Grady said. "So now the sheriff is looking for a car thief *and* a murderer." He laughed shortly. "And he's still looking for that escaped prisoner as well. Got his plate full, I'd say."

The convict! "Maybe that's who did this, Grady." Lizzy leaned forward excitedly. "Maybe the convict kidnapped Bunny at gunpoint and forced her into the car and drove away with her." She snapped her fingers. "I'll bet that's it! He grabbed her and made her go with him, as a hostage. She struggled, or tried to jump out of the car, and he shot her. Then he put her in the driver's seat and pushed the car through that barrier and into the ravine, in order to hide what he'd done."

"My goodness," Grady said mildly. "You've missed your calling, Lizzy. You oughta be writing stories for one of those true crime magazines." He chuckled. "You're right about one thing, though. The girl was in the driver's seat, but she wasn't driving that car when it went over the edge."

Lizzy stared at him. "How do you know?"

"Because the engine wasn't running."

"Wasn't . . . running? But how—"

"When we righted the car yesterday, I noticed that the key was in the ignition but it was turned off. Fact is, the motor wasn't running when the car went over the edge. Even if Doc Roberts hadn't spotted the gunshot wound, there still would've been a big question about that wreck." He hoisted himself out of the chair. "Well, I guess I'd better go. I've got work to do, and you have, too." He looked toward Mr. Moseley's closed office door. "Where's the boss?"

"He's not here," Lizzy said. "He said he was coming in a little late this morning and—"

She didn't get to finish her sentence. Grady bent down, put his hands on her shoulders, and kissed her. Then he kissed her harder, and his arms went around her, lifting her to her feet, pulling her against him. She tried once or twice to push him away, but only briefly, for she found herself melting against him, tingling suddenly as if there were an electrical charge pulsing between them, giving herself to the reckless, unruly moment, wanting it to go on and on endlessly.

"Ahem," said a dry voice. "Excuse me, but I believe I work here. If you don't mind, that is."

Lizzy pulled away from Grady, feeling herself blushing furiously, mortified. How long had Mr. Moseley been standing there, watching? She clenched her fists, trying to steady her breathing.

But Grady was grinning broadly. "Hello, Bent," he said. "It's been a while, hasn't it? Nice to see you."

"Same here," Mr. Moseley acknowledged. He didn't sound enthusiastic.

Grady picked up his hat and put it on his head, tipping the brim to Lizzy in a rakish way, his eyes glinting. "Later, doll." He put his hands in the pockets of his pants, strolled out the door, and clattered noisily down the stairs.

"Doll?" Mr. Moseley's brown eyebrows arched. "Later, *doll?*" he repeated, amused.

Lizzy, her face hot, pushed her hair out of her eyes. She sat back down at her typewriter table and turned the platen on the machine, bending over to look as if she were searching for the place where she had left off typing. But to tell the truth, she was trying, not very successfully, to catch her breath. She was still feeling the hardness of Grady's body against hers. It was as if they had simply picked up where they had left off on Saturday night in the car.

Mr. Moseley hung his hat on the rack and shrugged out of his jacket. He turned, studying her for a moment, as if he were seeing her in a new way. "Doll," he said, half under his breath. Then he smiled crookedly and put the morning's mail on her desk. He began to roll up his sleeves.

"Well, now," he said in a businesslike tone, "what about telephone calls? Anything urgent?"

Lizzy reached for the collection of telephone notes and

handed them to him. He went through them, nodding, until he got to his wife's two calls. His mouth hardened. "She didn't leave a message?"

"Just that she'd like you to call as soon as you got in."

"Right," he said sarcastically, and wadded up the note and threw it, forcibly, into the wastebasket. He looked at Lizzy. "Did you do what I told you to do at the bank this morning?"

"Yes, thank you. I've put the money in the safe. In an envelope with my name on it." She took a breath. "What's it all about, Mr. Moseley? I've heard something about a bank examiner—"

"You've heard that?" he asked in some surprise. "People are talking about it? Who told you?"

"I'd rather not say."

He grunted. "This damn town. People talk all the time. You can't keep private affairs private." He glanced at her. "Not *that* kind of affair," he added archly. "Business affairs, I mean."

"Yes, sir," she said. Not wanting to be put off, she persisted. "But what about that bank examiner?"

"Is this the Cooper file?" He picked up a manila folder from her desk.

"Yes, sir. But what about—"

He gave her a hard, straight look, his courtroom look. "I can't talk about it, Lizzy. There is a problem at the bank, yes. It may be a serious problem. That's all I can say. And even if I knew the whole story—which I don't, not yet—I couldn't tell you. And that's a fact."

She frowned. A serious problem? Of course it was a serious problem! Something was going on at the bank and nobody was supposed to know anything about it. But the bank was the heart of the town. If it failed—

He paused, pursed his lips, and regarded her narrowly. "I don't suppose it's any of my business, Liz, but have you been seeing Grady Alexander long?"

The suddenness of the question startled her. She swallowed. "A . . . while."

"How well do you know him?"

She tilted her head, catching the clear implication, which offended her, although she wasn't sure why. "Pretty well," she replied defensively.

But it was a silly question. She'd have to know a man very well before she let him kiss her like that, wouldn't she? She wasn't the kind of girl who went around kissing everybody who wore pants.

Half-defiantly, wanting to show him that she had some important news, too, she straightened her shoulders and added: "Grady found a dead girl in Pine Mill Creek yesterday, and I identified her. It was Bunny Scott. He stopped in just now to tell me that she didn't die in the car wreck. She was shot."

What happened next was totally out of the blue.

"Bunny—The dead girl—" Mr. Moseley stared at her, first disbelief, then dismay written across his face. "Bunny? She's . . . dead? Good Lord!"

Lizzy was jolted. It sounded as if— "You knew her?"

He half-turned away, his hand over his mouth, as if he were gagging. "Yes. I mean, I know who she is. Was. The blonde who worked at Lima's. Right? You say she was . . . shot? Somebody *killed* her?" His voice was gruff and shaky, and then half-pleading. "Oh, God. Jesus, Liz. You're kidding, aren't you? You're making this up?"

It took a moment to persuade him that she wasn't kidding, a little longer to tell him the full story. About Grady coming to town for the sheriff and for Charlie Dickens. About going out there with Grady and Charlie and seeing the body and knowing who it was from the hair and the rhinestone bracelet. And then about Grady telling her that Bunny was shot and the car pushed into the creek, with the ignition key off.

"Grady says it was a twenty-two. Dr. Roberts retrieved the bullet." Lizzy swallowed. Her mouth had gone dry and she was trembling. "From inside Bunny's . . . skull." Somehow it was that detail that made it so much more horrible, the finding of the bullet that had killed her, somewhere inside her head.

"Good Lord," Mr. Moseley said, very low. He passed his hand across his forehead, wincing as if he himself were feeling the pain of the bullet. His words were ragged, as if his throat was clogged. "She was so *alive*. I can't believe—"

"I'm sorry," Lizzy said, feeling inadequate, trying to think of what to say. "If I'd known that you knew her, I wouldn't have—"

"I didn't *know* her," he cut in harshly. He put up his hand as if to stop her, physically, from going a step farther. "Not in the way you're thinking."

"I'm sorry," she said again, now thoroughly confused. She bit her lip. "I didn't mean . . . I wasn't—"

"Listen to me, Lizzy." He gave his words an abrupt staccato emphasis. "I did not know that woman. Do you understand me?"

She blinked, speechless. Her heart was pounding. After a moment, she whispered, "Honestly, Mr. Moseley, I really didn't think—"

"Then don't," he snapped, striding toward his office. "You're not paid to think." He opened the door and went in, closing it behind him, not quite slamming it, but almost.

Lizzy sat for a moment, almost in shock, feeling bruised and swollen, as if he had hit her. Mr. Moseley had never spoken to her like that before. He had always been courteous, respectful, even attentive, as if he cared what she thought, how she felt, even if she was only his secretary. He had helped her handle the purchase of her house and offered her advice on the remodeling work. He had given her time off when her mother was sick. He had never—

She stopped.

All of that was true. And all of it made what had just happened entirely inexplicable, another of the entirely inexplicable things that seemed to be happening in the past couple of days.

But it wasn't inexplicable, was it? If Mr. Moseley had been secretly seeing Bunny Scott—

She pushed her chair away from the typewriter, feeling a sharp stab of anger that she might have recognized as jealousy, if she had been a little more experienced in that emotion. Well, to hell with him. She hadn't meant anything by what she said. The thought of Mr. Benton Moseley and Bunny Scott had never once come into her mind—not until he had put it there himself, just now, with all those denials.

She took a deep breath. The world might be going to hell in a handbasket, but there was work to be done. And work was the sheltering wall behind which Lizzy Lacy had always taken refuge when things became difficult. She reached for the stack of mail Mr. Moseley had brought from the post office and began to open the envelopes, slitting each one with careful precision, taking out and unfolding the contents and neatly paper-clipping everything to the envelope before putting it in the appropriate stack, concentrating on this task as if it were really important, pushing everything else out of her mind.

There were two checks from clients, and she set them aside to be entered in the office accounts ledger. There was the six-month invoice for the lease payment for the office space, to be paid to Charlie Dickens, who owned the building. There was a bill for the repair of Mr. Moseley's automobile, which she would pay from his personal account, and another from—

Dismayed, she stared at the envelope she had just opened. It was from Ettlinger's Fine Jewelry, in Mobile.

In it was an invoice for twenty-six dollars.

For a rhinestone bracelet, engraved with the initials *ELS*.

FOURTEEN

Verna and Lizzy: On the Case

When lunchtime came around, Verna was still trying to deal with the upsetting news she'd gotten from
Myra May and Ophelia's surprising revelation about Bunny
and Mr. Lima. She closed and locked the office and went outside, pausing to admire the summer annuals—zinnias, marigolds, and petunias—that were beginning to bloom in the
sunny strip along both sides of the walk. She bent down to
pull a couple of volunteer weeds. The Dahlias had planted
the beds six weeks before. They'd be blooming most of the
summer and would strike a bright and cheerful note in the
courthouse square—something the whole town would need,
if the unthinkable happened and the Darling Savings and
Trust failed.

She went to the usual lunchtime spot beneath the chinaberry tree and sat down. When Lizzy crossed the street and
sat down beside her, Verna looked at her friend in surprise.

"What's wrong?" she asked, as Lizzy pulled a paper bag
out of her purse and took out a sandwich and boiled egg. She

had so much to tell, but the look on Lizzy's face made her hold her tongue.

"What's *wrong?*" she repeated urgently.

"Nothing's wrong," Lizzy replied in a high, unnatural voice. She cleared her throat and repeated it. "Nothing's wrong. Whatever makes you think that?" She unwrapped a ham-and-sliced-tomato sandwich, laid it on its wax paper, and began peeling the egg. The shell flecked off unevenly, pulling chunks of egg with it.

Verna grunted. "Then why are you looking like somebody just socked you in the stomach? And the way you're attacking that poor, defenseless egg—there won't be anything left by the time you finish butchering it."

Lizzy didn't say anything for a moment. Then she put down the egg and pulled in a ragged breath. "Grady came to the office this morning to tell me that Bunny didn't die in the car wreck, Verna. She was shot. In the head. Point-blank."

"Shot!" Verna exclaimed, thunderstruck. "That's incredible!"

She listened to Lizzy, trying to comprehend the story that spilled out incoherently, the whole unbelievable thing, from somebody shooting Bunny and pushing the car into the ravine to Mr. Moseley being terribly upset by the news—and finally Lizzy's discovery of the invoice for the engraved rhinestone bracelet from Ettlinger's.

"Bunny and Benton Moseley!" By now, Verna was nearly weak from shock. "Gracious sakes, Lizzy! That girl had more men on her string than anybody can count. Do you think Mr. Moseley gave her the pearl earrings, too? Or was that somebody else? And who the devil *shot* her?" She leaned forward and dropped her voice, although nobody was listening. "You don't think it was Mr. Moseley, do you?"

"No, I do not think it was Mr. Moseley," Lizzy parroted in a bitterly mocking tone. "You can give a girl a bracelet without being suspected of murdering her, can't you? And Mr. Moseley simply couldn't *kill* anybody. I know him, Verna. He's not that kind of man."

Verna didn't want to say so, but Lizzy was probably still carrying a torch for Mr. Moseley, whether she knew it or not. And the truth was that somebody had shot Bunny Scott and tried to make it look like she had been killed in an accident with a stolen automobile. That required planning ability and intelligence, didn't it? Mr. Moseley certainly had plenty of both.

And now it was clear that he could have had a motive, too. Maybe he'd had a fancy for Bunny and she was trying to break it off. Or maybe Bunny was threatening to tell his wife. Then she remembered what Ophelia had told her about Lester Lima kissing Bunny behind the curtain. Mr. Lima could have had the very same motive. Mentally, Verna put both of them at the top of the suspect list.

Lizzy finished her sandwich and refolded the wax paper so she could use it again. "Well, if you ask me, Verna," she said in a definitive tone, "it was the escaped convict who killed her. He's been on the loose for over a week now, hiding somewhere around here. He's desperate to get away. He took Bunny hostage, stole Mr. Harper's brother's car, and when Bunny tried to escape, he shot her. Mr. Moseley had nothing whatever to do with anything—except that he . . . he knew . . ."

She took out a handkerchief and blew her nose. "He knew Bunny. I don't know how well, and I don't care." She blew her nose again.

"You may be right about the convict, Lizzy." Verna patted her hand sympathetically, mentally adding the convict to her suspect list. "And I certainly understand how you feel about Mr. Moseley. But listen, I've got some news, too. About Bunny—and about Alice Ann Walker."

She told Lizzy what Ophelia had told her—that Mildred

Kilgore had seen Bunny and Lester Lima kissing behind the curtain at the drugstore—and reported that Myra May had heard Hiram Riley and the bank examiner talking about Alice Ann Walker being questioned as a suspected embezzler.

"Alice Ann, an embezzler?" Like Verna, Lizzy was both incredulous and indignant. "Why, that's the most idiotic thing I've ever heard! The Walkers are poor as church mice. What in the world would she do with that kind of money? She couldn't spend it around here—somebody would see it and wonder where she got it. And she wouldn't do anything to endanger the bank, either. She knows how much Darling depends on it."

She paused, shaking her head sadly. "But Bunny and Mr. Lester—Somehow, that's easier to believe. Remember what Bunny said the other day?"

"About what?"

"That Lester Lima isn't the gentleman he's supposed to be?"

Verna was thoughtful. "And there was Nadine Tillman," she said slowly, thinking about what Ophelia had told her. "Remember her?"

Lizzy frowned. "She worked at the drugstore last summer, didn't she?"

"Yes, until she got fired. Nadine told her mother that Mr. Lima got fresh with her and her mother told Mrs. Lima. Mrs. Lima fired her. Nadine left for Chicago and hasn't been heard from since."

"Oh, my gosh," Lizzy said breathlessly.

"Yes. And now there's Bunny."

Lizzy's eyes widened. "You're saying that Mr. Lester—" She swallowed. "*Both* of them?"

"I'm not *saying* anything, Lizzy. We don't have enough facts to draw any conclusions." Nevertheless, Verna moved

Lester Lima to the top of her suspect list. "But I like your idea about the convict taking Bunny hostage and forcing her to help him steal the car. It makes sense, Lizzy." Mentally, she moved "escaped convict" to the Number Two position. Which left Mr. Moseley at Number Three.

"Well, I'm glad you think so," Lizzy said gloomily. "Nothing makes much sense to me. We know where the bracelet came from, but what about those pearl earrings? And the deposit book you saw in the drawer—where was she getting the money? That's all part of the puzzle, too. I have the feeling that Bunny Scott wasn't the person we thought she was. There are just too many mysteries floating around. We don't know enough about her."

Those pearl earrings. Verna felt a wrench of guilt. They were in her purse at this moment, in that little wooden box. She had been worrying about them since yesterday, wishing she hadn't foolishly taken them out of Bunny's dressing table drawer. Of course, Bunny was dead now and it wasn't likely that Mrs. Brewster or her girls were aware of them. If they had been, the pearls probably wouldn't have stayed in the drawer. Still, what she had done was stealing, and Verna knew it. She had to put them back, if she could only figure out how.

But there wasn't any point in bringing that up. What she said was, "I agree, Liz. There are too many mysteries, and more are popping up all the time. What's worse, we don't know if what we don't know about Bunny has anything to do with her being in that car."

Lizzy looked confused, but nodded.

Verna got up and brushed off her dress. "We have to clear up the mysteries. So I vote that we pursue our investigation, starting with the Palace. Maybe Don Greer will remember who Bunny was with on Saturday night."

"I'm with you," Lizzy said, getting to her feet. "Let's go."

*   *   *

The movie house was a long, narrow building fronted by a fancy marquee, with the words *The Palace* in pink neon and dozens of lightbulbs studding the canopy. The marquee also displayed the name of the movie, Alfred Hitchcock's *Blackmail*, which would be showing for the next two weeks.

The ticket taker's glass booth was empty and closed, but the theater's double doors were propped open. Verna led the way inside, into a thick dimness that smelled of dusty carpets, stale popcorn, and toasted peanuts. The ceiling was painted dark blue, with glittery silver stars pasted to it. The foyer walls were plastered with movie posters from recent shows: Charlie Chaplin's *The Circus*; *The Wind*, with the beautiful Lillian Gish; and the Buster Keaton comedy, *The Cameraman*. Verna had seen every one of them at least once.

Off to the right was the candy counter, where Mrs. Greer sold Mounds and Milky Ways and Milk Duds, as well as red-and-white-striped paper bags of popcorn out of the Butter-Kist electric popcorn machine and bags of hot peanuts out of the peanut toaster. Beside the counter stood a red Coca-Cola cooler, where customers could put in a nickel and get a bottle of icy-cold Coke. Mrs. Greer had been heard to say that they made as much money from candy, popcorn, peanuts, and Cokes as they did from movie tickets. It didn't seem to matter that some people were too hard up to buy groceries. They still came out to see the picture show, share a bag of hot peanuts, and escape for a couple of hours from the harsh reality of the world.

From somewhere inside the movie house, Verna could hear the sound of a vacuum sweeper running. She went to the leather-covered door that led into the auditorium and pushed it open. There were two narrow sections of red-plush seats, with a center aisle that led to a low wooden stage. On the wall at the back of the stage hung the silvery movie screen, now covered with a heavy red drape. A few dim lights in candelabra brackets shone along the walls, and in their dusty glow, she saw Don Greer pushing the vacuum over the carpet, down at the front, near Mrs. LeVaughn's black upright piano. He looked up when he saw them coming down the aisle toward him and switched off the Hoover. It shuddered into silence.

"Hello, Mr. Greer," Verna called.

"Hullo, gals," he said jocularly. The air was warm and stuffy, and he took out a handkerchief and rubbed it over his forehead and his nearly bald head. "We're closed on Mondays. Don'cha know that by now?" He refolded the handkerchief. "*Blackmail* opens tomorrow night. Come back then and bring your friends." He added, confidentially, "But don't bring any Baptists."

This was a standing joke in town, because Baptists weren't supposed to go to the picture show, where they could see people drinking and smoking and misbehaving—although of course they went anyway.

He stuffed his handkerchief back in his pocket, chuckling. "Y'all ain't Baptists, I reckon."

"Not this week," Verna said, matching his tone. "But we're not here for the movie. We're looking for some information. About a friend of ours."

"Oh, yeah? Well, maybe I can help. What friend? What's her name?"

"Scott. Eva Louise Scott. The blonde who worked at Lima's Drugstore."

"Oh, her." Mr. Greer narrowed his eyes. "The girl who stole that Pontiac from that fella at the bank and drove it over the cliff into Pine Mill bottom." There was sharp disapproval in his tone. "Dunno why Lester ever hired that one. Dead, ain't she?"

Verna and Lizzy exchanged glances, and Lizzy spoke up. "Yes, she's dead, Mr. Greer. And we're very upset about it. But nobody seems to know what really happened on Saturday night. We're hoping to get some information that might help to answer some questions."

"Well . . ." Mr. Greer hesitated. "Yeah, I did see her Saturday night, come to think of it. She was sittin' close to the back, where she allus sits. That purty yella hair of hers—it shines real bright when the projector's on." He grunted. "Had her head on some young fella's shoulder. Reckon he's feelin' kinda low about what happened."

"Oh?" Verna asked eagerly. "Who was the fella, Mr. Greer? Who was she with?"

"Dunno." Mr. Greer shrugged. "Didn't see who he was, or if I did, it didn't register. Them boys all look purty much the same when you see 'em from the projection booth. Anyway, she's with a diff'rent one ever' time she comes. Sees ever' movie more'n onct, too. Bet she saw *Applause* three, four times. Real tearjerker."

"Do you remember *anybody* she saw it with?" Lizzy asked.

He furrowed his forehead, thinking. "Well, I think it was Willy Warren one night. Hank Crawford's oldest boy, Pete, another night. Other'n that, I don't rightly remember. You might ask Mrs. Greer—she sells candy to purt' near ever'body who comes in. Or Gladys." Gladys was the Greers' daughter, who was still in high school. "Yeah, that's right. You come back tomorrow night when we're open and ask Gladys. She sees folks under the marquee lights when she sells 'em their tickets. Got a real good mem'ry, too."

"We'll do that," Verna said.

Mr. Greer grinned thinly. "O' course, people don't allus come in with the ones they sit with. You'd be mighty surprised to know how many folks come in by theirselves and just happen to end up cuddlin' with somebody in the back row. A tryst is what it's called, y' know." He enjoyed the word so much that he said it again, his grin broadening. "A secret tryst. At least, they like to think it's secret."

"And what time did the picture end on Saturday night?" Lizzy asked.

"Well, lessee." He rubbed his chin. "It was a double bill, *Applause* and *Tarzan*. Reckon it was all over by nine thirty." He frowned. "How come y'all wantin' to know?"

Verna didn't answer his question. She only said, "Thanks very much."

"Sure thing." Mr. Greer switched the Hoover back on and Verna led the way up the aisle, disappointed.

"I know both Willy Warren and Pete Crawford," she said, when they were outside the theater. "If you ask me, neither of them has the gumption to steal a car, much less shoot a girl. Especially Bunny. They'd a whole lot rather take off her clothes than shoot her." At that, she paused, struck by a thought. Turning to Lizzy, she asked, "When Grady told you about the way Bunny was shot, did he say anything about an assault?"

"Assault?" Lizzy asked, frowning.

Really, Verna thought. Sometimes Lizzy was so innocent. "You know. A sexual assault. A—"

"Oh, you mean rape," Lizzy said. "No, he didn't, so I guess there was nothing like that." She tilted her head. "Although maybe the doctor didn't do that kind of autopsy? Or maybe he couldn't tell? And even if the doctor had mentioned that, Grady might not have said anything to me. It's . . . well, you know."

"I know," Verna said, and sighed. Men didn't discuss things like that with women. At least, not Southern men.

"If she was raped, Charlie Dickens wouldn't print that in the newspaper," Lizzy said. "But I agree, Verna. I don't think either Willy or Pete could have anything to do with Bunny's death. Those kids are as lazy as all get-out. Anyway, no matter who she was with at the picture show, the movie was over by nine thirty. The car wasn't reported stolen until midnight. If she felt like dumping her date, she had plenty of time to get rid of him and go off with somebody else—somebody she couldn't be seen with in public."

"Exactly," Verna said. Somebody like Benton Moseley, she thought. Or Lester Lima. "Lizzy, let's go over to the drugstore and talk to Mr. Lima."

"Talk to him about what?" Lizzy asked. "He sure as shootin' wasn't with Bunny at the movie. And if he knows anything about how she died, he's not dumb enough to tell us about it."

"I don't mean *question* him," Verna replied. "I just mean . . . Well, we could just sort of casually ask if he noticed anybody talking to Bunny while she was at work. You know—probe a little. See how he reacts."

Lizzy looked at her watch. "Okay, but let's hurry. I've got to get back to the office."

Lima's Drugstore was across from the picture show, on the southwest corner of the courthouse square, at Rosemont and Dauphin. But when Verna and Lizzy got there, they discovered a piece of paper taped to the door, clumsily hand-lettered in red crayon: CALLED OUT OF TOWN. CLOSED UNTIL FURTHER NOTICE.

Lizzy blinked. "Closed?"

"Well, for pete's sake," Verna said, astonished. "What do you suppose?"

"Beats me," Lizzy replied, shaking her head. "I don't remember that Mr. Lima has *ever* closed the store, only at Thanksgiving and Christmas. He always said that he hated to take vacations because some of his patients might need their medicine."

Verna narrowed her eyes. "This certainly seems suspicious

to me, Lizzy. Do you think it has anything to do with Bunny? With what Mildred Kilgore saw behind that curtain?" She paused. "If Mr. Lima was getting after her hot and heavy at the shop, what do you think was going on after hours?"

But of course there was no answer to this question. The two of them crossed Dauphin and began walking across the courthouse lawn. After a moment, Lizzy broke the silence.

"I've been thinking, Verna." She stopped and cocked her head, giving Verna a sidewise glance. "This may seem like a silly question, but do you . . . well, do you ever miss it?"

"Miss what?" Verna asked, preoccupied with the puzzle of Mr. Lima. What could have made him close up the drugstore and leave town so unexpectedly? Had Mrs. Lima found out that he and Bunny had been having—

"You know. Sex." Lizzy colored and looked away. "Walter has been dead now for . . . how long? Ten years?"

"Ten years last month," Verna said. She was surprised at Lizzy's question but tried to answer it honestly. "Yes, I do miss it, I guess. Walter and I didn't always get along, but when it came to that, he was . . ." She smiled, remembering the pleasure. "He was just great. It may be awful for me to say it, but after he was gone, sex was what I missed most. Certainly wasn't his camellias." She paused. "Why are you asking?"

Lizzy's color deepened. "Oh, just wondering."

"Wouldn't have anything to do with Grady Alexander, would it?"

"Sort of." Lizzy sighed. "I have to decide what to do about him, Verna. I'm not sure I can put it off much longer." She laughed a little. "If I don't decide, the decision may get made for me."

Verna frowned, thinking about the possibility that Bunny had been assaulted. "Oh, come on, Lizzy. I'm sure Grady wouldn't—"

"No, he wouldn't. He's a gentleman." Lizzy's smile was crooked. "But I might. I'm sorely tempted."

Verna chuckled. "Would that be such a bad thing? I mean, Grady is sexy as all get-out. Not bad-looking, either. And he's got a real job. Pays real money."

Lizzy screwed up her mouth. "You're so practical, Verna."

"Hell, yes, I'm practical," Verna said shortly. "That's what it takes to get along in this world. Try falling for a hobo and see how long that lasts, kiddo."

"I know, I know." Lizzy sighed. "Just the same . . . I mean, I'm not a prude, and neither is Grady. But I know him. If we have sex, he'll start pushing me to marry him. He's old-fashioned that way. But I've got my own house, and a yard and a garden, and it's all just the way I want it. I enjoy my job, and I like earning my own money." She paused. "Grady's old-fashioned about money, too. He'd probably insist on being the breadwinner and want me to stay home and be a housewife. Maybe it sounds selfish, but . . ."

"It's not selfish at all," Verna said warmly. "Living alone gets a little lonely sometimes, but being your own boss can make up for a lot. If you're lonely, Lizzy, get a dog. Clyde never gets drunk, always shows up for dinner on time, and doesn't run around with other women." She paused, smiling a little. "What about Mr. Moseley? You used to carry a flaming torch for him, didn't you?"

Lizzy rolled her eyes. "That was years ago, Verna. Years and years. It's all over now, absolutely and utterly. My heart is safe. I couldn't care less about Benton Moseley."

Verna gave her a skeptical glance. "You're sure about that?"

"Don't be silly, Verna," Lizzy scoffed. "Mr. Moseley is married."

"It looks like that didn't stop Bunny," Verna said, half under her breath, as the courthouse clock began to chime.

"Oops. I have to get back to work. The boss is supposed to come in this afternoon."

"Me, too," Lizzy replied. "You can quit worrying your head about me and Mr. Moseley, Verna. But thanks for the advice about Grady. I do appreciate it."

"It's worth what you paid for it," Verna said carelessly. She looked back over her shoulder at the drugstore. "Listen, Liz— how about if we get together after work and walk over to the Limas' house?"

"Why? If Mr. Lima is out of town, Mrs. Lima probably went with him. If she didn't, she likely won't talk to us. If they're both gone, it'll be a waste of time."

"Maybe," Verna said. "But you never know. We might learn something. You don't have to come along, of course. I just thought—"

"No, that's okay," Lizzy said. "Give me a call or stop by the office when you're finished for the day, and I'll go with you." She grinned. "You know, Clyde is really cute. Does he have a brother?"

FIFTEEN

Mr. Moseley Makes an Unexpected Proposition

When Lizzy got back to the office, Mr. Moseley's office door was propped open. He was leaning back in his chair with his feet propped on an open desk drawer, eating a sandwich. There was a brown bottle on the desk beside him, and a glass. Whiskey. Lizzy knew that he kept a bottle and a couple of glasses in his office, to be able to have a drink with friends when they dropped in. She had never seen him drink alone.

"Liz," he called. "Could you come in here for a few minutes, please?"

Hurriedly, Lizzy picked up her steno pad and pencil. She went into his office and sat down in the chair on the opposite side of the desk. She couldn't help thinking of that invoice from Ettlinger's, but she wasn't going to bring that up. It would likely provoke a worse storm than this morning. But there was something else she needed to ask.

"Have you heard anything about Alice Ann Walker,

Mr. Moseley? I heard that she's being questioned about embezzlement at the bank, but I really don't think—"

He shook his head. "I can't talk about that. It's bank business." He paused, tilting his head. "This gal a friend of yours?"

"Yes. A good friend. A Dahlia. And I just know she wouldn't—"

"It's nice that you're willing to go to bat for your friends, Liz. Sorry. That's all I can say."

She sighed. "Okay, then." She poised her pencil over her steno pad. "I'm ready for dictation."

"I didn't call you in here for that, Liz." He swung his feet to the floor and gave her an apologetic half-smile, studying her over the tops of his gold-rimmed reading glasses. "It's about what happened this morning. I am truly sorry for being rude. It was unforgivable. I apologize. And I owe you an explanation, as well as an apology."

Lizzy was so startled that she dropped her pencil. "Oh, no," she protested, bending over to get it off the floor. "Really, Mr. Moseley. Please don't feel you have to—"

"Be quiet," he said mildly, "and let me talk." He picked up his whiskey glass, drained it, set it back on the desk. "To start with, I need to tell you that my wife and I are . . . Well, we've been having our problems lately. I won't go into the details, but it's possible that we may divorce. Or rather, I should say that it's likely. Adabelle is in Birmingham, staying with her parents." His lips quirked. "It seems that she is consulting a lawyer—her uncle. Her father is encouraging this, of course. He wasn't happy when I left the legislature. He rather liked being able to brag about it. And I was a handy pipeline to the state capitol for projects he had in mind."

"Oh, I'm sorry!" Lizzy exclaimed. She meant it, too. She may have once cared for Mr. Moseley in a romantic way, but as she had told Verna, that was in the past. All she wanted was for him to be happy. And nobody could be happy when there was a divorce on the horizon. She knew that for a fact, because the people who consulted Mr. Moseley about getting a divorce all seemed miserably unhappy. Another reason not to get married, she thought. It might not work out and then—

"Don't be sorry, Liz," Mr. Moseley said. "Whatever happens is fine with me, although of course I'll miss the children. The girls will be heartbroken."

"Of course," Lizzy murmured. She wondered whether this was true. Mr. Moseley didn't bring the children to the office very often, but when he did, the girls didn't seem especially interested in their father. They exhibited what Lizzy thought of as a flippant, almost disrespectful attitude toward him. It bothered her. She might be old-fashioned, but she felt that children ought to look up to their fathers—although it had crossed her mind that perhaps he wasn't as attentive a father as he might be. He was often in the office during the evenings and on weekends.

He leaned forward on his elbows, pulling off his glasses and brushing his hair out of his eyes. "The fact is, Adabelle and I haven't had a real marriage in . . . well, quite some time." He cleared his throat, looking away. "I don't suppose you want to hear that, but it's true. I only tell you because of . . . well, because of the girl. The girl who died." He pushed the papers around on his desk until he found what he was looking for. He held up the Ettlinger's invoice. "The girl I bought this bracelet for. I had it engraved with her initials."

Lizzy fastened her eyes on her steno pad. She could feel the flush creeping up her cheeks. Mr. Moseley was right. She didn't want to hear this. She didn't—

"I lied to you, Liz," he said steadily. "I *did* know that girl, as I'm sure you have already guessed. Eva Louise Scott. Bunny." He sighed. "I met her in the drugstore and thought she was very pleasant. Pretty, too. A little flashy, but—" He sighed. "She laughed a lot, and I liked that."

Lizzy started to say something, but he held up his hand, stopping her.

"One night after Adabelle had gone back to Birmingham, I was driving home late from the office. I happened to see Bunny walking back to her boardinghouse. She had been to the picture show. It was dark and beginning to rain, and she didn't have a raincoat or an umbrella, so I stopped and gave her a lift. We started talking and—Well, I suppose you could say that I lost my head."

Lizzy pulled in her breath, trying to steady herself. Why was he telling her this? Why—?

"It was a mistake, of course, and I knew it." He picked up the bottle and poured a generous slug of whiskey into his glass. "Couldn't help myself, I guess."

"Please," Lizzy managed. His words were sounding slurred. "Please don't—"

"They say confession is good for the soul, Liz. So let me confess." He turned to look out the window, sighing, putting his fingers together under his chin as if he were saying a prayer. His voice was low and heavy with sadness—and whiskey. "You know, I can't really believe she's dead—much less that anybody could actually *shoot* her. She was such a sweet, delicate little thing, and she'd had such a damned hard time in her life."

He was silent a moment, then swung his chair around so he could look at Lizzy. "Did you know that her daddy was a drunk? And that her momma ran away from home when she was nine years old and left her with four young children to take care of—including a pair of twins? The family lived out in the country, and Bunny had to walk miles to get to school every day. But she did it, and kept her brothers and sisters fed and clothed, too. That took courage. Real courage."

Lizzy was staring at him. Bunny's mother ran away from home, leaving her with four children?

"But that's not true!" she protested. "Bunny was an only child, and her mother was a widow. They didn't live in the country—not at all. She and her mother lived in Monroeville, where—"

Mr. Moseley acted as if he didn't hear her. "I know that's no excuse," he said. "For what I did, I mean. The world isn't fair, and lots of young women have a hard time."

"Really, Mr. Moseley, she didn't—"

He waved her objection away. "I just felt sorry for her, that's all." He picked up his glass and drank the whiskey in one gulp, then set the glass down hard on the desk. "She seemed to have a genuine appreciation of finer things, pretty things. I wanted to show her a good time, give her some pleasure. When we went to Mobile a couple of weeks ago, we walked past Ettlinger's. She saw the bracelet in the window and liked it, so I bought it and had it engraved for her."

Lizzy's heart had stopped at the words *We went to Mobile*. Mr. Moseley had taken Bunny to Mobile? You didn't drive all that way just for one day. They must have stayed overnight, in a hotel. But even if they didn't stay in the same room, he was married, and that made it wrong! And not only wrong, but dangerous. Lizzy wasn't very sophisticated about affairs of the heart, and she hadn't had much experience of her own. But she knew that a girl who would deliberately lie to a man about her family situation in the way that Bunny Scott had lied to Mr. Moseley—well, a girl like that couldn't be trusted not to make trouble, that was all. If she had lied, what else might she have done?

Her heart started again with a painful thud and she straightened her shoulders. "She must have liked it," she said almost desperately, trying to think of something to say. The words felt thick on her tongue. "The bracelet, I mean. I saw her wearing it the other day. And she was wearing it when she . . . when she died. I saw it. On her . . . her arm."

"When she died?" Mr. Moseley closed his eyes, then opened them again. He looked haunted. "Then I'm sunk, Liz. Completely sunk, damn it. That bracelet has Ettlinger's stamp on it. They'll trace it. The police will find out I bought it for her."

Lizzy stared at him, trying to focus. Why was he so upset? So what if they found out he had bought Bunny that bracelet? It might be embarrassing, but that was all. It was only because he was drinking and feeling sorry for Bunny and even sorrier for himself. It was the whiskey talking. Buying the bracelet wasn't smart, but a person could surely buy a present for another person without being accused of—

"They'll trace the bracelet," he said again, as if he were talking to himself. "They'll talk to Ettlinger's. The salesclerk will remember that we were together. In Mobile." He took a deep breath. "They'll search her room at the boardinghouse. They'll find my letter."

She felt raw. "You . . . You *wrote* to her?"

"I knew it was foolish. But I had to tell her—I had to explain why we couldn't . . . why I couldn't give her what she wanted. A place of her own, where we could . . ." He passed his hand across his eyes. "So stupid," he muttered thickly. "How could I have been so all-fired *stupid*? After all the times I've told my clients never to write incriminating letters—" He reached for the bottle, then pushed it away. "I guess I'm just lucky she didn't try to blackmail me."

"Blackmail?"

"Make me pay for my sins," Mr. Moseley said in a sour tone. "But the really bad thing is that I don't have an alibi for Saturday night."

She stared at him. "An . . . alibi?"

"I was home. Alone. Adabelle and the kids were in Birmingham." He rubbed his eyes with the back of his hand.

"The woman who cooks and keeps house for us was gone for the weekend. I didn't see anybody, didn't talk to anybody. I got good and drunk. Nobody can vouch for me."

She didn't understand. "But what . . . what does that matter?"

"Can't you see, Lizzy? It matters because I can't prove I had nothing to do with Miss Scott's death. If the police find out I was involved with her, I'll be at the top of their suspect list."

He dropped his face into his hands. Lizzy could think of nothing to say.

A moment later, he lifted his head, leaned forward, and looked at her. His eyes were red, bloodshot. His voice was thick. "Liz, my dear Lizzy, I really hate to ask you this, but could you bring yourself to—That is, would you be able to—" He stopped.

She couldn't bear it. "To . . . do what?"

"To lie." He took a deep breath. "To say we were together. You and I. On Saturday night. Just the two of us. At my house—or at yours, doesn't matter."

"Together?" Her heart was thudding against her ribs. Together? In the same way he and Bunny had been together? In the way she herself had once dreamed of being with him?

He regarded her for a moment, then gave a long, shuddery sigh. "Ah, hell. Forget it, Liz. I can't ask you to do that. It's embarrassing to you. People would assume that—Well, they'd assume, that's all. And they'd keep on assuming, for a damned long time."

Another sigh, longer. "And if worse came to worst, you might have to swear to it in court, and that would mean perjury."

Numbly, Lizzy shook her head. "I couldn't anyway, Mr. Moseley. I was . . . I was with Grady on Saturday night. We went to the picture show, and then we—" She swallowed. "It was probably midnight by the time I got home."

"Ah. The ubiquitous Grady."

"Pardon?"

"Never mind." He took a deep breath. "It's all right, Liz. I shouldn't have asked you. Please forget I said anything." He picked up his glasses and put them on again. "I suppose we'd better get back to work. We've got a filing due today."

She nodded. There was a long, uncomfortable pause. "I wonder . . . Could I . . . Do you mind me asking a question?"

He was moving papers around on his desk. "What?" He didn't look up. "What's your question?"

"Did you—" She clenched her fingers around her pencil. It was an impertinent question. A question she didn't have any right to ask. And either way, she didn't want to hear the answer. But she had to know. "Did you buy Miss Scott a pair of earrings, too? Pearl earrings, from Ettlinger's?"

"Buy her what?" He found the paper he had been looking for and glanced up. He seemed genuinely surprised. "Earrings? No. Why are you asking?"

"No reason," she said hastily, and stood up.

He frowned. "You must have had a reason, Liz. What is it? Did somebody else buy her—"

She shook her head. "Please. If there's anything else I can do—"

"There isn't," he said, and picked up his pen. "Yes, there is. You can pour me a cup of coffee, black, no sugar. Then make another pot. Make it strong. Oh, and cancel the afternoon's appointments. I don't want to see anybody. Understand?"

"Yes, sir."

He gave her a look. "Except you, of course."

SIXTEEN

Verna and Lizzy Have a Narrow Escape

Verna's afternoon was uneventful. She closed the probate office at the usual time and went across the street and up the stairs to the office of Moseley and Moseley to pick up Lizzy. Mr. Moseley was in but his door was closed. Lizzy put her finger to her lips, and they left silently.

"He's not feeling well," Lizzy said, as they reached the street. "It's been a . . . a difficult afternoon." She didn't offer to explain, and Verna didn't like to ask. In fact, Lizzy didn't seem to want to talk at all, even make small talk, so they turned onto Robert E. Lee in silence, walked two blocks east on Dauphin, past Beulah's Beauty Bower, to Peachtree Street. The Limas lived in the middle of the block in an attractive, two-story frame house with a pretty porch and a yard filled with blooming azaleas and gardenias, carefully kept, no doubt by a gardener.

The door was opened by a plump maid in a neat black dress and white apron, with a white beribboned cap pinned to her hair. Verna thought the costume was pretentious. People who could afford it employed colored women to cook and clean, but only a few required them to put on little white caps in the afternoon and pretend that they didn't have anything to do all day but answer the front door.

"I'm Mrs. Tidwell and this is Miss Lacy," Verna said, gesturing at Lizzy. "We've come to talk to Mrs. Lima about becoming a member of our garden club." That was the reason she and Lizzy had made up for their visit.

"Miz Lima ain't here," the maid said. "Her and the mister has gone out of town."

"Why, my goodness," Verna said, pretending to be surprised. "We didn't know they were planning a trip. Not a family emergency, I hope?"

The maid shook her head and the ribbons on her cap bobbed. "No, ma'am. Miz Lima had jes' got back from her sister's over in Repton, where she been for the past three, four days. But this mawnin', right after breakfast, she was took sudden-like with the urge to go agin. The mister, he said he thought it was a right smart idee—they could have themselves a nice vacation, just the two of 'em. So they drove on down to Mobile. Said they might be goin' to Pensacola after that."

"Did they say when they'd be back?" Lizzy asked.

"No, ma'am. Jes' said they'd phone."

And that was that.

"Well," Verna said, when they were out on the street again, under the overhanging canopy of oak trees. "I call that interesting, don't you? Kinda sudden, seems to me."

Lizzy frowned. "And peculiar. Verna, I'm sure it has something to do with Bunny's death. I'm thinking about what Ophelia told you. If Mrs. Lima found out about Mr. Lima and Bunny, and then she heard that Bunny was dead, she'd want to get Mr. Lima out of town." She took a deep breath. "Especially if he didn't have an alibi for Saturday night."

"An alibi?"

"You know. If Mrs. Lima was in Montgomery and Mr. Lima was here by himself, nobody could vouch for him. For what he was doing at the time Bunny was killed, I mean."

Verna was surprised. So far as she knew, Lizzy didn't read detective novels. What had made her wonder about Mr. Lima's alibi for the night Bunny was killed? She was even more surprised when Lizzy turned to her and said, with an unexpected eagerness, "I've got an idea, Verna. Let's go over to Mrs. Brewster's and see if we can get into Bunny's room."

"Why?" And why was Lizzy suddenly getting into the investigating mood?

"Because—" Lizzy looked away. "Because I'm curious. If I could see where Bunny lived, maybe I'd feel I know her a little better. You went there, didn't you?"

"Well, yes, but that was before anybody knew she was dead. I don't think—"

Verna stopped. She had no idea why Lizzy wanted to check out the room. But if they did, maybe she could return the earrings she was carrying around in her purse. The earrings that somebody might think she had stolen.

"I don't think that would be a problem," she said, changing what she had intended to say. "But by this time, Mrs. Brewster has probably heard that Bunny is dead. She'll never let us into that room. And besides, the sheriff has likely sealed it off. The police do that when they're looking for evidence." She knew this from reading *True Detective*.

"Maybe," Lizzy said, and picked up the pace. "Or maybe not. As you said at lunchtime, we won't know unless we try, will we?"

As it turned out, Mrs. Brewster never even knew they were there. As they came around the corner of Plum Street, they saw the lady walking purposefully in the direction of the courthouse square. She was carrying an empty basket.

Going to Hancock's for groceries, maybe? Whatever her mission, it was important enough to make her move swiftly. And it gave Verna and Lizzy their chance.

They went up the stairs to the front door. Verna rapped, very softly—just so they could say that they had knocked. When there was no answer, she pushed gently on the door. It opened, as she thought it would. Nobody locked their front doors in Darling—and Mrs. Brewster's girls would have to be able to enter and leave.

So they entered. The main hall was dark and quiet, since most of the residents were still at work. Verna put her hand on Lizzy's arm and motioned to the steep, narrow staircase. They crept up to the second-floor hallway and down the empty hall to the last door on the right.

Still unlocked, luckily. They went in, quietly, and shut the door behind them.

"Oh, dear," Lizzy whispered, looking around the tiny room. "Oh, my goodness."

"Yes, exactly," Verna said sadly. "Poor kid."

It didn't look as if the police had been here. If they had, they hadn't neatened anything up, for the room was as littered as before. Bunny's clothes were still scattered across the floor, the bed was still unmade, the air still reeked of My Sin. Verna stood for a moment, then went to the dressing table and pretended to look over the cosmetics. Furtively, she opened her purse, took out the small box containing the pearl earrings, and slid it into the drawer, breathing a secret sigh of relief.

Success! She could stop feeling guilty. Now nobody would ever know that she had taken those valuable pearls. She raised her eyes and glanced in the mirror, to see if Lizzy had noticed.

She needn't have worried. To Verna's surprise, Lizzy was pulling open the dresser drawers, one after the other, pushing things aside and looking among Bunny's clothing as if she were searching for something specific. In the third drawer down, she seemed to have found it. She took out a white envelope, held it in her hand for a moment, then, without turning around, quietly tucked it into the front of her dress.

Verna cleared her throat. "Find something interesting?"

"Oh!" Lizzy jumped, startled. "Oh, gosh. I didn't think you'd—" She turned, shamefaced, and pulled out the envelope. "It . . . It's a letter, Verna. From Mr. Moseley to Bunny. I should have told you. It's the reason I wanted to come here this afternoon. To see if I could find it."

"A letter?" Verna rolled her eyes. "For pete's sake, Lizzy, the man's a lawyer. Doesn't he know any better than that?" Incautious letters sometimes led to blackmail. And blackmail led to murder. At least, that was the plot of a recent mystery she had read.

"I don't think he was thinking," Lizzy said. Her face was pale. "I think maybe his brain shut down. He said he had to tell her that he wanted to break it off."

"What does the letter say?"

"I don't know," Lizzy replied in a quavering voice, and handed it over. "You read it, Verna. Read it out loud."

Verna opened it. The letter was handwritten and dated two weeks before. It was short and to the point. She read in a low voice.

" 'Dear Bunny, I'm sorry. I can't give you what you want, or what you deserve. You need to find someone else. We can't see each other again.' It's signed with his initials," she added. "B.M."

She handed it back to Lizzy. "Sounds pretty definite to me. If I got a letter like that, I'd be upset. Maybe frantic, depending on whether I really liked the guy." But maybe it wasn't a case of Bunny really liking—or even loving—Bent Moseley. Maybe she'd seen him as a meal ticket, and when he dumped her, she had threatened to tell his wife about their relationship. If she threatened him, how would he react? Would he be scared? Would he be scared enough to kill her? To Lizzy, she said, "What are you going to do with that letter?"

Lizzy straightened her shoulders. "I'm going to give it back to him." She put the letter into her purse.

Verna frowned. "You're absolutely, positively certain that he didn't have anything to do with Bunny's death?"

"I am positive." Lizzy's voice was firm. "I know Mr. Moseley, Verna. He would never do something like that. The trouble is that he doesn't have an alibi for Saturday night. His wife was in Birmingham with the girls and he was home alone."

So that explained her unexpected remark about Mr. Lima's alibi, Verna thought. She opened her mouth to tell Lizzy to put the letter back. If she took it, she'd be obstructing justice or something awful like that.

But she didn't. After all, she herself had taken those earrings—who was she to tell Lizzy what to do?

Instead, she turned back to the drawer. "Here are the earrings I told you about," she said. She took the box out of the drawer, and opened it.

"Oh!" Lizzy exclaimed, in an awed tone. "Oh, my goodness. They're beautiful!"

"Do you think Mr. Moseley gave them to her?"

"I asked him point-blank," Lizzy replied. "He says he didn't."

"That must have been some conversation," Verna said with a dry chuckle. "Wish I'd been a fly on the wall." She pulled the deposit book out of the drawer. "Just look at how much she was socking away every week, Lizzy. Where in the world was she getting it?"

Lizzy leafed through the book. "Do you suppose she was . . . was blackmailing someone?"

Verna eyed her. "What made you think of that?"

"Mr. Moseley said he was lucky she hadn't tried to blackmail him."

"Hmm," Verna said. She wondered, briefly, if Mr. Moseley had said that to Lizzy in order to allay any suspicions she might have had.

"I think he was telling the truth," Lizzy said, turning the pages in the deposit book. "He seemed to want to tell me everything. Too much, really. I didn't want to hear it, especially the business about him and his wife getting a divorce."

"My goodness," Verna said softly, wondering if this would change Lizzy's relationship to him—or to Grady Alexander.

"What about Mr. Lima?" Lizzy asked.

"What about him?"

"Maybe Bunny was blackmailing him." She turned another page.

"It's a possibility," Verna replied. In fact, the more she thought about the abrupt departure of the Limas "on vacation," the more suspicious it looked.

Lizzy glanced down at the paper Bunny had been writing on. "Maxwell Woodburn," she mused, frowning. "I'm sure he doesn't live in Darling. I wonder who he is."

"Amanda Blake thought he might be Bunny's pen pal in Montgomery," Verna replied. "Maybe he's the source of that extra ten dollars a week. Maybe Bunny was blackmailing *him.*"

"I doubt you'd blackmail somebody you thought you might marry," Lizzy said. "I wouldn't, anyway."

"Maybe she was using blackmail to get him to marry her," Verna suggested.

"Well, if he was her pen pal," Lizzy said reasonably, "there ought to be more letters around here somewhere."

Agreeing, Verna pulled out the drawer of the dressing table and began to rummage through it. As she did, she uncovered the photograph. "See?" she said, holding it up.

"It's Bunny!" Lizzy exclaimed.

Verna chuckled wryly. "Bunny in her teddy. And that's the teddy, over there on the floor. Shocking, isn't it?"

"Yes, in a way. You wouldn't catch me sitting on the hood of a car in my teddy, letting some guy photograph me." Still holding the deposit book, Lizzy took the photo and began to study it. "You know, Verna, there's something about—"

"Shhh!" Verna put a hand on Lizzy's arm. "Somebody's coming!" From the direction of the stairs, they heard the *clack-clack* of pumps on bare wood, and the sound of Mrs. Brewster's voice.

Lizzy gasped. "What do we do?"

"Quick!" Verna whispered. "We have to hide! Come on!"

Grabbing Lizzy, she pulled her behind the curtain that was strung diagonally across one corner. There was barely room for them. Holding their breaths, they crowded against the wall, behind Bunny's dresses. Verna hoped to heaven that the curtain wasn't moving and that their shoes couldn't be seen below its hem.

"—the only room I have available at the moment," Mrs. Brewster was saying, as the door opened. The footsteps came into the room, but not very far. "The unfortunate girl's belongings are still here, as you can see. But I can have the room cleaned and thoroughly aired for your daughter, whenever you need it."

A woman's high-pitched voice said, critically, "Is this the largest you have? I'm not sure that my Sue Ellen would be happy in such a small room." She sniffed. "And what *is* that odor? Some sort of exotic perfume, I suppose." Without waiting for an answer, she went on, "You say that the young woman was killed in an automobile wreck?"

"Yes," Mrs. Brewster said shortly. "My girls are usually quite trustworthy and follow the rules of the house without question. But this one—" She made a disdainful tsk-tsk. "I am sad to say that she was almost incorrigible."

The scent of Bunny's My Sin was overpowering, and Verna felt her nose tickling.

"Rules of the house," the woman repeated thoughtfully. "You are strict with your boarders, then, Mrs. Brewster?"

Verna took a deep breath and pinched her nose to stop the tickle.

"Oh, absolutely," Mrs. Brewster replied. "In fact, you can ask anyone in Darling. They will all tell you that I am extremely strict with my girls. Curfews, meals, visiting hours, the presence of young men in the house—I consider myself *in loco parentis*, and I watch over the young women with as much care and attention as their mothers. Your daughter is a treasure," she added sanctimoniously, "and I pledge to guard her virtue with my life."

Verna pinched harder, feeling that she was about to explode.

"Well, then," the woman said, sounding mollified, "perhaps the room will do after all. My Sue Ellen is, as you say, a treasure, but she is a bit wild, and it would be a comfort to me to know that she is being watched carefully. One young man in particular is making quite a nuisance of himself. I have forbidden him to—"

The sneeze came just as the door closed behind them.

"Whew!" Lizzy breathed out. They listened as the *clack-clack* of heels receded down the hall. "That was a narrow escape."

"What wretched old women," Verna said in disgust. "Remind me never to behave that way when I get old."

After a moment, they came out from behind the curtain. Verna went to the door and opened it a crack. They could hear the women's voices drifting up from downstairs. "Sounds as if they're in the parlor," she whispered.

"In the parlor?" Lizzy's eyes widened. "Then we can't go down the stairs without being seen! We're stuck here."

"Maybe not," Verna countered. "How good are you at climbing?" She stepped out into the hall and raised the window sash. It went up smoothly. "The girls use this as their secret exit, when they don't want Mrs. Brewster to know that they've been out past curfew. You see that trellis? That's how they do it."

Lizzy looked out the window, onto the porch roof. "I've always been good at climbing trees, and this isn't much different." She hiked up her skirt. "And it seems like the easy way out, compared to trying to sneak past those two old dragons. Let's go!"

A few minutes later, Verna and Lizzy were safely on the ground and out on the street, strolling nonchalantly down the block, arm in arm, and trying not to giggle.

SEVENTEEN

Myra May Organizes the Dahlias

Myra May's shift at the switchboard behind the diner began at four in the afternoon five days a week and ended at midnight. Darling was a small town. Only about half of the residences had telephones and most of these were on party lines. Given people's habit of listening in, a single phone conversation could keep as many as half a dozen people busy at once. Which meant that the switchboard operator's job was normally pretty light, except when there was an emergency—like the day the convicts escaped and everybody was calling everybody else, trying to find out what was going on. Most afternoons and evenings, there were only five or six calls in an hour. Myra May got a lot of reading and knitting and letter-writing done during her shift.

This week, for instance, she was reading a book she'd gotten at the library. The library was small and Miss Rogers couldn't buy many books, but this one had been donated. Myra May had picked it up, read the first page, and checked it out immediately—in spite of Miss Rogers, who had told her that it was written for children. It was called *The Secret of the Old Clock*, by Carolyn Keene, and featured a courageous, quick-witted sixteen-year-old girl named Nancy Drew. Myra May would've loved to have taken part in a few of Nancy's adventures: finding a will hidden in an old clock, having a run-in with thieves, being overpowered by criminals and locked in an abandoned house. And all because Nancy was trying to help a poor, struggling family denied their share of a wealthy relative's estate.

This afternoon, though, Myra May was having a hard time concentrating on the adventures of Nancy Drew, exciting as they were. She kept worrying about her friend Alice Ann and wondering whether the sheriff had arrested her yet. It didn't seem so, for Mr. Johnson at the bank had telephoned Hiram Riley the accountant, and their conversation suggested that they still didn't have all the evidence they needed to make an embezzlement charge stick. Mr. Johnson seemed certain, though, that Alice Ann had stolen the money—if only he and the bank examiner could figure out what she had done with it.

"Damned clever woman," he had growled angrily. "Covered her tracks so well that we can't follow. And she won't tell us a blasted thing. Just cries and cries and claims to be innocent."

"What's the situation at the bank?" Mr. Riley had asked nervously.

"Same as it was." Mr. Johnson sounded weary. "Precarious, I don't mind telling you, but keep that to yourself. If we don't locate that money . . ." His voice became dramatic. "We'll all be in for it, Hiram. The whole town. Bad times comin', like a big black winter cloud rollin' down from the north."

Listening, Myra May thought that Mr. Johnson sounded just a bit too dramatic, which was unlike him. He usually talked like butter wouldn't melt in his mouth, and here he was, sounding like a Hardshell Baptist preaching Armageddon.

A few moments later, Mr. Johnson asked Myra May to connect him, long distance, with a man in the banking division of the state comptroller's office in Montgomery. The conversation was too technical for Myra May to follow, but the gist of it seemed to be that Darling Savings and Trust was about to be put on the list of "troubled banks." Myra May recognized this term because she had read it in the Mobile *Register* when a half-dozen Florida banks had failed the previous year. There was something about "undercapitalization" (she had no idea what that meant) and "unsecured loans" (that one she understood). But the central problem for the bank seemed to be, as Mr. Johnson put it darkly, the "malfeasance of a trusted bank employee," who would be arrested as soon as the investigation was completed.

They hung up and Myra May sat there at the switchboard, feeling so sorry for poor Alice Ann that she could cry. And so angry at Mr. Johnson—that proud, puffed-up little man who was rich enough to buy and sell half the town and didn't hesitate to foreclose on any poor soul who got behind on his payments—that she could just about spit nails.

While she was thinking this, there was a call from Florence Henderson, asking to be connected to her elderly mother so she could see if she needed any groceries from Hancock's, since Florence was coming to town to shop. Her mother asked her to get a loaf of bread, a pound of sugar, and a box of Kellogg's Corn Flakes, which should come to a total of eighteen cents (five cents for the bread, five for the sugar, eight for the corn flakes), which Mrs. Hancock should put on her mother's account. Then Mr. Snow at the Farm Supply wanted to talk to Calvin Combs so he could ask about payment on an overdue bill for seeds planted the year before. It was a big bill, too, nearly nine dollars, but all Mrs. Combs could say

(Mr. Combs was out in the field) was that they would try to pay something—maybe fifty cents—the next week or the week after. Last year's crop hadn't done too well because of the drought.

As she plugged in these calls, Myra May kept thinking about Alice Ann, trying to come up with something she could do to help. She knew very well that Alice Ann didn't have it in her to steal money. What's more, she was a Dahlia. The Dahlias ought to stand up for one another when there was trouble.

Finally, she rang Alice Ann's number. When Alice Ann said hello, in a tired, unhappy voice, she said, "Alice Ann, honey, I've been hearin' about your troubles. I wish there was something I could do, but I just can't think what. Still, I want you to know that your friends don't believe a word of it. Not a single, solitary word."

There was a click on the line and then another and another, and Myra May said firmly, "Miz Perkins, is that you? Mr. King? One of the Barrett sisters? This is a private call, if y'all don't mind. Miz Walker and I would appreciate it if you could just hang up now."

Then she waited, counting the clicks. One, two.

"One more," Myra May said sternly. "Maybe you don't know it, but listenin' to private conversations is against the law." The third receiver went down.

By this time, Alice Ann was crying as if her heart would break.

"Oh, Myra May," she sobbed, "I can't thank you enough for callin'!" The words came tumbling out, all in a hurry. "Yours is the first friendly voice I've heard all day, and it sounds so sweet. I've been feelin' all alone out here, just me an' Arnold, and neither one of us knowin' what in the world we ought to do. They won't let me work at my window at the bank and I know I'm goin' to be fired. Mr. Johnson took me into his office and him and the bank examiner kept askin' me how was it I took all that money and what did I do with it, and I kept sayin' I didn't take any money so how could I tell them where it was?" She gulped. "But they say they've got evidence against me, Myra May! They say I might could get arrested!"

"What kind of evidence?"

"They say it's in the bank records, although they won't tell me exactly what records. And Arnold, poor man, he wants so bad to help but he can't do a blessed thing. Seems like everybody is against us! It's a terrible, helpless feeling. Why, I'm so discomboobilated that I can't even think what I'm goin' to feed poor Arnold for his supper!"

At last! Myra May had finally found something she could help with. She spoke firmly. "Don't you bother your head one bit about supper, Alice Ann. I'll call a few Dahlias and somebody'll bring y'all some supper. But before I do, I wonder if you've given any thought to who might've taken that money. I mean, from the way I hear them tell it, it's really gone, and it didn't just disappear by magic, poof! If you didn't do it, who did?"

Myra May's question seemed to calm Alice Ann down a bit. "Well," she said slowly, "there's only the two cashiers, me and Mr. Harper, but he hasn't been here very long. There's the bookkeeper, Mr. Swearingen. And Mr. Johnson. But of course the president of the bank wouldn't—" She stopped. "At least, I don't think he would," she said slowly.

Myra May frowned, remembering Mr. Johnson's dramatics. What if that had been an act? What if he had been stealing money from the bank and got scared that the bank examiner was going to find out? It would be all too easy for him to manipulate the bank records so that the trail led to Alice Ann, rather than to him.

But she had just thought of another possibility. "What about Imogene Rutledge?" she asked. Miss Rutledge was a former cashier who had worked at the bank since Mr. Johnson's father had opened it, back in 1902. The whole town had been surprised when she left her position as head cashier the previous fall, but she had explained it by saying that her mother (who lived over in Monroeville) needed her at home to help, which was something that everybody could understand. Mr. Harper had taken her place.

"Miss Rutledge?" Alice Ann sounded hesitant. "Well, we haven't seen much of her lately. She moved over to Monroeville, to live with her mother."

"But she was with the bank for years and years, wasn't she? She probably knew the accounts better than anybody. And the way I heard it, her mother wasn't the only reason she left."

"Well, that's true. I didn't hear what really happened, but there were plenty of rumors flying around. Somebody said she got fired for sassin' Mr. Johnson once too often."

Myra May frowned. "And don't I remember hearing that she bought a new Dodge from Kilgore Motors right after she quit? Must've cost nearly three hundred dollars."

"Yes, I heard that, too. But—"

"And you don't know for sure why they're pickin' on you?"

"No," Alice Ann said. "I don't have an idea in the world about it." And she began to cry again.

Myra May could understand why Alice Ann was crying, although she herself made it a personal rule never to cry. When you cried, they (usually some man or another) knew they had you in their power, and she was never going to give them that kind of satisfaction. She said gently, "Now, you just stop cryin', Alice Ann, honey. Go lie down on your bed with a wet washrag on your eyes and you'll feel better. The Dahlias are goin' to take care of your supper. Somebody'll be round with a basket in an hour or so."

Myra May unplugged the call and swung into action. She

rang up Beulah's Beauty Bower, the one place in town where she could expect to find the regular Tuesday afternoon Dahlias gathered together. Bettina answered the phone.

Myra May said, "I'm organizing a basket supper for Alice Ann and Arnold. If any Dahlias there would like to help out, let me speak to them."

As it happened, both customers in the beauty chairs—Bessie Bloodworth and Aunt Hetty Little—were Dahlias, as of course was Beulah. She had just shampooed Bessie and was trimming her, but she interrupted her work long enough to go to the phone and offer a big bowl of stewed hen and dumplings (tonight's dinner at the Trivettes') for the Walkers' supper. Bessie spoke up from her chair and offered some black-eyed peas cooked with fatback and onions and a pint jar of home-canned pickled beets. Bettina was curling Aunt Hetty Little, who offered a garden salad and some fresh tomatoes and green onions, if somebody would come and pick it up. Beulah offered Hank's services as a driver.

Which left dessert, but since Myra May knew there was plenty of Euphoria's pie on the shelf in the diner, there was no need to ask anybody else for that. So she told Beulah to tell Hank to stop by on his way out to the Walkers' and pick up half a pie.

"Tell everybody thanks," she said. "Alice Ann can sit down to supper now without worrying her head or lifting a finger—and all on account of the Dahlias!"

But Myra May wasn't quite finished. Before she hung up, she asked to speak to Aunt Hetty Little, whose white hair was now wound into what looked like shiny little white caterpillars all over her head. She was more than willing to come to the phone, step up on the stool that was kept under the phone for short ladies, and spend a few minutes talking—without fear of the neighbors listening in, since Beulah had a private line.

"You know about Alice Ann bein' investigated for stealin' money from the bank, I guess," Myra May said.

"I do," Aunt Hetty replied tartly. "Biggest load of cow poop I have ever in all my life encountered."

Myra May heartily agreed. "Well, if Alice Ann didn't do it, seems to me the question is, who did? I was goin' down the list of possibles and wondered what you know about why Imogene Rutledge quit the bank."

"Imogene Rutledge," Aunt Hetty said thoughtfully. "My, my. Well, what Dorothy Rogers told me is that Imogene got pretty free with her tongue one day and Mr. Johnson ordered her to turn in her cashier's badge. Imogene always did have a way with words. Used 'em the way you'd use a flaying knife. Didn't make her a whole lot of friends. And if she happened to make a few, she didn't always keep 'em."

"So she talked back to Mr. Johnson. You're sure there was no more to it than that?"

Aunt Hetty was silent for a moment. "Well, there's that new Dodge she bought the week after she left the bank."

"A new car," Myra May asked. "How well do you know her, Aunt Hetty?"

"Not as well as Dorothy does," Aunt Hetty said pointedly. "You want to know about Imogene Rutledge, you go over to the library and talk to her."

"Thanks, Aunt Hetty," Myra May said. "I think I'll just do that. You tell Beulah we'll have that pie waiting for Hank when he comes to pick it up."

Aunt Hetty said good-bye to Myra May, hung up the receiver, and told Beulah what Myra May had said about Hank and the pie. Then she went back to sit in the beauty chair so Bettina could use the electric hair blower to finish drying her hair. It made a fearful racket, but it worked so quick that nobody minded.

But since Beulah was using the other hair blower to dry

Bessie Bloodworth's hair, the two hair blowers together made it impossible to talk unless you shouted. And everybody wanted to talk, because everybody had been listening to Aunt Hetty's end of the conversation.

"What does Imogene Rutledge's new Dodge have to do with Alice Ann?" Bessie Bloodworth shouted, getting straight to the point.

Aunt Hetty shouted back: "Myra May is doing some investigating on her own, seems like. She's looking for other suspects."

"Suspects in the embezzlement?" Beulah asked, and when Aunt Hetty put her hand to her ear, repeated the question in a shout.

Aunt Hetty nodded vigorously.

"Well, Imogene Rutledge would be at the top of my list, just on gen'ral principles," Bettina shouted, then added, "O' course, I'm just jokin'." Everyone knew she wasn't really, though. When Miss Rutledge lived in Darling, she had not patronized the Beauty Bower, but had gone to Conrad's Curling Corner, on the other side of town. In Bettina's eyes, this was an unforgivable sin.

"Well, there's that new Dodge she bought before she left town," Bessie shouted. "It must've cost a pretty penny. Bet Kilgore Motors was happy to see her comin'."

"And I heard she bought her and her mother a house over in Monroeville," Beulah shouted. "A big house. They're meaning to turn it into a rooming house." She turned off the hair blower halfway through her sentence and the last part of it was very loud.

"A new car, a new house," Bessie shouted, which also came out too loud, because Bettina had shut off her blower. "Sounds pretty incriminating to me," she added, in a lower voice. She turned her head, admiring her reflection in the mirror. "My, Beulah, but that is pretty."

"Well, if I say so myself, I do know hair," Beulah said modestly, picking up a soft brush and whisking hair off the back of Bessie's neck. "Listen, ladies, I want to know if either of you have heard anything about that escaped convict. Bettina and I ask everybody who comes in here, and nobody seems to have heard a blessed thing."

"There wasn't even anything about him in Friday's *Dispatch*," Bettina complained, beginning to unwrap Aunt Hetty's little white caterpillars, which by now were nice and dry and very springy. "You would think Mr. Dickens would give us at least one little clue, wouldn't you? Why, I don't know whether it's safe to sleep with my window open at night, or whether I ought to lock all the doors and take the stove poker to bed with me."

"Oh, pooh," Aunt Hetty said dismissively. "You can stop worrying about that escaped convict, Bettina. He probably hopped a freight train and is havin' a high old time with the ladies in Memphis or St. Louis by now."

"I agree," Bessie Bloodworth said, getting out of the beauty chair and allowing Beulah to unfasten her cape. "Nothing for any of us to worry about, Bettina."

Bettina breathed a sigh of relief. "Well, I am glad to hear that. I guess I can put that big ol' stove poker back where I got it, can't I?" She unwrapped the last caterpillar. "Now, Mrs. Little, I need you to tell me what I'm doin' wrong with my eggplants. They just don't seem to be growin' as good as they should. They're just little bitty things."

"Don't you fret about those eggplants, dear," Aunt Hetty said in a comforting tone. "The mornings have been chilly lately, and they don't like cold feet. They love summertime, and they'll perk up real good when it heats up some. Look for 'em to grow like a house afire along about the Fourth of July. Come hot summer, you'll have more eggplants than you know what to do with, and you'll be askin' everybody for recipes."

"I've got a good one for you, Bettina," Beulah said, hanging Bessie's cape on the hook. "Tomato and eggplant pie, with eggs and a little milk and cheese rubbed through the grater, if you've got cheese. If you don't, you can do without, but maybe put in an extra egg so the custard sets up. I have a hard time getting my children to eat eggplant, but they do like that pie."

"Thank you, everybody," Bettina said gratefully. She looked around, smiling. "I guess I owe just about everything I know about gardening and cooking to Beulah's Beauty Bower."

It is true, however, that while the Dahlias know quite a lot about growing vegetables and making pies, they don't know all there is to know about escaped convicts.

EIGHTEEN

Lizzy and Verna Plan an Expedition

When Lizzy and Verna stopped giggling about their narrow escape from Mrs. Brewster's boardinghouse, they discovered that they were hungry—which might be expected, since the sandwiches they had eaten at lunchtime were a distant memory. Lizzy's house was closest, so she invited Verna to have supper with her.

"Nothing fancy," she said, "but there's cheese and ham, and tomatoes and green onions and lettuce from the garden, and I can scramble some eggs and open a pint jar of Sally-Lou's canned peaches. She always puts up more than we can eat."

"Sounds perfect to me," Verna said. "I think we need to talk, don't you?"

Lizzy nodded. She had been wondering how much of what Mr. Moseley had told her she should share with Verna. He expected her to keep it in confidence, but she felt she owed Verna an explanation for taking that revealing letter, which she knew should be left for the police to find. But she and

Verna had been friends for a very long time and Liz felt that she could be trusted. After all, they were both Dahlias, weren't they? Dahlias were loyal. Dahlias could keep a confidence.

So while she fed Daffodil and then got busy scrambling eggs with cheese and bits of ham and green onions and Verna assembled a garden salad from lettuce, fresh tomatoes, and chopped green peppers, along with a handful of fresh raw peas and more green onions, Lizzy told Verna about her conversation with Mr. Moseley. Some of it was . . . well, torrid, she thought, especially the part about Bunny and Mr. Moseley going to Mobile together.

But as Lizzy had said earlier, she wasn't a prude. If Mr. Moseley wanted to have an affair with Bunny, who was she to sit in judgment? After all, she was thinking of Grady in pretty much the same way—although she had to admit that there was a difference. Neither she nor Grady were married. Mr. Moseley was, and Bunny knew it. That was what made it torrid, in Liz's opinion.

Verna, however, was not very interested in the seamy stuff. In fact, she hardly blinked. She seemed to be much more interested in the story Bunny had told Mr. Moseley about her life on a farm outside Monroeville, with a drunk for a father and a runaway mother who had left her with four younger brothers and sister to care for, including a pair of twins.

"Bunny told him she kept them all fed and clothed and walked miles to school every day," Lizzy concluded. "He was impressed by her courage. I guess that might have been what attracted him to her in the first place."

"Courage, smourage," Verna scoffed. "He was impressed by her—" She glanced at Lizzy. "By the way she looked in that red dress. What's more, she lied to him. Bunny lived with her widowed mother, not with four little kids and a drunk."

"How do we know?" Lizzy asked, pushing scrambled eggs onto two plates.

"What do you mean, how do we know?" Verna put the salad bowl on the kitchen table. "Because that's what she told us."

"Well, yes. But how do we know whether the story about her widowed mother is true, or the story she told Mr. Moseley?"

Verna frowned. "I guess we don't," she said slowly. "That girl was such a liar—I wonder if she told Maxwell Woodburn she'd marry him."

"Or told Mr. Lima that she would run away with him. Or—" She put the skillet in the sink.

"Or promised something to somebody we don't even know about yet," Verna said. She looked around. "What's to drink, Lizzy?"

"Lemonade in the fridge. Glasses on the first shelf in the cupboard. Oh, and while you're at it, pour some milk in a saucer for Daffy."

"Your fridge is a lot bigger than mine," Verna said enviously, taking out the pitcher of lemonade and a bottle of milk. "This Monitor-top is really a beauty. Quiet, too. My Kelvinator works fine but it growls." She opened the cupboard and took two glasses off the shelf.

"I lived with Mother's icebox for too many years," Lizzy replied. "Somehow, I was the one who always got to empty the pan, because it was too heavy for Mother, and Sally-Lou always spilled water all over the floor. So when I moved in here, I got the best fridge I could afford, figuring I'd have it for a while." She put a plate of corn muffins on the table and took the cover off the butter dish. "We could ask Mrs. Bledsoe about Bunny. They were cousins. She'd know."

Verna poured the lemonade and Daffodil's milk. "We can't ask Mrs. Bledsoe because she's up in Nashville with a new grandbaby." She put the glasses on the table and the saucer of milk on the floor. With a rumbling purr, Daffodil began to lap it up. "Looks like there's nothing further we can do as far as the Limas are concerned," she added. "So what would you think of going over to Monroeville to do a little snooping? I'm sure it wouldn't be hard to locate somebody who knew Bunny. She's not exactly the shrinking violet type, you know. Probably *everybody* knew her."

Lizzy opened Sally-Lou's home-canned peaches and spooned them into two bowls. "Monroeville," she said thoughtfully. "Well, I guess we could. But it would have to be after work." The two sat down. Lizzy took some salad and passed the bowl to Verna. "And how would we get there?" She occasionally rode her bicycle to work, but neither she nor Verna had a car.

"How about going tomorrow? We might could ask Myra May to drive us, if she can get away from the diner and the switchboard. Maybe stop for supper at Buzz's Barbeque?"

"Sounds like a good idea to me." Lizzy felt in the pocket of her dress for her hankie and pulled out something else.

"Oh, dear," she said. "It's Bunny's photo. And the deposit book." She put it on the table between them. "I guess I had these in my hand when we heard Mrs. Brewster coming and we had to hide in the closet. I must've stuck them in my pocket."

Verna chuckled. "Well, I don't suppose anybody is going to put you in jail for stealing a photo, Lizzy. And now that Bunny's dead, she's not going to be withdrawing that money." She picked up her fork and took a bite. "Hey, these are good scrambled eggs."

"I get eggs from Mrs. Freeman, down the street," Lizzy said. "Her rooster wakes me up in the morning, so I figure the least I can do is eat his hens' eggs." Fork in one hand, she looked down at the photo, then picked it up and held it closer, studying it. "You know, this car looks a lot like—" She put down her fork, frowning. "Oh, my gosh! You're not going to believe me, Verna, but I would swear that this is the same car—"

"Yeah?" Verna added another couple of tomato wedges to her salad. "The same car as what?"

"The same car that I saw wrecked in the ravine yesterday." She took a deep breath. "With Bunny in it."

"It can't be the same one." Verna took the photo, looking at it closely. "The car she was in was *stolen*, Lizzy. It was reported stolen hours before she turned up in it, dead."

"But it *is*! I'd swear it is, Lizzy! Look. It's a Pontiac—there's the Indian hood ornament. The one I saw was green, and this one might be, too, although you can't tell from this photo." She pointed with her fork. "And it's got an Alabama license plate. See there? Alabama 10-654. White numbers on black. Big as life."

"Well, there you go. If it's the same license plate number as the one in the ravine, you've got a match. Is it?"

"I don't know," Lizzy said regretfully. "There was no reason for me to notice that plate. I'm sure the sheriff did, though—he had already matched it with the one that was reported stolen." She paused. "I don't want to ask Sheriff Burns, but Charlie Dickens was there, too, taking pictures and making notes. He might've written it down."

Verna gave her an intent look. "Lizzy, I think you should call Charlie right now. He's probably still at the newspaper. The sooner we get this question settled, the sooner we'll know for sure."

"You're right about that." Lizzy was already on her way to the telephone on the wall. She rang the exchange—one short ring. "Myra May, this is Lizzy. Would you ring the *Dispatch* office for me, please? I need to talk to Charlie."

"Sure thing," Myra May said. "Listen. I need to talk to you. I'll call you back after you're through with Mr. Dickens. Okay?"

"Sure," Lizzy said. "Anyway, Verna's here and she's got the idea that maybe we should all drive over to Monroeville tomorrow evening." She laughed. "She's playing detective."

"Okay," Myra May said. "I'll ring you back."

Charlie was at the office, working on Friday's paper. Yes, he had made a note of the Pontiac's license plate. Give him a minute and he'd hunt it up. There was the sound of papers rustling. A moment later, Lizzy had her answer. She wrote it down as Charlie read it out of his notebook.

"How come you're askin', Lizzy?" Charlie wanted to know.

"Just tying up a couple of loose ends," Lizzy said evasively.

"Hey, wait a minute," Charlie said. "If there's something important here—"

"Thanks a lot, Charlie. See you soon." She hung up and went back to the table. "It's the same," she said, sitting down at the table. "Alabama 10-654. So it *is* the same car, Verna."

Verna picked up the photograph and studied it. "Which means that Bunny knew the owner of the car she died in."

"And she knew him pretty well," Lizzy put in. "You don't strip down to your underwear to pose for just anybody." She paused. "I wonder when this was taken."

"Not too long ago, I'd guess," Verna said. "Had to be a warm day." She pointed to the photograph. "That's a man taking the picture. You can see his shadow. Looks like he's wearing a fedora."

"That doesn't help," Lizzy said. "Lots of men wear fedoras. Grady, for instance." She frowned. "The sheriff said that the car belonged to Mr. Harper's brother, over in Monroeville. That must be the connection."

"Makes sense," Verna said. "But what I don't understand is why—"

The phone rang and Lizzy got up. "Probably Myra May."

It was. "Lizzy, do you know anything about Imogene Rutledge?"

"Wait a minute," Lizzy said, listening for clicks on the line. There were none so she went on, with a little laugh. "Miss Rutledge? Well, all I know is that a lot of people breathed a sigh of relief when she left the bank last year. She had a habit of telling people what they didn't want to hear, I guess. Why are you asking?"

"Because I'm trying to think who else—besides Alice Ann—might have been taking money from the bank. If you still want to go to Monroeville tomorrow evenin', I'll be glad to drive—if we can spend some time checking out Imogene Rutledge. She lives over there now, with her mother."

"It's okay with me," Lizzy said, "although I hope you're not planning to walk straight up to her and ask her if she's an embezzler. She'll tell you where to get off."

There was a silence on the other end of the line. "I'll think of a way," Myra May muttered. "So we're goin' to drive over there and poke around?"

"If you're agreeable. Oh, and could you do a couple of things for me? Telephone-operator type things? Remember last night when we were playing hearts and Verna was telling us about Maxwell Woodburn, the guy who might be Bunny's pen pal? One of the girls at Mrs. Brewster's told Verna that she thought this fellow lived in Montgomery. Could you find a telephone number for him?"

"Great idea!" Verna applauded from the table. "Wish I'd thought of it."

"Sure, I can do that," Myra May said. "Let me write that down. Maxwell Wood-b-u-r-n?"

"Right. And also, last night you mentioned that the Pontiac that Bunny Scott is supposed to have stolen belonged to Fred Harper's brother."

"He lives in Monroeville, too," Myra May said. "He's a dentist."

"Could you get a phone number for him?"

"And an address," Verna put in.

"Verna says we need an address, too," Lizzy repeated.

"What's all this about?" Myra May asked.

There was a click on the line. "Lizzy, could I break in?" Mrs. Freeman asked, in her old-lady's quivery voice. "Myra May, I need to get hold of Mr. Lima at home, quick. Howard's stomach is real bad again, and Doc Roberts is here. He says Howard has to have some new medicine and wants to tell Mr. Lima which one to order."

"Mr. Lima isn't at home, Mrs. Freeman," Lizzy said. "He and Mrs. Lima drove down to Mobile this morning, on a little vacation. There's a sign on the drugstore door that says it's closed."

"Actually," Myra May put in, "they drove on to Pensacola. Mr. Lima telephoned his sister not twenty minutes ago to let her know where they were." She sounded apologetic. "He says they plan to stay for a week, at least. Mrs. Lima wants to sit on the beach."

"A week!" Mrs. Freeman exclaimed. She sounded frightened. "Mr. Lima has *never* closed that drugstore before! He always says he's here to take care of this town, regardless. What are we supposed to do for medicine while he's gone?"

"Tell you what, Mrs. Freeman," Myra May replied. "I'm here at the telephone switchboard, and Tommy Ryan is sittin' out front in the diner, polishin' off a piece of Euphoria's chocolate meringue pie. Tommy works out at the Coca-Cola bottling plant, but he lives over t'wards Monroeville and drives back and forth every day. If you'll put Doc Roberts on the phone, he can tell Tommy what he needs and Tommy can pick it up at the drugstore in Monroeville tomorrow morning and bring it to you."

"Oh, what a wonderful idea, Myra May," Mrs. Freeman said, with a sigh of relief. "I'll go fetch the doctor."

"I'll go get Tommy," Myra May said. "Lizzy, see you tomorrow at five."

"I'll get off the line now," Lizzy said. "Mrs. Freeman, I hope Mr. Freeman gets to feeling better."

"I do, too, dear," the old lady said fervently. "Howard suffers so with that stomach of his. And I sure hope Lester Lima gets back from that vacation real soon. There'll be lots of folks in town needing medicine." She sighed heavily. "Oh, and Lizzy, there's a few more eggs for you here, if you want them. The hens are laying good right now."

"Thanks," Lizzy said. "I'll get some extra for Mother, if you can spare them." Going back to the table, she said, "Myra May says that Mr. Lima called his sister and said they'd gone to Pensacola so Mrs. Lima could sit on the beach."

"I really would like to know why they left town so suddenly," Verna said.

"We may never know," Lizzy replied. They finished their meal in silence, the deposit book and the telltale photograph on the table between them.

NINETEEN

Bessie Bloodworth Bags a Ghost

Evenings were always quiet at Magnolia Manor—so quiet, in fact, that the younger folks (the ones who liked to go out to the Watering Hole or the Dance Barn to dance and drink bootleg booze in the parking lot) might have called them dull. Bessie didn't see it that way, of course, for her days were full of chores, sunup to sundown. When supper was over and the evening work was done, she was glad to go out to the front porch and join the Magnolia Ladies (that's what they called themselves) for a relaxing hour or two before bedtime.

Besides Bessie herself, there were five other ladies living at the Manor at the present time: Dorothy Rogers, Mrs. Sedalius (the one who had heard the Cartwright ghost digging in the Darling Dahlias' garden), a retired schoolteacher named Leticia Wiggens, Maxine Bechdel, widow of the previous editor of the *Dispatch*, and Roseanne, the Negro lady who had cooked and cleaned for Bessie's family for over forty years.

None of the Magnolia Ladies was "well fixed," as Leticia

put it delicately, and all of them had their own chores at the Manor, to help out with the cost of running the old place. Roseanne did the cooking and the laundry, as she had done for many years. Leticia and Maxine washed the dishes and cleaned the kitchen and dining room. Mrs. Sedalius cleaned the upstairs, Miss Rogers dusted the downstairs, and Bessie did the downstairs floors, the shopping, and the outside work.

In addition, everyone (even Miss Rogers) worked in the garden that supplied the Manor's table, and they all helped to tend the dozen hens that gave them their breakfast eggs. One year, they had a milk goat named Belle, but while everyone loved Belle for her sweet manners and soft ears, none of them was crazy about her milk ("tastes like old socks," Miss Rogers said). So Belle lived a lazy life in her backyard pen and Roseanne walked the two blocks to Mr. Wellgood's barn every morning and brought back a quart of straight-from-the-cow milk for breakfast.

Magnolia Manor was the name Bessie had given to her family home after her father died, taking with him to the grave the Civil War military pension that had supported them both. Trying to come up with an idea that would earn some money, Bessie turned the place into a boardinghouse, which suited her own minimal needs and brought in enough to pay the taxes, buy coal and electricity, and buy meat and such staples as flour, sugar, coffee, and tea.

The ladies didn't pay much, because they didn't have much. Mrs. Sedalius' son (a doctor in Mobile) sent a small check once a month (just the check, never a letter). Miss Rogers earned a few dollars a week at the library. Leticia was a Civil War widow and got her husband's pension, while Maxine owned two small houses and the tenants usually (but not always) paid rent. Roseanne had once lived in Maysville, but after her husband died and her daughters got married, she moved in with Bessie and traded her cooking and laundry talents for board and room. Both Roseanne and Bessie were satisfied with the arrangement, especially Roseanne, who was scared to death of ending up in the poorhouse. Cypress County had a poorhouse, of course—all the counties in the state were required to have one—but there wasn't enough money to manage it right and nobody in her right mind wanted to end up there.

Bessie had once read that in England, the government gave its elderly citizens an old-age pension. She thought this was a very good idea and wished that America would do this, too, the sooner the better. In fact, she had recently written an urgent letter to Senator Bankhead, telling him that he ought to get behind Huey P. Long's proposal that everybody over sixty should receive a pension. But she wasn't surprised when she didn't get an answer. Huey Long thought that the government should guarantee every family in the nation five thousand dollars a year, and that nobody should earn more than a million dollars a year. People who had money didn't like him. They thought he was dangerous, and he probably was, and a Communist and maybe he was that, too (although he said he wasn't). But Bessie liked his ideas and wished that Huey P. Long could come over and take charge of Alabama, because Louisiana did not deserve him.

She had even heard Huey P. Long on the radio. Two Christmases before, Mrs. Sedalius' son (who probably felt guilty because he never came to visit) had sent his mother a Crosley five-tube table model radio. The ladies were scandalized, because Miss Rogers had seen an advertisement in *Popular Mechanics* and knew that it sold for fifty dollars. "See it, hear it!" exhorted the advertisement. "View the refreshing beauty of its solid mahogany cabinet. Watch the stations, written in on the graphic dial, parade before you and usher in their programs with unerring accuracy. Sharpen the reception with the Crosley Acuminators. Release inspiring volume by means of the Cresendon."

It took a while for the ladies to learn how to manage the acuminators and the cresendon and to replace the tubes when they burned out. But they persevered, and now they were very glad to have it. Bessie put the radio on the parlor table, and on warm evenings after supper, they liked to sit out on the front porch with the window open, listening to radio shows. *The Aldrich Family* was a favorite (they all chimed in with Mrs. Aldrich's "Henry! Henry Aldrich!" and Henry's quavery reply: "Coming, Mother.") They enjoyed popular music, too, particularly the older songs: "I'm Forever Blowing Bubbles" and "I'll Be with You in Apple Blossom Time" and "Smilin' Through."

While they listened, Leticia and Maxine played games— Parcheesi, pinochle, canasta. Tonight they were playing checkers, betting heavily with pieces of colored cardboard marked as ones, fives, and tens. Roseanne, piecing another quilt, sat on the porch swing next to Mrs. Sedalius, who was knitting caps for the poor children at her church. Since the yarn was donated, it came in wild colors that nobody else wanted, and since Mrs. Sedalius didn't have much color sense, the caps were even wilder combinations. Bessie always wondered whether even the poor children would wear them. Miss Rogers sat off to one side, reading a library book. Bessie herself brought out a small table and worked on her local history scrapbook.

It was nice that the ladies were such a companionable lot, Bessie thought as she turned the pages of her scrapbook. Oh, there was the usual good-natured bickering about the checkers game, and Miss Rogers was always imploring someone to *Please! Turn the radio down, if you don't mind.* But they had lived together for several years now and they were more like sisters than housemates—although of course, sisters had their differences. Even Miss Rogers (who Bessie knew was disappointed in the way her life had turned out and would have preferred to live alone if she could have afforded it) usually managed to keep her contrary opinions to herself in the evenings.

So by unspoken agreement, they all sat together on the porch for an hour or two before bed, while the softly scented evening grew darker and the birds sang themselves to sleep in the cucumber tree in front of the Dahlias' clubhouse next door. It was at this time in the evening that Bessie missed old Dahlia Blackstone very much, for she had often come through the gap in the cherry laurel hedge (*Prunus caroliniana*, according to Miss Rogers) to listen to the radio with them, bringing along her knitting or crocheting.

Of all the Darling Dahlias, Bessie herself had probably been the closest to the old lady, which was only right, seeing that they had been next-door neighbors as long as they could remember. Of course, they were more than just neighbors, for they had shared a love of local history and of gardening. Bessie had spent a great many pleasant mornings in Mrs. Blackstone's garden, listening to her stories about the old days and helping her with various garden chores, until she became so infirm that she couldn't manage a rake or a hoe or a pair of clippers. Mrs. Blackstone was a good teacher and generous with garden advice.

Now Bessie always felt sad when she glanced out her bedroom window at Mrs. Blackstone's overgrown back garden, or out her parlor window at the cucumber tree in front of Mrs. Blackstone's house. The old lady had loved that tree so much and always looked forward to its blooms. This spring was the first in over eighty years that the cucumber tree would dress itself in all its beautiful blossoms and Mrs. Blackstone wouldn't be here to see and appreciate it.

A noisy automobile went past on Camellia Street, coughing

out a cloud of oily white smoke. Miss Rogers lifted her head and sniffed the air distastefully. Bessie sighed. It wasn't just the passing of Mrs. Blackstone that made her sad these days. It was the inexorable passage of time, and the many changes time had brought to Darling, unwelcome changes, in her opinion. She remembered when people could sit out on their front porches in the evening—or during the day, for that matter—and not hear any noise at all, except for the laughter of the children at their games, or the barking of one of the neighborhood dogs, or the soft *clop-clop* of a horse's hooves in the dust of the street. Oh, they might hear the railroad train, but the tracks were on the other side of town, and the train ran only once a day.

Now the motor cars were everywhere, and trucks, too, and motorcycles. And even airplanes flying low overhead on their way between Mobile and Montgomery, or landing at the grassy airstrip out at the county fairgrounds. Barnstormers might delight the young boys in town, but when the planes did loop-the-loops over the town, the earsplitting noise rattled everybody's windows and scared the horses and dogs. And while Bessie liked their own radio, she wasn't all that fond of the across-the-street neighbors' choice in music. Jazz, and they turned it up so loudly that half the neighborhood complained. Bessie often longed for the days before the Great War, when the world seemed so much quieter and slower than it did now. But she was enough of a realist to know that modern life was upon them. The world was whirling like a kaleidoscope, faster and faster, everything blurring together. Nobody could stop what was happening—and worse, nobody seemed to want to.

When nine o'clock came, Miss Rogers (always the first to leave, since she wanted first turn in the bathroom) closed her book, and went upstairs. Mrs. Sedalius yawned and said that tomorrow was going to be busy, since the visiting nurse would be in town and it was her day to volunteer. "And with the Cartwright ghost wandering around, we'd all better get into our beds," she warned, stuffing her knitting into her bag.

"I'd personally be more concerned about that escaped convict," Maxine said. "He could be hiding out in half a dozen places around town."

"Why would he hang around here, where somebody could catch him?" Leticia asked reasonably. "He's probably in Memphis or Nashville by now. Or Chicago." She jotted some numbers on a slip of paper. "You owe me thirty-seven dollars, Maxine."

Maxine, who hated to lose, scowled at the piece of paper. "I thought it was thirty-four. You'd better add it again, Lettie. Don't forget what happened last time."

"What happened last time was that you added wrong," Leticia replied. She grinned amiably. "Come on, Max. Don't be a sore loser. Fork it over. Thirty-seven dollars."

"Not until you add it up again," Maxine retorted, but she began counting her pieces of colored cardboard.

Mrs. Sedalius got up. "You girls can sit here and argue all you want. *I* am going to make my nightcap and go to my room, where I don't have to worry about that ghost." She went off to the kitchen to heat up a pan of milk on the gas range and make herself a cup of Ovaltine. It helped her sleep, she claimed, although everybody knew it was really the bootleg rum that she kept under her bed that put her to sleep.

The business about the ghost was nonsense of course, although Bessie didn't contradict her. Roseanne, however, was deathly afraid of ghosts, so she went quickly to her room and shut the door and put a chair against it—a practice Bessie discouraged (in case of fire) but could not stop.

By the time Mrs. Sedalius carried her nightly cup of Ovaltine out of the kitchen, Leticia and Maxine were headed in that direction to make the toasted cheese sandwiches and cocoa that they enjoyed before bedtime. Bessie and Roseanne were partial to popcorn, and they always made sure that there were enough of these little treats on hand so that everyone could have what she wanted. The world might be going to hell in a handbasket, as Bessie's father liked to put it—in fact, judging from the stories she read in the *Dispatch* about people losing their jobs and their houses, that was exactly what was happening. But if they could afford just a few little treats, Bessie told herself, maybe they could fool themselves into feeling that they were rich. Or at least, not poor. You couldn't be poor if you had a toasted cheese sandwich and cocoa every night.

Bessie herself always put up her gray hair in spit curls before she went to sleep, sitting at her dressing table and twisting the hair neatly around her finger and pinning the curls to her scalp with bobby pins. She used a setting lotion made of boiled flaxseed and always set two rows in the front, three over each ear, two in the back. Then she covered the curls carefully with a ruffled pink net cap, put on a pair of pink cotton summer pajamas, cold-creamed her face with Pond's in a ritual battle against wrinkles, and opened the window, enjoying the wafting fragrance of the moonflowers and nicotiana blooming in the garden. The window open, she crawled into bed and went to sleep.

But not for long.

It was not quite midnight, according to the clock on her bedside table, when she heard it. The *clank-clank-clank* of a spade against stone—muffled, as if whoever was digging was trying to be quiet. She lay there for a moment, pretending that she wasn't hearing it. But then there was a hesitant rap on her door.

"Bessie?" asked a voice. "Are you awake? It's Leticia."

"And Maxine," said another voice.

Bessie got out of bed and opened the door. Leticia was

wearing a red plaid flannel dressing gown, belted around her thick middle. Maxine's dressing gown was the same style, but flowered blue and purple. Maxine's hair was twisted up in rags. Leticia's long gray hair was braided into a single braid, over her shoulder.

"Somebody's digging," Leticia said in a low voice. "In our garden."

"We heard him from our window," Maxine added. The two of them shared the largest room at the far end of the hall.

"Not in *our* garden," amended Miss Rogers, coming out of her room. "In the Dahlias' garden, next door." She was wearing a silky gray gown and her hair was down around her shoulders. Bessie thought she looked ten years younger.

Another door opened and Mrs. Sedalius joined them, her roly-poly self engulfed in a voluminous gold wrapper. "It's not a him; it's a her!" Mrs. Sedalius squeaked excitedly. "It's the ghost! I saw her. Just now! Out my window!"

"We thought you went to bed and covered up your head," Maxine said. She flicked on the hallway ceiling light, and Bessie reached over quickly and flicked it off.

"No lights," she warned. "Whoever that is out there, we don't want him to know we're awake. Or her," she added.

"What ghost?" Leticia asked with interest. "The Cartwright ghost again?"

"The one looking for her buried baby," Mrs. Sedalius said mournfully. "Buried in a little wood box."

"Or the Cartwright family treasure," Bessie replied, remembering the story Dahlia had told her once. "It was buried."

"Or her shoes," Maxine said. "I heard that the ghost lost her shoes. That's what she's looking for."

"With a shovel?" Leticia asked. "Why does she need a shovel to look for her shoes?"

There was the sound of a chair scraping, and Roseanne, her brown face almost gray with fright, came into the hall, clutching her flannel nightgown to her. "I heard y'all talkin' 'bout that ghost," she said tearfully. "Is that po' Miz Cornelia out there agin, diggin' for that sweet lit'le chile?" She shivered.

"It's all right, Roseanne," Maxine said in a comforting tone, and put an arm around her. "Whatever it is, it's out there, not in here. You're safe."

Roseanne whimpered.

"This is all nonsense, you know," Bessie said firmly. "There are no such things as ghosts."

"That is not necessarily true," Miss Rogers put in, in her dry, precise tone. "Ghosts are a phenomenon of the imagination. To the person who believes that there is such a thing, it is a fact, not a fancy. However, in this case, it was the Cartwright family silver that was buried, not a baby."

"It wa'n't no silver, it was a baby!" Roseanne cried. Despite Maxine's steadying arm, she was trembling. "*Her* baby! The one Miz Cornelia birthed while Miz Dahlia was down there in Mobile."

"Oh, really?" Bessie asked, interested. "I've never heard that. What Mrs. Blackstone told me was that she was sent to Mobile because her mother had consumption."

"It's a tale ain't often told," Roseanne retorted, "an' maybe the white folks don' know it. But it's true. My grandma tol' me, an' she was there. Miz Cartwright birthed that baby while her husband was off to the War. Miz Dahlia was sent away so she wouldn't know nothin' 'bout it." She shook her head. "She knew all the same, though. She knew."

"Ah," Bessie said, remembering that Dahlia had never liked to talk about what happened during the war years. She always said it was too painful. Bessie had assumed that it was the pain of the armed conflict the old lady was referring to, but of course pain came in all shapes and sizes.

Maxine released Roseanne and regarded her curiously. "If Colonel Cartwright was off killing Yankees with General Lee, who was the father of the baby?" She paused. "Or shouldn't I ask?"

Roseanne pressed her lips together.

"Come on, Roseanne," Leticia coaxed. "You brought it up. You have to tell the rest of it. Who was he?"

"Please, Roseanne," Bessie said. "This could be important. It's a bit of local history that people don't know." Everyone always said that the colored help knew more about their white folks' families than the white folks' friends and relations. And if this story about Cornelia Cartwright were true, she could understand why Dahlia didn't like to talk about the ghost.

"Yes, Roseanne," Mrs. Sedalius said. "You have to tell us."

There was a long silence. "Well, I reckon they's all dead now, even Miz Dahlia, so they ain't no point in keepin' it hid," Roseanne said finally. "Baby's daddy was the colonel's plantation manager." Her voice dropped almost to a whisper. "Name of Adam. He had a white daddy, colored mama. Was a slave, 'til Mr. Lincoln set him free. Handsomest man ever was in this world, they say. Won Miz Cornelia's heart."

"Oh, my goodness gracious!" Miss Rogers recoiled in horror. "How *could* she?"

Maxine looked at Miss Rogers and shook her head. "I guess you don't know about love," she said quietly.

"Forbidden love," said Leticia with a longing sigh. "What a sad, sad story."

"Which is why we've never heard it, I reckon," Bessie said drily. "Because it was forbidden."

"Meaning . . . ?" Maxine asked.

"Meaning that the Cartwright friends and family—if they knew it—would never permit it to be talked about," Bessie said. And of course, the fact that the relationship (if it had existed) was secret made it likely that all sorts of fictional embellishments would be added to the story. As an amateur historian, she had encountered many such tales and knew that they were usually 20 percent fact, 80 percent fancy. There was a ghost, so there had to be a sad story. There was a sad story, so it had to be forbidden love.

"How did the baby die?" Leticia asked.

Roseanne shrugged. "Babies jes' die. Happens ever'day."

"And then *she* died?" Leticia persisted. "Cornelia Cartwright, I mean."

Roseanne nodded wordlessly.

"How?" Maxine demanded.

"Consumption," Bessie said. That was what Dahlia had told her.

Roseanne didn't say anything for a long moment. Then: "Kilt herself, whut my mama tol' me. She dead an' buried by the time Miz Dahlia come back from Mobile. Everybody was tol' it was consumption, but it wa'n't."

"What happened to Adam?" Leticia asked. "Mrs. Cartwright's lover?"

Roseanne's face became stern. "Whut y'all think?"

"He went north with the Union soldiers," Miss Rogers said.

"He died of grief," Leticia hazarded.

"He was . . . he was strung up," Maxine guessed, in a low voice.

"In the cucumber tree," Roseanne said starkly. "The one at the back of Miz Dahlia's garden. The col'nel, he come home after the war an' done it hisself, one dark night."

They all fell silent. Bessie wasn't sure she believed what Roseanne was telling them. But she shivered, thinking of the many times she and Mrs. Blackstone had stood beneath that very same tree, looking up into its branches, laden with beautiful blossoms—too beautiful to be the site of so much ugliness. Did Dahlia know the story? Could it be true?

Well, of course it could, and Bessie knew it. If Colonel Cartwright had gotten wind of illicit goings-on between his plantation manager and his wife, he would have ordered the man hanged without a second thought and felt perfectly justified in doing so. The fact that his wife was already dead might even have given him some secret satisfaction: she had paid for her terrible crime with her life. And of course, he would have gone to great lengths to keep his daughter from finding out what he had done. But you couldn't keep a secret from the servants.

"And the baby is buried out there somewhere?" Maxine asked.

"In a little wood box," Mrs. Sedalius said with relish. "That's what the ghost is looking for. The baby's coffin."

"Under the cucumber tree," Roseanne said unexpectedly.

"Really?" Leticia and Maxine asked, in wide-eyed unison.

Bessie made up her mind. "I've had enough of this," she said. The story was interesting—more than that, it was fascinating. But it had nothing whatever to do with whoever was digging out there in the garden. "I'm going out there and get rid of that trespasser, for once and all."

"Oh, no!" Roseanne wailed desperately. "Oh, Miz Bessie, you gots to leave that po' lady be! She lookin' for her *chile*!"

Without a word, Bessie went back into her room. She put on her shoes, then went to the closet and found what she wanted. While she was there, putting on her shoes, she heard it again—the *clank-clank* of a shovel. She went back out into the hall.

"I really wish you wouldn't," Miss Rogers said faintly, seeing what she was carrying.

Roseanne whimpered.

"A shotgun?" Maxine asked, both eyebrows going up. "My gracious, Bessie."

"My daddy's favorite duck-hunting gun." Bessie held it out

for them to see. "Browning twelve-gauge pump. He taught me how to shoot it. I've bagged many a bird in my day. I'm out to bag a ghost."

"You can't kill a ghost," Mrs. Sedalius said firmly.

"Who said anything about killing him?" Bessie retorted. "All I want to do is scare him. The gun is loaded with bird-shot, and I'm going to fire over his head." She grunted. "Anyway, it's not a ghost. It's somebody dressed up like the Cartwright ghost."

"Maybe it's the escaped convict," Miss Rogers ventured timidly.

Roseanne whimpered again.

"That's it!" Leticia exclaimed, snapping her fingers. "The convict!"

This had not occurred to Bessie, and it gave her momentary pause. A convict might not scare easily. A convict might—

But then she shook her head. "I don't think so. Why would an escaped convict dress up like the Cartwright ghost and dig in the Dahlias' garden? Doesn't make any sense."

"Doesn't make sense for *anybody* to be doing it," Leticia pointed out, and Bessie had to agree.

"Okay." She narrowed her eyes at the ladies. "You can go to the windows and watch. But keep out of sight, and don't say a word. I'm going to sneak up on him. I'd like to be close enough to see his face."

"Her," amended Mrs. Sedalius, still clinging to her belief that this was a ghost. "She's wearing that same dark cape she wore the other night." She paused, considering. "I guess ghosts don't have much choice in what they wear."

"You're going to look pretty silly out there yourself, Bessie," Maxine remarked critically. "Pink ruffles on your curler cap, Ponds on your face, pink pajamas, and shoes. And that shotgun."

"I don't care how I look," Bessie retorted. "And neither will that intruder, when I get through with him. Now, you stay here. And keep still."

Carrying her shotgun cradled in the crook of her arm, she went down the back stairs, out through the kitchen, and onto the back porch, silently shutting the door behind her. The only streetlights in town were on the courthouse square, and they were turned off at ten o'clock every night to save on electricity and because nobody was on the streets at that hour. There was a moon, but its silver face was covered with a curtain of racing clouds, and the garden was bright, then shadowed, then black as pitch. On the other side of the street, Mrs. Hamer's dog, General Lee, was barking fitfully, but that didn't seem to bother whoever was digging, for Bessie could hear the intermittent metallic clanking of the shovel against stone.

She crept through the gap in the hedge and into the Dahlias' back garden and down the path. She had come this way so often over the years that she knew the path without seeing it. She was breathing faster than usual, though, and in spite of her bravado in front of the others, she knew she was afraid. But she hadn't lied when she'd said she knew how to handle the gun. She hadn't fired it for a while, but it felt like an old friend.

She could see the figure in the dark cape, digging away under the cucumber tree, in the same place where she and Mildred and Ophelia had noticed the newly turned earth. The form was ghostlike, yes. But the sound of the shovel was very real, and Bessie crept closer, until she was within twenty yards of the figure. As she watched, he dropped the shovel, fell to his knees, and began digging in the dirt with his bare hands.

At that moment, the curtain of clouds parted and the moon came out, flooding the entire garden with its white brilliance, almost as bright as daylight. Whether by accident or because Bessie made some sort of small movement, the kneeling figure turned and saw her. With a menacing curse, he scrambled to his feet and half-turned in her direction, grabbing up the shovel and holding it in front of him like a weapon, as though he might be going to charge her.

Afterward, Bessie couldn't describe exactly what happened next, or why. Was she afraid she was being attacked? Was she acting by instinct? All she could remember was jerking up her gun and firing—well over the man's head, she was sure.

But he stumbled and fell forward and the curse became a loud, pained howl.

She gasped. Somehow, she didn't know how, she must have hit him!

But not fatally, obviously. In the space of a breath, he was back on his feet, turning, hopping, lurching, running toward the woods at the bottom of the garden, his cape flying out like the wings of an injured bat.

Bessie had bagged her ghost.

TWENTY

Ophelia Takes Bold Action and Lucy Takes Charge

Wednesday, May 21, 1930

It was Wednesday morning, the time Ophelia often set aside for sewing. She was studying her old yellow piqué sundress with the idea of cutting it down for Sarah. There was a stain on the skirt, but she could cut around it. Sarah was growing so fast, but if she used red rickrack on the hem, letting it down for next summer would be easy.

And then her glance strayed and a totally different idea occurred to her. She had stopped at the dress goods counter in Mann's the day before and bought a cute short-sleeve Butterick blouse pattern for herself, to make up one of the cotton plaids she'd been saving, either the yellow or the green.

As she looked at it now, she thought that the green plaid would be lovely with Lucy's stunning red hair. Wouldn't it be a friendly gesture to take the pattern and the material and her sewing basket out to Ralph's place and show Lucy how easy it was to sew up a blouse? Emma had a Singer—she had kept it in the bedroom, in front of the window, with an embroidered cloth over the top. It was certain to be there. Ophelia could show Lucy how to lay out the pattern on the material (it was always tricky to match a plaid) and cut it out. They would spend a companionable day sewing and chatting. By the end of the day, they would have two very nice blouses to show for their effort and they'd be fast friends.

Not stopping to wonder whether this really was a good idea, Ophelia changed into a clean cotton dress, brushed her hair, and put on her third-best hat, since the road was bound to be dusty. She packed the two bolts of material, the pattern, and her sewing box into a large basket. Then she went to the kitchen pantry and got a loaf of Florabelle's soda bread as a gift for Lucy (Ophelia's mother had taught her that it was rude to go anywhere without taking something to eat) and a dozen oatmeal cookies for the boys. While she was there, she picked up a pint jar of red raspberry jam made from berries that grew in the big patch behind Lizzy's house. The jam was extra good on slices of Florabelle's soda bread, buttered and toasted in a skillet. The boys would enjoy it for breakfast. She put the bread and cookies and jam in her basket.

Florabelle was finishing the ironing she hadn't done the day before. Ophelia told her that she didn't expect to be home for noontime dinner, and would she please see to Mr. Snow's and the children's meals. She would've called Lucy to let her know that she was coming, but Ralph's house was at the end of the road and the telephone didn't go out that far. Anyway, Ophelia knew that Lucy—who was certainly lonely out there by herself all day—would be grateful for the company and happy to be surprised.

Ophelia set off gaily, thinking that it was such a pretty morning for a drive into the country, the late-spring flowers blooming along the road, the sun bright with the eager promise of summer to come. When she noticed a particularly lovely patch of flowers not far from a noisy creek rippling through the woods, she pulled off to the side of the road. She got out and picked a large handful of orange butterfly weed, white Queen Ann's lace, yellow coreopsis, and purple verbena, with some bright green ferns for foliage. Smiling, she pictured Lucy's delight when she saw the flowers. They would brighten her kitchen windowsill. Hurrying a little now, she got back in the car and drove on.

But the Model T didn't quite make it all the way. Ophelia came around a corner and over the low-water crossing about a quarter-mile from Ralph's place. The front left wheel hit a hole and the tire blew out with a sharp bang.

"Oh, drat!" Ophelia said aloud, exasperated, and then realized that she was in trouble. This was the third blown tire on the Ford in the past month, the second in a week. There was a spare wheel on the back of the car, but she knew she'd never be able to put it on all by herself. At breakfast that very morning, Jed had told her that he had ordered a pair of new tires and suggested that she not drive the car until they arrived. But she had been so taken by the idea of treating her new friend Lucy to a pleasant day of sewing that she had forgotten all about it.

Well, now what? Ophelia sat for a moment, trying to decide what to do. The nearest telephone was at the Spencers' house, a good half-mile behind her and uphill all the way. She could walk back there and call Jed, who would send somebody out to change the tire—although of course he would lecture her sternly about not paying attention when he told her not to drive. Or she could go on to Lucy's, spend the day, and when the boys got home from school, send them to make the telephone call.

The walk to Lucy's was shorter—only a quarter-mile—and definitely easier, since it was all downhill, and she wouldn't have to listen to Jed's lecture. So she left the Ford where it was, one wheel in the ditch at the side of the dirt road, picked up her basket and flowers and began to walk toward Lucy's.

She stayed in the shade of the pine trees, but by the time she got to the bottom of the hill, she was sweaty and tired and very much wished that she hadn't worn her pumps. Her everyday flat-heeled oxfords would have been much better suited to walking over this uneven ground.

When she had driven up on Monday, Ophelia had tootled the horn at the gate—always the polite thing to do, so the people in the house would know they had company and could come out on the porch to see who it was. But by the time she had reached the gate at Ralph's place, her mouth was too dry to even summon up even a weak shout. All she could think about was getting something cold to drink.

Ophelia opened the gate and trudged up the rock-bordered path to the porch. Lucy had washed this morning, and sheets and towels—nicely white, Ophelia noticed with approval—were pinned to the clothesline. Three fat hens were catching bugs in the flower bed under the watchful eye of a rooster, perched on the arm of the wooden porch swing. The white goat had finished nibbling the leaves off Emma's rosebush and was now working on the large althea beside the fence.

The morning was warm, and the front door stood open. Ophelia went up the steps and rapped with her knuckles on the screen door. "Lucy," she called. "Yoo-hoo, Lucy. It's me, Ophelia. Thought I'd come and keep you company."

Inside, back in the kitchen, Ophelia heard a barely stifled shriek and the scrape of a chair across the bare floor. There was the sound of a muttered curse in another voice. A shriek? A curse? Something was wrong!

Alarmed, Ophelia yanked the screen door open and stepped inside. "Lucy? Lucy, are you all right?"

"I'm fine," Lucy called breathlessly. "Don't come in, Ophelia. Please! You just wait right where you are. I'll be right out. I—"

But it was too late. Ophelia had reached the doorway to

the kitchen, where she saw Lucy, backed up against the wall, her eyes wide with fright. And just getting up from eggs and ham and grits and biscuit and coffee on the kitchen table was a strange young man, someone Ophelia had never seen. He was dressed in regular clothes—a blue work shirt and bib overalls—but Ophelia recognized him anyway, for his head was shaved bald.

The escaped convict! He had forced Lucy to cook breakfast for him. He must be holding her hostage!

And then Ophelia—who was not by nature a bold person— did something she had never done before, had never thought of doing, had never even *imagined* herself doing. She took bold action.

She reached into the basket she was carrying, grabbed the pint jar of red raspberry jam she had brought for the boys' breakfast, and flung it with all her strength at the escaped convict, exactly as David might have flung the rock at Goliath, except that David used a slingshot and Goliath was larger— except that, at this moment, this fellow seemed as big as a bear and twice as menacing.

The jam jar hit him right square between the eyes. He stood stock-still for a moment, eyes wide-open and slightly crossed. Then his knees crumpled and he pitched forward, knocking the table over, the eggs and ham and grits and coffee cascading onto the floor. The convict fell facedown into the mess and lay there unmoving.

And then Lucy did an entirely unexpected thing. Instead of flinging her arms around Ophelia and crying, "Oh, thank you, Opie! Thank you for saving my life!" she shrieked "Oh, no! Oh, my God, Opie, you've killed him!" Frantically, she ran to the man's side, knelt down, trying to roll him over.

"I certainly hope so," Ophelia said defensively. "He was holding you hostage, wasn't he? Why, the man could have raped you!" A horrifying thought struck her and she felt her knees go wobbly. "He didn't, did he?" she asked, in a trembling voice. "The kids are all right, aren't they?"

Then another thought. She forced herself to be brave, to take more bold action. "Quick, Lucy, we need some rope! We have to tie his hands and his feet before he comes to."

"We do not need rope," Lucy said, in a scathing tone. "The kids are in school, and no, he didn't rape me or hurt them." She made a disgusted noise. "Look at him, Opie, for crying out loud. He's only a boy. He's barely fifteen." She scrambled to her feet and went to the white enamel water bucket on the shelf beside the door. She grabbed a towel, the dipper, and the bucket and carried them back to the man. "Help me roll him over."

"A boy?" Ophelia asked uncertainly. She knelt beside Lucy and together they rolled him onto his back. The jam jar had left a three-inch gash on his forehead. It was oozing blood, but he was beginning to open his eyes.

To Ophelia's dismay, she saw that Lucy was right. She had not knocked down a towering Goliath but a slight, pale boy, not much older than her own son, Sam. No beard yet, his features as shapely and delicate as a girl's.

Lucy dipped the dipper into the pail and splashed cold water on his face. "Come on, Joey," she commanded urgently. "Wake up. Wake up, please!"

"Joey?" Ophelia swallowed. "You . . . You know his name?"

"Of course I know his name, you goose. He's been living here with us. Hiding out. He's been so sick. Really sick, I mean. Once or twice, I actually thought he was going to die." She wrung out the towel in the bucket and folded it across his forehead. The gash was beginning to swell. "Joey," she crooned. "Come on, Joey, wake up!"

Ophelia sat back on her heels, trying to come to terms with what she was seeing and hearing. He had been living here? *Hiding out?* And there was Lucy, speaking as gently to this escaped convict as she would to one of Ralph's boys. What was going on here?

It took a few moments, but at last the convict—Joey—was sitting up, taking little sips of water from the dipper Lucy held to his lips, and trying not to cry. With Lucy's arm around him, he looked even younger than fifteen. Twelve, maybe.

"Sit tight, Joey," Lucy said, getting to her feet. "I'll fetch the iodine." She was back in a moment, iodine bottle in her hand. She doctored the gash as he winced.

"It hurts," he whimpered. His voice squeaked, and he ducked his head, embarrassed.

"Of course it hurts, silly," Lucy said warmly. "Iodine is supposed to hurt. Kills the germs that way. You don't want to get infected, do you?" She finished with the iodine. "Now, let's get you off to bed. I don't think you ought to try to eat right now, with your head like that. Okay?" She frowned at Ophelia. "Well, don't just stand there, Opie, help me!"

"Oh, sorry," Ophelia muttered, already beginning to wish that she hadn't been so quick to act. Obviously, she had walked into something that was entirely different from what she had thought it was.

Between the two of them, they got the boy to his feet, his arms over their shoulders. He was tall, yes, taller than Ophelia, but much lighter than she would have guessed, almost skin and bones. Ophelia thought he must have been sick, to have lost so much weight.

Or maybe they didn't feed them very well at the prison farm. She'd heard that the farm raised its own food, but that the best of it—the meat, especially, and the freshest vegetables—went to the guards and the higher-ups and their families. Of course. That was just the way things worked. The prisoners would always come last. They probably didn't get any milk, either. And she had heard horror stories about the prison doctor who tended the prisoners when they got sick—not somebody you'd want to look after somebody you loved.

They put the boy to bed in one of the kids' beds. Lucy covered him lightly and smoothed his gashed forehead with a tender hand. "He doesn't have a fever anymore, thank goodness," she said, half to herself. More loudly, she said, "You have a nice rest now, Joey. I'll fix you something else to eat when you're awake." She glanced at Ophelia. "And then we're going to do what we talked about. Remember what that was?"

The boy's eyes lit up. "Today?" he asked eagerly.

"I hope so," Lucy said, with a glance at Ophelia. "But first you have to rest."

They went back into the kitchen. Without a word, Lucy set about cleaning up the mess. She scooped the food into the slop bucket by the door, where it would go to feed the pigs, and put the plate and fork and spoon into the enamel dishpan, to be washed later.

Ophelia stood by, feeling helpless and more than a little guilty, not knowing what to say. When Lucy was finished, she helped her right the table, and managed, in a small voice, "I'm sorry, Lucy. I didn't know—I mean, I thought he was . . ."

"I know what you thought," Lucy said in a chilly tone. "And you were wrong. That poor boy nearly died in that prison farm. He didn't belong there in the first place. Do you know what he was sentenced for?" She answered her own question. "He got six months for stealing a chicken, that's what. One lousy chicken. He was hungry. The poor kid hadn't had anything to eat for several days."

Ophelia stared at her. At her house, things were pretty much the way they always had been, so it was easy to turn a blind eye to the problems that were cropping up everywhere else. Men without jobs, mothers without food for their children, children without proper clothes and shoes.

"They sentenced him to the juvenile home," Lucy continued, "but it was full, so they sent him to the prison farm with all those tough, seasoned criminals. He wasn't strong to start with, and they made him work terribly long hours, in all kinds of weather, until he could barely stand up. There was worse abuse, too, because he's young and slender and some of the other prisoners, big bullies, men who—" Her voice broke and she turned away.

A moment later, she turned back, wiping her eyes with her hand. "I don't want to tell you what they did, but you can imagine." Ophelia could, and shuddered. "It was more than he could take," Lucy went on. "When the other fellow made a break for it, he ran, too. He told me he was running for his life." She turned to look squarely at Ophelia. "And if you'd been me, Opie, you would've taken him in, too. You're a kind person—you couldn't have helped yourself."

"What happened?" Ophelia asked quietly.

Lucy finished wiping the table. "Sit down and I'll pour us some coffee and tell you," she said, and Ophelia obeyed.

What happened, it turned out, was that when the two convicts escaped, the sheriff and Buddy caught the older man right away, at the low-water crossing on the road between Ralph's place and the Spencers'. The other convict, Joey, managed to get away and hide out in the woods before the dogs arrived.

Normally, of course, the dogs would have tracked him down and the sheriff would've hauled him back to the prison farm before supper time. But Scooter and Junior found him first, hiding under a sweet gum tree in the swamp about a mile away. They saw how young and scared and pitiful he was and immediately felt sorry for him.

"I was proud of them," Lucy said quietly. "They knew they couldn't let that boy go back to the prison farm, and they were right."

It was Scooter's idea to trade shoes with him, to keep the dogs from following. Each of the boys put on one of Joey's shoes—such as they were, almost no heels and soles flapping loose—and gave him one of theirs to wear. Then Junior took the boy on his back and carried him to another tree, where they boosted him up high. Scooter ran off in one direction and Junior ran off in the other, circling around through the marsh and crisscrossing their trails until they got back home.

This tactic naturally confused the dogs, of course, when they were brought in. They tracked Joey off the road and into the swamp, but when they got to the sweet gum tree, they lost the scent completely, circling around and sniffing. They never did pick up the trail. When the dogs were pulled off for the night, the boys went out and brought Joey back and hid him under Lucy's bed.

"So he wasn't already here when Jed came," Ophelia said, trying to get the sequence of events straight in her mind.

"No, he was still out there in the swamp." Lucy met her eyes. "To tell the truth, Opie, I wanted Jed here so that the sheriff wouldn't suspect Scooter and Junior of having anything to do with Joey getting away. Jed doesn't know anything about Joey." Her forehead puckered. "Say you won't tell him. Please!"

Ophelia hesitated. She knew her husband, all too well. He took his duties as Darling's mayor very seriously. She didn't like keeping secrets from him—it made her feel disloyal. It made her feel . . . Oh, it was hard to describe, almost as if she were disobeying one of the Ten Commandments. But if Jed knew, he'd insist that the boy be sent back to the prison farm immediately.

"I won't tell him," she said at last. "It feels like being between a rock and a hard place, but I won't tell him."

Lucy looked relieved. "You should have seen the poor boy, Opie," she said soberly. "He was skinny as a fence rail, scratches all over him and welts on his back from the over-seers' whips. Wrists like sticks, too, and his eyes all hollow, and of course not a hair on his poor shaved head. Once I started feeding him, though, he began to look a little better."

Which must be why, Ophelia thought, Lucy had run out of food and had been desperate to get to the grocery store. "What are you going to do?" she asked. "He can't stay here forever. Ralph will be back in a week or so, won't he?"

Lucy sighed. "Yes. Joey has to be gone before Ralph comes home. He'd be furious if he ever found out what the boys and I have done. They won't tell, of course. They'd be scared of a thrashing." She looked grave. "I have a plan, but I need help, Opie. Ralph's Studebaker still isn't running. I was going to take Junior's horse, but that foreleg is still pretty bad. I need you to drive Joey and me to—"

"No, no!" Ophelia protested quickly, shaking her head. "Not me. I can't help, Lucy. Jed would . . ." She shivered, imagining what her husband would say—and do—if he caught her aiding and abetting a convict's escape. "Why, he'd be as mad as Ralph. Maybe madder."

"I don't give a hoot about Jed Snow, Opie," Lucy said fiercely. "And now that you've discovered our secret, you're obligated. You are going to help me get Joey out of here, to a place that's safe. It's not hard—your part of it. All you have to do is drive the car. I'll do the rest. And I don't want to hear any excuses. Got that?" She leaned forward, looking stern. Her voice no longer sounded like lemon-meringue pie. "Got that?"

Ophelia gulped. Lucy was much tougher than she had thought. "I guess so," she said in a small voice. She heaved a heavy sigh. "Yes, I guess so. When do we have to do this?"

"Today," Lucy replied. "Like you said, he can't stay here forever. Every day makes it more likely that somebody'll stumble over him, the same way you did." She pressed her lips together. "Next time, he might get shot, instead of just getting beaned with a jar of jam."

Ophelia pretended she didn't hear that. "Today?" She gave a rueful little laugh. "Well, that lets me out, I'm afraid. If it's a car you need, and if you want it today, you'll have to find somebody else."

Lucy narrowed her eyes. "Why?"

"Because the Ford has a flat." Ophelia made a face. "I parked it beside the road and walked the rest of the way here. There's a spare on the back but I have no idea how to change it—Jed always handles things like that. I was going to call him later today and ask him to send somebody out to do it for me."

"A flat?" Lucy laughed. "Is that all? Well, you can stop worrying your head about that. I'm a champion tire changer. And don't you think it's something you should learn, too?" She pushed her chair back. "In fact, it would be a good idea if we put the spare on now, while the boy's asleep. Come on."

And Ophelia—still wishing she'd worn her other shoes— had no choice but to follow. Lucy had taken charge.

TWENTY-ONE

Verna, Myra May, and Lizzy: On the Case in Monroeville

That same afternoon, right after work, Verna, Lizzy, and Myra May all met outside the diner, where they piled into Big Bertha, Myra May's 1920 green Chevrolet touring car. Bertha had belonged to Myra May's father, who had taken very good care of her. Even though she was ten years old and was on her fifth set of tires and her second carburetor, she still had a good many miles left in her. Big Bertha was roomy, too. There was ample space for all three of them with room left over, and they started off for Monroeville in high spirits.

It was a warm, sunny afternoon, and they were dressed for an outing in light summer dresses with frilly collars—all except Myra May, who wore her usual trousers and tailored blouse. They all wore summer straw hats, too. Myra May's was narrow-brimmed and mannish, Lizzy's was decorated with flowers, and Verna's sailor hat sported blue and red grosgrain ribbons.

"Did you hear about the excitement in the garden behind

the Dahlias' clubhouse last night?" Myra May asked when they had all piled into the car and were driving off.

"Excitement?" Lizzy asked, startled. "No! What was it? Is everything okay?"

"Somebody was digging in the back garden, under the cucumber tree," Myra May said. "The ladies at the Magnolia Manor heard it and they all got up to see what was going on. Bessie Bloodworth took her shotgun out there and actually shot at him."

"Shot at him!" Verna exclaimed.

"Right. She meant to shoot over his head, but she thought she might've hit him, according to Miss Rogers. She's the one who told me the story." Myra May giggled. "Would you believe? This fellow was dressed up like the Cartwright ghost."

"Well, my goodness," Verna said. She shook her head, frowning. "Who would have done such a thing? And why? Do you suppose it was the escaped convict?"

"Could've been, I suppose," Myra May replied. "That's what Miss Rogers thinks, anyway."

"But *why*?" Verna persisted. "It doesn't make any sense."

"We'll have to get Bessie to tell us all about it," Lizzy said. "No word about the convict yet?"

"Nope," Myra May said. "It's as if he's dropped off the face of the earth."

"And Alice Ann?" Verna asked, concerned. "She hasn't been arrested yet, I hope. Have you heard anything about the situation at the bank?"

"I heard Mr. Johnson talking to the bank examiner," Myra May said soberly. "They're still looking for evidence. Alice Ann has been warned not to leave town."

"As if she would," Lizzy said. And with that, they settled in for the ride to Monroeville.

Route 12 took them to Route 47, through the village of

Mexia and into town on West Claiborne Street. Monroeville, the county seat for Monroe County, was the major market town for the whole area, and anything that couldn't be bought in Darling was sure to be found in one of the Monroeville stores. Around the square were the First National Bank ("The Only National Bank in Monroe County"), the Monroe County Bank ("Promoting the Progress of Monroe County"), the U.S. Post Office, the Commercial Hotel, the office of the Manistee & Repton Railroad Company, the Monroe Journal building, Dawson's Drugs, and a dry goods store. In the center of the square: a grand brick courthouse, a twin of the one on Darling's courthouse square, with a large white-painted dome and a clock.

"Well, ladies," Myra May asked as they came into town, "where do we start? Sounds to me like we have a long list of things to do."

Myra was right. On the way over from Darling, they had gone over all the questions that needed answers, and Verna had jotted them all down.

Which of the stories about Bunny is true? Was she really her widowed mother's only child or the abandoned daughter of a runaway mother?

Fred Harper's brother (Dr. Wayne Harper, a dentist) owns the green Pontiac that Bunny was supposed to have stolen. Did he know Bunny? Did he take the photo of her sitting on his car in her teddy?

Did Imogene Rutledge have anything to do with the money problem at the Darling bank? Could she have taken the money Alice Ann is suspected of taking?

Scanning the list with a critical eye, Verna thought it seemed pretty silly and amateurish and doubted that Miss Silver would approve. It wasn't very likely that Dr. Harper would tell them anything about Bunny (if there was anything to tell), and it was altogether *un*likely that Imogene

Rutledge would even condescend to speak to them, much less give them any real information. Why should she—especially if it incriminated her? And would anybody tell them *anything* if all three of them marched up to the person and began clamoring for information?

But then she had an idea. Instead of all three of them trying to answer all three questions at once, why not split up? She was the one who was most interested in Bunny's background—she could look into that. Lizzy had brought the photo of Bunny sitting on the car, so she could talk to Dr. Harper. And Myra May had already spoken to Miss Rogers about Imogene Rutledge (at Aunt Hetty Little's suggestion), so she could look up Miss Rutledge.

"Well, what do you think?" Verna asked, when she had proposed this division of responsibilities.

"Sounds good to me," Myra May replied with a little laugh. "I have a very good reason to knock on Miss Rutledge's door. I want to see her face when I tell her that Miss Rogers sent me."

Lizzy tilted her head to one side. "You know, I've done some reporting for the *Dispatch*. I could pretend to be on assignment from the newspaper, interviewing Dr. Harper for a human-interest piece on the theft of that car. That would give me a reason for having the photograph. I wonder how he'll respond to it."

"And I'll see if I can track down Bunny's old neighbors," Verna said. "I'll start at the drugstore. She used to work there." She looked at her watch. "Two hours? Will that be long enough, do you think?"

"If we can't find out something in two hours," Myra May replied firmly, "we're not going to find it out at all."

"You're probably right," Verna said. "How about meeting at Buzz's Barbeque for supper when we're done? It's just down the street, across from the railroad depot."

"Or we could eat in the Commercial Hotel," Lizzy put in. "It's a little more . . . civilized, maybe."

"I vote for the barbeque joint," Myra May said. "They've got good ribs and catfish, fresh out of the river. And there's nothing better in this world than Buzz's pulled pork sandwiches." She grinned. "There's something to be said for being uncivilized."

"Buzz's, then," Verna said. "Let's meet in two hours."

Dawson's Drugstore was brighter and more attractive than Mr. Lima's store, Verna thought, as she opened the door and went in—about the same size, but well lit, the walls painted a light color, and with a nicely arranged front window display of Euthymol, Colgate, and Pepsodent toothpastes, with a big cardboard advertisement for Pepsodent's new radio show, *Amos 'n' Andy*, and a pyramid of bottles of Lavoris mouthwash. The soda fountain counter boasted a half-dozen stools and a pair of patrons, a teenaged couple sharing a milk shake with two straws. They were trading jokes with the soda jerk, a pimply faced, dark-haired teenaged boy in a white apron.

The pharmacy at the back of the store had already closed for the day, but Verna began to casually browse the cosmetics displayed on the shelves opposite the soda fountain, picking up a small rectangular box that held Maybelline Eyelash Darkener for "eyes that glow with enchantment." She wondered whether her eyes would glow if she used it, but she doubted it. She rarely bothered with makeup, which took a long time and didn't seem (to her, anyway) to make that much difference in the way she looked. The eyelash darkener cost fifteen cents, so she put it down.

"Gloria ain't here just now," called the soda jerk. He was polishing a glass with a white towel. "If there's anything I can help you with, just holler."

"Thanks," Verna called back. She pretended an interest in a dark red Cutex nail enamel until the teenaged couple finished their milkshake and left, trading noisy good-byes. Then she went to the counter and sat down on one of the red leather–covered stools.

"What'll it be?" the soda jerk asked pleasantly. Behind him was an array of sparkling glassware—glasses for sodas and milkshakes, dishes for sundaes, plates for sandwiches and cake—on glass shelves. A large wall mirror reflected the glassware, the boy's back, and Verna's own image.

"How about a cherry Coke?" Verna replied, and fished a nickel out of her coin purse.

"None of that makeup stuff?" the boy countered, obviously eager for a sale. "Make you look real purty."

"I kinda like myself the way I am," Verna said with a little laugh. She wasn't priggish—she just thought it was silly to spend money to paint your face and pretend to be somebody you weren't. If you were married, what did your husband think when the eyelash darkener came off and your eyes no longer glowed with enchantment? "Just the Coke, please," she added firmly.

"Comin' up." The boy took down a glass and held it under a spigot on the chrome-plated soda dispenser. Dark Coca-Cola syrup squirted out. Another spigot for the cherry syrup. Then a lever for fizzy carbonated water. The boy plopped in a maraschino cherry, added a paper straw, and pushed the glass across the black marble counter. He rang the cash register with a flourish and dropped the nickel into the drawer.

"Nice place," Verna said, looking around.

"Been here since 1908," the boy said proudly. "My dad's place. He wa'n't much older 'n me when he started it." He wiped off the counter with a white cloth. "The soda fountain's only a few years old, though. Dad likes to keep up with the times."

"He's smart," Verna murmured in an appreciative tone. "You've been working here long?"

"Off and on since I was a kid," the kid said, squaring his shoulders. "Want somethin' to go with that Coke? We got sandwiches. Ham and cheese." He gestured to a plate of white-bread sandwiches covered with a glass dome. "My mom makes 'em. Real good."

"No thanks," Verna said. "I'm meeting someone later. Listen, I'm wondering . . . Didn't a girl named Bunny used to work here? Seems to me somebody told me that."

"Oh, yeah," the boy breathed. "She sure did." From the evident longing in his voice, Verna guessed that he wished she still did. "That was before Gloria," he added. "She's our cosmetics girl now." He grunted disdainfully. "Not much of a girl, though. Gramma's more like it. Dunno what an old lady like her is s'posed to know about cosmetics."

"Did you know Bunny very well?"

The boy gave her a crooked grin. "Not as well as I would've liked."

"Yeah?"

"Yeah. But she had bigger fish to fry. Which you can't blame her for." Another grin, this one with a cynical edge. "You got it, you better use it—that's my motto. She had it. And believe you me, lady, she used it."

Verna couldn't argue with that. "Big fish?" she asked casually. "Like who?"

The boy shrugged. "Like guys with money. Al, the guy who runs the parts department over at the Ford dealership. The dentist down the street. Salesmen who stayed at the Commercial." He frowned. "I'm not sayin' there was anything wrong. Guys like me, she was always real nice. Laughed and teased, flirted, even. But what she really liked was a good time. You couldn't show her a good time, you weren't gonna get to first base with her. Bottom line."

Verna stirred her Coke with the straw, thinking that Bunny hadn't changed one bit when she moved to Darling. She'd still liked a good time, and she'd still preferred guys with money. "She grew up around here, I understand."

"Yeah. Went to school with my sister. Lived with her mom over on Oak Street, next to Doc Myers' animal hospital— 'til her mom died a while back." The boy cocked his head curiously. "Hey. How come you're wantin' to know about Bunny?"

Verna had already guessed that the news of Bunny's death had not yet arrived in Monroeville. She wondered briefly if she should tell the boy, but decided against it. Bunny had been found late Monday, and today was only Wednesday. He'd find out soon enough, probably when the *Monroe Journal* came out at the end of the week.

"Just curious," she replied, and slurped up the last of her drink. "I met her at the drugstore over in Darling. She was working there."

"Darling. So that's where she went. I wondered. She kept sayin' she was goin' to Mobile or Atlanta. New York, even." The boy picked up a glass and began to polish it. "Listen, you see her, you tell her Jerry the soda jerk said hi. She'll remember me. Tell her she oughtta come back over here and see her friends sometime. We'll all chip in and buy her a dinner or something."

Verna stood up, feeling a sudden impulse to tell the boy that Bunny would never come back—here or anywhere. That she was dead. That somebody had killed her. She felt a sharp anger rising inside her.

"I sure will," she lied, thinking urgently that she had better get out before she said more than she intended. "Thanks for the Coke."

The boy raised his hand. "You bet."

Verna thought then of giving up the search. The boy had

already answered the question she'd come to ask—which of Bunny's stories about her life was true? Bunny had lived with her mother on Oak Street, not in an old farmhouse outside of town, the brave caretaker of four small children. Anyway, what did that matter now?

But Oak Street wasn't far away, as Verna learned when she asked directions to the animal hospital, and she had an hour to kill before she was supposed to meet the others. So she began to walk.

The animal hospital—a regular house with a big fenced-in yard, dog houses here and there—was on the corner. The house next door was small, no more than three rooms, and it hadn't been painted in many years. The front door was open and Verna rapped at the screen. The woman who answered the knock was well past middle age and her dark hair was going gray. Her hands were square and work-hardened, the hands of a farm wife. She didn't offer to open the screen door.

"Sorry to bother you," Verna said. "I'm looking for Miss Scott. Eva Louise Scott."

There was a sudden chorus of barking from the animal hospital next door, and the woman raised her voice. "Eva Louise don't live heah no more. Her mama died a while back and she moved out. Went over to Darling is what I heard." She cocked her head to one side. "How come folks're askin' 'bout Eva Louise all of a sudden? She gone an' got herse'f in some kinda trouble?"

The barking stopped. "Folks?" Verna asked. "What folks?"

"Some man, jes' this mawnin'. Said he was a lawyah from over in Darlin'." The woman shook her head. "Allus bad trouble when lawyers come 'round askin' questions." She peered at Verna. "Don't reckon you're a lawyah," she said, and then chuckled at her own joke.

Something clicked. A lawyer. "Wouldn't have been Mr. Moseley, would it?" Verna guessed.

The woman nodded vigorously. "Moseley. Yep, that'ud be him. You know him?" She made a clucking sound with her tongue, and Verna saw that she was missing most of her teeth. "Eva Louise—her mama raised her right an' she's a good girl, down deep in her heart. But she don't allus use the sense God gave her, 'speshly where menfolks is concerned." She laughed. "That lawyah fella—he seemed right surprised to find out she lived heah, her 'n' her mama. Got it into his head some way that her mama done run off years ago an' Eva Louise was takin' care of a big bunch o' brothers an' sisters somewheres out in the country. He was gonna stand right theah an' argue with me 'bout that, 'til I showed him that photo of Eva Louise an' her mama."

Verna chuckled to herself, imagining Mr. Moseley's surprise when he learned the truth. Good enough for him, she thought with a kind of acid pleasure—allowing himself to be taken in by a pretty girl on the make. But why had he come here?

"You're related to Miss Scott?" she asked, wondering if this woman should be told about Bunny's death. Obviously, Mr. Moseley hadn't told her—and she wondered why.

"Not related." The woman shook her head. "Knew her mama from church is all. She sang in the choir, helped out with Bible School. That picture I showed that lawyah is one that was took last summer at the church picnic." She frowned. "That girl is in trouble, I reckon," she said sadly. "Like I said, she's a good girl, but she's got no sense."

"Thank you," Verna said, and decided against saying anything about Bunny's death. She hated to be the bearer of bad news. And, like the soda jerk, the woman would find out soon enough.

"No sense a-tall," the woman muttered, and turned away from the door.

* * *

Earlier that day, Myra May had done as Aunt Hetty Little suggested. She had taken a break from the diner after lunch and gone to the Darling library to ask Miss Rogers what she knew about Imogene Rutledge.

The library was located in two small rooms at the back of Fannie Champaign's milliner shop, Champaign's Darling Chapeaux, on the west side of the courthouse square. In one room was Miss Rogers' desk, a rack of wooden drawers that held what she called the "card catalog," and a table where a person (only one, because there was only room for one chair) could sit and read in front of the window. The other room had shelves on all four walls, from the floor as high as a person could reach. The books were mostly donated, but the City Council set a few dollars aside for new books every year and sometimes people gave a little money. Miss Rogers was frugal. She bought mostly nonfiction. The year before, she had bought *We*, by Charles Lindbergh, *A Preface to Morals*, by Walter Lippman, and (on the lighter side), *Believe It or Not*, by Robert L. Ripley. But she did buy two best-selling novels: *The Bishop Murder Case*, by S. S. Van Dine and *Joseph and His Brethren*, by H. W. Freeman.

When Myra May came in, Miss Rogers had immediately told her what had happened at the Magnolia Manor the night before—or rather, in the backyard of the Dahlias' clubhouse. Bessie Bloodworth had fired on an intruder and had hit him—accidentally, of course. She had aimed over his head.

"Any idea who he was or what he was doing?" Myra May had asked.

"It was the escaped convict, if you ask me," Miss Rogers said. "Now, Myra May, what can I help you with today?"

When Myra May told Miss Rogers what she wanted, the

librarian frowned. "Imogene Rutledge," she mused. "Well, I'll tell you this much. That woman still owes a library fine. It just keeps getting bigger, too." She opened her desk, took out a ledger, and consulted a page. "It's up to forty cents."

"My goodness," Myra May said, and something occurred to her. "I'm going over to Monroeville late this afternoon, Miss Rogers. Would you like me to see if I can collect?"

"That's very thoughtful of you, Myra May." Miss Rogers wrote some numbers on a slip of paper and added them up. "Here's the fine and a list of the penalties. I doubt if she'll pay it—she is such a negative individual. But of course it's worth a try." She handed the paper to Myra May. "Why are you asking about her?"

"Because," Myra May said, and told Miss Rogers that Alice Ann was accused of embezzlement. While some of the Dahlias were thinking of possible suspects, Imogene Rutledge's name had come up and Aunt Hetty Little had suggested that Miss Rogers might know something.

Miss Rogers sniffed. "Well, what I know," she said tartly, "is that Imogene Rutledge has a very sharp tongue and doesn't mind using it. And in addition to not paying her fine, she stole a book. Took it right off the shelf in the other room."

"Stole a book!" Myra May exclaimed. "Oh, my goodness!" She was shocked by the theft, of course, but even more shocked that Miss Rutledge had dared to take the book out from under Miss Rogers' nose. "How did she manage to—"

"Simply put it in her bag and walked out the door with it," Miss Rogers said darkly, and it was clear from her expression that this was an exceptionally malevolent transgression. "I missed it immediately, of course, for I had seen it on the shelf not a half hour earlier. It happened to have been a personal favorite of mine—a book that everyone in Darling enjoyed reading and rereading. *Further Chronicles of Avonlea*, by Maud Montgomery."

"I see," Myra May said, thinking that somebody who was bold enough to walk past Miss Rogers with a stolen book— and one of the Anne of Green Gables series, at that—was bold enough to embezzle. "Is there anything else that might point to . . ." She hesitated. "Well, to Miss Rutledge being involved in shenanigans at the bank?"

"You mean, anything in addition to that brand-new car and the house she bought for her mother in Monroeville?" Miss Rogers' tone was acid.

"She bought a house?" Myra May asked, surprised.

"She certainly did. Quite a large one, too. New, from what I heard. Must've cost a great deal of money. Of course, I have no information about what might or might not have happened at the bank, and whether the car and the house have anything to do with that. I suppose she might have made her little bundle in the market, before the Crash."

Miss Rogers pressed her lips together, turning her head, and Myra May knew that she was thinking of the money she herself had foolishly invested in stocks and the little cottage she had hoped to buy with all that money she was going to make in the market. No wonder she was angry at Miss Rutledge, who had committed three terrible sins. She had not paid a fine, she had stolen a book, and she still had plenty of money, when Miss Rogers had lost every penny of hers.

Myra May had thought about this all afternoon, while she was working. She had even gone so far as to call the operator in Monroeville and get Miss Rutledge's telephone number and street address. So when Verna suggested that they split up to do their investigating, she had been glad to volunteer to talk to Miss Rutledge.

The Rutledge house, it turned out, was indeed quite large, although it was by no means new. In fact, it was old and in urgent need of repair. But there were pots of red geraniums on the front porch, red and green chintz cushions on the porch swing, and a small brass plate beside the front door, engraved with the words RUTLEDGE'S RESIDENCE FOR GENTEEL LADIES.

Miss Rutledge herself answered the door. In her fifties, she was erect and firm-featured, with a braided coronet of still-dark hair. She wore a gray skirt and tailored white blouse with a dark, mannish tie. "Yes?" she asked pleasantly. "May I help you?"

Myra May introduced herself and said, in a deeply apologetic tone, "Actually, I'm here at the request of Miss Rogers, at the Darling Library. I hope I'm not offending you, but I mentioned that I was coming to Monroeville and Miss Rogers asked me to stop in and remind you about the library fine."

Miss Rutledge rolled her eyes. "Oh, for pity's sake," she said. "Dorothy Rogers. She'd rather send somebody than spend two cents on a stamp. Such a parsimonious old dragon!"

Myra May gave a little laugh. Clearly, Miss Rutledge's reputation as a woman who spoke her mind was well earned. She herself liked Miss Rogers, but the librarian was strict and she made sure that everyone obeyed her rules to the letter, whether the rules made sense or not. Lots of people would probably agree that she was a dragon—and parsimonious to boot.

"Forty cents!" Miss Rutledge heaved a sigh. "Well, that's what I get for forgetting. Since you're here, I suppose I might as well pay up, so Dorothy can scratch my name out of her little black book. Come into my office, and I'll get the money for you."

Somewhat surprised that collecting was going to be so easy, Myra May followed Miss Rutledge into the hallway. An older woman, obviously quite genteel, sat in the parlor, embroidering what looked like a napkin. Another, equally genteel, was reading aloud to her while she worked. A fat spaniel lay at their feet, snoring.

"The Bigood sisters," Miss Rutledge whispered. "My first residents. There are two others, but they're napping right now, as is my mother." She gave what sounded like a snicker. "Genteel old ladies nap quite a lot, it turns out."

Myra May found herself liking this woman. She was leading the way into a room behind the parlor, just large enough for a neat little writing desk and chair, a wooden filing cabinet, a bookshelf, and a straight chair. On the wall over the writing desk hung a plaque from the Monroeville Chamber of Commerce, welcoming Rutledge's Residence for Genteel Ladies to the roster of outstanding Monroeville businesses, and a large framed photograph of Miss Rutledge and an older woman (who must be her mother, Myra May thought) cutting a ribbon across the front porch. There was another photograph, too: Miss Rutledge high on a ladder with a brush and a bucket, painting the shutters on a second-story window.

Miss Rutledge followed her glance to the plaque and the photographs. "It's not exactly a genteel life for me," she said wryly. "Managing Mama and the rest of these old ladies takes just about all my strength. My patience, too. Sometimes I tell them if they don't behave, I'm going to run away and join the circus." She shuddered. "But it's better than the bank, I'll tell you. Mr. Johnson was never an easy man to work for, and when the money situation got worse, he got to be a real bear."

"When the Crash happened, you mean?"

"No. Before. That bank has a problem. There are a couple of unsecured loans to Mrs. Johnson's father and brother. Loans that Mr. Johnson should never have made. I told him he'd be in trouble the next time the bank examiner came," she added crisply. "At which point he tried to fire me for sassing him." She straightened her shoulders. "But I quit first. Told him what he could do with his old job."

"Then you bought this place?" Myra May asked.

Miss Rutledge nodded. "Mama sold her house and I had made a little money in the market." She smiled crookedly. "I didn't make much, but I was lucky to get it out before everything came crashing down in October. Mama and I pooled what we had and bought this house. I took my savings out of the bank and bought a car, too—although maybe I shouldn't have. We could have used that money to get the roof fixed." She opened a drawer and began to hunt. "I don't have forty cents here. I'll look in my purse." She left the room.

Myra May glanced around the room. She had already begun to revise her opinion of Imogene Rutledge. She liked her frankness and her independent spirit and felt she was not at all the stealthy, conniving person Miss Rogers had pictured. Maybe the librarian was jealous of what she imagined to be Miss Rutledge's freedom, not to mention her success in the stock market.

The bookshelf was right by her elbow and Myra May began idly to browse the titles on the spines. There were several of Mary Roberts Rinehart's mysteries, a book on gardening, and another on dressmaking, along with several *Ladies' Home Journal*s and—

Myra May pulled in her breath. And *Further Chronicles of Avonlea*, by Maud Montgomery.

She leaned forward and took the book off the shelf and opened it. It was clearly stamped *Darling Public Library* and had one of those little envelopes glued to the inside back, with a library check-out card in it, the kind where you write your name and the due date and give it to the librarian for filing in her calendar file so she'll know when the book is overdue and she can start charging you with the fine.

But this one wasn't overdue. It was stolen. Miss Rogers might have given the wrong impression about Miss Rutledge in some ways, but she had her story straight about this. Myra May frowned. Somebody who stooped so low as to steal a book from a public library might not balk at stealing money from the bank—especially when she thought it was badly managed.

Myra May was still holding the book when Miss Rutledge came back into the room and put three dimes and two nickels on the desk—and saw what Myra May was looking at.

"You're a fan of Maud Montgomery?" she asked, smiling pleasantly. "I loved all the Green Gables books—so delightful to watch Anne grow up in those wonderful stories." She sighed. "It's such a shame about that one."

"Really?" Myra May turned it over in her hands, now very curious. "What's wrong with it?"

"The publisher put it out without Miss Montgomery's permission," Miss Rutledge replied. "The book has stories in it that the author decided she didn't want published, so she's suing."

"Suing?" Somehow, Myra May had never thought that an author might actually sue a publisher. It was a new idea to her.

"Yes. The case is still in the courts. That's why I took the book back." When Myra May frowned, she added, "I donated it to the library when it was first published, you see. That was back in 1920 or '21. Last year, I learned that the stories were published without permission. So I told Miss Rogers that I thought the book should be withdrawn from the library—at least until the lawsuit was resolved."

"Ah," Myra May said, beginning to understand.

Miss Rutledge chuckled. "Of course, she didn't agree. She never agreed with me, no matter what. We argued about it several times, and when I saw she wasn't going to give in, I took it back. Since I donated the book in the first place, I felt perfectly justified." Miss Rutledge gave a rueful smile. "Poor Miss Rogers. I don't think she has ever forgiven me."

"I think you're right," Myra May murmured, and replaced the book on the shelf.

Miss Rutledge scooped the coins off the desk and handed them to Myra May. "You'd better give me a receipt. Just in case Miss Rogers forgets to cross me out of her little black book." She found a scrap of paper and wrote *Rcvd of Imogene Rutledge 40¢ for library fine,* and handed it to Myra May.

Myra May signed and dated the receipt and gave it back. "I wonder," she said, pocketing the coins. "If I told you that Alice Ann Walker was suspected of embezzling money from the bank, what would you say?"

"I'd say that's crazy, that's what I'd say!" Miss Rutledge hooted. "Alice Ann is as honest as the day is long. And I'd tell whoever 'suspects' her to look a little higher up in that bank. At the man at the top. The man who made those bad loans and thinks he can move money around to cover up the losses."

Myra May gave her a straight look. "There's a bank examiner in town right now. Would you be willing to tell him what you know about those loans?"

A smile spread across her face. "Would I be willing to tell? You bet I would. Any day of the week." She eyed Myra May. "What exactly did you have in mind?"

Myra May told her.

Lizzy's experience as a *Dispatch* reporter was mostly confined to the Darling Flower Show and the Peach Festival that took place at the Cypress County Fairgrounds every year. In addition, Charlie always had her cover the Watermelon Roll and the Tomato Fest and the Garden Tour—and of course, there was her weekly column. But Dr. Harper didn't need to know that she mostly wrote garden pieces.

Now Lizzy stood on the street in front of the dental office, with its sign: DR. A.V. HARPER, D.D.S., GENERAL DENTISTRY. There was a light inside, and a man—a patient, she thought—had just come out, slamming the door behind him and jamming his hat on his head with a pained expression. It was late in the day, but Dr. Harper must still be there. She checked to be sure that she had her notebook in her purse, took a deep breath, opened the door, and went inside.

The room was small, with only a couple of straight chairs for people who were waiting to see the dentist and an empty receptionist's desk with a chair behind it, a small vase of wilted flowers on one corner. A man wearing a white coat came through a door in the back and into the waiting room. He was in his forties, thin-faced and slightly balding, with gold-rimmed glasses perched at the end of his nose and a droopy dark moustache on his upper lip. Behind his glasses, his eyes had a red-rimmed, squinty look, as if he had been rubbing them.

"We're closing now, miss." His voice was oddly high-pitched. "Miss Thomas, my receptionist, has gone home for the day. Please come back tomorrow. Or you can leave your number, and Miss Thomas will call you."

"Oh, thank you, Dr. Harper," Lizzy said breathlessly. "But I'm not here to make an appointment. My name is Elizabeth Lacy. I'm from the *Dispatch*, over in Darling, and Mr. Dickens—Charlie Dickens, he's our editor—sent me to see you."

This was a lie, of course, but Lizzy thought it was justified, under the circumstances. Anyway, she could write up something from the interview and give it to Charlie. He might find a way to use it.

"Oh, he did?" Dr. Harper asked, raising his eyebrows. "About what?"

"He wants to run a human-interest story about what happened on Saturday night. About your car being stolen, I mean, and that poor young girl dying in it. Would you have a few minutes to talk to me?"

Under his moustache, Dr. Harper's mouth tightened. "That was a bad thing," he said. "A real sad situation. I could hardly believe it when Fred telephoned me yesterday to tell me what'd happened. My brother was so distressed, poor fellow, that he couldn't give me any of the details."

"It must have been terribly upsetting for both of you," Lizzy murmured. He didn't seem to notice that she had taken her notebook and a pencil out of her purse.

"Oh, it was. Yes. Very," he said fervently. He frowned a little. "Miss . . . Lacy, you say?"

"Yes. Elizabeth Lacy. The girl stole it from your brother's house, the way I understand it," Lizzy said. "That was Saturday night, around midnight. On Monday afternoon, the car was found in the ravine at Pine Mill Creek, where the bridge had washed out."

"She crashed right through a barricade, my brother said." He looked away, chewing on his moustache. "Drinking. Killed in the wreck."

Not true. Bunny had been shot—murdered. But since Dr. Harper didn't seem to know this already, Lizzy didn't think she'd tell him. Not just yet, anyway.

"A sad situation," Dr. Harper said again, shaking his head gloomily. "I feel very sorry for my poor brother."

But not for the poor girl who was dead? "You loaned the car to him, I understand," Lizzy said.

"Well, yes. I suppose you could put it that way."

Put it that way? That was the way Fred Harper had put it to the sheriff.

"We shared the car, you see," the dentist added. "When he was living here with me."

"Of course." Lizzy tilted her head. Well, that wasn't so unusual. Lots of people—sometimes whole families—shared cars. "When he was living here," she repeated. "That was . . ."

"Last year. I don't drive the automobile very often these days—my eyes, you know. When I need to go out of town,

Fred takes me. We went to Montgomery two weeks ago. He wanted to keep it, and I agreed."

Lizzy wondered briefly how, if Dr. Harper couldn't see well enough to drive a car, he could see well enough to fix somebody's teeth. She wasn't sure she'd want him poking around in her mouth. But she only nodded sympathetically.

He sighed. "I suppose I'll have to think about getting another car, though. The Pontiac is a total wreck, my brother tells me. The frame is bent. Can't be repaired."

"That's too bad," Lizzy said. She put her pencil to her notebook. "You purchased it here in Monroeville?"

"No, from the Pontiac dealer in Mobile. I've always been partial to Pontiacs. Every car I've ever owned has been a Pontiac. It's that Indian on the hood. It appeals to me." There was a gleam in his eyes. "You can put that into the story if you like. When I was a boy, I wanted to be an Indian fighter. I suppose that's human interest, isn't it?"

She nodded and wrote that down. *Wanted to be an Indian fighter.* "Did you know the girl?"

"The girl who stole the car? No, of course not." He sounded slightly indignant, as if an acquaintance with a common thief was beneath him. "My brother said she worked in Darling. I don't get over there very often." The way he said *Darling* made it sound as if the town was beneath him, too.

"You're *sure* you didn't know her?" Lizzy asked, managing to sound just a little doubtful.

"Of course I'm sure." Now he was definitely indignant. He eyed Lizzy. "Why are you asking? How would I know a girl in Darling when I don't go over there?"

"I'm asking because—" Lizzy opened her purse and took out the photograph of a smiling Bunny perched on the hood of the car. "Because the *Dispatch* came into possession of this photo." She held it out. "Your car, Dr. Harper. The date on the license plate is 1930, so the photo was taken earlier this year. And the young lady sitting on the hood is the one who was reported to have stolen the car. The one who died." She paused, and then repeated her question. "You're sure you don't know her?"

He took the photograph and bent over it, squinting. "Good Lord!" he exclaimed. "I can't believe—" He closed his eyes and passed his hand across his forehead. "This is the girl who—?" His voice squeaked and he gulped, trying again. "It's . . . it's Eva Louise! She's . . . she's *dead?*"

"Yes, she is," Lizzy said very politely, withholding censure from her tone. "So you do know her, then?"

He nodded dumbly. He was still peering at the photograph.

"And that *is* your car?"

He nodded again.

"Did you take the photo?"

"Oh, no!" Another squeak. "I've never seen . . . I wouldn't—" He swallowed hard, making an effort to control his voice. "I've never seen her wearing . . . whatever that thing is called."

"It's a teddy," Lizzy said quietly. "It's her underwear."

"Oh." He was still looking at the photo, hungrily, Lizzy thought. "Her underwear," he repeated. He licked his lips.

She gently took the photo away from him and put it back in her purse. "Eva Louise was a friend of yours?"

He sank down in one of the straight chairs and put his head between his hands.

"She was a friend?" Lizzy asked again.

"A . . . friend." His voice was muffled. "Yes. We . . . we went out to dinner sometimes. We used to go to Mobile, until my eyes got too bad to drive." He pulled off his glasses and rubbed his eyes. "Beautiful. She was a beautiful girl. She loved pretty things."

Lizzy felt she was taking advantage of him, but she did

it anyway. "Did you give her gifts? A pair of pearl earrings, maybe?"

He nodded, sniffling. "She looked so beautiful in those earrings." He sat up, putting his glasses back on, hooking them over his ears. "But I never expected to see her sitting on a car—*my* car—in her . . . in her underwear!"

Lizzy was beginning to get an idea of what might have happened. "Could it have been your brother who took the photo?"

"My brother?" he repeated incredulously. "No! Of course not! Fred knew that Eva Louise and I were seeing each other. He wouldn't—"

"Well, then, who else drove the car?"

"Nobody! Nobody else! Just—" He stopped.

"Then it must have been your brother who took the photo, don't you think?"

The idea was beginning to sink in. He stared at her. "I—I suppose—"

She took a chance. "Tell me, Mr. Harper. Do you own a gun?"

"A gun? Well, yes. A twenty-two revolver. But I can't see to use it now. Anyway, it's not here. I . . . I gave it to—" He broke off.

"You gave it to your brother?"

"Yes. Fred said he wanted it for target practice, so I gave him the gun and the ammunition. Why? Why are you asking? Why—"

"Because Eva Louise wasn't killed when your car went into the ravine, Mr. Harper. She was shot in the head. The bullet was a twenty-two caliber."

"Oh, no!" he cried. "Oh, no!"

When she left, he was still sobbing.

TWENTY-TWO

The Dahlias Clear up a Mystery or Two

Thirty minutes later, Verna, Lizzy, and Myra May gathered in front of Buzz's Barbeque, an unpainted, tin-roofed wooden building on a dusty street across from the Monroeville railroad depot. Hungry people getting off the train—especially city folks—might turn up their noses at the idea of sitting down to a meal in a place that looked like a good puff of wind might blow it over. But they changed their minds when they caught the enticing fragrance wafting from behind the shack: the pig Buzz was roasting over a hickory fire in a brick barbeque pit.

"Ah," Myra May said appreciatively, taking a deep sniff. "Doesn't that smell wonderful?"

"Heavenly," Verna agreed, raising her voice over the loud huff-and-puff of the just-arrived steam locomotive, which was taking on the mail, goods, and passengers for the evening run to Montgomery and points north. The same railroad spur that served Monroeville also served Darling, built to connect with the Pine Mill Creek sawmill outside of Darling. The spur joined up with the main L&N line twenty miles to the east at Repton.

Just at that moment, a black Ford sedan came around the corner and pulled up in front of the depot, across the street from where they were standing.

Verna frowned, looking at it. "Hey, take a look, girls. Isn't that the Snows' Ford?"

"It sure is," Lizzy said, surprised. "And that's Ophelia behind the wheel. Who's that with her? That redhead—I don't recognize her."

"That's Ralph's wife, Lucy," Myra May said. She grinned. "I heard that Ophelia went out to her place and brought her into town to get groceries—Ophelia's way of scotching a few nasty rumors. Ophelia said she was going to ask Lucy to join the Dahlias now that we've lowered the dues, so I guess we'll get acquainted with her."

"Who's that with them?" Verna asked curiously. "I don't recognize her."

Clambering awkwardly out of the Ford's rear seat was a tall, gangly woman in a faded cotton dress and an old-fashioned green slat bonnet—the kind that allowed a woman to shield her face and neck from the hot sun while she worked in the garden. This one completely hid the woman's hair and most of her face, so it was impossible to tell whether she was young or old. She turned back to the auto and took out a small cardboard suitcase.

"I don't think she's anybody from Darling," Lizzy said, studying her. "Maybe one of Lucy's family. Or a relative of one of the neighbors." Out in the country, when somebody was driving to Darling or one of the nearby towns, they always asked if the neighbors needed a ride or something from the grocery or the hardware or the feed store. "Let's see who it is."

"Yoo-hoo!" Myra May put up her hand and waved. "Hi,

Ophelia! It's us! The Dahlias!" And she started across the dusty street, with Verna and Lizzy right behind her.

And then something odd happened. Lucy and the strange woman turned, put their heads down, and hurried toward the depot. Lucy had her arm around the woman's shoulders. The woman was leaning on Lucy, walking with her ankles turned out, clumsily, as if she wasn't accustomed to wearing pumps.

Ophelia greeted them beside the Ford with an oddly nervous smile. "Lucy's cousin is hurrying to make the train." The breeze had come up again and she put a hand on her straw hat to keep it from blowing off.

"Where's she going?" Lizzy asked conversationally.

Ophelia frowned. "Uh, to . . . to Memphis, I think."

"Been here for a visit?" Myra May tilted her head, studying Ophelia.

"I . . . I think so," Ophelia said. She took a deep breath and changed the subject. "Pretty afternoon, isn't it? What're y'all doing in Monroeville today?"

The three of them exchanged glances. "We were just about to discuss that," Verna said, and made a grab for her own hat as the wind gusted. "Maybe you and Lucy would like to join us. We're going to Buzz's."

"Well, I don't know . . . That is, I—" Ophelia bit her lip. She seemed more than usually flustered.

By now, Verna was feeling suspicious. "What's going on here, Ophelia?" she demanded. "There's something you're not telling us. What is it?"

"Oh, no!" Ophelia exclaimed, widening her eyes innocently. "Oh, not at all! It's just the way I said, honest, Verna. Lucy's cousin is going to Nashville—No, Memphis, I mean. She's been staying with Lucy and the boys for the past few days. They've been having such a marvelous time together, hunting mushrooms, picking flowers, going fishing. She's really just the nicest person, even if—"

She broke off and looked from one to the other. "I'm babbling, huh?"

"You're babbling," Myra May said in a kindly tone. "Tell us what you're hiding, Ophelia."

Ophelia began to color. "Nothing," she protested. "I'm not hiding anything. Honest!"

"Ophelia," Verna said sternly, "we have played hearts together almost every Monday night for nearly ten years. I know when you're lying. You're hiding something. So what is it?"

"No, really! I—"

But Verna had left the group and was already on her way into the small frame railroad depot. It had an office and a ticket window at one end and a couple of benches so that waiting passengers could sit inside, out of the weather. The depot was empty, so she went through the opposite door to the wooden platform beside the railroad track.

The evening train was a short one, as usual—just the locomotive, the coal car, a baggage car, a soot-stained passenger car, and a red-painted caboose. Lucy was standing beside the nearly empty passenger car, helping her cousin up the steps. The conductor was standing at the head of the train, checking his watch and talking to the engineer, while the steam hissed and puffed from beneath.

"Have a good trip," Lucy said to her cousin. "Be sure and write to me when you get there, so I'll know you're safe."

"Thank you," the cousin said, in a curiously high-pitched voice. "Really, I'm jes' so grateful for all you've did. I'll try to live up to it." She bent down to take the cardboard suitcase out of Lucy's hand.

But at that moment, a gust of wind caught her slat bonnet. The strings must not have been tied securely, for the bonnet went sailing off. Lucy, with great presence of mind, caught it one-handed in midair, while Verna gawked, openmouthed.

Lucy's cousin was as bald as a billiard ball.

* * *

They all got their food and sat down together. While they ate, Lucy told the story, with a little help, now and then, from Ophelia. It didn't take long.

"And that was why I felt I had to take him in, poor boy," she said at the end. "I simply couldn't let him go back to that awful place, where the overseers flogged him when he couldn't work and where the other inmates—" She turned her face away, swallowing tears.

"You should have seen him," Ophelia put in. "Skin and bones, with open welts on his back."

Lucy took out a hankie and blew her nose. "I felt I had to get him away from here as soon as he was well enough to travel. I know it was wrong, legally speaking. If the sheriff or the prison people find out, I'll be in hot water. They'll put me in jail, too." She gave them a defiant look. "But you can say whatever you want. I don't care. It was the right thing to do."

"It was the only thing to do," Ophelia said firmly. "I for one am glad that he's safely on that train and on his way north."

There was a long silence. The five of them were sitting on wooden benches on both sides of a scrubbed wooden table, Ophelia and Lucy on one side, Verna, Myra May, and Lizzy on the other. Everybody but Verna had a sandwich of Buzz's pulled pork with white sauce, along with side dishes of cabbage slaw and fried okra. Verna had ordered grilled chicken and poured white sauce over it, too. Before he moved to Monroeville, Buzz had worked for Big Bob Gibson, up in Decatur, Alabama, where he learned how to make the famous white sauce. Everybody raved about it.

"Well," Verna said finally, "I have to admit that it was quite a sight. That bonnet flying off, and your cousin standing there on the train steps, bald as the day she was born."

She grinned. "Bet those shoes are going to kill her feet before she gets to Memphis."

Lucy shook her head ruefully. "I had to warn her not to take them off. Her feet will swell so bad she'll never get them on again. I wanted to give her a pair of Ralph's but I was afraid a man's shoes under that dress would be a dead give-away." She sobered, looking at them across the table. "You're not going to tell on me, are you?"

"Tell what?" Myra May asked. "Seems to me that it was really nice of you to buy a train ticket for a cousin who was down on her luck."

"I think so, too," Lizzy put in. "I hope she gets where she's going safely and never has to come back."

Verna shook her head. "Too bad she had such a terrible experience during her visit here. Couldn't have been much fun."

"Thank you," Lucy said simply.

Ophelia nodded, her eyes nearly filled with tears. "Yes, thank you, thank you! Y'all are the best friends anybody could have."

"That's for durn sure," Myra May said emphatically. She finished her sandwich and wiped her fingers with her napkin. "And now, you two get to hear what the three of us have been up to this afternoon." She looked at Verna and Lizzy. "Okay if I go first?" When they nodded, she reported on what she had learned from Imogene Rutledge, then summarized her conclusions in one sentence.

"Miss Rutledge thinks that the bank's money problems were created by Mr. Johnson, who made a couple of unse-cured loans to family members. She thinks he's been moving money around to cover up his misdeeds, and she's willing to tell the bank examiner what she knows. In fact, she's agreed to drive over to Darling first thing in the morning and talk to him."

"Sounds a little vindictive to me," Verna said critically.

"Who cares?" Ophelia asked. "If she can get poor Alice Ann off the hook, she can be as vindictive as she likes."

"Anyway," Lizzy said, "he's got it coming. Silly man— firing an outspoken woman who knew about those loans. That's asking for it, seems to me. You'd've thought he'd have more sense." She looked at Verna. "So what did you find out about Bunny?"

"That she lied to Mr. Moseley," Verna said promptly. "And what's more, he knows it—now. He was here this morning, asking about her at the house where she and her mother used to live." She told what she had learned from the soda jerk about Bunny's time as a cosmetics clerk at the drugstore and from the woman at Bunny's old house. "The woman kept saying that Eva Louise was a good girl who didn't have any sense at all when it came to men," she added. "I guess we can take that for true, can't we?"

"I sure can," Myra May said dryly.

"I can, too," Lizzy said. She leaned forward and lowered her voice. "And I can tell you who the man was in that photograph, as well."

Lizzy and Verna Hire a Lawyer

Thursday, May 22, 1930

Lizzy and Verna were waiting for Mr. Moseley when he came into the office at seven thirty the next morning, folding his umbrella, shaking the rain off his hat. They had discussed whether Lizzy should talk to Mr. Moseley alone or whether Verna should be there. Lizzy thought it might be less embarrassing for him if she did it alone, but Verna thought that the two of them might be able to put more pressure on him to do what needed doing. They had finally decided to do it together.

"Strength in numbers," Verna said, and Lizzy agreed.

"Mornin', girls," Mr. Moseley said cheerfully. He had met Verna often, of course—he had regular business at the probate office, and she dropped in to visit with Lizzy every now and then.

Knowing that Verna resented being called a "girl," Lizzy spoke up. "We need to talk to you, Mr. Moseley. We're hoping you can help us."

Mr. Moseley smiled and rubbed his hands. He seemed to be feeling better. Lizzy wondered if his trip to Monroeville had anything to do with it. And perhaps he no longer feared that he was in danger of being targeted as a suspect.

"Sure thing," he said, in what just missed being a patronizing tone. "What's up? Did one of your pets run away? Got a little problem with the girls in your garden club?"

Lizzy replied quickly, because it looked like Verna might explode. "Oh, no, nothing like that," she said, dismissing his offensive remark sweetly. In her experience, even the nicest of men often had lapses. The best thing to do was ignore them. She smiled at him. "But the subject is a little . . . well, touchy, I'm afraid. May I get you a cup of coffee? Then we can sit down and talk about it."

"Wonderful," Mr. Moseley said warmly, returning her smile and proving (in Lizzy's mind, anyway) that you really can catch more flies with honey than with vinegar.

"Now, then," he said, as they sat down in his office, he behind his desk with a steaming cup of coffee, Lizzy and Verna across from him. "How can I help you two pretty ladies?"

Lizzy and Verna exchanged glances, Verna trying not to roll her eyes. Then Lizzy leaned forward and laid Bunny's photograph on the desk in front of Mr. Moseley. She sat back, not saying a word.

He frowned. "What? What's this?" He was staring at the photo now, his eyes getting big.

Verna spoke up. "I think you can see what it is. Or who it is, rather. Bunny Scott, posing in her underwear."

He set his coffee cup down so hard that the coffee sloshed into the saucer. "Yes, of course. But—"

"The car is the Pontiac that was reported stolen by Fred Harper," Verna went on.

"How do you know?" Mr. Moseley asked sharply.

"It's the same license plate," Lizzy said. "You can confirm that with Charlie Dickens. He copied it from the wreck."

"Her underwear," Mr. Moseley muttered, still staring

at the photo. "Out in public like that. Such a sweet little thing—I wouldn't have thought she could be so—" He sighed. "But she lied to me. Her whole story was a lie, from start to finish. So I don't suppose I should be surprised that she'd pose for . . . for cheesecake."

"You are entirely missing the point, Mr. Moseley," Verna said firmly. "This has nothing to do with underwear or cheesecake. We found the photograph in the drawer of Bunny's dressing table. It proves that she was associated with that car before last weekend. It was no accident—if you'll pardon the pun—that she died in it."

"The car belongs to Dr. Harper, the dentist in Monroeville," Lizzy said gently. "I've spoken to him. It turns out that he knew Bunny quite well—well enough to give her a pair of pearl earrings."

Mr. Moseley made a noise deep in his throat.

Lizzy gave him a sympathetic look, but went on. "Bunny also knew the owner's brother, Mr. Fred Harper. He lives here in Darling now. He works at the bank."

"He's the man who reported the car stolen," Verna put in. "He told the sheriff he didn't know the woman he saw stealing it, even though he described her to a T." She added, with only the slightest hint of sarcasm, "Harper knew her, all right. In fact, his brother says that's him." She pointed to the shadow of the man in the fedora. "The man who took this photo."

Mr. Moseley raised his eyes from the photo. "You say you found this in Bunny's room?"

"Yes," Lizzy replied. She put an envelope on the desk. "The same place we found this letter."

Mr. Moseley leaned back, breathing out a gusty sigh of relief.

"We didn't think," Lizzy said softly, "that it was a good idea to leave it where we found it. Since we knew that your connection to Bunny had nothing to do with her death, we thought you ought to have it back."

Quickly, as if he were afraid that she might snatch the letter away from him, he picked it up and slipped it into his desk drawer. "Thank you," he said. His glance went to Verna and back to Lizzy. "I know I've been . . . foolish. I'm grateful for your help."

"That's good," Verna said. "Because we need yours."

He tilted his head warily. "What kind of help?"

"We think Fred Harper shot Bunny Scott," Lizzy said, and told him about the .22 revolver Dr. Harper had loaned his brother.

He stared. "How do you . . . Why—?"

"We'll tell you," Verna said, and when she had finished, he shook his head.

"How in God's name you managed to find—" He swallowed. "So Dr. Harper is willing to say that his brother was having an affair with Miss Scott? Why would he do that?"

"Because he was in love with Bunny, too," Lizzy said quietly. "He wants to see that the man who killed her pays for what he did."

"But even if Fred Harper and Bunny were having an affair, that doesn't prove he killed her," Mr. Moseley protested. "What possible motive could he have?"

Verna put the deposit book on the desk. "She was blackmailing him. He was putting money into her bank account. Here's the proof."

He picked it up and began turning the pages, shaking his head in disbelief. "Ten dollars a week? On the salary of a bank teller? Where in the world was he getting it?"

"From other accounts at the bank, maybe," Lizzy suggested. "We think he might have been stealing money. And if the sheriff searches his house, we think he'll find that gun."

He looked up. "The sheriff?"

Verna leaned forward. "Sheriff Burns will never listen to Lizzy and me. But he'll listen to you. If you show him the photograph and the deposit book and tell him what Dr. Harper said about the gun, he'll have to pay attention."

"But how am I going to explain all this?" he asked. "Where am I supposed to have gotten this information?"

"That's easy," Lizzy said. "Tell him that one of Bunny's friends brought you this stuff and told you that she was sure that there was something fishy about Fred Harper's story."

"If he asks who," Verna put in, "tell him that's a matter of attorney-client privilege." She put a quarter on the desk. "Here's our retainer. We'd like a receipt, please."

Within the half hour, Mr. Moseley was at the sheriff's office, presenting the photograph and the deposit book, and reporting Dr. Harper's oral statement about the gun and the car. When the sheriff asked him where all this came from, he said the information was privileged—although his client might be willing to consider revealing his or her identity if the matter could not be resolved in any other way.

But it was resolved. The sheriff, feeling as if he had just been handed a present (which he had), got into his car and drove straight to Monroeville, where he spent the better part of an hour obtaining a signed affidavit from Dr. Harper, who decided that voluntary cooperation was better than the alternative. Then he drove straight back and got the county judge to sign a search warrant.

The search of Fred Harper's house was successful, at least as far as the sheriff was concerned (Mr. Harper would not have agreed), for a .22 revolver was discovered in the springs of the parlor sofa. Confronted with that, and with the photo, the bank book, and the statement that his brother provided, Mr. Harper broke down and confessed to shooting Miss Scott.

His motive? He had made the mistake of bragging to her that he had taken some money from the bank in Monroeville, and she knew that he was continuing the practice at Darling Savings and Trust. She was already blackmailing him to the tune of ten dollars a week. Thinking that this ought to be a family affair (and recalling the sight of Miss Scott in her teddy), he had asked her to marry him. She refused. She wanted more money or she would tell what she knew. He killed her to keep her from spilling the beans.

The day after Mr. Harper was arrested and charged with murder, an additional charge of attempted embezzlement was filed against him. He was accused of taking nearly five thousand dollars in small amounts from various depositors' accounts and depositing the money here and there. Some of it had gone into Bunny's account, the rest into various inactive accounts, some of them belonging to dead people. The money, however, was still in the bank. Mr. Johnson was able to reverse these deposits and the cash was returned to the accounts from which it had been stolen. Nobody lost a dime. And best of all (as far as the Dahlias were concerned): Alice Ann was invited to come back to work, where she was promoted to head cashier and given a raise of ten cents an hour.

In the end, even the bank examiner was satisfied. Miss Rutledge (vindictive or not) made good on her promise to discuss the bank's loan portfolio with him. After hearing her story and her threat to go to the Banking Commissioner in Montgomery, the examiner met with George E. Pickett Johnson. Their discussion must have been an interesting one, for the next morning, the two unsecured loans that were the bank's most potentially damaging liabilities—one to Mrs. Voleen Johnson's father, the other to her brother—were paid in full, righting the bank's capitalization-to-debt ratio and allowing Darling Savings and Trust to be removed from the "troubled banks" list. This was a good thing, because the examiner was a longtime friend of Mr. and Mrs. Johnson. He would have hated to close their bank.

TWENTY-FOUR

The Dahlias Plant Their Sign

Sunday, May 25, 1930

There were several other little mysteries, but they were cleared up over the next few days. Mr. and Mrs. Lester Lima came back home from their Florida vacation—a "second honeymoon," Mrs. Lima called it, as she proudly displayed the diamond ring that Mr. Lima had bought her as a pledge of his undying love and affection. ("And an abject apology," as Mildred Kilgore put it to Ophelia.) Mr. Lima reopened the drugstore and got busy filling all the prescriptions for the sick people who had gone without their medicines in his absence. Mrs. Lima put herself in charge of hiring, and after an exhaustive and highly competitive search, she found Miss Scott's replacement, Mrs. Priscilla Prinney, age fifty-seven, mother of three and grandmother of eight.

Nadine Tillman, meanwhile, finally got around to letting her mother know where in the world she was. Her postcard arrived from Los Angeles, with a picture of the H-o-l-l-y-w-o-o-d L-a-n-d sign on the front (thirteen huge white letters planted on the side of Mount Lee, publicizing the new real estate development). Nadine had written a few lines on the back, saying that she was well and happy and hoping for a career in the movies. But she was broke and would really appreciate it if her mother could send a money order for ten dollars so she could pay her rent.

Maxwell Woodburn had no telephone, but Myra May was finally able to locate an address for him. He was very, very sorry when he learned about Bunny's death. They had been corresponding for several years, he said, having met through the Baptist Sunday School Pen Pals list. He was a little surprised to hear that Bunny had been practicing her signature as Mrs. Maxwell Woodburn, for he was serving four years in the state penitentiary (he was truly a "pen pal," he joked) and would not be able to marry anybody until he got out. But he appreciated the thought and wished that Bunny was still alive so he could tell her so.

Which leaves the mystery of Bessie Bloodworth's ghost, the one she fired at with her twelve-gauge shotgun. Bessie was right, of course. The cloaked figure with the shovel was no ghost. He was Beatty Blackstone. He would not have revealed himself, except that he was wounded in his encounter with Bessie—not because she shot him (she really did shoot over his head when she discharged her gun) but because he somehow managed to slice his leg quite badly with the sharp edge of his shovel when he was trying to get away from Bessie's twelve-gauge.

Beatty (who never liked to admit to weakness and didn't like to spend money on doctors) put off treatment for several days. But when his leg became seriously infected and he could no longer walk, his wife Lenora insisted on taking him to the doctor. Doc Roberts scolded Beatty for not coming in earlier, then cleaned and stitched the wound and painted it with iodine. He had done all he could, he said, but Beatty would be lucky not to lose his leg. It was touch-and-go for a couple of days, but gradually the leg improved, and after a while, Beatty could get around again without too much trouble. But forever after, he walked with a limp.

This ghostly misadventure might not have come to light if it hadn't been that Beatty, out of his head with pain, told Doc Roberts that he'd been injured when he was digging under the cucumber tree in Mrs. Blackstone's garden. When Doc Roberts asked him why he was doing such an outlandish thing, Beatty, by that time rambling and incoherent, told him the whole story. Doc Roberts' assistant, Maureen Wiggins, was helping the doctor sew Beatty up and overheard the tale.

Maureen told her mother-in-law, Leticia Wiggins, who had witnessed the ghost-bagging episode from the window of the Magnolia Manor.

Leticia told Bessie Bloodworth.

And Bessie told the Dahlias, when they met at the clubhouse the following Sunday afternoon.

"Dressed up like the Cartwright ghost!" Aunt Hetty Little exclaimed. "Why in the world?"

"And what was he looking for?" Earlynne Biddle wanted to know.

"He was looking for the Cartwright treasure," Bessie explained. "Cornelia Cartwright's mother's family silver, which Cornelia buried in the garden when she thought that the Yankees were about to overrun the place and steal her blind."

"I thought it was a baby she buried," Mildred Kilgore said.

"She did bury her baby," Bessie replied. "But she buried the silver, too."

"But why was Beatty digging under the cucumber tree?" Lizzy asked, puzzled. "What made him think he'd find it there?"

"Because he had inherited a big box of papers from Mrs. Blackstone. Most of it was Blackstone family letters and

278   *Susan Wittig Albert*

diaries. But one of the items was a letter that Cornelia Cartwright wrote to Colonel Cartwright, telling him that the family silver was buried under their favorite cucumber tree. The poor woman died before the letter could be sent, and nobody ever saw it—until Beatty discovered it. He was hoping to find the Cartwright treasure."

"Maybe that was why Beatty was looking at the plat books!" Verna exclaimed. "He must have been trying to determine the bounds of the property, to locate the tree."

"Well, he obviously didn't find the silver," Myra May said. "Yesterday, his wife telephoned the grocery with an order. Mrs. Hancock reminded her that they owed four dollars, but Lenora said they could only pay half because it cost so much to doctor Beatty's leg. If he had found what he was looking for, they'd have sold it to pay the bills."

Aunt Hetty Little cleared her throat. "Speaking of paying bills," she said, "we'd better talk about how we're going to fix the roof on this house. We have a serious situation here, ladies. This afternoon, I mopped up a big puddle of water on the kitchen floor. That roof can't wait."

"We could hold another plant sale," Ophelia suggested hopefully.

"We only made two dollars and thirty-five cents at the last one," Bessie replied. "It was a lot of work, too."

"How about a rummage sale?" Mildred Kilgore asked.

"The Methodist ladies are planning two rummage sales this summer," Beulah Trivette reported. "They wouldn't take competition kindly."

"We could raise the dues," Mrs. Johnson proposed.

A collective sigh ran around the group and several shook their heads. But nobody could come up with any more ideas. Mrs. Johnson looked pleased.

"I move that we raise the dues," she said.

"Let's table that motion while we give the matter some

more thought," Aunt Hetty Little said, and the motion passed.

"Well, then," Lizzy said, "if there's no other business, the chair will entertain a motion to adjourn, so we can go out front and plant our sign." Zeke still hadn't gotten around to it.

A few moments later, they were all gathered out front. Bessie brought a shovel. Lizzy had her Kodak. Beulah and Verna placed the sign where it was supposed to go, and marked the spots where Bessie could dig the holes. Everybody else stood around and offered suggestions and encouragement as Bessie began to dig.

"Well, that was easy enough," Bessie said, when the first hole was completed. She had dug about eighteen inches down. She handed the shovel to Lizzy. "Your turn, Liz."

"Sure," Lizzy said, and gave her Kodak to Verna to hold. She pushed the point of the shovel into the dirt, then cut out a small circle of turf. That done, she began to dig the hole, dumping the dirt off to the side. The job went easily until her shovel struck something. She put her foot on the shovel and pushed harder. It didn't budge.

"A rock," Alice Ann suggested.

"Doesn't feel like a rock," Lizzy said. "It's a root, I think."

"Probably a cucumber tree root," Bessie said fondly, looking up at the tree overhead.

"*Magnolia acuminata,*" Miss Rogers corrected.

Lizzy got down and began to pull the dirt out with her hands. "Yes, it's a root. Must be huge."

"Oh, dear," Beulah said distractedly. "Will we have to put the sign somewhere else?"

"Maybe," Lizzy said, still digging. "Or maybe—" She looked up. "I don't think it is a root, after all. It looks like a box. A wooden box."

"A box?" the Dahlias exclaimed, in unison.

And that's what it was. The hole had to be enlarged, which

required quite a bit more digging. Verna took over from Lizzy and Mildred Kilgore took over from Verna, and by the time Mildred handed the shovel over to Earlynne, they were nearly ready to lift it out. It was square, about two feet by two feet, and about eighteen inches deep.

A few moments later, the box, rotten and splintering, was sitting on the grass. Eager hands were opening it—carefully, for it was obviously very old. And when the lid was lifted, there was a collective chorus of awed ohs and ahs.

"Why, it's the Cartwright silver!" Bessie cried in great excitement.

That's exactly what it was: a set of thirty-six place settings of sterling silver flatware, Gorham's Chantilly pattern, engraved with an ornate C. It was stained black from nearly seven decades underground but otherwise undamaged. And when they began to look more carefully, they found several pieces of old-fashioned jewelry—a bracelet set with a square-cut emerald, a pair of pearl earrings, and a small diamond ring—and a bag of twenty-dollar gold coins. Ten gold coins. Two hundred dollars' worth of double eagles, still as perfect as the day they were minted, in 1852.

"Yankee money," Earlynne Biddle said, and sniffed. Earlynne's mother had been a charter member of the United Daughters of the Confederacy, and Earlynne had inherited her distaste for all things Yankee—even money.

"It's Cornelia's legacy," Bessie said in a reverential tone. "Right where she said it was. Under the cucumber tree."

"It's *Magnolia acuminata*," Miss Rogers said sharply.

"It's our roof," Aunt Hetty Little said happily. "Glory be, it's our roof!"

Makin' Do:
12 Ways to Stretch
Whatever We Have
Compiled by the Darling Dahlias

May 1930

1. Save all your bits of bread, the heels, crusts, etc. Use them for bread pudding, in stuffing, and to bread catfish. With the right care and attention, you will never run out of bread crumbs. (Lizzy Lacy)

2. Don't throw away old feather beds or feather pillows. You can wash the feathers and they'll be good as new. Take out the feathers and wash in a tub of real hot suds. Then spread them in the attic to dry, in a single layer. Do not dry in the wind, or you will have feathers all over the place. (Bessie Bloodworth)

3. If you have old woolen coats that have already been cut up for children's wear and will no longer serve as garments, cut the fabric into strips and braid for doormats and rugs. Children love to help with this. Worn-out tablecloths can be hemmed and made into nice napkins. (Ophelia Snow)

4. After you've done your laundry, throw the soapy water on your bushes and young plants. They will appreciate the suds, but the bugs won't. Also, pour the soapy water into a bucket and wash your brooms. A clean broom sweeps better! (Mildred Kilgore)

5. Keep moths away from your woolens by packing them in a tight box with pepper, cedar chips, tobacco, santolina, wormwood, or lavender—or a mix. In fact, almost anything with a strong, spicy smell will work. Camphor is good, too, but some people object to the way it smells—and you can't grow it. (Miss Dorothy Rogers)

6. Save old letters and envelopes and use the backs for notes and lists. But be careful not to use a letter you don't want someone else to read. (Myra May Mosswell)

7. Do not turn up your nose at hand-me-downs. Give an item to someone else if you can't use it. (Aunt Hetty Little)

8. You can have a supply of horseradish all winter. When you dig the roots, grate them, put the gratings into a bottle with a good lid, and cover with strong vinegar and a tight-fitting lid. Do the grating outdoors—you'll know why if you've ever tried it. (Earlynne Biddle)

9. Don't spend money on expensive hair-setting lotions. Simmer 1 cup flaxseed in 3 cups water for a few minutes. Strain the flaxseeds and add back enough water to give the desired consistency. Comb through your hair and roll in rags or curlers as usual. (Beulah Trivette)

10. Be a string saver! Wind it into a ball and you'll always have some handy. Buttons, too: keep them in bag or a box, so you'll know where to go when you want one. (Mrs. George E. Pickett Johnson)

11. If you have cockroaches, don't spend money on expensive bait. Boil up some poke-root and mix it with molasses, then set it out in the kitchen and the pantry in saucers. Be sure and keep the cats and the kids out of it. (Alice Ann Walker)

12. Keep a soup pot going on the back of the stove. That's where you should put all the bits of food left from the day's dinner. By supper time, you'll have a thick, rich soup. Add some of those saved bread crumbs to thicken it up some more. (Verna Tidwell)

The Dahlias' Favorite Recipes

Verna Tidwell's Molasses Cookies

Molasses is a by-product of the sugarcane refining process. The cane is crushed to remove the juice, which is then boiled and the sugar crystals extracted. The syrup becomes molasses. Its flavor and color depends on whether it is extracted early or late in the process. Until the 1880s, it was the most popular sweetener in the United States, because it was cheaper than refined sugar. Now it is more expensive.

¾ cup butter or lard, melted
1 ⅓ cup white sugar, divided
1 egg
¼ cup molasses
2 cups all-purpose flour
2 teaspoons baking soda
½ teaspoon salt
1 teaspoon ground cinnamon
1 teaspoon ground ginger
½ teaspoon nutmeg

In a medium bowl, mix together the melted butter, 1 cup sugar, and egg until smooth. Stir in the molasses. Combine the flour, baking soda, salt, cinnamon, ginger, and nutmeg; blend into the molasses mixture. Cover, and chill dough for 1 hour. Preheat oven to 375°F (190°C). Roll dough into walnut-sized balls, and roll them in the remaining white sugar. Place cookies 2 inches apart onto ungreased baking sheets. Bake for 8 to 10 minutes in the preheated oven, until tops are cracked. Cool on wire racks.

Euphoria's Peanut Butter Meringue Pie

The peanut (not a nut, but a legume) came to America from Africa, via the Caribbean. It became an important crop in the South after the boll weevils devastated the cotton fields. Peanut butter was a locally produced food until the 1920s, when it began to appear on grocery store shelves.

CRUST

½ cup peanut butter (modern cooks may use crunchy)
1 cup confectioners' sugar
1 9-inch pie shell, baked

FILLING

⅔ cup brown sugar
¼ cup cornstarch
½ teaspoon cinnamon
¼ teaspoon nutmeg
¼ teaspoon salt
2 cups milk, scalded
3 egg yolks, beaten

2 tablespoons butter or margarine
1 teaspoon vanilla

MERINGUE
3 egg whites
3 tablespoons sugar
⅛ teaspoon cream of tartar

Combine peanut butter and confectioners' sugar, blending well. Spread all but 3 tablespoons over the bottom of the baked pie shell.

In a medium saucepan, combine brown sugar, cornstarch, cinnamon, nutmeg, and salt. Slowly stir in scalded milk. Cook over medium heat until smooth, stirring constantly. Stir about ⅓ of the hot mixture into the beaten egg yolks. Add this mixture back to the pan, along with the butter or margarine. Continue cooking and stirring until thickened. Remove from heat and stir in vanilla. Pour into prepared peanut butter crust.

Preheat oven to 300°F. Beat egg whites, sugar, and cream of tartar until stiff but not dry. Spread over filling. Place in oven until meringue is lightly browned. Serve chilled or at room temperature. Refrigerate the leftovers.

Beulah's Tomato and Eggplant Pie

The eggplant (a member of the nightshade family, related to the tomato and the potato) was grown in Virginia as early as 1737. The Virginia House-wife *(1824), by Mrs. Randolph, included a recipe for fried eggplant. A warm-weather plant, it became a favorite in the South, perhaps because of its use in Creole and Cajun cookery.*

Salt
1 small eggplant, peeled and sliced thin
1 large tomato, sliced ¼-inch thick
½ large onion, sliced thin
Melted butter (modern cooks may wish to use olive oil spray)
1 tablespoon finely chopped fresh basil
½ teaspoon dried oregano
½ teaspoon dried thyme
½ teaspoon dried summer savory
Pepper
Crust for a 9-inch pie, unbaked
¼ cup grated yellow cheese
3 eggs, beaten
¼ cup milk
1 teaspoon prepared mustard

Generously sprinkle salt over both sides of the eggplant slices. Place in a colander for 15 minutes to drain the bitter juices. Rinse and pat dry. Brush both sides of the eggplant, tomato, and onion slices with melted butter (or spray with olive oil). Arrange eggplant on a cookie sheet, leaving space for the tomatoes and onions. Bake at 350°F for 10 minutes. Remove from oven and add the tomatoes and onions. Sprinkle with herbs and pepper and return to the oven until lightly browned. Remove and cool slightly. Layer the egg-plant slices on the crust. Cover with grated cheese, reserving a few tablespoons, and the tomato and onion slices. Mix the eggs, milk, and mustard and pour over the slices. Sprinkle with the remaining cheese. Bake at 350°F until the egg/milk mixture is firm (about 35 to 40 minutes).

Florabelle's Soda Bread

Cornbread, hoe cakes, spoon breads, biscuits, and other forms of non-yeast quick-cooking breads were popular throughout the South. However, the "light" bread made with baking pow-der and baking soda was baked in a loaf and could be easily sliced, making it more suitable for sandwiches and toast.

4 ½ cups all-purpose flour
⅔ cup sugar
4 ½ teaspoons baking powder
1 ½ teaspoons baking soda
1 ½ teaspoons salt
3 cups buttermilk
3 large eggs, lightly beaten
4 ½ tablespoons butter, melted and cooled

Preheat oven to 350°F. In a large bowl, mix the dry ingredi-ents. Make a well in the center of the mixture. Add butter-milk, eggs, and butter, stirring just until thoroughly blended and almost smooth. Pour into 2 lightly greased 8½ x 4½ -inch loaf pans. Bake for 45 minutes, or until a long wooden pick inserted in the center comes out clean. Cool in pans on a wire rack for 10 minutes. Run a knife along edges of loaves to loosen from pans. Remove from pans to wire rack and cool completely (about 1 hour) before slicing.

Buzz's White Barbecue Sauce

This tangy white sauce is an Alabama favorite that dates back to the 1920s. It is served with pork, beef, chicken, and even vegetables.

½ cup mayonnaise (modern cooks may use low-fat)
2 tablespoons white vinegar
1 teaspoon lemon juice
1 to 2 teaspoons grated horseradish
½ teaspoon freshly ground pepper
Dash salt

Combine ingredients. Refrigerate unused portion.